THE ISLAND GOSPEL ACCORDING TO SAMSON GRIEF

THE ISLAND GOSPEL ACCORDING TO SAMSON GRIEF

STEVEN MAYOFF

radiant press

Editor: Dave Margoshes
Cover art: Tania Wolk
Book and cover design: Tania Wolk, Third Wolf Studio
Printed and bound in Canada at Friesens, Altona, MB

The publisher gratefully acknowledges the support of Creative Saskatchewan, the Canada Council for the Arts and SK Arts.

creative SASKATCHEWAN   Canada Council for the Arts   Conseil des Arts du Canada   sk arts

Library and Archives Canada Cataloguing in Publication

Title: The island gospel according to Samson Grief / Steven Mayoff.
Names: Mayoff, Steven, 1956- author.
Identifiers: Canadiana 20230509304 | ISBN 9781989274972 (softcover)
Classification: LCC PS8576.A89 I85 2023 | DDC C811/.54—dc23

radiant press
Box 33128 Cathedral PO
Regina, SK S4T 7X2
info@radiantpress.ca
www.radiantpress.ca

"The greatest blessing granted to mankind
comes by way of madness, which is a divine gift."
–Socrates

"A man without land is nobody."
–Simcha Kravitz to his grandson, Duddy
in *The Apprenticeship of Duddy Kravitz*
by Mordecai Richler

For Thelma

PART 1:

OUR COLLECTIVE INNOCENCE

1

I KNEW SOMETHING wasn't right when I looked out the window that bright summer morning and saw the three of them. They were standing in the open field behind my building. I recognized them by their hats. The blue baseball cap, the coral bucket hat and the yellow porkpie hat. *Really?* I thought to myself, *this again?* I decided to go about my usual preparations for the day. My favourite L. Cohen CD, *The Future*, was playing in the paint-spattered boom box. Breakfast was a cup of lapsang souchong and a toasted fried egg sandwich. Slurping the dregs of my tea, I looked out the window again.

They were gone.

I surveyed the rickety table displaying a clutter of brushes, palettes, cans of turpentine, tubes of paint, as well as a variety of scissors, rulers, drawing utensils, etc. Through the boom box speakers, the gentle croak of the Jewish lo-fi blues poet made the deceptively simple observation that everything has a crack which functions as an aperture, allowing light to enter. I was grateful to hear this, since it was my habit to play this CD every morning and considered the observation to be a daily affirmation, inviting me to cross the threshold into a hallowed zone of creativity. As usual, I made the same backhanded remark, a superstitious part of the preparatory routine: "Except for the *tuchus* crack, Lenny, 'cause that's where the sun don't shine."

I removed the drop cloth covering the canvas on my easel and experienced an odd shiver somewhere between the hairline at the back of my neck and the slight depression between my shoulder blades. No doubt this was because I couldn't stop thinking about the three figures I had just seen outside my window. There really was no earthly reason why that business should be starting up again after almost thirteen years.

Had it really been that long? I realized it was exactly thirteen years to the month and wondered if it had anything to do with the number thirteen. I didn't want to go down this rabbit hole, so I forced myself to stare at the unfinished painting before me.

It depicted a specific area at North Cape. Normally a narrow strand of ruddy, stone-encrusted shoreline tapers toward a divide where the waters of the Northumberland Strait meet those of the Gulf of St. Lawrence. In my painting, rather than merging, the two bodies of water part – waves rising in rapid brush strokes of shimmering aquamarine tinged with yellowish-white streaks, climaxing into a silvery Biblical scroll of oceanic sputum – to reveal a stretch of iron-rich red soil strewn with seashells, beer bottles, crustaceans and other detritus from the watery depths.

The original concept of the painting was yet another fantasia of Jewish iconography set on modern-day Prince Edward Island. The problem was I still couldn't make up my mind: should I depict Moses leading his people onto the shores of North Cape or should they be escaping it? And if the latter, who were they fleeing from? Lobster fishermen? Potato farmers? Japanese tourists? The longer I surveyed this half-baked creation, the more I came to realize that my indecision was rooted in a personal conundrum I could no longer ignore, no matter how many tubes of acrylic I slathered onto the canvas.

I looked out the window again. Thankfully the three figures had not reappeared.

The first time I became aware of them was in 2002 when I was still living in Charlottetown. I had created a painting called *Anne of Bergen-Belsen*. It was a portrait of an emaciated Anne Shirley, complete with straw hat and ginger pigtails, the twisted plaits rendered in excruciating detail. I had her dressed in rags and sporting a yellow Star of David armband. Her left forearm, skeletal and pale, was imprinted with blue tattooed numbers. It was the eyes that filled me with pride. Simmering orange-green embers for irises with dilated coal-black pupils at their centers, like twin abysses of unspeakable terror. I imagined them burning into the viewer's soul, evoking mixed reactions of pity and revulsion. Behind her was a dull grey barbed wire fence, the iron mesh made all the more menacing by being outlined with a sickly bluish-white. In the distance was a candy-striped lighthouse, complete with a machine-gun toting German soldier standing guard at the top and a red flag flying a black swastika in a white circle.

By the time I laid on the last stroke of paint, I knew I had turned a corner in my creative life. I decided to treat myself to a bubble tea in the Cradletown Court Mall. It wasn't my usual choice of refreshment, but I was in the mood to celebrate with something different. I purchased a kiwi-flavoured tea at the Red Pearl stand on the mall's uppermost level and sat in the food court seating area. As I slowly sipped through the wide plastic straw, I thought about my creation. Something in the painting scared and excited me. I had never done anything like it and revisiting the image in my mind's eye made the hairs on the back of my neck tremble.

Since moving from Toronto to PEI in 1997, the year the Confederation Bridge opened, my output was more "whimsical", according to a profile in *The Drone*, our monthly arts newspaper. Typical subject matter were watercolours of a swaddled infant Moses in a dory floating past channel markers and buoys on Malpeque Bay or Joseph wearing his rain slicker of many colours. I also tried my hand at sculpture with a model of Noah's Ark made entirely out of lobster traps, which won first prize in an Island-wide competition held at the Cradletown Art Gallery, hosted by Kerrie-Jo Campbelljohn, Minister of Tourism and Culture. There was a cash prize of five hundred dollars and a photograph of my ark was used on a tourism poster. The competition's judge, Digger Docherty, host of the long-running TV gardening show, *A Patch of Red*, and still PEI's biggest local celebrity, called my sculpture "clever" and suggested "a garden gnome playing Noah might give it a cute final touch."

My growing reputation led to an article in the *Charlottetown Parrot*, with the headline *The Monet from Away*. A freelancer for the *Toronto Satellite,* looking to do a human-interest piece on Toronto ex-pats, dubbed me *Cézanne of Green Gables*. Hungry as I was for the recognition, I felt that my work was being misrepresented as mere kitsch and wondered if it wasn't my own fault. In 2001, after the attacks on the Twin Towers and the Pentagon, it was clear to me that something had to change and *Anne of Bergen-Belsen* was definitely a bold departure from my creative status quo.

As I was going through all of this in my mind, I had become aware of three men sitting at a nearby table by the food court railing that overlooked the level below. My first clue that they were not locals was their clothing, which bore the distinct signs of tourist attire: colourful short-sleeved shirts and casual headgear – a baseball cap, a straw porkpie hat and a denim bucket hat. Everything looked oddly random, maybe even too random as if the outfits were chosen from a theatrical wardrobe department or a Goodwill shop. Then I noticed they all had scraggly facial hair. Trying not to stare, it dawned on me that their hats were doing a bad job of concealing their long hair. When I realized their hair were various shades of red, I truly became uneasy.

The one in the yellow porkpie hat, whose gaunt and tanned leathery face tapered to a spade-like goatee, making him look like an ancient hipster, glanced my way. I did a quarter turn away from him in my seat, feigning interest in something or other before turning around again. Their table was now empty and they were nowhere to be seen. I extended my search to the level below. There was no trace of their garishly distinctive attire among the wandering shoppers.

Snapping out of this reverie, I was brought back to the task at hand: trying to finish this painting of the parting waters at North Cape. The voice of the Jewish lo-fi blues poet sang of "signs for all to see." Scanning the ocean floor that tapered into the illusory perspective of distance, a different idea slowly began to dawn on me. Cohen's observation in the song's refrain, about everything having a crack to let in the light, took on a new meaning. It wasn't that each single thing had its own individual crack. There was only one crack that ran throughout the world. It was the singular crack that simultaneously divides us from and connects us to each other. And this reddish strand that stretched out to the canvas's point zero of infinity, this strip I had been pondering for the last five minutes was exactly that: the crack that ran through everything.

I was wrapping my mind around this notion when I saw it. I had to crouch down and bring my face right up to the painting. I couldn't quite make it out, so I found a magnifying glass among the chaos on my worktable and inspected that section of the canvas more closely.

There, among the detritus was a starfish. But not just any starfish. This one had six arms. Like a Jewish star. A Starfish of David, if you will. It looked to have been painted with a fine detail brush. The only thing I knew for sure was that it wasn't me who painted it.

A thick noxious fog of fear, anger and general bewilderment erupted in my brain.

"Nobody tampers with my work!" I cried while fumbling with a tube of paint. I squeezed it directly on the canvas, grabbing the closest brush and mashing the fanned bristles into the oily blob until the image of the six-armed creature was obliterated from my sight.

WANDERING ORCHARD STREET, Mount Russet's main thoroughfare, I struggled to clear my head and tried to make sense of the mysterious starfish. Could I have painted it and just forgotten? Impossible! What with seeing those three strangers outside my window and now this, the morning was taking a very strange left turn. I did the only sensible thing and made a bee-line for Sadie's Tea Room, one of my favourite daytime haunts. Once settled in, I decided to take my mind off the starfish by concentrating on those three mysterious figures. That first sighting thirteen years ago at the food court had not been my last.

The Manson Gallery in Charlottetown, newly situated in an old warehouse at Queen and Water Street in 2002, agreed to display *Anne of Bergen-Belsen* with a few other works of mine. Some were scandalized, declaring it an unprovoked assault on the good character and gentle nature of their beloved island. Others insisted that it had some artistic merit.

A vitriolic op-ed piece appeared in the *Charlottetown Parrot*, penned by local entrepreneur Reuben Arsenault, best known for building the Silver Springs Club golf course and the Evangeline Estate Lodges, twelve state-of-the-art summer cottages. He loved the popular description of Charlottetown as the Cradle of Confederation so much, he came up with the nickname Cradletown, which was used for the downtown mall, the arts centre (home to the Montgomery Repertory Festival that ran every summer) and the art gallery, all of which were built by his company, Freeland Corporation.

In his op-ed piece, Arsenault condemned *Anne of Bergen-Belsen* for depicting Islanders as Nazi sympathizers. He characterized the citizenry of PEI as good old-fashioned lovers of freedom and declared this portrayal of Anne Shirley a slap in the face to the memory of Lucy Maud Montgomery, strongly suggesting that the L.M.M. Licensing Trust sue me for all I was worth. The piece ended with a plea that the painting be burned in public.

Ah yes, nothing says loving freedom like the good old-fashioned public burning of art.

No legal proceedings were ever brought against me for *Anne of Bergen-Belsen* because we all expected the controversy to die down. It most likely would have if I hadn't won the NovaBank Art Award that year, which quickly shone national attention on *Anne of Bergen-Belsen*, sparking a larger debate on the sacrosanctity of beloved cultural icons. During an interview on the national current affairs radio program, *So It Goes*, I tried to make it clear that the image was in no way meant to disparage the good people of Prince Edward Island or Lucy Maud's creation. Rather, it was a statement "on the post-911 world we're living in, where nobody is safe anymore and the primary victim is the delusion of our collective innocence."

As sincere as that statement was, in truth, I had pulled it out of my ass at the last minute. Like everyone else, I'd been swept up in the lingering aftershock following those horrifying attacks. And yet, I also knew, in my heart of hearts, that I said the first thing I thought would get me off the hook.

It had been gallery owner Angus Manson's idea to nominate me for the NovaBank Art Award and it proved to be a shrewd gamble, business-wise. After my win, almost overnight, a stampede of art lovers and curiosity seekers descended upon Charlottetown. Whatever Islanders may have felt about the way I had besmirched their beloved icon, they could not argue with the influx of tourist dollars. They came by the carload to see "that Holocaust painting," as some had labelled it.

Around this time, those three figures started to pop up whenever I least expected it.

When I made appearances at the Manson Gallery, there they were, usually standing at the back of the room, away from the gawking tourists. The renown, such as it was, that *Anne of Bergen-Belsen* brought me had been, at first, a novelty. The payoff amounted to many lucrative commissions, a slew of free drinks from a handful of admirers, and the attention of many a nubile art groupie, who found a neurotic Jew from away exotic enough to follow to bed. Through it all I kept seeing these three weirdos and it got to the point where I couldn't stop thinking about them. My work began to suffer. The couple of times I tried to approach them, something or someone always got in the way, and the three figures mysteriously disappeared before I could get to them.

One night, while leading a blonde Prince Edward Island University creative writing student back to my studio for some nude portraiture, I found them lingering under the street lamp opposite my front door. It was the last straw. I charged across the street at them, screaming at the top of my lungs, only to run smack into the lamppost. I woke up in the emergency room of Queens County Hospital. I explained that I was trying to protect the young lady I was with, but she had told the EMTs that I suddenly went berserk and ran at the lamppost. She didn't say anything about three strangers.

According to the on-call doctor, I had had a "mini-breakdown," probably brought on by the stress of "dealing with the demands of sudden fame." He prescribed Valium and a change of lifestyle.

Eventually, I packed my belongings and moved out of my spacious upper duplex on Pownal Street to Mount Russet, a modest community thirty kilometres west of Charlottetown. I took refuge in an open apartment in the rundown Mount Russet Arms, known to locals as the Mount Russet Body Parts: a crumbling, ash-coloured brick two-storey walk-up situated at the end of Morningstar Crescent, an unwelcoming cul-de-sac at the down-at-heel north end of town.

It was at the Body Parts that I found some stability and was able to work again. For the next thirteen years, I happily traded in my status of local art star for that of reclusive journeyman, working steadily without hindrance, until the morning I saw those three figures outside my window, and a mysterious six-armed starfish on a painting I couldn't finish.

THE NEXT FEW DAYS, following my disquieting discovery, were a kind of limbo. I made a couple of half-hearted attempts to touch up the smear that covered the six-armed starfish, barely managing to blend it in the painting. Beyond that I couldn't bring myself to do any more work on the picture. The touch-up sapped all my energy and concentration.

So I went for walks, but not idle wanderings. If I wasn't able to work, then my days had to have a purpose. I resolved to wander through Mount Russet and see it through new eyes. Maybe this would help me return to the painting with a renewed dedication. On my initial jaunts, everything that had first attracted me to the town seemed the same. That in itself went some way toward restoring my equilibrium. I took refuge in familiar landmarks. The iron statue of Senator Milius Bertram (a founder of the town, whose descendants still reside in the Mount Russet area), which stands at the foot of Bertram Park, greeted me with its usual stoic countenance. The 1952 Ford half-ton that sat in the empty lot beside Bulger's Tire Sales & Service was painted fire engine red and shone like a beacon. The mauve sign over the door of Merchant and Sons Fine Jewellers sported white angular Art Deco lettering surrounded by a reflective border that sparkled in the sunlight.

Just as these and other familiar sights began to make me believe I might be able to get back to work, I saw them again, those three redheaded strangers in their gaudy summer shirts and goofy headgear. I had been innocently picking up a few groceries at the Co-op and there they were in the household items aisle, passing around a double package of paper towels to each other, puzzling over the cellophane-wrapped rolls as if they were the Dead Sea Scrolls. Another time, in Bertram Park, they were sitting on a bench in the distance. I tried not to look, but when I did, the portly one with the bucket hat looked my way.

Soon, no matter where I turned, there they were: at the Albion Dairy Bar; in front of the Holy Jordan River Baptist Church; at Luke Gallant's John Deere dealership on Highway 7.

Things came to something of a head the morning I received an email from our local library telling me a book I had put on hold was now available to pick up. It was a wonderful picture book called *The Golden Book of Illustrated Bible Stories*. I had owned a copy as a boy, a present for my eighth birthday from

Zaide Jakob, my paternal grandfather who lived with us. He was a survivor who always wore long sleeves, but secretly let me look at the numbers tattooed on his arm. My copy of *The Golden Book of Illustrated Bible Stories* had long since been lost, but when I found out another one was floating around the Island-wide library system, I made a point of taking it out any chance I could.

One of my favourite illustrations in the book had always been a depiction of Moses parting the Red Sea. The perspective was from his eye level, making the rising waves that much more dramatic. One could see all manner of marine life being swept up in the towering walls of ocean. Crowning the azure sky above was a white heavenly light fringed with fiery crimson.

This was the visual effect I had in my mind for my Red Sea-inspired depiction of North Cape. I thought if I could look at the original illustration it might help me break through my creative block.

As I entered the Mount Russet Public Library, Marcie, the assistant librarian, smiled, knowing what I was there for, and raised a finger for me to wait. She returned without the book.

"I could have sworn we had it back here," she said. "We have a new volunteer here. She might have returned it to the shelves by mistake. I'll see if I can find it for you."

I told her I knew exactly what shelf it might be on and proceeded to make my way toward the rear stacks in the children's section.

I all but recoiled to see the three strangers sitting at the table situated next to the corkboard, on which children's crayon drawings were attached with candy-coloured pushpins. The strangers were hunched over an open book. Without really looking, I knew they were perusing *The Golden Book of Illustrated Bible Stories.* Then I realized the picture that engrossed them so deeply was of Moses parting the Red Sea.

A white rage flared up behind my eyes. My first impulse was to reach down and grab the book off the table. Then the one in the blue baseball cap looked up and pushed the book toward me. His finger pointed at something in the picture. To my horror, there at Moses's foot was the same six-armed starfish that had mysteriously appeared on my painting. I had looked at this picture more times than I could count and had no memory of seeing such a creature.

"Rum looking bugger, ain't it," said baseball cap.

I ran along the library's main aisle. Marcie called out my name, but I pushed through the front doors and didn't stop until I reached home.

I liked the Body Parts well enough because it was cheap, remote and I rarely saw any of my neighbours. Which was why I was unpleasantly surprised to see a moving van parked in front. Two men carrying an ugly green sofa were about to block the front entrance. I managed to sidle past them just in time to race up the stairs, fumble with my key in my door and slam it shut as soon as I was in my apartment.

Bounding up the short flight two steps at a time took the wind out of me. I bent over, bracing my hands against my knees, while I caught my breath.

"We was wondering what took you so long, my dear."

It was them. In my apartment. The speaker was the one in the baseball cap. He spoke in a cockney accent and had *The Golden Book of Illustrated Bible Stories* in his hand. He held it out. "You forgot something."

"How did you get in here? What do you want?"

"We doth harbour no ill tidings toward thee, signor" said the stout one in the coral bucket hat.

"Who the hell are you?" I demanded. "Why are you talking like that?"

The third took off his yellow straw porkpie hat. "Perhaps we might be seated at the table," he said in a deeply mellow voice. His hooded eyelids carried the weight of having seen too much in his lifetime. "All shall be revealed by and by."

The table he was referring to was the old-fashioned folding kind, usually used for playing cards. There were two metal folding chairs and a stool by the kitchenette counter where I usually had breakfast. "The three of you can sit. I'd rather stand."

Baseball cap and bucket hat took the chairs. The other one laid his porkpie hat on the table and perched on the stool. His compatriots hesitantly followed suit, removing their headgear and setting them on the table. Without their hats the three of them, with their various shades of red hair, looked oddly vulnerable and unsure of themselves.

"I believe it is best to begin with introductions," said the one on the stool. "My name is Judas." He pointed to the stout one. "This is Shylock." Then gesturing to the other: "And this is Fagin." The sharp, high-pitched yelp that leapt out of my throat was as close to laughter as I could manage, considering three lunatics were in my apartment and I had no idea how to get them out.

"So, when you say... Judas, you mean Iscariot?"

"That is the name by which I have come to be known."

"And Shylock? From *The Merchant of Venice?*"

The stout one rose. He had thick eyebrows resembling burly caterpillars, from which stray hairs sprang out like twitching antennae. "Verily, signor, I did hail from that ghetto within fair Venice. And yet, I was no merchant, but a moneylender, as I had no other means of livelihood."

I looked at the other one. "Let me guess, Fagin. Dickens' pickpocket?"

"I have acquired many talents, my dear. But I always preferred to think of myself as an educator, passing on me hard-won experience to the next generation." He touched the bill of his baseball cap.

"I have no idea how you got here before me or even how you got in here at all. I assume one of you is good at picking locks."

"I can assure you we did not enter by any criminal means," said Judas.

"Well, you weren't invited either," I said. It was then that I noticed the discoloured scar circling the base of his throat. I must have been staring because he tugged at his collar with gloomy humility. "In any case I think you all should leave now."

Shylock stood and rested a meaty hand on Judas's shoulder. "We hath no wish to overstay our welcome. Yet we beg thy indulgence to hear with good patience the purpose of our mission."

The notion of bolting out the door and running flitted briefly through my head. Either the one called Fagin could read minds or the impulse was clearly visible in my expression.

"And doing a runner won't help you none, my dear. Why not save everyone time by hearing us out?" He also stood and pushed his chair toward me. "You'll need this more than me."

I sat. Judas slid down from the stool, took the chair that had been vacated by Shylock and placed it in front of me, settling onto the seat while the other two stood behind him. Judas spoke patiently, explaining that the three of them could be best appreciated as figments of my imagination, and yet they also had free will. "While we originate from your mind, we are also capable of independent thoughts and actions."

"How is that possible?" I asked.

"It is a mystery that may become revealed to you within this lifetime or perhaps the next. That is all I can say to any satisfaction."

"So, all those times I saw you appear and then disappear..."

"We were trying to introduce ourselves to you. That was why we had to adopt this form of dress, so as not to alarm you and ease our way to your attention. Yet we sensed you were not ready to be approached."

"But then you left me alone for all these years. Why are you back?"

"I ask that you be patient and listen. There is much for you to take in."

His tone was gentle, yet insistent, making it clear that any further questioning or discussion was futile. This only brought more questions to mind, but I pushed those thoughts out of my head and forced myself to listen. I was not prepared for what he was about to tell me. The mission that Shylock had mentioned was no small thing. The three of them were messengers of the "Supreme One."

"You understand of whom I speak?" Judas asked and tried to smile.

"God?" I said.

"If that is the name you prefer."

"God spoke to the three of you?" I looked at the other two. Their faces revealed nothing. "What did His voice sound like?"

"I have no words to describe this. It is not the voice of a man."

"God's a woman?"

"It is not the voice of man or woman but that of an all-pervading silence."

He allowed me to ponder this before going on to explain that, for the past few centuries, the Supreme One had been very disturbed by the state of this world. The destruction of natural resources caused by rampant greed, the dwindling of compassion and the ever-growing reverence for self-interest in most of its inhabitants had signalled a point of no return.

"Centuries?" I said. "If it's been going on for centuries why this sudden concern?"

Judas's patience was waning at all my interruptions. "The length of a century in this world passes in a mere instant where the Supreme One dwells."

"'Tis the truth, signor," said Shylock. "Those thirteen years that marked our absence, of which you spoke earlier? They passeth in the instant it takes to scratch the Supreme One's nose."

Fagin leaned in a bit closer. "That is, my dear, if the Supreme One had a nose or a reason to scratch it."

Before I could ask anything else, Judas waved his compatriots back. He continued by pointing out that the Middle East, which many have long considered the Promised Land, was, in particular, a great cause of distress. Apparently, in the Supreme One's estimation, the tensions there were far beyond any reasonable solution.

"Henceforth, that part of the world will no more be distinguished by that name. The Supreme One has seen fit to bless this small red mote as the new Promised Land."

"What red mote?"

"This very one we are now on."

"Red mote? You mean here? PEI? This nothing little island? The new Promised Land?"

What began as a slow chuckle soon escalated into fits of gasping hysteria that threatened to spill into heaves of panicking sobs at any moment. I started to hyperventilate and hugged my knees. When I looked up again, I could see the worried creases registered on the three faces staring at me. I kept my hands braced on my knees as I struggled to get a grip. Little did I know the *coup de grâce* was about to be delivered.

"Before this consecration can be made final, one task must be completed. This island has churches of various denominations, a mosque, a Buddhist monastery, a variety of places of worship except one. A synagogue must be built and you have been chosen to erect it."

"Chosen?" The word lacked any meaning. "Why me?"

"Why, because of the girl, of course," said Fagin. "That bone-thin, ginger-haired urchin you painted. That picture caught the Supreme One's attention right smart."

Now Shylock stepped up and towered above me. "Forsooth, signor, rarely has paint and canvas made palpable such vulnerable despair and grim pride. It most nakedly expressed what thou hadst described so artfully as..." He turned to Fagin. "How went that pithy statement?"

"'The delusion of our collective innocence,'" Fagin quoted. "Your way with words, my dear, is almost as dexterous as your handling of the brush."

Hearing those words echoed back after all these years made something inside me go icy. "But I just said that... I was on the radio, I had to think of something..."

Judas looked at his other two compatriots and they both stepped back. "I sympathize this may be more than you can comprehend in a sitting," he said.

What I couldn't understand was, if a supreme deity was going to choose messengers, why these three? And what were they doing in my psyche in the first place? Each was a famous Jewish character in literature, each a prime example of anti-Semitic sentiment throughout the ages. But only two of them were definitely fictional characters, while there is enough historical evidence to verify that Judas was a real person. I mentioned this to them.

"It is factual that I did exist," Judas said. "And yet my history took its own path through the telling and retelling by others to portray the version of a Judas other than me. While Shylock and Fagin, though fictional they be, had their origins in people who existed."

"And if I weren't based on one model, my dear, then perhaps it was a composite of many to make a single portrayal," said Fagin. "But that's the case of everyone, innit? You yourself are just a result of many who came before you."

"'Tis a great problem of our philosophy, signor," added Shylock "What form doth reality take and what may be said to be a fiction? Is one a mirror for the other or are they clothed by the opposite ends of a single thread?"

I closed my eyes and rubbed my temples. "Am I going crazy?"

I opened my eyes to find myself alone again. Relieved at first, I walked around the flat, opening the doors to the bathroom and the tiny space I used as a bedroom, checked the closet, bathroom cabinet, pulled aside the shower curtain, even flung open the kitchenette cupboards and rummaged through the drawers.

Not a sign of them anywhere except for the copy of *The Golden Book of Illustrated Bible Stories* on the kitchenette counter. I opened it to the page with the picture of Moses parting the Red Sea. There was no sign of the six-armed starfish.

My attention was drawn to the large picture window, the one letting in all the natural light that makes this apartment such a perfect studio space. An unusually bright beam illuminated the drop cloth on the canvas. Hoping against all hope, I removed the cloth, but there on the canvas was the six-armed starfish again, now a good deal larger and more centered from where I had blotted it out last time.

I stepped back, allowing my eye to follow along the tapering reddish strip between the rising waves. If before I saw it as the crack running through the world, I realized it now symbolized a stretch of unknown from which there was no turning back.

2

Almost a week had passed since Judas, Fagin and Shylock, or the figments – *Figs* for short – as I came to think of them collectively, first rudely appeared in my apartment. I kept expecting them to show up at any moment and my constant state of anticipatory dread was beginning to take its toll on my nerves. To forget my troubles, I dropped in at my local watering hole the Crazy Diamond Bar & Grill. I settled onto my favourite stool and my spirits brightened when I read the sign over the cash register: *Try our Harvest Moon cocktail. You'll take a real shine to it.* I never failed to get a kick out of that. It was a welcome, if brief, respite from my bewildered state of mind.

The Crazy Diamond was a ramshackle roadhouse bar on the outskirts of town at the end of the Mount Russet Road before it jigs over to become Highway 7. I'd heard about it while I was still in Charlottetown, so when I moved to Mount Russet it was one of the first places I checked out and quickly became a regular. Maggie Beairsto and her husband Pius Duffy ran the joint and it was Maggie's obsession with the British psychedelic rock band Pink Floyd that gave the place its name. But it was Pius's brainchild to refit a vintage Wurlitzer jukebox with a computerized, non-stop MP3 playlist of all the classic prog rockers' albums, covering the gamut of their career. At that moment a disembodied voice sang softly through the speakers about a lunatic being in his head, followed by someone else's creepy, disturbed laughter (presumably the lunatic in question).

Only one lunatic in his head? Lucky bastard.

Pius also had a talent for distilling his own shine, which kept him in an adjacent area behind the Crazy Diamond. If you understood the Floydian connection between "shine" and the bar's name then you understood Maggie and Pius's particular sense of humour. And if you shared that sense of humour, you were okay in their book.

The Crazy Diamond's peculiar atmosphere was what can only be described as Maritime psychedelia: a décor of lava lamps on the tables, lobster traps, nets and buoys hanging from the ceiling and prints of vintage Pink Floyd album covers – including some rare European and Japanese editions – on the walls. Most of one wall was taken up by a large mural reproduction of the famous back cover of their double album, *Ummagumma* with all of the Floyd's gear: musical instruments, amplifiers, microphones, etc, as well as two roadies, symmetrically arranged on an airport tarmac.

The unique combination of Maggie and Pius's shared obsessions brought in a stream of faithful customers every night and made the Crazy Diamond the success it had been for the past fifteen years.

Maggie was a sturdy, middle-aged ex-biker chick with a Medusa-like mane of greying curls brightened by streaks of blue, red, green and mauve. This colourful coif was often echoed by a black *Dark Side of the Moon* prism rainbow tank top, at least one size too small, if the escaping peekaboo pink bra strap was anything to go by. We had a friendly, sometimes playfully flirtatious, barmaid/barfly relationship, bordering on the protective. A couple of times in the past, when some rum-soaked yahoo gave me lip about my paintings and their "Jewed up" depiction of "the Island way of life", Maggie was not slow to take out Lorie, her prize 9-iron (named after women's golfer and favourite PEI daughter, Lorie Kane), from behind the bar to show everyone who ran this establishment.

This particular night I noticed a wide-mouthed jar in front of the cash register.

"New tip jar?"

Maggie flashed her trademark smirk: shorthand for don't be such a schmuck. She turned the jar so I could see the large computer-created sign taped to it. In big block letters it read: ASHLYNN'S CAMP FOR KIDS FUND.

"Who's Ashlynn?"

"Didn't you hear Chet and Chad this morning?"

I shook my head. Although the radio turns on automatically to wake me, I preferred not to listen too closely to *Good Morning PEI* with hosts Chet Affleck and Chad Peladeau. I tend to keep it low as background noise during my morning ablutions, stopping only to listen to local news and weather updates. I'd grown annoyed by Chet and Chad's stiff banter of forced hilarity and the show's non-story filler items about local sports awards, spelling bees and food bank drives, all delivered to make whatever was being said sound more interesting than it was.

"It was a story they did about that poor little girl who died of leukemia. Her one last wish was to go to summer camp with her friends," Maggie said.

"Yet another cheery item from *Good Mourning PEI*."

"They did an interview with Reuben Arsenault. The girl's mother works in one of his restaurants. He was so moved by the story he's heading a fund-raising drive to get a summer camp built in her name."

"And there's the money shot in this morass of sentimental porn," I said. "Rich douchebag builds kid's camp. That should buy him a lot of PR."

"He challenged all local businesses to see who could raise the most money to help build the camp."

"Don't tell me," I said. "The winner gets to open a concession stand in the new camp. I'll bet your Virgin Margaritas would go over like gangbusters."

"You can put on that cynic act all you want, but deep down I know you got a heart of gold."

"Yeah, I'm like a walking Fort Knox." I drained my stein and, good bar hostess that she was, Maggie replaced it before I could wipe my mouth. "Does Pius know you're raising money for one of Reuben Arsenault's PR stunts?"

"He runs his end and I run mine."

Maggie set up four highball glasses and the ingredients to make a shaker of Harvest Moons. I swallowed the rest of my IPA and savoured the momentary rush of alcohol saturation with a sloppy grin. Once the Earth's axis righted itself, I eased down from my stool and reached across the bar to take one of Maggie's hands, with their stubby sausage-like fingers, and planted a chivalrous kiss on her wrinkled knuckles. "One day you'll make some lucky *mamzer* a good wife," I said. "But for the time being you're stuck with that S.O.B. in the back."

"I'll tell Pius you send your regards."

With that I swivelled on the soles of my paint-splotched Blundstones and made my way past the crowded tables toward the door.

AN AMBER THUMBNAIL paring of crescent moon darted between spectral branches, its teasing grin playing peek-a-boo against the star-pocked violet night, as my VW Golf sputtered homeward. I was reminded of my first visit to the Island in the summer of 1993, almost twenty-two years ago, after graduating from the Ontario College of Art. Construction on the Confederation Bridge was due to start that autumn, so I had to take the ferry from Cape Tormentine, New Brunswick to Borden. How I loved tooling around the back roads in the trusty Lada that managed to get me from Toronto to PEI and back. It was love at first sight (with the Island that is, although I did have an odd fondness for that Lada, beat-up piece of *dreck* that it was).

Back then I had recognized something both virginal and vulgar in the rich rusty shorelines, the verdant needles of spruce trees with their glistening sap and the birches' dappled, ashen bark peeling like dead skin. Something in my painter's soul was shaken awake by the cobalt rivers and cerulean bays (both revealing patches of the Island's rubicund inner life) and the mountain range of clouds – with their bleached cotton folds sloping to smoky grey – rising against an endless sky of washed-out robin's egg blue. From the moment I arrived on that first two-week holiday, I swore I would return some day to become an Islander by Choice, as those of us from away are now known in politically correct circles. After toughing it out in the art department of Fennimore-Paisley (at the time, one of Toronto's up-and-coming ad agencies) for almost three and a half years, while paying my parents minimal rent to save my meagre wages, I finally cashed in some Israel bonds that had been accruing interest since my bar mitzvah and made good on that promise.

"I was young," I said as I negotiated the gradual bend of the road leading into town. "I was full of hope, rife with dreams." This habit of consciously talking aloud while alone was a coping mechanism during times of stress. I often talked to myself in public, although I was careful to keep the conversation inside my head. If I noticed people staring at me, I knew my vigilance had been lowered and I was silently moving my lips. The best thing was to restrict the one-sided conversation to private moments like this.

"What the hell did I know anyway?"

"More than you might think, my dear," said a voice beside me.

A sharp swerve punished my shock absorbers on some bumpy dirt roadside before I jammed my foot on the brake. With one hand gripping the wheel, the other hand shot up and switched on the overhead light. The first thing I noticed was the blue baseball cap and beneath it, Fagin sitting in the passenger seat.

"You nearly gave me a heart attack!" I shouted.

"You don't seem happy to see me," he said. "And here I rather paid you a compliment."

"What compliment?"

"You asked what you knew back then as your younger self and I said more than you think. I was giving you some credit, me."

"I was talking out loud," I explained with a snort of impatience. "I wasn't asking anyone anything. Least of all you."

Back on the road, a minute of nothing but the Golf's rumbling engine made me wonder whether I had chastised him into silence. Then I remembered that Judas had said they were figments with free will. As if on cue, my passenger proved I had no idea what I was up against when it came to him and his cohorts.

"Didn't you have any inkling you were following a path what had already been laid out before you, my dear?"

His raspy East London drawl came from behind and I saw that the passenger seat was now empty. In the rear-view mirror I could see Fagin's glinting fox eyes.

"By the way, where are Larry and Moe?" I asked, realizing he probably wouldn't get the cultural reference. Sure enough, he scratched his scraggly beard in bewilderment. "I mean why are you here alone?"

"Truth be known, my dear, we was worried we may have sent you over the bend. Thought it might be more prudent to take turns confabbing with you rather than coming at you all at once."

"So, you drew the short straw?"

"Nothing as arbitrary as that." Fagin leaned close to my ear and spoke in a conspiratorial whisper. "Fact is, I'm here to lay out the opportunity what's being afforded to you, seeing as opportunities is something of my personal expertise."

I could feel his hot breath on the back of my neck. What irked me most was the possibility that this little Cockney *ganef* might be right. That thing he said, something about a path being laid out. It struck a nerve. The first thing that popped into my head was my unfinished painting. Was that what it was trying to be, the path that had been laid out for me, the path leading to PEI? If this painting was merely a way of assessing the past eighteen years, with the realization that it has all come to nothing, could that be the source of my block? If I finished the painting, was I, in essence, finishing myself? I waited for my passenger to say something further, but he sat there, taking pleasure in the silence of me wrestling with my own artistic mortality.

"So..." I ventured. "What did you mean before by opportunity?"

"Well, it's like your picture, innit?" he said and I wondered yet again if he could read my mind, which wasn't so far-fetched since he sprang from some dark recess inside it. "You can't push ahead with it, right? It's become this massive obstacle. But the truth of it is, obstacles are really just opportunities in disguise."

I gave him a cursory glance in the rear-view mirror. "Great, now I've got the Tony Robbins of Petticoat Lane in my car."

"Who?"

"Never mind."

"Mock me all you like, my dear, but your whole life has been leading up to this."

"To what?"

"The synagogue, what else? It's all well and good to be painting fantasies of a Jewish Island, but now you have the opportunity to turn that into a reality."

"I'm not an architect. I don't build things."

"What about that Noah's Ark made out of oyster crates?"

"Lobster traps," I corrected. "Besides, I haven't stepped inside a *shul* since my bar mitzvah in 1974. I'm still scarred by memories of my thirteen-year-old falsetto cracking in front of the entire congregation while I struggled to follow Torah with my rabbi's silver-plated pointer in my trembling hand."

"Them's the trials of life what builds character," he said. "You can do whatever you got a mind to, my dear."

Was that what I'd been doing all along with my paintings, envisioning a Jewish PEI? That never felt like my intention. To me it was a simple juxtaposition of cultures, a way of assimilating my otherness to the Island's bucolic splendour and simple quality of life. The paintings were my way in, while maintaining my place on the outside. Artists need to have that foot in both worlds or else we suffer from a creative claustrophobia brought on by too much comfort and contentment.

Then it hit me. Maybe that's what the strip of land in my painting indicated. No beginning and no end, just a very comforting and noncommittal strand of limbo. The muddle of the road, so to speak. And yet something in me rebelled against the idea that I had lost my creative fire. Was I really going to let this fast-talking phantasm poison me against my own work for the sake of some synagogue pipedream? I pulled over.

"Get out."

Fagin's sympathetic tongue clicking brought no comfort. "I had a notion this might happen, my dear."

"I said, get out."

"Let's not be hasty." He shifted over in his seat, wisely keeping his distance. "You're feeling particularly vulnerable right now. No profit in making knee-jerk decisions."

"I don't need you and your motivational mumbo-jumbo to pull me out of the red mud I'm currently mired in. I've weathered more creative blocks than you've buggered street urchins!"

"Oi, easy on," he said darkly. "There's no call for that filthy sort of aspersion!"

Obviously, I hit a nerve, found a weakness. There was no backing down now. I knew I had to stand my ground.

"I can sit here all night if I have to, but I am not going to budge an inch until you have extricated your Dickensian keister out of my car and out of my life."

"Tell you what," he said with a conciliatory manner that only served to irk me all the more. "How about you come back here so we can have a genuine heart-to-heart?"

"If I go back there it'll be to drag you out of my car by the scruff of that rusty steel wool you call a beard."

"Fine, suit yourself." With that he crossed his arms to indicate an infinite reserve of patience. "Maybe after you've cooled off, we can continue this little chat in a more civilized-like manner."

I glared at him in the rear-view mirror, but the imaginary laser beams shooting out of my eyes refused to ricochet off the silvered-glass rectangle into the back seat. It was obvious that I was going to have to be proactive about this and show that I was a man of my word. I unbuckled my seat belt, opened my door and got out, slamming the door shut for dramatic effect. I heard a familiar click, which didn't register until I pulled the back door handle, nearly yanking my arm out of its socket. When I realized the door was locked, I tried to get back into the driver's side, only to find it was also locked. I peered in through the window and saw my keys dangling from the ignition. I could see Fagin still sitting cross-armed in the back seat. I went around to the other side and tried both those doors only to find them locked as well. I had no idea how he did it and I didn't care as I pounded on the window until he finally deigned to turn his head in my direction. I yelled at him to unlock the doors, but he merely shrugged his shoulders and turned his head away from me.

I became aware of the blasé rhythm of distant crickets. Every chirp mocked my situation. "Fagin!" I screamed. "You let me in this instant! I can last as long as you can." I waited, but only the crickets responded to my questionable bluster with a high-pitched chorus of scepticism.

"Was it the crack about buggering urchins?" I asked. "You brought that on yourself. Okay, maybe not, but I spoke in the heat of the moment. You want an apology? Is that it? Will that settle things between us? Fine. You win. I... I'm sorry."

Peering into the back seat, I could see Fagin had done a disappearing act. I heard the tell-tale click once more and was relieved to discover the front door unlocked. I opened it and slipped back in behind the wheel.

IN MY APARTMENT, I stood at the kitchen sink with the tap running for what felt like an indefinite amount of time until I had the presence of mind to fill the kettle and set it on the stove. I was physically and mentally drained and leaned all my weight against the counter. The whistling kettle nearly split my head in two and, in my haste to pluck it off the burner, seared the side of my hand.

Sitting up in bed with gauze wrapped around my ointment-smeared hand and my laptop balanced on my thighs, I scanned my various bookmarked sites but could not find anything suitable to divert my attention. I scrolled down the bookmark menu under the Miscellaneous heading, contemplating favourite websites on archaeology, ornithology, gerontology and a number of other ologies, most of which interested me as passing curiosities and ways to induce sleep.

At the end of the menu was a link for a site called annesurly.com. I couldn't remember visiting, never mind bookmarking such a website. Had I been hacked? Was this a phishing scam? I decided it was probably best not to click the link and checked out a few of my favourite museum and other artistic websites, but curiosity kept nagging me to return to this strange new link.

I looked closer at the URL and was able to decipher it as Anne Surly. Some kind of website satirizing Anne Shirley? There are a plethora of works for the stage, page and other media that play fast and loose with Lucy Maud's world-famous fictional waif (including my own infamous creation), so what could it hurt to have a look?

The screen loaded to a dark metallic-grey page wallpapered with yellow straw hats, orange pigtails and blood-red lips curled downward into snarls that bared sharp white fangs. In the middle of the page was an old-fashioned picture frame surrounding quaint needlepoint letters: ENTER AT YOUR OWN RISK. I clicked the needlepoint and there appeared a melon pink page with black letters in a stencilled font: *Please Wait.* I stared patiently at this page for almost a minute then decided to go somewhere else and check in later. Before I could do so, the screen flickered, then showed a room being filmed on a webcam. The grainy wall was bare, and the only furnishing was a leatherette sofa with a green diamond pattern. Something about this sofa seemed oddly familiar.

The picture blurred slightly and refocused. Someone was obviously adjusting the webcam lens.

A female figure appeared from the side of the screen. She wore an *Anne of Green Gables* straw hat with orange pigtail attachments one can find in most souvenir shops. Her face was partially covered by an opaque half-mask that exposed a slim jaw and mouth enhanced by gaudy blood-red lipstick, like on the homepage's wallpaper. The rest of her attire was less traditional. She wore a crimson bodice that pushed up a well-shaped cleavage, matching fishnet tights and knee-high black patent-leather boots. The outfit was completed by elbow-length metal-studded black leather gloves and a black riding crop, which she used to cut the air with a menacing swoosh or punctuate her speech with a smack against the side of her boot.

"Hello, fans, freaks and fuck-knobs. Anne Surly here for my weekly rant, so listen the hell up! I know you're sitting there with your hands down your boxers, fiddling with your pathetic junk and fantasizing that you're gonna get your dinky stinky. But first you gotta eat your vegetables and I have a lot to get off my chest."

I could not believe what I was seeing and especially what I was hearing. Who in the Supreme One's name was this foul-mouthed hellion and how did this link end up being bookmarked on my laptop?

"So, first of all, to the mouth-breathing shit-for-brains dickwads who broke into my previous location to screw up my operation: don't think for a minute I don't know who you are, you Neanderthal nut-sacks! And don't think I don't know who's paying you to fuck my shit up. Same big money that thinks they can squeeze another golf course or amusement park or pizza joint out of these world-famous little titties."

She did a frenzied shimmy and her cleavage jiggled accordingly.

"Well guess what? This little orphan ain't yours to pimp out any more! I'm the one calling the shots now. Gentle Island, my ass! More like a stinking sewer of politics and dirty deals beneath the nineteenth century façade of homespun bullshit. For too long now they've appropriated my image to bring in clueless tourists and their deep pockets, but now I'm taking it back and I'm going to blow this whole sick co-dependent tourism-and-culture cycle wide open! Tonight, there will be a new feature to my weekly rant: Anne Surly's Top Ten Enemies of the Island."

She cracked the riding crop against the side of one leather boot and began to do a slow seductive grind, listing off the names starting at number ten. The first few names didn't mean much to me. There was the president of a novelties company that distributed Anne merchandise, ironically like the straw hat and pigtails she was wearing. A couple of names from the L.M.M. Licensing Trust and some general manager in charge of Green Gables Family Land. At each name she sliced the air with the riding crop while her body's grinding rhythm grew more suggestive. Its effect on me was starting to feel uncomfortably obvious, but my attention was seriously diverted by the next five names.

"Number Five on my enemies list has earned his place because of his newly-appointed volunteer position as Project Director of Ashlynn's Camp for Kids, a supposedly innocent charity with a possible connection to a number of silent political and business partners. Enemy number five is one half of the *Good Morning PEI* radio team... Chet Affleck!"

She turned around to reveal satin-clad buttocks and shook them vigorously. As mesmerized as I was by the sight of that, I was more stunned by the mention of Ashlynn's Camp for Kids and wondered what Maggie Beairsto would make of this.

"For the number four spot we're keeping it in the family. His alleged involvement in the Waterslide Scandal at Sarsaparilla Springs was quickly glossed over by the media but not forgotten here. And now that Sarsaparilla Springs has closed down, it's been named as the possible new site for Ashlynn's Camp for Kids. Can you say nepotism? If you can then it should come as no surprise that enemy number four is none other than the big brother of enemy number five, our own premier of Prince Edward Island... Nathan Affleck."

Now she seesawed the riding crop between her legs. I could have happily watched that all by itself, but I kept wondering how she could make these allegations and was she opening herself up to a charge of slander? No wonder she wore a mask. The Waterslide Scandal was a highly publicized news story, where two young people were seriously injured at Sarsaparilla Springs Water Park due to poor maintenance of the waterslide as a cost-cutting measure. But Premier Affleck's connection as a one-time adviser to the company that ran the water park was mentioned only in passing and then quickly dismissed by the local media.

Did this webcam wiggler know something everyone else didn't? It's true the water park was closed and its future was in question, but the idea that it might become a children's camp sounded like a spurious rumour at best.

The next two enemies of the Island were also familiar names. Number three was the CEO of the PEI Board of Health, Dr. Humphrey Becker, who apparently also had a tenuous connection to the Waterslide Scandal. Anne Surly alleged that he publicly downplayed the seriousness of the victims' injuries as part of a shady patronage deal with the premier, because Becker had his eye on the Minister of Health portfolio.

The penultimate enemy was, not surprisingly, Kerrie-Jo Campbelljohn, Minister of Tourism and Culture, or as Anne Surly dubbed her, "The Reigning Bitch-Queen of Golf Carts and Yogurt." Campbelljohn had been the Tourism and Culture Minister pretty much since I had moved to PEI. The portfolio, her first and only so far, had been handed to her by then-premier Alan MacSorley, whose Retro-Progressive Party was in power at the time. He was later narrowly defeated by Loyalty Party upstart Nathan Affleck. Everyone expected Campbelljohn to be relegated to the backbenches, but she pulled off a bold about-face: a Walk of Shameful Opportunism across the floor of the Legislature to join the newly in-power Loyals.

It was not enough to turn their minority government into a majority, but it did strengthen Affleck's hand somewhat. All the same, he would still have to work within a coalition comprised of the Retro-Progressive opposition and the Neo-Egalitarians to get anything done.

For her "bloody-minded head-lock on the Tourism and Culture portfolio," Campbelljohn earned her position as Anne Surly's Number Two Enemy. So venomous was her opinion of the minister, I couldn't imagine who she had slotted in the top spot. Considering the major league players in the lower ranks, I could not even hazard a guess as to who it might be.

"And now wankers, weasels and wimps, that leaves us with only Island Enemy Number One. Or should I say Island Enema, because this one has been a pain up PEI's fundament for a long, long time. Get ready to grab your peckers for the big reveal. The number one enemy of the Island is the Donald Rump of Island unreal estate and other forms of crass materialism, none other than… Reuben Arsenault. He's got a top-secret development deal in the works that ties into all our previously named enemies. Stay tuned to this website for further…"

A noise startled her, diverting her attention to something off screen. Two balaclava-masked intruders charged into the picture. If Anne Surly felt any fear, she didn't show it. Instead, she wasted no time swinging the riding crop at them. She connected with one intruder's shoulder and neck, sending him reeling off screen. I'm pretty sure I heard him yell, "The camera!" and suddenly the other one loomed large on the screen before it went black altogether.

I became aware of a commotion above me. There was stomping and shouting. Domestic squabbles and other disturbances were commonplace at the Body Parts and normally I wouldn't have bothered to even look through the peephole on my door.

But this sounded like a continuation of what I had just witnessed on my laptop. My curiosity won out against my better judgement and I opened my front door a crack and slipped through, as if that would somehow keep me invisible and safe. I went over to the staircase leading to the next floor up and heard the same stomping and shouting.

Common sense dictated that I hurry back into my apartment and lock the door behind me, but some other compulsion – something stronger than mere curiosity – propelled me up the stairs. As soon as I reached the next floor, the door of the apartment facing me flew open and two balaclava-masked figures scrambled past me, almost tumbling down the stairs. I managed to flatten myself against the wall to keep from being knocked over. My first inclination was to somehow get even farther away from the stairway, but I was suddenly confronted by Anne Surly. She raised her riding crop, ready to strike.

"What the fuck are you looking at, arse wipe?"

Any words I might have uttered at that moment were cowering somewhere in the coils of my lower intestine. Yet, in a dark, damp corner of my brain I was able to ascertain that this was not an entirely unreasonable question. All

I knew for sure was that in a relatively short period of time – where I had been confronted by three figments of my imagination, claiming to have free will and be messengers of some heavenly deity – a riding crop wielding *Anne of Green Gables* as dominatrix was by far the strangest thing I had witnessed to date.

I had a queasy feeling in my lower intestine, huddling somewhere in the coils along with my power of speech, that far stranger sights were going to come.

3

A LITTLE LATER, in my apartment, I was joined by none other than Anne Surly, now fully dressed in jeans and sweatshirt. Without her straw hat and pigtails and opaque half-mask, she had closely cropped hair dyed canary yellow, almond-shaped eyes and fine cheekbones, accentuated by her light olive complexion that was more apparent in person than on the screen. A perfectly beautiful young woman, although I have to admit her shaved eyebrows, the left one being pierced by a row of small gold rings, left me cold. I guess I'm a bit of a square in that way. All that remained of her cyber alter ego was the blood red lipstick.

When she had confronted me upstairs, rather than thrashing me with her riding crop, she let me explain that I lived on the floor below her and was only standing outside her door because I had heard the commotion in her apartment. I said nothing about watching her on my computer. I offered to call the police, but she said there would be no point. She told me to wait in the hallway and went inside, closing her door behind her. I waited and soon felt foolish standing there. I was about to head back downstairs when she emerged fully dressed and unmasked and asked if she could sit in my place until she felt safer. That threw me for a loop. The way she had handled herself, it would have been more humane to offer refuge to those two masked goons. She told me her name was Aziza.

Aziza wandered around my apartment, peering closely at my brushes and paints and glanced at some of the paintings on the wall, as well as the ones leaning against each other near a corner. She stopped at the drop cloth draped over the canvas on my easel. My anxiety mounted at the thought of her peeking under it. Noticing how I was watching her and probably sensing my uneasiness, she made her way to the kitchenette counter.

"Would you mind if I lit this up?" she asked, producing a half-smoked joint from the small string purse slung over her shoulder. "I'm feeling a bit shaky and this would help calm me down."

Normally, I don't allow smoking, tobacco or otherwise, in my apartment, but considering what she had just been through I acquiesced and handed her a saucer to use as an ashtray. She sat at the card table and lit the joint, quietly sucking in the smoke – a delicate hissing not unlike a slow leak in a party balloon – and held out the joint to me. I declined and told her I was strictly a beer man. She took a couple of quick tokes, gently extinguished the joint's lit end in the saucer and returned what was left in her purse. I was secretly glad to have the thing extinguished and out of my sight. Not that I'm a prude about drugs, but considering how life was currently unfolding, my reality was already being altered beyond the point of credulity.

"So," she said and looked at the chaos that made up my studio. "You're an artist."

"Either that or I need a new housekeeper."

"Wait a minute." She looked at me with narrowing eyes. "You said up there that your name is Samson? Are you Samson Grief? You painted *Anne of Bergen-Belsen*?"

It was as much a statement as it was a question. I merely nodded and slouched in my chair, wishing I could disappear under the table.

Far from escalating into an uncomfortable confrontation, it turned out that seeing *Anne of Bergen-Belsen* had been a turning point for Aziza. She had been twelve and already impressively well-versed in much of the feminist canon, including Simone de Beauvoir, Betty Friedan, Kate Millet and Susan Sontag, among others. The moment she saw *Anne of Bergen-Belsen* she could not believe that a man had painted it. I assumed this was meant as a compliment.

"Well, I guess that's not entirely true," she quickly corrected herself. "On first viewing, the painting seemed to victimize Anne, which was in keeping with a certain patriarchal viewpoint that, in my opinion, has entrapped her all these years."

My ego felt as if it was being pumped with an air hose, only to have the nozzle suddenly pop out, leading to rapid deflation.

"Why patriarchal? Lucy Maud Montgomery was a woman."

"I guess I'd always been on the fence as to whether *Anne of Green Gables* could be considered feminist literature," she said, her hands gesturing emphatically. "I mean, she's headstrong and all that, but in the end, she does what's expected of her. She gives in to the conventions she's trapped in."

"I guess," I said, trying to remain as non-committal as I could. In truth, I couldn't even get through the whole book although I had tried a number of times.

"Still, something intrigued me about your painting," she continued. "The more I looked at it, the more I saw you were trying to depict her as a survivor of the Island's patriarchal capitalist agenda that had imprisoned her image purely for monetary gain."

I wanted to tell her that wasn't what I was trying to do at all but opted to keep my mouth shut. Nothing devalues art more than making the mistake of trying to explain it.

"Oh sure, at one time she was probably the right image for the innocence that was part of life here," Aziza said. "But that eventually was spun off into a thousand merchandising opportunities, all for filthy tourist lucre that would keep us chained to our fake nineteenth century quaintness for as long as it paid off. I mean even your painting, irony of ironies, brought in a lot of tourists. That's when I realized what you were doing. I couldn't help feeling like a torch was being handed to me. I felt this overpowering compulsion, a real fire in my belly, to rescue her from mere survival into a state of empowerment."

For a minute it sounded like she was going to resort back to her Anne Surly persona. I tried to nod indifferently, but in my mind's eye I couldn't erase the image of Anne Surly in her dominatrix regalia and tried to reconcile that with the affable twenty-something sitting before me. As much as I attempted to adopt a poker face, I grew fearful that something in my body language must have a tell, betraying my inner thoughts.

"You know, you haven't asked me about what happened up there," she said.

"Why I was dressed up like that."

"To be honest, I didn't really think it was any of my business. You were in distress and that's all that mattered."

"In distress? Me?" At first, I thought she was angry, but then she laughed. "You should have seen the look on your face. You were terrified I was going to use that riding crop on you."

"Guilty as charged."

"So, what did you think was going on?" I didn't know what to say and my eyes must have signalled their helplessness, because a sudden look of disgust twisted that blood red mouth of hers. "You didn't think something freaky was going on with those two jokers, did you?"

I assured her I thought nothing of the kind and tried to steer the topic back to her political-feminist-economic interpretation of my painting. She was having none of it and persisted in questioning me, chiding me for my lack of curiosity, much to my obvious discomfort, in which I'm pretty sure she was taking a certain amount of delight. I found myself blurting out that I had seen everything on my computer right up until the screen went black, then heard the commotion above me and put two and two together.

I was preparing myself to be verbally lambasted for being a perverted creep, since that was obviously what Anne Surly thought of her viewers. Instead, her manner was gentle and sympathetic to my obvious mortification. She asked how long I had been one of her viewers and I explained that night was the first time. I worried she wouldn't believe me. Instead, she confessed that she was proud that I had seen her, since it was *Anne of Bergen-Belsen* that had inspired her to create Anne Surly.

"How long have you been doing this?" I asked, while still trying to wrap my head around this revelation.

"I've been evolving the character for a few years. At first, I tried a much tamer version called Surely Anne as a performance piece I did in friends' living rooms and a couple of coffee houses. It was mild satire with some political commentary. After a while I tried to push the political element more, but audiences were bored. I knew I needed a new approach. I invested in a webcam and started to broadcast. I made the character edgier and called her Anne

Surly but realized no one was really watching. That's when I decided to go for broke and added the bustier and riding crop. I've been doing this version of her for almost six months now."

I asked about her audience, if she knew who was watching and how many of them there were. She couldn't say with any accuracy. She had made the mistake of having a Twitter account to promote Anne Surly and get a sense of who was watching. She wasn't naïve enough to think there wouldn't be some perverts trying to connect with her, but she wasn't prepared for the onslaught of filth that came her way. She tried to deflect the tide by staying on message and stubbornly engaged them in political discourse. But in the end, she closed her Twitter account and decided to continue her broadcasts without worrying about who, if anyone, was watching. But the whole Twitter thing had embittered her more than she imagined, and this resulted in the dominatrix-like style I had witnessed that evening.

"I decided to treat them like the scum I knew they were and say anything I wanted. The more outrageous the better. No one believes what I'm saying is true anyway so being fearless comes easy."

During her online diatribe, she alluded to the fact that this was the second time someone had tried to stop her broadcasts. The first time was a couple of months ago when she was broadcasting out of an apartment in the west end of Charlottetown. She came home one night to find the place broken into and the webcam gone. She decided to get another webcam and take her act out of Charlottetown.

She was surprised how quickly they found her this time, but she knew who they were. She didn't want to involve the police because it might have led them to ask too many questions.

"When they broke in, my first thought was to hide behind the sofa, but I guess my adrenalin was rushing and I started lashing out with the riding crop. I hit one of them, on the neck I think, but the other one stomped the webcam with his boot. It's smashed to pieces. Don't know if I can afford a new one."

When she mentioned hiding behind the sofa, it jolted my memory about where I had seen it before. It was the same sofa that was being carried by those moving men the day I'd rushed back to the Body Parts after seeing the three

Figs in the library. She was moving in that day. It really didn't take long for whoever was trying to stop her from finding her. A mere week.

"Who's behind the break-ins?" I asked. "And why are they trying to stop you?"

"The goons in balaclavas are a couple of lowlife brothers. Mostly petty B&E offences with some dealing on the side. Reggie and Kelvin Muir. Reg'n'Kel to everyone who knows them."

"If you know who they are, why not call the cops?"

"They're just a couple of hired stooges. The one who's paying for their services is someone much higher up the food chain."

"What food chain? Who is it?"

"I'll give you a hint. My last name is Arsenault."

"Aziza Arsenault? Has a nice ring to it, but not very helpful. Arsenault is one of the most common Island names next to Gallant. They're the Smith and Jones of PEI."

"Then I'll narrow it down a bit. The person in question has the same name and was mentioned in my Top Ten list tonight."

I had to think back to the list for a moment, running down the names as best as I could remember them until I got to Island Enemy #1.

"Reuben Arsenault is trying to shut you down? Just because he's number one on your shit list?"

"No," she said and unclipped her purse. She took out what was left of the joint, sparked it up and drew in a sizable toke until it sizzled down to a miniscule roach. Her voice strained under the smoke being held in her lungs. "Because he's my father."

MUCH OF THE NEXT morning was taken up sitting in front of my painting while going over in my mind the previous night's events. The majestic rise of the waves seemed to reveal the six-armed starfish, which had now assumed a prominent place in the picture. This was as puzzling as the appearance of Anne Surly's URL in my bookmark menu. I could not for the life of me see how the Starfish of David and Anne Surly were connected, but I somehow suspected at the center of it was this proposed synagogue that I was determined to have nothing to do with.

The Jewish lo-fi blues poet croaked in the background but stirred nothing resembling a creative urge within me. I wondered if it would be possible to continue working on the painting. The very suggestion of picking up a brush, let alone futzing around with tubes of paint, palette, turpentine and whatever, instilled an anathema for any artistic labour, while oddly rousing my stomach juices.

It was eleven o'clock on a Saturday morning. There was only one thing that could satisfy the hunger gnawing at my insides.

All through the twenty-five-minute drive to Charlottetown, my growing appetite – sharpened by this one culinary craving – managed to temporarily take my mind off the existential quicksand into which my life had been hopelessly sinking. The parking lot of the Farmers' Market had all the orderliness of bumper cars at an amusement park. I managed to steer the car through an obstacle course of vehicles, edging into a space between a mud-encrusted Dodge half-ton and a Toyota RAV4. A confederate flag decal on the half-ton's bumper read KWITCHER BELLYACHIN'. The SUV's vanity plate was I♥CZRS. A political endorsement to bring back the Russian monarchy? When I sounded it out, I understood the owner's only connection to Russia was a taste for Stoli mixed with Clamato juice.

Heading toward the market I noticed a Harley-Davidson chopper with JESUS TAKE THE WHEELIE in fiery gold lettering across the gas tank. I guess if I was of that ostentatious temperament, I'd paint the Golf with something like GO CRAZY OR GO HOME.

Inside the market, I shuffled along with the crowd of people who idled in front of vegetable stands; purveyors of cheese, bread, sausages; artisans hawking various crafts and any number of stalls offering a vast array of ethnic foods from samosas to pizza, cabbage rolls to spring rolls, as well as various blends of coffee, smoothies, fresh juices and deep fried mini-donuts sprinkled with your choice of powdered sugar or cinnamon.

Finally, I reached the stall that offered the one reason I came all this way. The Latke Lady was Frieda Greenglass, one of the first people I got to know during my first year on PEI. Back then I gave no thought to the fact that I was moving to a small rural island populated by Scottish, Irish and English descendants who probably never heard of Jews. It never occurred to me that other Jews might have got the same idea to settle here. After all, there was no synagogue on the Island, the nearest one being in Moncton, which was no deterrent to me, but for some reason I assumed it would keep other *landsmen* away.

If I'd been trying to assimilate through painting Jewish stories on Island settings, Frieda adopted a culinary approach. She took PEI's sacred fruit, the thing it's most known for (aside from lobster suppers and *Anne of Green Gables*), the lowly potato, and transformed it into that most Jewish of edible delights: potato latkes. She was an instant success at the Farmers' Market, as this line up of twelve patient customers attested. I took my place in line and waited as the aroma of golden-brown potato latkes, sizzling in three large cast iron frying pans, tortured my olfactory senses and caused my stomach to growl in rebellion.

To take my mind off my hunger, I went over some of what Aziza had told me after I got over the shock of her being Reuben Arsenault's daughter. That was reason enough for wanting Anne Surly to stop shaking her satin-clad ya-yas on the Internet, but apparently there was more and it had to do with some of the allegations integral to her Top Ten list. As one might assume, there was also a certain amount of personal baggage there as well.

Reuben had been separated for almost two years from Aziza's mother, Zaina, a daughter of the prominent Lebanese-Canadian Mahmoud family, who had lived on PEI for five generations. There had been no doubt that Reuben was a philanderer, with a number of extramarital affairs under his belt. After Zaina had had enough and filed for divorce, Reuben agreed to a separation, but always managed to avoid signing the papers that would make their divorce final, fearing Zaina could take him to the cleaners, even though, according to Aziza, all she wanted was a clean break from their marriage.

Aziza also claimed that her father had political aspirations and to that end was having an affair with Kerrie-Jo Campbelljohn. It wasn't hard to imagine that Campbelljohn's inclusion on Anne Surly's Top Ten Enemies list was personally motivated.

Aziza admitted that many of her allegations were, to some degree, the product of strong hunches, rather than hard evidence. But she knew, through some contacts she had been cultivating (which she preferred not to divulge), that there were a lot of unsavoury deals being forged. Many of these deals centered around something called the Blue Point Society, a private club for PEI's powerful white male elite. Aziza knew her father was a member and so were most of the men on her Top Ten list.

She wouldn't say how she got her information, but she had read some of Reuben's emails that referred to a building project for a resort specifically for members of the Blue Point Society and their out-of-town guests. What raised her suspicions was an email that mentioned Ashlynn's Camp for Kids, although it didn't say anything specific. Aziza speculated that there was a connection between raising money for the camp and building the Blue Point Society's resort, possibly a siphoning of funds from the former for the latter.

"Hello? Earth to Samson." Frieda Greenglass's voice shook me from my reverie and I realized I was next to be served. "Still daydreaming as usual."

"I'm merely meditating on the soul-soothing effects your heavenly latkes will soon be working on my taste buds and my general well-being."

"Good answer, you silver-tongued liar," she said with a bittersweet chuckle. "I always could tell when you were lost in your little world where no one else could go."

"What can I say, Frieda? You know me better than I know myself."

"And yet we're still friends," she said. "The usual?"

I replied in the affirmative and she said there would be a short wait while she fried up a fresh batch of latkes. She asked me about the bandage on my hand and I mentioned my mishap with the kettle.

"How is it you've lasted this long without someone to take care of you?" she asked as she patted the raw mixture of grated potatoes, egg, matzo meal, onions, salt and pepper into patties and plopped them onto a hot pan, well-greased with schmaltz. The instant hiss and sputter underscored the criticism in her question.

"You know me, I like to live dangerously," I said, hoping to bring back some levity to the conversation.

We first met, purely by accident, when I saw her reaching for a box of matzo in the Maritime Super-Mart's ethnic food section (a relatively new product back in those days, which the store, sadly, has discontinued). I struck up a conversation and that, as they say, got the ball rolling. She was in her late forties, about fifteen years older than me, with thick hair the colour of muddy straw, now streaked with grey, which she wore in a thick braid that tapered just past her shoulder blades. Her square face was offset by pale, pillowy lips and a prodigious nose that curved like a graceful beak.

There was something shy, but imposing about her eyes that startled me at first. Possibly it was their perpetually moist rims or the way they were crowned by the arches of her eyebrows, but I could see that those eyes were the entryway to long-held pain and untold suffering.

She didn't bother to hide her attraction to me from the start. I was flattered, even tempted, by her interest and fancied myself a Benjamin Braddock to her Mrs. Robinson, allowing the usual young man's fantasies of having an older, more experienced lover, but one also infinitely grateful for the attentions of a younger man who could magically stoke once more the fires of her youth.

We went on one date, having a quiet supper at a backroom table in Maguire's, a decent pub that no longer exists, but at the time was one of the nicer eateries in the city. By any standard it would have been a no-brainer for me to pay the cheque and take Frieda straight to my bed. The conversation flowed easily.

I was intrigued to discover we had something in common in our familial pasts. Frieda's father had been a young rabbi from Warsaw who had spent some time in Amsterdam, where my grandfather was born and raised. During the war, the Nazis put Rabbi Greenglass in Westerbork, a transit camp in the Netherlands where many Dutch Jews were first kept en route to Auschwitz, Treblinka and other camps. I recognized the name Westerbork from my grandfather's stories when I was a boy. I wondered aloud whether Frieda's father and Zaide Jakob might have actually met. Expecting an agreement or at least a nod to acknowledge this coincidence, I was momentarily taken aback by Frieda's brooding silence.

She then went on to describe her father as she remembered him during her childhood in Montreal during the mid 1950s. He continued being a rabbi at their local synagogue in Côte St-Luc. He was a man of extreme moods, often depressed, but also prone to inexplicable fits of rage toward his wife and children. Later, when Frieda was entering adolescence, allegations by a reporter from one of the small local newspapers came out about her father's time in Westerbork. It was alleged that he had colluded in some way with the Nazis, possibly by being a sort of stationmaster who designated which Jews would go to which camps.

Her father had tried, unsuccessfully, to sue the reporter but ended up dropping the suit. After that, his behaviour became more erratic. In 1966, he was hit by a bus and died instantly. Reports by eyewitnesses differed. Some said he looked disoriented and wandered into the street. Others swore that he purposely walked in front of the bus. Suicide could never be proved and he was buried in the consecrated ground of a Jewish cemetery.

Frieda's younger brother, Avi, steeped himself in his Jewish studies and later became a rabbi at the same congregation, until their mother passed away. The stigma that had attached itself to their father's reputation was never entirely obliterated in the congregation's mind. Avi decided to accept a position in a synagogue in Moncton. Frieda herself went through two unsuccessful marriages and then headed east to the Maritimes as well, stopping in Moncton for a short time to be near her brother before continuing on to settle on PEI.

Not surprisingly, our date ended shortly after that. It wasn't so much that I was turned off by the fact that Frieda Greenglass's father might have been responsible for my grandfather going to Auschwitz (although the horror of that possibility clung to my mind like a film of cold sweat). Revealing this damaged part of herself so soon in the relationship overwhelmed me in such a way that I was afraid to imagine what it would be like to see her naked. She had already bared more of herself than I could deal with. In a sense she was everything I'd been trying to exorcise through my paintings. I felt a profound sorrow for Frieda, but it was accompanied by a terror that becoming intimate with her meant I would be swallowed up by something beyond my imagination. I was in awe of that damaged part of her, but could only view it from a remote angle, the way one does a blindingly brilliant stone or piece of jewellery dug up from a mass grave.

After a brief cooling off period, where I merely smiled and nodded whenever I saw her, we did indeed become friends after Frieda opened her latke stand in the Farmers' Market (although that first date remained as something unspoken between us).

"Here, try," said Frieda, holding out a small paper plate with a single sizzling latke on it. I received it gratefully, edged the tip of the potato pancake off the rim of the plate and took a tentative bite.

"Careful, it's hot," she warned.

I juggled the burning morsel between my tongue and soft palate, chewed quickly and swallowed. "To die for," I kvelled.

"Should I pack up a nice Frieda's Dozen for you?" she asked, by which I knew she meant a container of fourteen latkes (like a Baker's Dozen, except for her superstitious nature), something she only did for me. I nodded, while gobbling down the rest of the latke.

"Listen..." I said. "You're still a member of the Collective, aren't you?"

The Collective was the Prince Edward Island Jewish Collective or PEIJC, a group of Jews living on the Island who got together for the High Holidays or important cultural events, such as Yom HaShoah or the local Klezmer Festival. When a rabbi's services were required, Frieda put in a call to her brother Avi, who was always happy to make the two-hour drive across the bridge to minister to the leaderless PEI congregation.

"Since when are you interested?" Frieda's smile was warm but wary.

"More curious than interested," I answered, thinking it was a good save, but realizing the reply was open to misinterpretation and hastened to add: "Not in joining, mind you."

"Then what?"

I squirmed inwardly for a moment then decided to come right out with it. "I was wondering why the PEIJC never tried to get a synagogue built on the Island."

Frieda's expression of genuine confusion could have easily been construed as one of concern over my mental health.

"Why the interest all of a sudden in a synagogue?"

My sigh carried the weight of a thousand unspoken misgivings. "Call it curiosity," I began and gritted my teeth beneath a grimace. "I've been wondering what it would take to actually build one."

"You mean for an art project?" Frieda asked. "Like an installation or something?"

"No," I said patiently. "I mean an actual house of worship. A shul."

Frieda fell silent and went about packing the latkes into the container. I didn't know how to interpret this but was grateful for the silence. She put the container on the counter and placed on top of it a plastic cup of sour cream and a plastic knife and fork. I asked for a can of iced tea and paid for everything.

"I don't know what to tell you, Samson," she finally said. "The Collective has talked about the possibility of finding a vacant building for a shul, or even building one from scratch, especially after the mosque was built. But when we saw the vandalism that happened, the spray paint..."

"That was an isolated incident," I said. "It happened once and never again. Besides, the way everyone rallied around the Muslim community showed real support."

Frieda looked at me in a way that was hard to read. There was suspicion in her eyes, but her mouth pouted with the corners sagging downward in a way that was alternately sad, wistful and pitying.

"Maybe some things are better left the way they are. Now if you don't mind, you're holding up business."

Indeed, a line of three or four impatient customers had formed behind me. With an apologetic smile, I took my Frieda's dozen and drink and beat a hasty retreat.

My original idea was to get in the car and drive home to eat the latkes there, but once I stepped into the mild sunshine, I decided on lunch alfresco instead. I spotted a vacant picnic table away from the throng and made a beeline for it. As soon as I settled down, I flipped the container's lid open and used the plastic knife to spread some sour cream on a latke. No sooner had I popped a healthy bite in my mouth, I heard a sadly familiar voice in my ear.

"'Tis a good sign, signor, to hear thou pursue the inquiry regarding the synagogue." I turned to see the bucket hat angled jauntily atop Shylock's shaggy head. The stray hairs of his burly carrot-coloured eyebrows twitched hopefully. "Hath thou, in this instance, been convinced to join our cause?"

"I hath not," I replied through a second mouthful of latke. "And I wouldst be grateful to the maximum if thou couldst kindly shoveth off so I can enjoy my lunch in peace."

I must have said that out loud, because I noticed a couple passing by turn their heads toward me. I made a mental note to keep the conversation out of earshot, although I dared to hope that might not be necessary. Despite my previous experience with these figments, I dared to hope he might just disappear. What little I could tell of Shylock's personality suggested that he was different from, say, Fagin. He possessed more of a gentlemanly bearing. Still, he merely folded his beefy hands in front of him on the picnic table and sat staring at them silently. As I continued my feast, I tried not to look at him, but the occasional glance revealed a thoughtful expression on his porcine features. He was actually waiting while I ate, ready to sit quietly for as long as it took until I polished off every last latke.

"Don't you Figs ever break for lunch?" I asked, sotto voce, and slid the Styrofoam container towards him, looking around to see if anyone passing by was taking notice. Shylock inspected the latkes, sniffing warily at first, but then I could have sworn I heard a grumbling from that enormous girth of his. "Going once, going twice..."

He reached over, broke a latke in half and crammed it into his mouth. His eyes lit up and a smile formed as he chewed. I slathered a bit of sour cream on the other half.

"If you think that's good, try this."

He ate the other half and his eyes closed in heavenly exultation. I invited him to help himself and we ate in silent communion. This didn't last as long as I hoped it would.

"Allow me to offer thee humble thanks," said Shylock. "Thou hath a most generous nature, signor."

"You're welcome."

This came as close to a civilized exchange as I'd had with any of the Figs. It confused me, because I could not entirely accept them as real, and yet here I was breaking bread, or splitting spud in this case, with one of them. I knew I needed to keep up my guard, but I also needed the illusion of normalcy in this anything-but-normal situation.

"If you don't mind, could you call me Samson?"

"A name well chosen by as loving a mother and proud a father as ever drew breath," he said gleefully, licking some sour cream off his fingers. "A Biblical hero of powerful virtue who did serve well his Lord."

"And who came to a bad end because of his frailty," I added, washing down the latkes with a long swig of iced tea. "I'm happy to share my lunch. No need to spread it on so thick. I'm not a potato pancake and that ain't sour cream you're spewing, if you get my drift."

"Drift?"

"Hey, we're having a nice friendly lunch together. Is there any way we could put aside this whole synagogue business for the time being?"

"I well apprehend thy meaning. And yet..." He paused to make short shrift of a latke. "And yet, a curiosity in regards to the synagogue hath been pricked, if that conversation with the serving wench may be taken as testimony. To what end, if I may be so bold to inquire, didst thou embark on this topic?"

"First of all, she's not a wench," I corrected. "She happens to be a good friend of mine and someone of good standing in the Island's Jewish community."

I had no intention of admitting that Shylock and his two cohorts had put a bug in my ear. I told him I had assumed he or one of the other two were following me and I merely wanted to show them I wasn't the one for the job. They were coming to the wrong guy. There was a whole organization of Jews on the Island who had already been considering the question of having a synagogue. As usual, things move slowly in a collective, but if it was really in the cards for PEI to have a shul, these were the people to do it. I scarfed down the last latke with the self-satisfaction of a sated appetite and the belief I had made an unassailable case. Shylock cocked his head sceptically.

"Either thou hast adopted a mask of modesty or the cloak of deceit." His manner was good-natured, but tempered with an underlying disappointment that I was being less than forthright. "As I perceive the matter, what lies at stake is the all-encompassing aspect of Principle."

At that moment I felt a raindrop on my nose. I looked up and another fell on my cheek. Soon a rapid succession of raindrops followed and quickly became a blinding downpour, sending everyone scrambling for cars, doorways and whatever shelter was nearest. Shylock and I huddled against the wall of an elevated outer nook that had doors leading into the market's dining area. A couple of others took shelter there as well, but we were able to stake out a corner to ourselves where we could continue our conversation in relative privacy.

"What principle are you talking about?" I asked in a hushed voice.

"I speak not of a principle, but of the thing itself. Principle. Morality's marrow. I lost everything at the altar of Principle."

I leaned toward his ear. "You were given everything you asked for, and more, but you wouldn't be happy with anything except your pound of flesh."

His eyes were imploring. "For the Principle of it."

"You were pig-headed," I said. "That's why you lost everything."

"I was victim of a most vile trickery on the part of the law!" he fumed.

Luckily, the downpour ended abruptly. The day turned bright once more and we ventured out from under the shelter.

"Words may be misconstrued to suit a purpose for ill or good," said Shylock. "Yet 'tis in Nature we find direction to Destiny's true path." He raised his hand and pointed toward the sky. "Behold!"

I looked up and saw the wide arc of a rainbow that stretched out protectively over the city of Charlottetown.

"Beautiful," I said. "But what's your point?"

"Surely thou doth glean the rainbow's significance."

"These days it's Gay Pride."

He stared at me as if at a stupid child. "My reference is to its Biblical origin."

"Are we talking flood? The big one?"

"As an artist, thou must surely take inspiration from this many-hued spectrum. 'Tis also an argument most powerful for the true purpose of a synagogue on this divinely chosen isle."

"So, the rainbow was God's covenant, his promise to never destroy the world again." I said. "What does that have to do with me building a synagogue?"

"Doth thou see not, good cousin Samson? The promise is the thing. Throughout a myriad of centuries, the Supreme One hath been witness to the precipitous decline of the lowly creatures who inhabit this great orb. Great as it may be in scope, it encompasses the bottommost plane of existence. Verily, the Supreme One expresses fits of wrath through one natural disaster or another. Yet, 'tis all that can be done. If ever a moment when the temptation to destroy all comes over the Supreme One, the rainbow hangs there. A veritable albatross blazing its colors like a poxy peacock."

I listened with growing interest. The notion that the Supreme One's hands were tied when it came to dealing with the state of the world ricocheted in my mind like a stray bullet in a steel enclosure.

"So, you're saying that building the synagogue would initiate a cosmic loophole that would allow the Supreme One to have a do-over without destroying the planet?"

"The Supreme One hath created yonder covenant to ensure a benevolence eternal, not as a resort to trickery." Shylock smiled sadly. "Hath thou never suffered the urge to strike a blade into thine own canvas when utter frustration o'erpowers thee?"

"If you're referring to the one sitting in my apartment with the mutant starfish stubbornly affixed to it, the worst I ever did was try to cover it up with paint. Unfortunately, the thing reappeared bigger than before, like a humongous zit on some teenager's nose on prom night."

"The mutated sea creature?" He stared at me with genuine confusion. "'Tis thy covenant thou hath pledged to the Supreme One. Doth thou not recognize the work of thine own hand?"

"I didn't paint that thing." My patience was beginning to wear thin. "I would have remembered that."

"The reason the creature obstructs the path afforded by those parting waters is to ensure thou shalt carry out the Supreme One's will."

"Are you saying if the starfish goes then I'm off the hook?"

"'Tis more complicated," he said and his round face grew long with worry. "Alas, I can speak of it no further."

I stared at his insufferable hangdog expression. I thought about what he'd said before, about being tempted to take a knife to the canvas. To be honest, I'd never had the compulsion to do that to any of my paintings no matter how fed up I was with them, but I had just about enough of this business.

I stormed off through the parking lot. In my mind I played over and over the scenario of what would happen when I got home. I knew which knife I would use. That fat butcher's knife I had sitting in my kitchen drawer. It was going to be carnage. It was going to feel bloody marvellous.

4

THE DRIVE BACK to Mount Russet – during which my lead foot shaved a good ten minutes off the usual twenty-five – did little to dampen my resolve to destroy the painting. I kept thinking of the ending of *The Picture of Dorian Gray*, when Dorian takes a knife to his decrepit portrait and instantaneously breaks the illusion of eternal youth that had led him into a moral abyss. Slashing the cursed work of art was the only way of setting himself free, although as soon as Dorian destroyed the painting he died and his corpse turned old and withered, like the painting had once been, while the painting itself was magically restored to its original youthful image.

My intention was to also free myself by ripping that painted path to nowhere – rising waves, scattered detritus, mutant starfish and all – into ribbons. I would metaphorically step through the canvas's gaping slashes into a new life devoid of imaginary figments, speculative synagogues and the unpromising concept of Prince Edward Island as the new Promised Land. I could only hope things would not end the same way as in Wilde's novel. Would I turn into some primordial sea creature with a pair of paint-spattered Blundstones dangling from two starfish appendages?

When I stood in my kitchenette with the butcher's knife in my hand, hefting its weight, enjoying the way its contoured handle fit perfectly in my palm, I mused briefly on what had possessed me to purchase the thing in the first place. After I made the decision to abandon the not-so-dazzling lights of Charlottetown for Mount Russet, I was determined to change my lifestyle, which included eating better and economizing by cooking more meals at home rather than running out for something quick whenever I got hungry. I bought the knife, with that purpose in mind, at the Bitchin' Kitchen, a store in the Cradletown Court Mall selling state-of-the-art culinary instruments. The sales person, a young man with tattoos on his neck and huge wooden rings embedded in his earlobes – stretching them out as if for some primitive initiation rite – and who, much to my surprise, said he was studying at the Island School of Culinary Arts, told me the knife would be perfect for boning certain cuts of meat and slicing the most impenetrable of root vegetables, as well as gourds and coconuts.

Not surprisingly, my resolution to cook more at home came to nought and the blade remained in my kitchen drawer until this very moment when I was holding it in my hand.

Perhaps some dark corner of my psyche anticipated such a day coming and now I was ready.

I approached my easel and pulled away the drop cloth. I stared at the rising waves, strip of land and six-armed starfish, summoning up the courage to make the first slash. My concentration was rudely interrupted when Judas stepped from behind the easel and stood off to the side. In my recent encounters with Fagin and Shylock, it was their ridiculous headgear, the blue baseball cap and the coral bucket hat, that I had recognized first. What struck me right away this time was the fact that Judas was bareheaded.

He held his yellow straw porkpie hat in both hands, almost as a sign of respect, the way one might in the presence of somebody deceased. I found it disconcerting but returned my attention to the painting. If my resolve to finish what I'd come to do was beginning to wane, the sight of Judas pumped a renewed urge to do some bloody-minded damage through my veins.

"I'm glad you're here to see this," I said, expecting him to reply with some form of protest. He stood there in silence, which I took as a provocation.

This was now a game of chicken. We would see which one of us was going to sprout feathers.

"Anything you'd like to say before I slice 'n' dice this half-baked thorn in my side and forever wash my hands of you figments, the Supreme One, synagogues and the whole Promised shooting match?"

He said nothing, made no gesture. He studied the unfinished painting, calmly imprinting its details in his memory before it was no more.

"Can you at least answer me one question?" I asked with the sinking realization that I was stalling for time.

His only reply was to turn his head to look at me. I pressed on.

"Is it true what Shylock said? That this starfish was painted by me?"

He nodded slightly, slowly blinking for emphasis.

"What's up with the silent treatment? Normally I can't shut you Figs up, except for when I want to know something."

"We have done our best to explain what can be explained."

"Then explain how I could have painted this starfish when I have no recollection of doing it. The original was so small I couldn't even see it without a magnifying glass. The detailing was so fine I couldn't have done it using all my concentration while wide awake. Was it hypnosis?"

"It was a test."

"I don't understand," I said, still holding the knife, poised to strike the canvas lest his answer didn't satisfy. A ridiculous stance, since Judas didn't seem to care one way or another if I destroyed the painting or not. "What kind of test?"

"A test of your faith and your devotion. The reason you cannot remember painting the starfish is that it was a different version of you who executed the painting of it. A version of you who dwells in another plane of existence. This is the best explanation I can offer. The starfish also exists in that same plane of existence. The only reason you can see it, the reason you cannot erase it, the reason it can be miniscule in one instance then grow larger or appear in a book as well as on your painting the next moment, is because the Supreme One is allowing you to see it. The Supreme One controls all these perceptions. This is the Supreme One's way of confiding in you. Humans only have faith in empirical evidence. This is the Supreme One's manner of meeting you half way."

I lowered the knife. It dropped out of my hand and clattered to the floor. A dappled mist swam before my eyes. In a daze, I shuffled toward the card table, pulled out a chair and lowered myself onto it, not wholly conscious of what I was doing.

Judas picked up the butcher's knife, set it on the card table and sat in the other chair.

"I fear I may have said too much."

I wasn't sure if this meant he said more than he was allowed to reveal or whether he said more than I could comprehend. Possibly both were true. The idea that the Supreme One was confiding in me, meeting me half way, was hard to take in. I should have felt honoured, blessed even, and I did, maybe too much so. If the Supreme One was making all this effort, then how could I refuse to build the synagogue?

The weight of the obligation was becoming oppressive. Is this how Noah felt? Thankfully, the Supreme One had not specified how big this synagogue was supposed to be. Not yet anyway. I desperately tried to remember what size a cubit was and realized I needed to get a grip on reality.

"I have said too much," Judas repeated and shook his head to himself. "It has long been a weakness of mine."

He was genuinely distraught and I wasn't sure whether I should be concerned for his wellbeing or whether I should be angry, since I was the one who was dealing with more than I could handle at the moment. Unless this was a tactic on his part to take my mind off all this new and unsettling information that he had just laid on me. I decided that focusing on Judas's problem might be a welcome departure from my own sense of helplessness.

"What do you mean weakness? Does this have to do with... um... you know? What you did?" He glared at me then looked away. "Sorry. I guess that's been tough to live down after all these centuries."

"I knew what would happen to me and how my reputation would be tarnished for all time. He told me I would be cast as a villain throughout history. He also said I was predestined to play this role and that, in sacrificing my good name, I would be doing him the greatest service one could ever perform."

"He? You mean Jesus?"

"To me, to all of us, he was Yeshua. It means 'the rescuer' or 'the deliverer.' I loved him better than a brother. Our camaraderie created a bond unlike any ever known. I was everything to him. Friend. Advisor. Confidant. More so than the others. In turn, he told me things he did not reveal to anyone else. The spiritual path laid out for him. How I was going to be instrumental in helping him travel that path. What would happen to him after death released his spirit. So many wondrous secrets it made my mind spin. In some ways, to be branded as the worst traitor in history was a small price to pay. The greater burden was to wonder, in my darkest moments, whether indeed it was he who had betrayed me."

He covered his face with his hands and I watched his shoulders tremble for a few seconds. I fetched a glass of water and placed it in front of him. Once he had gained control of himself, he took a tentative sip then another and thanked me.

"Forgive me for asking," I said and by his slight nod I knew it was okay to continue. "Is it true that you did it with a kiss?"

"Many did not understand his contrary sense of humour." I was amazed by his wry, albeit grudging grin. "He did not often reveal it to others."

"The kiss was his idea?"

"Even though all outward evidence had to look like I was betraying him, he said it would help me to remember this was, in reality, an act of great love and true loyalty."

"So why did you say talking too much has been your weakness? What does that have to do with the 'betrayal'?" I was careful to modify the last word with air quotes in the context of what he had just told me.

A different silence engulfed him. I assumed that would be the end of it, but he spoke again. "After I had been approached by the Pharisees and offered the thirty pieces of silver, I immediately told Yeshua. That was when he told me I had to accept their offer. When it was done and they took him away, I purposefully demonstrated my true feelings by throwing away the silver pieces in public. Then I knew I could not show my face and travelled to Bethel, assuming a disguise. A story had spread that I killed myself out of guilt. While in Bethel, I heard much about the trial and the crucifixion. There was news of his body being taken to a cave and the body later disappearing. This was not part of the plan he had imparted to me. Out of this came stories of a resurrection and yet other stories that he had not actually died but escaped far away to the east. I did not know what to think and I became agitated, not knowing what I should do."

He paused for another sip of water. I could see the emotional toll it was taking on him to relate the story. I was on the verge of telling him not to go on if he didn't want to, when he took up the tale again. As difficult as it was to continue, I could also see that he somehow needed to tell me the rest. I sensed that, possibly, I was the first person to whom he had revealed this story.

"Not knowing what else to do, I disguised myself and returned to Jerusalem for whatever factual information I could discover. There were still many conflicting stories. It is difficult to say why I did what I did next. It was at this point that my morale had ebbed to its lowest depth. I harboured many ill feelings toward Yeshua and I convinced myself that I had been used as a fool. As you may imagine, I thought of all the secrets he told me, universal truths that are beyond the knowledge and understanding of mere humans. Had he been feeding me these stories to gain my trust? Such doubts were beginning to set in. I wondered if everything he ever told me was a lie. The only way I could think of putting it to the test was to spread this gospel myself. I stayed in disguise and presented myself as a travelling sage. If I had been using even a small amount of reason, I would have understood that it was too soon after Yeshua's death for anyone to care for these words. His influence had dissipated among the general public. People merely laughed and when my true identity came to light, they called me a charlatan. They said I spread the rumour of my own suicide, so it would look like I had been resurrected the same as it was said of Yeshua. They assumed I was trying to copy him and this made my return appear all the more trivial. It was declared publicly that I had betrayed Yeshua because I was jealous of him and wanted to set myself up as a messiah for profit. I knew then it was my own folly that had made my situation worse. It was more than I could bear. I found myself a good strong piece of rope and fled into the wilderness until I came across the first tree in my path with high sturdy limbs. Now I truly did feel all the weight of guilt on my shoulders. If Yeshua was still alive, I felt I had no right to dwell in the same world as him. And if he was indeed dead, all I wanted was to present myself before him, wherever he might be, prostrate my wicked soul at his feet and beg forgiveness for spreading his secrets so shamelessly."

"Listen, I've met my share of Messianic Jews or Jews for Jesus or whatever you want to call them. Me, when I was growing up, the best thing I ever heard about Jesus..."

"Yeshua."

"Whatever. Back in the day the story us Jews all agreed on was that he was some kind of rabble-rousing rabbi. A rebel rebbe. After that we didn't give him a second thought."

I couldn't help but shift my gaze at the horrible scar ringing his throat like a necklace of twisted flesh. He noticed where my eyes fell, but this time he made no movement to cover up the disfigurement. In fact, I sensed that, in some way, he was daring me to stare at it for as long as I could. If this suddenly felt like another game of chicken, I lost all too quickly, turning away but not knowing where to look.

My sight finally took refuge on my painting. The starfish welcomed me with all six arms. I pondered what Judas had said earlier, about the starfish being the Supreme One's way of reaching out to me, a way of making His/Her/Its presence felt. And yet, much like week-old egg salad, something was not sitting right with me.

"I'm trying to understand something," I said. "Why you three? Why were you summoned from my psyche? When Fagin was in my car last night he kept talking about the synagogue as an Opportunity. And today Shylock spoke about building it in terms of Principle. What's your argument or theme or whatever you want to call it? Are you meant to represent Betrayal? But that doesn't make sense, in light of what you just told me. In that case, maybe with you it's about Sacrifice? Is that why you told me your story? To sell me on the idea of sacrificing myself for the greater good? Or maybe it's Forbearance. You dealt with your sullied reputation with great aplomb. Maybe I'm supposed to just suck it up and do what's expected of me."

There was a knock at the door. I decided to ignore it to see what Judas was going to say, but a second series of raps, sharper and louder this time quickly followed the first. I went to the door to ask who it was.

"Police."

I cracked the door ajar. The light in the hallway revealed a uniformed officer's sharp nose upturned between two icy blue eyes. Trim, greying sideburns were exposed beneath the band of his cap.

"We're making inquiries about a break-in in this building last night. Can we ask you a couple of questions?"

"I'm just..." I glanced back quickly and saw that Judas's chair was now empty. "...um, getting ready to go out. But I can answer a couple of questions."

The police officer craned for a look in the apartment.

"I'm Officer Schurman," he said. "This is Officer Roy."

The female cop standing behind him was younger and sported lightly tinted aviator glasses. I could see that her blonde hair had been pulled back in a ponytail, perhaps to make her look more authoritative, although a few strands peeked out from under her cap, almost strategically, as if she had come straight from a photo shoot for the cover of *Modern Policewoman*.

"We're investigating a report of a break-in last night," Officer Schurman continued. "It was in the apartment upstairs. Can you tell us if you heard or saw anything?"

Again, he tried to look in the apartment. I made a concentrated effort not to let on that I was unnerved by his question, since I had witnessed the whole thing.

"Look," I said. "You guys are here a couple of times every month. You know better than me that something is always going on here. I just try to shut it out and get on with my life, if you know what I mean."

"That doesn't answer my question. Did you hear or see anything or not?"

I decided it was best to say only enough of what I knew to extricate myself from the situation, without giving myself or Aziza away. I mentioned only that I'd had a long day and decided to call it an early night, made tea and got into bed with my laptop.

"About twenty minutes later I heard some noises and shouting from the apartment upstairs, then footsteps running down the stairs. Then it all went quiet."

The whole time he was writing down what I was saying in his notepad. He noticed my bandaged right hand and pointed at it with his pen.

"What happened there?"

"Burnt myself on the kettle when I was making tea last night."

He wrote that down and underlined it twice.

"Do you know the tenant who lives above you?"

I assured him I made it my business not to know who any of my neighbours were. Whether or not this satisfied him and his partner, he decided the questioning was over and thanked me for my time. They turned and left, allowing me to shut my door at last. The first thing I did was hurry to the table and returned the butcher's knife to its drawer, where, I had no doubt, it would stay unused for as long as I owned it.

AFTER WALKING aimlessly and trying to make sense of things, I found myself mentally exhausted in Sadie's Tea Room. Being late afternoon on a Saturday, there were several customers, but I managed to secure a table by the window. I became aware of an odd sound: a tapping so insular I could only imagine it was a section of my brain being literally chipped away from all the recent mental and emotional stress.

When the sound grew a bit louder, I looked up and saw it was the tip of a fuchsia-painted fingernail belonging to Aziza Arsenault tapping on the window. The expression on her face was grave. For a moment it was as if we were trapped in different dimensions with no way of communicating other than this bleak Morse code. I motioned for her to come inside and join me.

She entered the tearoom with shoulders hunched and head down. The tension in her body language made me wince inwardly. She sat with her back angled to the window.

"I just biked past the Body Parts and saw a police car parked outside," she said. "Apparently they've been looking for me?"

"They're knocking on everyone's door and asking about the break-in."

"You talk to them?"

I nodded. "I stonewalled them as best I could."

She took a couple of deep breaths and added that the police had gone to Mario's, the sandwich joint on the far south end of Mount Russet where she worked, before she showed up for her shift. Her boss had also received an anonymous phone call about her.

"So, guess what? I've been canned."

The call to her boss referred to her Internet activities without giving any details, basically portraying her as an online sex worker.

"At first, he came across all holier-than-thou," she said. "About how he couldn't have such an immoral element defiling his family friendly establishment. I kept trying to defend myself, trying to convince him the caller was lying. But the bug was planted in that speck of dirt he calls a brain. The only way I was going to keep my job with this upstanding business owner and pillar of the community was if I agreed to some 'unofficial overtime' at his convenience. Hypocrite slime ball. Maybe an anonymous call to the board of health about the roaches in his backroom might be in order."

The big question for me was who made the call to the police about the break-in. Aziza's eyes widened in the most sarcastic display of awe I'd ever witnessed. Obviously, I was missing the obvious. She explained with an exaggerated patience that whoever actually made the call was beside the point. It was her father, Reuben Arsenault, who ordered the calls to be made. The dubious expression on my face must have spoken louder than anything I could say. She then produced her phone and quickly went through her text messages from that day. A text from her father mentioned something about a job opening for her in his office.

"I got that right after Mario fired me," she said with a note of triumph in her voice, as if that explained everything. "Or maybe you'd rather put that down to a coincidence?"

She seemed to be daring me to do so.

"Okay, let's say your father's the one who got you fired," I reasoned. "Then he offers you a job with him. To what end?"

"To keep an eye on me, why else? First, he gets rid of Anne Surly then he keeps me on a tight leash so I won't embarrass him any further."

"Which brings me to my other question. If he's the one who ordered the two goons in balaclavas to break into your place, why report it to the police? Wouldn't that risk exposing him too?"

"Obviously, you don't know Reuben. He's all about risk management. The police are meant to put the fear of God in me. A way to intimidate me. He knows it won't go so far as to implicate him."

"But he, or whoever made the call, told the police about the webcam."

"That's just his way of telling me I've been a bad girl. To him it's all about letting me know who's in control."

I tried to connect this new picture of Reuben Arsenault to the author of that op-ed rant against *Anne of Bergen-Belsen* from all those years back. The fact that Aziza and I had both created rogue versions of PEI's favourite fictional daughter, which both happened to be thorns in Reuben Arsenault's side, made me feel a bit closer to Aziza.

Her immediate problem was finding a new job. Stupidly, I asked if the offer from her father was legitimate but immediately rescinded the question. I didn't get the reprimand I expected. In fact, she had worked for her father before, which was how she became privy to those emails she had mentioned, the ones where she had first read about Ashlynn's Camp for Kids and this new project for a secret resort for the Blue Point Society. When she questioned her father about them, he tactfully rebuffed her, then laid her off with a healthy severance package, assuming she would forget the whole thing. Now he was offering her job back, realizing it was better to keep her close.

"Keep your friends close, your enemies closer and your family closest," I said putting a new spin on that famous Machiavellian quote from *The Godfather*.

Aziza was not amused. "I have to regroup. There's no point buying another webcam if they know where I am. Finding another place to broadcast isn't an option either. I'm going to have to lay low until I can figure things out. And to top it all off I need to find another job."

"I think I know someone who can help," I said. "What do you say we get something to eat first?"

We decided to try a restaurant that had recently opened in Mount Russet called Fusion Wok. It featured mainly Chinese dishes with touches of Middle Eastern and Indian cuisine. The proprietor, Wayne Mao, greeted us and showed us to our seats. We split an order of tandoori pot stickers and the Wok Like an Egyptian sizzling platter.

Aziza was surprised when I suggested the Crazy Diamond for drinks after our meal.

She had heard of it because her father had a longstanding interest in becoming a partner in the business with Pius and Maggie, but this was her first time inside.

"Reuben has to have a finger in every pie he sees," she said. "Especially if he sees them as potential competition. He doesn't understand the meaning of no and that tends to rub some people the wrong way. Might be better not to let anyone here know I'm his daughter."

I assured her that everything would be fine. We found a couple of stools at the bar. I noticed Aziza suspiciously eying the Ashlynn's Camp for Kids fund jar. I allayed any fears that I had lured her into an enemy camp and introduced her to Maggie Beairsto. A pint of Beairsto's IPA and a white wine spritzer quickly appeared and soon we relaxed into casual conversation. I happened to mention, though not as subtly as I hoped, that Aziza was looking for a job.

"We're looking for a waitress," Maggie said. "Any experience?"

Aziza said she did and Maggie went off to find an application form. At first, Aziza feigned annoyance at my ulterior motive for bringing her here, to which I feigned complete innocence. Then she thanked me for helping her out. We clinked glasses as the speakers throbbed with synthesizer strings trilling over stately horns. A voice sang of a lack of pain and a distant ship and finally a comforting sense of numbness. In that moment I could see my whole life drifting happily before my eyes and toasted it by polishing off the rest of my beer in one self-satisfied quaff.

Aziza surveyed the room as it slowly filled with more people. Suddenly, she swivelled around on her stool and hunched her shoulders over the bar while keeping her head down. I asked her what was up and she shushed me and told me not to look.

"Look at what?" I asked. "What's going on?"

"They're here." she said.

"Who?"

"Reg'n'Kel," she said. "The goons who broke into my place."

"Where?"

"Don't look."

Maggie brought the application form and a pen. I ordered another beer. Aziza kept her head down and concentrated on filling out the form when someone in an orange ball cap and black hoodie sidled up to the bar next to her. He was thin and wiry with long greasy hair. He craned his neck to read over Aziza's shoulder.

"Looking for a job then?" he asked. "Must be some wicked to work in this joint."

Aziza looked up and saw the angry red welt on the side of his neck.

"Looks like you had an accident, Reggie. You need to be more careful."

"Sounds like good advice for all of us," he said, then noticed me listening in on their conversation. "Something I can do for you?"

He walked past Aziza and edged himself between her and me. "You look familiar."

"Never mind him," said Aziza.

"This the good Samaritan?" he asked her without taking his eyes off me. "Or just a nosy neighbour?"

Then someone in a sleeveless jean jacket and black ball cap with the peak turned backward was standing next to Aziza. He had the same wiry build as Reggie but he was younger with a mop of curly hair.

"How you doing, Kelvin?" said Aziza.

"Hey, Zeez," he said shyly. His face reddened slightly.

"I told you to stay at the table, Kel," said Reggie. "Now we're gonna lose our seats."

"I thought you might need help with the drinks," said Kelvin.

"Aw, don't gimme that," said Reggie. "Everyone knows you're sweet on Zeez here."

"Just shut up about that," Kelvin growled. "Don't listen to him, Zeez."

"What can I get yez, boys?" Maggie asked. She was holding the shaft of a golf club in one hand and tapping its head in the palm of her other. "Never mind Lorie here. She just wants to make sure everybody's being nice and friendly."

"I think the boys were just leaving," said Aziza. "They came over to say good-bye."

"That's right," said Reggie. "Be seein' you, Zeez."

"What about our beers?" said Kelvin.

"Never mind, we'll stop by the Legion," said Reggie. He smiled and put his hand on my shoulder. "See you round, neighbour."

After they left Aziza filled out the rest of the form and gave it to Maggie. Considering how unnerved she was when she first spotted them, I was puzzled by how casually she acted when they were at the bar. I was a bit shaken by Reggie's menacing innuendoes. Aziza tried to assure me that Reggie put on a good tough guy act when he wanted to. Kelvin was basically a puppy dog trying to emulate his big brother. They'd had a rough upbringing with a mostly absent father and an alcoholic mother. It was Reggie who had raised Kelvin and whatever dismal road they were on they'd probably travel it together for the rest of their lives.

"I don't get how you can write them off like that," I argued. "I saw how they broke into your place, what they did to your webcam."

"They were acting on my father's orders," she explained. "I was never in any real danger, not while Reuben was paying them."

I tried to accept this simple explanation, yet I still couldn't shake off the nagging presence of something unspoken. An underlying dread followed us back to the Body Parts. I assumed it was just me, but when Aziza asked if she could hang out in my place, I could see that she was also feeling uneasy.

Inside, Aziza opened her purse and produced a half-smoked joint. She apologized and I waved the apology away, resigning myself that she was now the exception to my no-smoking rule. I wondered for a moment why she always produced half a joint. When and where did she smoke the other half?

She lit up and sucked in a couple of quick tokes. She offered me the joint out of politeness. My automatic refusal was halfway to my lips, but I found myself taking the joint from her. Not wanting to look too uncool, I took a wary toke, held it in and happily found that I could keep it down. I took another and passed it back to her. While she partook, I tried to rationalize this indulgence by telling myself that I merely needed to calm my nerves. But I knew there was more to it. It's not like we were on an official date or anything, but we did go out to dinner and then for drinks afterward. And here we were at my place. Accepting the joint seemed only logical, if the night was heading down the road that would be obvious to any two red-blooded human beings.

She sucked up the last of the joint and swallowed what little was left of the roach. A pleasant mist mushroomed in my head. For a moment we were facing each other with silly grins. Even her shaved eyebrows and series of tiny gold rings above one eye, which left me cold when I first saw her, now seemed exotic and strangely alluring. If there was ever a time for that first kiss, this was it.

"You know what would be great?" she suddenly said. "A cup of chamomile."

Perhaps the dope had jammed my telepathic powers. Nevertheless, I floated toward the kitchenette to fill the kettle. When I turned to ask what she took in her tea, she was standing in front of my easel and staring at my work-in-progress with great interest. That was when I realized to my horror that I had forgotten to replace the drop cloth on the canvas after nearly slicing it up with the butcher's knife earlier that afternoon. In any case, it was too late to cover it up now. She was staring at the thing.

"Is this supposed to be North Cape?"

"A version of it, in any case." I was hoping the edge in my voice would convince her to move away from the painting. I couldn't think of anything else to do so I retrieved the drop cloth.

"I realize it's not finished," she said before I could cover the canvas. "I mean, I like the rising waves. That part is very dramatic. But the rest..."

"What about the rest?"

"It's a bit empty," she said then put her hand on my forearm apologetically. "Sorry! I didn't mean to criticize. I know it's not finished yet. It's that stretch in the middle. There's not much going on, if you know what I mean. I assume you're going to put something there. Or is it supposed to be like that?"

What the hell was she talking about, not much going on? Couldn't she see that big six-armed monstrosity that was now filling up the space between the rising waves?

"I don't know," I said as casually as I could. "What do you think? Tell me what you see?"

She studied the canvas again. "Um, there're all those little things, bottles and shells and objects and whatever. I like the detail of all that. Is that supposed to be the point of the picture? All these little things that are under the water but now revealed? Does that represent our subconscious or something?"

"That's it? That's all you see?"

"I don't know what you mean. What else is there?"

I stared at the canvas with her, making it look as if I was pondering what she just said. In reality, I was staring at the Starfish of David and trying to let the fact that she couldn't see it sink into my head. Judas's explanation from that afternoon came back to me: how a version of me from another plane of existence had painted the starfish and how the starfish itself only existed in the same plane. I had no idea what he was talking about then and I still didn't entirely comprehend. But one thing was crystal clear to me at that moment.

I could see the starfish and Aziza couldn't.

I could see something that only existed on another plane of existence. Was this proof of the Supreme One meeting me half way, as Judas had said?

I covered the canvas with the drop cloth. Any thought of kissing her, or anything else that might naturally follow, had been unnaturally erased from my mind.

I've heard of divine intervention, but I never expected to be cock-blocked by an almighty deity (although, in retrospect, maybe that's part of their job). Instead, when I should have been getting tail and giving head, here I was endeavoring to make head or tail of the mysterious process of decision-making.

When exactly do we decide? Is there a subconscious process that leads us to the moment of realization? Are there bits of evidence that we pick up, like shells or stones or sea glass washed up along a shoreline? Was it various things that Fagin, Shylock and Judas had said, bits of argument that slowly swayed me?

Who knows? But whatever the process, the final realization was here: I was the only one who could see the six-armed starfish. It was a sign meant only for me. Even though this afternoon I was adamantly against the idea, I now knew beyond a shadow of a doubt that I was going to build the first synagogue on Prince Edward Island.

PART 2:

PASSIONS TO PASSIONS, LUST TO LUST

5

WHEN THE MEMBER of the Legislative Assembly for Mount Russet, Denise O'Hanley, stepped down after twenty years, a by-election followed and none other than Reuben Arsenault became Mount R's new MLA, swooping in on the promise to clean up Rossiter's Field, an unofficial dumping site on the outskirts of town. I myself didn't have to think twice about marking my X beside the name of anyone other than an art-hating Philistine like Reuben Arsenault.

It's debatable whether Reuben's penchant for wearing bolo ties played any part in his winning the election, but he himself may have felt this sartorial quirk did indeed give him an edge. He was reputed to own a large collection of them, which was apparently an exaggeration (according to Aziza) that Reuben liked to propagate as a way of embellishing his own mythology.

He had picked up a taste for this western accessory, not surprisingly, while studying Economics at the University of Calgary in 1985 (proudly claiming that he and Stephen Harper graduated together). Some of his bolo ties were custom made with PEI specific symbols, such as a brushed pewter potato, a silver buoy and a rust-coloured ceramic one in the shape of the Island itself.

Hot on the heels of Reuben's big political win, LovesterFest PEI was in full swing, running all of September as a way to extend the tourist season. It was created and promoted by Reuben himself with the full support of Tourism and Culture Minister Kerrie-Jo Campbelljohn. "Something they probably concocted after sweating up the sheets," Aziza confided to me with ill-disguised revulsion. After having his face plastered on posters, newspaper inserts and

TV ads during his political campaign, LovesterFest PEI provided a strategic segue to more public exposure for him, differentiated only by him showing off a special bolo tie that was copper with pinkish-red coral inlay, in the shape of the trademarked logo: a heart with two lobster claws and a lobster tail.

For an entry fee of $750, restaurants, dairy bars and pubs across the Island created variations on traditional lobster rolls and lobster burgers, as well as branching out into ethnic lobster-filled creations, such as tacos, gyros, calzones, egg rolls, bagels (or as pronounced by some Islanders, "baggles"). Customers voted online and the winning restaurant would have bragging rights until next year's competition.

The first year's winner was something called the Wreck 'N' Rollo Hoochie Koo from The Wreckage Patio Bistro in Rollo Bay. It was a lobster roll made with a maple-tinged mayonnaise and capers, pickled apple slaw, and seasoned with various herbs and cayenne, on a foot-long crusty cheese baguette. For the second year of the contest, the Crazy Diamond was entering as a way to promote their expanding kitchen menu. Nathalie Doiron, their head chef, kept with the Crazy Diamond's Maritime psychedelic theme by creating the Electric Lobster Acid Zest, a lobster salad brightened up with a lemon-lime vinaigrette and cocoa salt, served open-faced on tapenade-smeared Mediterranean flatbread wedges. The one I tried was delicious.

This was about a week or so after I committed myself to the synagogue challenge. Aziza had been waitressing at the Crazy Diamond and fitting in rather well, according to Maggie.

"Look at her go," she exclaimed, referring to how Aziza, wearing a tie-dye tee shirt and vintage bell-bottom jeans to fit in with the 60s décor, expertly made her way through the crowd while balancing a tray of drinks on one arm and a tray of food on the other.

Aziza was so busy that I sat at my regular stool, nursing my usual Beairsto's IPA, for a full twenty minutes before she was able to stop to say hello. I offered to buy her a drink and she asked Maggie for a white wine spritzer and ordered three Interstellar Overdrives for one of the tables. This was a new blender cocktail Maggie had recently invented and named after an instrumental cut from Floyd's first album, *Piper at The Gates of Dawn*.

Aziza hopped on the stool beside me. "Nice to get off my feet for a minute," she said, sipping her spritzer. "How goes the hunt?"

I motioned for her to keep her voice down, since she meant my furtive investigations into how I might get this synagogue built. Aziza was, so far, the only person I told about my desire to "found" (a word preferable to "build", since it implied less manual labour) a synagogue on PEI. She was intrigued but mystified by my motivation in this sudden interest. I was able to satisfy her curiosity by claiming that I was merely in the research stage as a way of taking my mind off my creative block.

"Not so good," I confided. "I've been looking into the possibility of turning some already existing building into a temple. Driving around Charlottetown and scanning the real estate section in the *Charlottetown Parrot*. I'm trying to keep my search casual and low key."

That was as much as I dared express about how helpless I felt. I hadn't seen any sign of Judas, Shylock or Fagin since I made my decision. My feelings about this were mixed. On the one hand, I would have loved nothing more than to be rid of those three boils on my psyche's backside for good. Still, I couldn't help but feel a sense of betrayal (maybe that was what Judas had been preparing me for during our last meeting after all). Once I finally made the decision that they had been pushing me toward, they suddenly up and abandoned me. One afternoon, I even took to wandering around Mount Russet, purposefully going to all those places where I'd previously encountered them, hoping they'd show up. On one desperate occasion I even stood in the middle of my studio and called out their names, to no avail except for deep embarrassment.

I checked my canvas to see if the Starfish of David was still there. For a brief moment, I dared to hope it had disappeared, but there it was like a stark reminder that I could not renege on my decision. It also told me that I was now entirely on my own. My reaction to that realization was, in retrospect, somewhat childish and bizarre. I decided to avoid the temptation of looking at my painting again by binding the drop cloth over it with bungee cords. It was my way of insisting that if I was to be abandoned then two could play that game.

"Well, I have some news," said Aziza with a sly grin. She leaned in close and spoke sotto voce. "Anne Surly's back in business."

"You bought a new webcam?"

"Not exactly." Her grin was of the shit-eating variety. "Best not to go into detail."

"Where are you broadcasting from? Not your apartment."

"You mean webcasting?" she said with a sarcastic smirk.

"Whatever," I said. "I left my Silicon Valley glossary in my other jeans."

"Come on, I'm just teasing." By this time, I was used to having Aziza break my chops, but her playful grin betrayed an unspoken happiness. I couldn't quite figure out what it was. I considered asking her, but Maggie signalled that the order of Interstellar Overdrives was ready. Aziza hopped off her stool and gave me a sly wink then hefted the tray of drinks with ease and disappeared into the crowd.

"I don't know, something about that one."

On the stool next to me sat Pius Duffy, making one of his rare appearances in the bar. His burly frame was exaggerated by his denim bib overalls, which he wore over a sleeveless checked work shirt. His potato-shaped head was bald on top but fringed by long thick blondish-grey hair that cascaded past his shoulders. His wild chinstrap of a beard, sans moustache, flared out around his face like the rays of a cartoon sun. Numerous tattoos, remnants of his biker days, covered his beefy arms, including RIDE spelled out on the knuckles of his right hand and HARD on the knuckles of his left hand. Normally he spent all his time in what he liked to call the Shine Shrine, or the Shrine for short, keeping a close eye on the quality control in the production of the shine that was at the heart of the Crazy Diamond's reputation.

"What do you mean?" I asked. "What about her?"

"What's she doing here anyway?" he asked. "Daughter of a big shot like that Reuben Arse-hole. What she want carrying trays in a place like this?"

"I told you she's okay," said Maggie, giving her husband a playful cuff on the ear. "She's an independent sort. Kinda reminds me of myself when I was that age. Besides she works some harder than most."

Pius turned to his wife. "I caught her nosing around in the Shrine the other week."

"Yes," said Maggie, trying to not sound too mollifying. "We cleared that up. She won't go in there again."

"What she want in there?" Pius grumbled. "She got no business in there."

Everyone knew that the Shrine was off limits to everyone except Pius and his two brothers, Casper and Alvin, who helped him distil. Maggie was allowed back there as well, but she mostly stuck to running the bar. She pulled a pint and slid it in front of Pius.

"Just curious, I guess," said Maggie. "Now drink up and get back in your cage."

"Yeah, curious," said Pius and knocked back a healthy swallow. "Like the cat."

"What is it you're suspicious about?" I asked.

"Apple don't fall far from the tree," he said.

I tried to vouch for Aziza, telling him what was appropriate about her feelings toward her father. "He offered her a job to work for him, but she'd rather do this."

"We don't know she ain't working for him now," he said and polished off his beer, then slunk back toward the Shrine. "Spying for her old man to see how he can horn his way into our business."

"Is he serious?" I asked Maggie.

"Never mind him." She cleared his empty glass and mine too. "Another?"

I declined and slid off the stool, noticing that big jar by the cash register no longer had its sign for the Ashlynn's Camp for Kids fund. I asked Maggie what happened. She shrugged in an oddly curt manner.

"I think you were right in the first place," she said. "Makes a better tip jar."

I MANOEUVRED THE CAR out of the Crazy Diamond's parking lot. In the back of my mind, I knew I had been wasting time doing this on my own. The first thing I probably should have done was approach the PEI Jewish Collective to get them on my side. Easier said than done. Many a time they had courted me to become a member only to be rebuffed, as nicely as I could. I knew that Frieda Greenglass, in particular, had been eager that I become an active part of the community. I had nothing against the Collective itself, it's just I have a general aversion to joining groups. I'm a natural loner. In some ways, I think that's what attracted Frieda to me (and perhaps still does), but it's also what irritated her to no end (and perhaps still does).

Nevertheless, sooner or later I was going to have to approach the Collective and I was going to have to do it through Frieda. I dreaded the thought. How was I going to explain this sudden interest in building a synagogue to her? Even when I mentioned it in passing the last time I saw her, it immediately aroused her suspicion. On the other hand, if I could convince her and the Collective that I was serious about doing this, it might appear like good faith on my part, which hopefully would bring me the support I was going to need.

I was now coasting along the curve of Highway 7 past Luke Gallant's John Deere dealership, heading toward Charlottetown on another fruitless search for some building that might magically scream out "Synagogue!" to me. I didn't want to waste any more time. What I really needed to do was see Frieda. I'd left it too long as it was. My best approach would be to meet her at the market after she closes the stall. Best thing I could do now was pull a u-ey and head home.

"Take the next right turn, my dear."

The voice came from behind me. Familiar as it was, I was startled and swerved to the side of the road, jammed my foot on the break and skidded to a halt. I had been expecting only Fagin, but all three of them sat shoulder to shoulder in the back seat: Fagin on the far right and Shylock on the far left, with Judas sandwiched in the middle. It was a tight fit, jammed in as he was with the knees of his long legs almost jutting against his chest.

"And here I thought you three rats had jumped ship," I said. "But if you're going to suddenly appear out of nowhere, may I suggest a moving vehicle is not the best place to do it. I assumed you would have learned that lesson from last time." I was staring directly at Fagin.

"I had such a lovely ride in this horseless hunk of metal I knew me two mates would enjoy their selves too," said Fagin with a smarmy grin.

"Signor, thou must forgive such an intrusion," said Shylock. "In truth, we meant no villainy. We come with a vital revelation to aid thine onerous task."

"A revelation," I said. "I'm almost afraid to ask."

"Now don't come the sceptic with us," said Fagin. "We heard you calling out our names."

"That must have been amusing for you," I said.

"Forsooth, signor, 'twas was no source of mirth. Had we a solution to thy distress we ne'er wouldst have kept our peace ere now. We hath made material a desire to be of assistance to thee."

While the two of them jabbered at me from both sides, my eyes never wavered from Judas, who, instead of meeting my stare, studied the fingers enlaced awkwardly on top of his upright knees.

"You've been suspiciously silent so far," I said to him. "You look pretty uncomfortable jackknifed like that. Wouldn't you prefer to stretch your legs in front?"

His eyes slowly looked up from beneath their hooded lids. "We are not far from our destination. We should continue while there is still light in the sky."

As Fagin had originally instructed, I took the next right. This was a narrow stretch of dirt road called Rossiter's Way. There was barely room for two cars to pass each other and I prayed no vehicle would be coming the other way. I couldn't imagine why we were taking this route as there really wasn't much here. On either side of us was desolate scrubland. The road ultimately led to the ruins of what supposedly was once a granary, which, according to local lore, had been destroyed in a fire well over a hundred and twenty years ago. Some said it had been torched for the insurance, others said it had been an accident, still others said the owner had been inside and the fire was set as an act of vengeance either over money or a love affair gone bad. That was about as much as I knew of the history of the place. The farther we drove, the more anxious I became.

"Where the hell are we going?" I asked aloud to my backseat navigators.

"Don't get your knickers in a twist, my dear," answered Fagin. "We're almost there."

"Almost where?" I asked, more as a reflex, knowing it was a question that wouldn't be answered. And sure enough, the only reply was silence for the next ten minutes until the road came to an end.

I stopped the car and got out. If this was where the granary had been situated, there was no evidence of it. Instead, a massive tract was overrun with weeds and sickly trees with brownish vegetation entwined around discarded kitchen appliances, junked automobiles, holey mattresses with rusty springs jutting out (looking like metallic flora), splintered furniture hardly recognizable from the trees around them. Strewn everywhere were all manner of broken bottles smashed into shards, punctured and dented plastic jugs that would be nowhere near to decomposing for decades to come, old telephones, metal that was twisted and tarnished beyond recognition and items too numerous or grotesque to mention.

So, this was Rossitor's Field. It had been used as an unofficial dumping ground long before I ever came to the Island. Every now and then, the government or the official opposition raised a hue and cry about the sorry state of the area and grumblings of cleaning up the place were heard, usually at election time. But the dumping had been going on for decades and eventually the problem of cleaning the place up seemed too insurmountable to undertake.

"What in God's name..." I started and caught myself. "Why did you drag me all the way out here to this unholy mess?"

"This be the place, my dear," said Fagin. He had a weird, self-satisfied smirk so wide that his springy mutton chops jutted out in fluffy angles at either side of his wiry face.

"What place?" My voice cracked in a desperate higher register that was not so much a question as a plea for help.

Shylock was beside me. "'Tis the ground sanctioned by the Supreme One," he said as if this would clear up everything.

"Sanctioned?" I said innocently. "For what?"

"Why for the temple, good cousin Samson," Shylock answered. "'Tis the very place where the temple must be erected."

"What kind of sick joke is this?" I moved toward the car. Judas stood in front of the driver's door.

"You have my word we are serious," he said. "This must be the site for the synagogue."

"Says who?"

"We already told you it were the Supreme One who made the decree," said Fagin, taking his place by Judas. "That's the bare-faced truth of it."

I ignored Fagin and kept staring at Judas, who made a slight nodding gesture to Fagin. He frowned and walked away.

"Look at all this!" I said and waved my hand at the vast entanglement of trash. "How am I supposed to build a synagogue on a garbage dump? Who's going to clean it up? You three?"

Judas said nothing.

For a moment it occurred to me that these three clowns could indeed probably clean it up with whatever hoodoo magic they possessed. For that matter, they could probably snap their fingers or twitch their noses, *Bewitched* style, and – poof! – there would be a spanking brand-new synagogue. There was no reason to drag me into this.

"We cannot do that," Judas said, interrupting my train of thought, which he apparently was privy to. "We are but mere messengers. We are not allowed to interfere with your task."

"Why not?"

Shylock stepped gently and stood to one side of me. "We beseech thee, good cousin, if it please thou to view our predicament with some sympathy."

"Your predicament?"

"Try to look at it from our boots, my dear," said Fagin at my other side. "We can only do as we are told. There would be rather severe consequences if we were to overstep our bounds."

I threw up my hands in disgust at the mound of garbage and trudged closer to it, the better to wallow in how insurmountable the task before me looked. I kicked an old porcelain toilet, which was lodged much more firmly in the muck than I thought, and nearly took my foot off in the process. I let loose a string of curses and saw I was once again alone. There was nothing to do but hobble over to the car and drive down Rossiter's Way to Highway 7. In my rear view mirror a cloud of dust trailing behind me obscured the garbage dump as if it was nothing but a bad dream.

Of course, there are theologies that believe – no matter where or how merrily you row your boat – life is indeed merely a dream and we are unable to see reality for what it is because we are mired in an all-pervading illusion perpetuated by the relentless cravings of our mortal appetites.

Dream or reality, one thing was clear: there was no way I could approach Frieda Greenglass, let alone the PEI Jewish Collective, with the idea of building a synagogue on Rossiter's Field. It would be tantamount to suggesting we build a holy temple on Gehenna, that site of human sacrifice and a burning trash heap from the Old Testament we Jews considered a literal Hell on Earth.

THAT NIGHT I SLEPT fitfully, thinking about Rossiter's Field and what I would say to Frieda. I remembered I was going to check in to see what Anne Surly was up to. I sat up in bed and opened my laptop. She was well into her rant. The first thing I noticed was an improvement in the production quality. There was something stark and theatrical about the lighting. It was mostly trained on her, while allowing her surroundings to remain indistinct. I didn't pay much attention to what she was saying, being focused on trying to figure out where she was. There weren't many clues: no furniture or distinguishing features. The only background was dark and rustic looking. Was she in a barn or a shed?

I also noticed a difference in her general performance. There was less bump and grind and more swagger in her body language. She was using the riding crop to greater effect, punctuating her words by slicing the air as an exclamation mark or smacking her boot as a full stop. Her delivery carried more authority in the way she spoke directly to the camera. It was both intimate and formal. She had obviously been practicing.

"And now, for all you sad little willy wankers and monkey spankers, here's your dose of medicine before you get to spunk your boxers. Now that our very own Island Enemy Number One, Rotten Reuben, is going to be the MLA of a place he's never set foot in, thanks to a big campaign promise to clean up Rossiter's Field that got the voters all fired up in the first place, gullible little golliwogs that they are, the question is: who's going to pay for the clean-up? The plan is that this will supposedly be the site for Ashlynn's Camp for Kids and that means jobs and economic growth for Mount Russet so the clean-up will eventually pay for itself. Sound too good to be true? Of course, there's more to this story than meets the eye. But like in any political fairy tale, if you want to find the dough you have to follow the trail of breadcrumbs. Tune in next time and I'll fill in some of the blanks and maybe let you lick my boot heels, if you're good little tool tuggers."

She cracked the riding crop against the heel of her boot and the screen went blank.

"Quite the performance," said Fagin, sitting at the foot of my bed. His leer showed off a couple of missing teeth, leaving only yellowish stumps glinting with saliva. "A bit too Soho for my taste. I prefer the original version in your painting."

"That's not the original," I explained. "She's based on a character in a book."

"Who ain't?" he said with a throaty cackle. "Still, the red hair is a dead giveaway that she's one of the tribe. That's the tradition, if you hadn't noticed." He gave his own long rusty locks a playful tug.

"Yes, I'm aware of the historical depiction of Jews as redheads," I said. "Still, I'm pretty sure *Anne of Green Gables* wasn't Jewish, despite her red hair."

"Then why paint her the way you did?"

I decided to ignore the question. "You know, this was the second time Anne Surly's webcast mentioned something I became aware of earlier. The last time it was Ashlynn's Camp for Kids that I'd heard about at the Crazy Diamond. Tonight, it was Rossiter's Field, where you brought me."

"What about it?"

"Could that be a coincidence?"

"As much a coincidence as that urchin having red hair and yet you claim she weren't Jewish."

"Anne Shirley was not Jewish!" I said with irritation. "Lucy Maud Montgomery made her a redhead because she was supposed to be a misfit, an outsider."

"Outsider, Jew, same difference," said Fagin. "Anyway, there ain't no coincidences, my dear, only well laid plans beyond the ken of mere mortals."

"What plans?"

"Didn't I just say they were beyond the ken of mere mortals?" he said with some annoyance.

"I can't help but notice how you and your two compatriots are conveniently short on details as to why the Supreme One wants this synagogue to be built on Rossiter's Field."

"If you must know," Fagin said. "This small area of the world, despite being reduced to a massive tip by you lot, is in actual fact a very hallowed spot."

"Hallowed? What makes it hallowed?"

"The Word of the Supreme One is what bloody well makes it hallowed ground, if that's all to your satisfaction," he said. "And since you ain't too swift on the uptake tonight, I will take the liberty of pointing out to you that it looks like a good bit of your work is going to be done for you."

I looked at him hopefully. "It is?"

"Didn't you hear what that young virago said? This Rotten Reuben bloke is going to have the tip cleaned up."

"Are you kidding?" I laughed. "They've been saying that for years. You expect a politician to keep his promises?"

"I may be a figment, but I ain't bloody gormless, am I. Politicians don't do shite when left to their own devices. It takes a larger hand to give 'em a nudge. Know what I'm saying?"

"You mean, the Supreme One?"

"Bingo, my dear."

"Man, this whole business is getting really convoluted."

"The Supreme One may work in mysterious ways, but it was a doddle to get the bugger elected so he could clean up all that pile of rubbish."

"The Supreme One got Reuben elected to MLA?"

"What did you think, it was them daft stringy ties he wears?" he said. "You just better be right geared up to make your move when the time comes."

"What move?"

"You're going to have to reckon some things out for yourself, my dear," he said and slowly began to sink out of sight behind my bed's footboard.

"Hold on! Wait a minute!"

Before I could finish, he disappeared completely. There was no way I could sleep, but I tried to relax and think. I wondered when Aziza would get home. I needed someone to talk to who wouldn't disappear whenever it was convenient. I decided to sit up and listen for her footsteps in her apartment above. I leaned back with my hands behind my head and tried to think up the best way to tell her what was going on without sounding like I had completely lost my sanity. Maybe I didn't have to go into too much detail. Just talk about voices inside my head, more in a spiritual sense than a lunatic one. Maybe it was better to make it one voice. More spiritual that way.

I WOKE UP THE NEXT morning with the duvet partially wrapped around my foetal-positioned body. The drool-soaked pillow felt cold against my cheek and the morning sun assaulted my sleep-encrusted eyes.

The radio was on low, but loud enough that I could hear the hosts of *Good Morning PEI*, Chet Affleck and Chad Peladeau, talking about Reuben Arsenault being named MLA for Mount Russet.

CHET: "Big news on the political front, don't you think, Chad?"

CHAD: "Certainly a controversial one, Chet. Ever since Reuben Arsenault's name was mentioned as a possible successor to Denise O'Hanley there have been a few grumblings about his lack of political experience."

CHET: "Too true, but now he's got the chance to prove himself."

CHAD: "What do you make of his promise to clean up Rossiter's Field?"

CHET: "Hard to say, Chad. This has been his main political promise and if he achieves it, he'll have succeeded where others failed lo these many years."

CHAD: "And if he does do it, rumour has it this will be the site for Ashlynn's Camp for Kids. You're the director of that project, so I have to ask... *heh, heh...*"

CHET: "Whoa, who, whoa. As Schultz used to say on Hogan's Heroes: *I know nussing. Nussing!*"

CHAD: "Ha ha! There you have it, folks. Charlottetown's own Rich Little.

CHET: "But in all seriousness, Chad, cleaning up Rossiter's Field would truly be a great thing for the camp and for the kids."

CHAD: "Not to mention the jobs it would bring to Mount Russet. And speaking of which, we'll be talking to Tammy Dennison from Labour PEI about a program that places seniors back in the work force... *as dog walkers?*"

CHET: "I guess you could say they're getting a new... *leash?* ... on life."

CHAD: "Ouch. But first we're going to hear a song from sixteen-year-old Treena Gallant, the winner of this year's *Tignish Idol*."

I quickly turned off the radio when I heard footsteps above me. I assumed Aziza must be awake, so I got dressed and headed upstairs. When I reached the top of the stairs, I saw her door was partially open. Had she just got home? I stepped inside, calling her name when Maggie Beairsto appeared from the bedroom.

"Samson?"

"Maggie, what are you doing here?"

"I could ask you the same thing."

"You could, but I beat you to it," I said.

Her hand covered her mouth. "You haven't heard..."

"Heard what?"

"About Aziza. I just came from the hospital."

Maggie led me over to the ugly green sofa. I sat with a thud and slumped down like a marionette whose strings had been cut. "What happened?"

Maggie paced. I wanted to ask her to sit as she was making me nervous, but even in my state I could see she was also on the verge of a meltdown and pacing was the only way she could keep it together. Eventually she was able to tell me that Aziza had had an accident while biking home after she helped close up the Crazy Diamond.

I mentally noted that she wouldn't have gone straight home after closing up because she first would have done her webcast, from where I didn't know, and then biked home.

"This is all my fault," Maggie moaned and then she did collapse on the sofa, which jolted me as much as the statement.

"Why do you say that?"

"Pius and his brothers had gone already. They always leave first on their choppers. Aziza helped Nathalie clean up the kitchen like she usually does and then helped me close up the place. After she left, I stayed behind to work on the books. I always told her it was dangerous biking home late at night on that friggin' Mount Russet Road, but she insisted it wasn't a problem. I always offer to drive her home in the SUV, but she's some stubborn when she wants to be. I should have never let her..."

Here Maggie stared straight ahead. I took her hand and told her to continue. She looked at me and tears welled up in her eyes. I got her some toilet paper to blow her nose. She managed to compose herself long enough to tell me how she spotted Aziza's bicycle lying by the side of the Mount Russet Road when she was driving home. She stopped, but she couldn't see Aziza. After she got a flashlight from her glove compartment, she could see that the bike's rear wheel had been mangled badly. After a bit of searching, she found Aziza's unconscious body a few feet away in some undergrowth. It looked like she went head first into a rock. There was blood on her helmet. She had obviously been thrown from the bike after whatever hit it had driven off.

"Motherfucken coward..." Maggie growled and blew her nose again. "I picked her up, poor dear hardly weighs a thing. Then I realized I probably shouldn't have moved her, but I couldn't leave her there in the bushes, could I?"

Maggie had managed to get a spare blanket from the back of her SUV, laid it on the ground, then laid Aziza on top of it and called 911 on her cell. It took the ambulance almost twenty minutes to get there. Maggie followed it to Queens County Hospital and then called Aziza's mother (having contact information for all her employees on her phone). "I sat up with Mrs. Arsenault in the ward by Aziza's bed. Later on, Reuben showed up. That's when I volunteered to come here and get Aziza some fresh clothes."

"How serious is it?"

"I think she's out of the woods, but she has a nasty bruise on her head. Her neck and one of her legs were in bad shape. I think they're going to keep her there."

I volunteered to take the fresh clothes to the hospital so Maggie could go home and get some sleep. "Don't think I could sleep," she said. "I'd rather find the low bastard that did this."

I finally convinced her to go home and promised to let her know if anything happened. She bundled the clothes in a shopping bag and gave it to me. All I could think of on the drive to Charlottetown was Anne Surly's webcast and Aziza's accident. My gut told me they were connected. But how?

6

STEPPING THROUGH the sliding glass doors at the main entrance of Queens County Hospital, I clutched the shopping bag of clothes Maggie had packed for Aziza, feeling lost. I passed the empty wheelchairs clustered near the glass doors and entered the main lobby. The waiting area itself, through which I passed, was more like that of an airport and added to my feelings of disassociation and transience. I looked down and noticed different coloured lines on the floor, which led me down an austere corridor to a bank of elevators.

Aziza had originally been put in a bed on a third-floor ward and I searched along the rows of beds, unable to find her. A nurse at the desk informed me she had been moved to a private room on the fourth floor. I assumed this had been done at the insistence of Reuben Arsenault.

Sure enough, when I reached Room 412, there he was pacing in the corridor, speaking furtively on his cell phone. His back was to me, and I entered the room, quietly enough that neither Aziza nor the woman in the pale headscarf (whom I assumed was her mother) noticed me at first. Aziza's head was bandaged. Her neck was in a brace and her leg raised in traction. They were speaking softly as I stood there like a ghost whose existence could not be felt in the living world. Although Aziza could not turn her head, I saw her eyes dart in my direction. Her mother noticed and turned my way. Suddenly the center of attention, I was seized by a mild panic. I held out the shopping bag in a gesture of self-protection and by way of explaining my presence.

"Maggie told me what happened," I said in a half-whisper. "She gave me this for you."

Aziza managed a smile. "You don't have to whisper. Put it on the bed. I think there's another chair."

"That's okay, I'd rather stand."

Aziza stared at me with a tight smile, clearly trying to put on a brave face, then allowed her eyes to take in the drabness of her surroundings. Her attention briefly drifted to the morning that brightened the window. I couldn't help remembering how happy she looked yesterday when I saw her in the Crazy Diamond. A secret happiness that I was not privy to yet made me feel closer to her. To see her like this now filled me with a despondent anger at whoever had done this to her. She noticed her mother staring silently at me.

"Ima, this is Samson. He lives in my building. Samson, this is my mother."

"Hello, Mrs. Arsenault."

She nodded then turned her attention to her daughter. "I think after they let you out you should come home and let me take care of you."

"That won't be necessary," said Aziza with the patience of someone who is having to repeat herself.

"How long will you have to stay here?" I asked. Her mother's eyes darted toward me, glowering for a split-second at my effrontery for interrupting a family conversation. I smiled weakly and trained my eyes on Aziza.

"Not sure," she said. "A couple of days probably, to see how things go."

"Do you remember anything? What happened?"

"Not much. Pretty sure it was a truck. The high beams were on so I couldn't get a good look, but I could tell it was crowding me. Next thing I know I'm flying through the air. After that..."

There was so much I wanted to ask her, about the webcast and its connection to the accident, but I decided it was more prudent not to say anything about Anne Surly with her mother there. According to Aziza, her father knew all about her online alter ego, but it wasn't clear to me whether her mother was aware of it. I dared only cast furtive glances in her direction. I assumed – mostly because of the headscarf, which gave her a severe and pious demeanour – she would be highly opposed to and deeply mortified by Aziza's behaviour in front of the webcam. She wasn't particularly pleased by my presence, and I have to admit this only made me want to ingratiate myself all the more to her, let her know that I was indeed a friend to her daughter.

"If you need anything..." I let the sentence hang unfinished, hoping Aziza would finish it for me, but she said nothing. "Like if you need a ride back home after they let you out or whatever."

"Thanks," Aziza answered. "And thanks for bringing my clothes." Clearly, this was meant as a signal that my visit had come to an end.

"I'll check in with you," I said and turned to leave just as Reuben Arsenault entered the room, flipping his phone closed and slipping it into his suit jacket inside pocket. The first thing I noticed was the bolo tie in the shape of the red LovesterFest PEI logo. It was a jolt of cheerful colour at odds with the hospital room's sombre atmosphere. I could feel the muscles around my mouth wanting to stretch out in a wide grin and clenched my jaw.

"Hello?" he said and offered his hand. "Reuben Arsenault."

I shook his hand. "Samson Grief." I noticed a gleam of recognition flicker at the corners of his grey-blue eyes. His head cocked ever so slightly and his thin lips curled upwards.

"And to what do we owe the honour, Mr. Grief?"

"I live downstairs from Aziza. Being a good neighbour and dropping off a few things for her. By the way, congratulations on your win. As a resident of Mount Russet, I look forward to the big changes you've promised."

"I'll try not to disappoint you, Mr. Grief," he said and shot the cuffs of his shirt so they peeked out from his jacket sleeves. I noticed his cufflinks were also shaped like the LovesterFest PEI logo, perfectly matching his bolo tie. He saw that I noticed them and looked appropriately pleased by what must have been the surprise on my face. "I'd be happy to hear any of your concerns. Feel free to send them in writing to my office."

Normally I would have left it at that, since all I wanted to do was get out of there as fast as I could. Instead, I found myself inexplicably rubbing my palms together and clearing my throat.

"I guess my biggest concern is your promise to clean up Rossiter's Field."

"Oh?" Obviously, he wasn't expecting this because his shoulders flinched slightly, but he quickly recovered. "It's one of my top priorities."

"I'm glad to hear that," I said and knew I should just say good-bye, but instead pressed ahead. "I was there only yesterday and I have to say you've got your work cut out for you."

"You were?" said Aziza. She tried to turn her head to face me but couldn't manage it.

"Yes," I said. "After I left the Crazy Diamond. I'd never seen it before and thought I'd go out of curiosity."

Reuben Arsenault grinned good-naturedly, holding his body erect with hands folded in front of him: a self-protective stance that feigned attentiveness. "I hope you weren't dumping anything there. As you say, I have my work cut out for me as it is."

"No dumping," I said. "I just wanted to have a look."

"What for?" asked Aziza.

I smiled at her and wondered what I was going to say. My brain didn't even have a microsecond to think up some flimsy excuse before my mouth blundered ahead.

"I wanted to see if it would be a good site for the synagogue I'd like to build. I mentioned it to you."

Aziza's face screwed up in confusion. "Yeah, you did..." She started to laugh but grimaced in pain, then continued to laugh some more. "But I thought you were looking somewhere more..."

I saw that her mother's face also betrayed bewilderment. Her laughter was quieter, after which she politely covered her mouth, as if she had coughed or sneezed. Even with her hand blocking the lower half of her face, I could see she was still amused. Although I knew I was being laughed at, I found her modesty endearing, almost respectful.

I turned to Reuben Arsenault to find those steely eyes scrutinizing me, like he was still considering whether I was even worth the effort of laughing at.

"A synagogue? Why in the world would anyone want to build a synagogue there?"

"I don't know," I said. "But I'm on my way to meet with a prominent member of the PEI Jewish Collective to discuss the idea."

I couldn't read his face, impassive as it was, but I could sense the turning gears of his mind processing this information.

"Well, I'd love to discuss this with you further, Mr. Grief, but I'm here to see my daughter and I think it's best if Aziza gets some rest."

At that moment the nurse entered the room with a sedative. All attention was now on Aziza. I said my good-byes, but they either didn't hear me or chose to forget my existence. I heard Aziza say she'd be in touch before I quietly exited.

Out in the hallway, I suddenly felt flushed and a little dazed at the memory of what had just happened. Was that really me squaring off against Reuben Arsenault? What was I thinking, telling him about the synagogue and saying I was going to meet someone from the PEIJC, like this idea was already on the table? It was true that I planned to meet Frieda Greenglass at her Latke Lady stall, this being Saturday morning and the Farmers' Market was already open. It's also true, though, that she didn't know I was coming, so I may have bent the truth a little. Still, the market was a neutral enough place to meet with her and I had a couple of hours to think about what I was going to say.

"Thou were most heroic, cousin." Shylock was walking beside me. "Thy steadfast fashion, in sooth, did make a deep impression. How firmly thou held to thy noble principle. I was most enthralled."

"I was flying by the seat of my pants," I said. "Things were just coming out of my mouth like it wasn't me saying them."

I stopped suddenly in the middle of the hallway. An orderly pushing an empty gurney behind me swerved to avoid hitting me. He glowered in my direction as he passed and muttered something about it being a good thing I was already in a hospital.

I ducked into a small empty corridor off the main hallway. Shylock followed.

"Was that you making me say all that stuff? Or one of the other two *dybbuks*?"

"Signor! Methinks 'tis a great disservice to malign the power of thy oratory. 'Twas thee alone, good cousin, and thy own voice thus rang true with such valorous self-possession."

I allowed this flattery to go to my head until I remembered who was talking to me.

"I shouldn't have given myself away so quickly," I said and continued back in the main hallway, hoping to shake him off. He kept pace right beside me.

"Nay, mighty Samson, nay. The first stone hath been laid to the groundwork and strong is thy position."

"What position?" I said quietly, looking around to see if anyone heard me. "I have no position. My position is that I'm flying by the seat of my pants. In case you didn't know, that's a piss poor position to be in."

"The man hath been well knocked off-kilter, if not in evidence of his frame, then most surely in the maze of his brain." Shylock laughed. "Even now the persistent gnat of such a notion as this synagogue buzzes maddeningly within his bonce."

"I'm sure he thinks I'm just a kook."

"By all the heavens, signor, 'tis thy position of strength." He rubbed his hands together like a general concocting a strategy. "To the eyes of the world, the fool's lower rank best conceals his upper hand."

Great. I'd been cast in the role of undercover fool. The question was, what leverage did I really have? Since I already told Reuben that I was going to see a member of the PEIJC, I wondered if it was possible to play both ends of the field. No doubt Frieda was going to think I'd lost my nut, wanting to build a temple on Rossiter's Field, but if I could tell her I had already mentioned the idea to Reuben Arsenault, then it might give me a modicum of credibility.

I suddenly felt a strange warmth emanating from some dark corner within me, like an ember among the cold ashes that has caught onto a stray bit of kindling. If I wasn't mistaken, this was what the faint glow of self-confidence felt like. With a bit of finessing, I might be able to soften up both sides.

Shylock loved what he was hearing. He hunched close beside me as we wandered the hospital hallway like a couple of conspirators. He went on at length about maintaining a course of subterfuge while remaining true to the principle of my mission. He got so carried away that, to be honest, I couldn't entirely follow everything he was saying to me. At some point, I realized he was going on and on about how he had been tricked into giving up his Jewish faith and it slowly became clear that he viewed building this synagogue as the ultimate vengeance for what he had gone through. I said as much to him, and he became highly offended.

"Why doth thou wound me so, cousin? 'Tis not revenge of the heart, but rejuvenation of the spirit. What hath been robbed shall be restored. Our mission is larger than either of us. This synagogue will mark the single link to a much greater chain of events."

With that, he disappeared down a small side corridor and was gone.

Outside the sliding glass doors, I needed to pause before heading toward the crowded parking lot, to get a sense of where I had left the car. I couldn't help replaying in my head my conversation with Reuben Arsenault, when I realized I was looking right at him. He was standing in a distant section of the lot in front of a cream-coloured BMW, which undoubtedly was his. He was not alone. I had to squint to get a good look at whomever he was talking to, somebody younger and not as well dressed. I could make out an orange baseball cap and a black hoodie. The longer I stared, the more certain I became that this was Reggie Muir.

Judging by their body language the conversation was animated, even heated, considering the way Reuben would start to turn away from Reggie only to move back toward him as Reggie stepped away with his shoulders sagging. It looked like Reggie was trying to say something, but Reuben was violently shaking his head and raising his arms in such a way that shut Reggie down. Presuming that it was Reggie at the wheel when Aziza got smucked on her bike, I surmised that Big Daddy Reuben was giving old Reg an earful for nearly killing his daughter. Presuming also that it was Reuben who had ordered Reg to merely scare her, then that would give Big Daddy even more reason to chew his henchman's ear off. Not just giving vent to anger, but probably a goodly amount of guilt to boot.

All this surmising was interrupted by my twigging to the presence of Aziza's mother, who was standing a couple of feet from me, equally concentrating on their conversation. Her severe expression almost made me want to believe that she could hear what they were saying. I became more interested in her reaction than in the conversation itself. I admit I couldn't help studying her finely shaded cheekbones, the angle accenting the bridge of her nose, the tapering fleshiness of her slightly downturned mouth. She turned to see me staring at her and I averted my eyes, too late I realized, then looked at her again, not knowing where else to look.

"Sorry," I said and wished I had something else to add. Instead, I smiled, felt stupid and wondered if I shouldn't just walk away.

"No," she said. "I'm the one who should apologize."

"For what?"

"Earlier. When I laughed. Because you mentioned the synagogue."

"That's okay," I said. "I probably sounded pretty foolish."

"I was also laughing at Reuben's reaction," she said. "You really threw him off guard. It's not often I've seen him like that." A trace of a smile played at the corners of her mouth. "It was refreshing."

"I threw myself off guard too. I hadn't actually planned to... what I mean is..." I searched desperately for some way to save face.

"It's still in the early stages?" she asked helpfully, and I could have thrown myself at her feet. Instead, I merely nodded like a grateful fool. There was a silence then and a strange awkwardness fell between us. She turned back toward the parking lot and I did too.

The conversation between Reuben and Reggie was winding down and Reuben got into his BMW. Reggie walked off and got into the driver's side of a half-ton pickup truck. Reuben drove off, but Reggie's pickup sat there. I squinted until I could feel a headache coming on. It looked like he was alone. Maybe waiting for someone? Then it struck me, something I remembered Aziza saying about how Reggie and his brother Kelvin were almost inseparable. Reg'n'Kel she called them. I looked at her mother.

"Mrs. Arsenault?"

"I prefer Zaina."

"Zaina," I said, trying it out, liking the way it sounded, then remembering what I wanted to ask her. "How was Aziza when you left her?"

"They gave her a sedative," she said. "She was sleeping,"

Without saying another word, I turned and rushed back into the hospital. Rather than bother with the elevator, I took the stairs two at a time and ran to her room. I opened the door to see someone in a sleeveless jean jacket and backward ball cap standing over her bed.

"Excuse me?" I said.

He turned, startled. It was Kelvin. He rushed past, slamming me into the doorjamb, and ran down the corridor before ducking into a stairway. I thought about going after him, but figured it was better to check on Aziza first. She was asleep and didn't seem to have been interfered with. Then I noticed an envelope beside her. It was unsealed and I opened it to discover a card. It had a drawing of a cartoon duck with a bandaged head and shedding a single tear. Inside the card was a childish scrawl in blue ballpoint ink that read: *Zeez. get bettur soon ok?*

After making sure Aziza was all right, I rushed back down to the hospital entrance, only to find Zaina gone. A scan of the parking lot failed to turn up any trace of her. I even wandered around for a bit, peeking into cars. After about ten minutes I realized that I might be mistaken for a carjacker. That was when I noticed Reggie and Kelvin talking to each other in front of a black half-ton pick-up truck. Their exchange seemed to be as heated as Reggie's was with Reuben. Things got physical when Kelvin pushed Reggie, who then shoved his younger brother back with greater force. Reggie capped it off with a slap to the side of Kelvin's head. That's when Reggie saw me staring. I quickly turned away and found the car and drove out of the parking lot.

SITTING AT A WOODEN TABLE in the dining area of the Farmers' Market, Frieda Greenglass stared at me with an expression that was mystified, angry and pitying, not necessarily by turns, but rather, in a single look that made the whites of her puffy eyes extra moist, as if welling up from some inner struggle.

"What?" I said.

"I don't know who's crazier," she said. "You, or me for even sitting here listening to this. I know artists are supposed to be a bit crazy, but normally they put that craziness in their work."

"I thought you'd be more supportive. You always wanted me to take more of an interest in the community."

"And you think building a synagogue on a pile of garbage is taking an interest? What did you expect from me? A medal and a kiss on both cheeks?"

Far from playing both sides or concealing my upper hand, as Shylock had suggested, I seriously overstepped my self-confidence by blurting out my plan to build a synagogue at Rossiter's Field, making myself look merely foolish. In my defense, if I have any at all, my focus was not entirely on the task at hand, my mind having been distracted by thoughts of Aziza's mother.

I couldn't honestly pinpoint where my attraction lay. Of course, she was beautiful. The headscarf gave her the appearance of being unattainable. I like to think I was smart enough to see beyond that. What I kept returning to was the modest laugh when I mentioned the synagogue in the hospital room. On one level, that laughter was at my expense, but it was also strangely encouraging, considering what she said later, about her laughing at Reuben being thrown off guard. And here I may have been projecting my own wishful thinking, I freely admit that, but there was almost a sense of gratitude on her part. After all, she confessed that it wasn't often she saw him like that. I guess that's what clinched it for me. In her own way, and probably without meaning to, she made me feel special. I kept telling myself not to make too big deal of it, but that sense of feeling special, as most likely fabricated by my frail ego as it was, clung to me like a piece of lint or a speck of glitter that I couldn't easily brush away.

"Hey, are you listening to me or what?"

I stared at Frieda, feeling like a deer caught in her headlights, and tried to cover my shock by waving my finger, as if I was about to make an important point. Frankly, I had no idea what to say and yet that didn't stop my mouth from sounding off.

"For your information, Reuben Arsenault seemed somewhat interested when I mentioned the synagogue to him."

"Who, the big shot from the *treyf* festival?"

Although Frieda wasn't strictly kosher, she had a deep disgust for all manner of shellfish, including lobster, having grown up in a conservative

Jewish household. This was recently hammered home to me when I innocently suggested that she make a lobster latke or croquette for LovesterFest PEI and practically had my head bitten off.

"Anyway, what does he care from synagogues?" she asked.

I had to explain to her about Reuben's ascent to political office and his promise to clean up Rossiter's Field.

"A politician making a promise, this is what you're basing all this interest on? You really think that if this gets done, the first thing he's going to do is build a synagogue? The next thing you'll be telling me is that Mount Russet is sister city with Tel Aviv."

Striking a note of what I hoped was jovial patience, I explained that I had merely put a bug in his ear and what I needed now was support from the PEI Jewish Collective so we could flex a bit of cultural influence, create a buzz, so to speak, and maybe even get public opinion on our side so he couldn't ignore us. To my astonishment, Frieda didn't laugh off my argument right away and even appeared to be seriously mulling it all over. I wondered what I had said to make her consider this a plausible idea, but I was too afraid of undoing whatever I'd done to interrupt her thought process.

"Personally, I still don't get why you want to do this and I'm pretty sure the Collective will think you're a nutcase, which you are. But, if you want, I could arrange a meeting with them, and you can present your case."

"Really?" I said and grabbed her hand, which she yanked away before I could plant the first of many kisses I had planned. "I can't tell you how much I appreciate this."

"Save it for the Collective," she said. "All I'm asking is that you don't make me sorry I'm sticking my neck out for you like this."

"You won't be."

"But in all honesty, I can tell you right now, the idea of a synagogue all the way in Mount Russet isn't going sit well with them, garbage dump or not. I mean, why not build it in Charlottetown or somewhere more central?"

"Being out of the way means it might be cheaper to build." I said, amazed that I could come up with something on the spur of the moment. Frieda curled her lip and reluctantly nodded. I was feeling pretty good about myself when she threw one at me out of left field.

"So, if this Arsenault guy just became the MLA for Mount Russet, when did you talk to him?"

"Lucky coincidence really, I ran into him at Queens County Hospital."

"Why were you there? Is everything okay?"

I explained about having Reuben Arsenault's daughter as a neighbour, the accident and my visiting her this morning as a good Samaritan gesture.

"So, you and this *neighbour...*" She let the word linger briefly, but still long enough for some unspoken assumption to make itself felt. "You know each other well? Enough maybe to borrow some milk for your tea? Or a cup of sugar?"

"Frieda, what the hell are you talking about?"

"So, is this whole thing with the synagogue just a pathetic attempt to impress some *tsatskele*, this object of your desire?"

"What?" I tried to laugh, but all I could come up with was something between a croak and a snort. "You're making a *tsimmes* out of nothing."

"Don't patronize me, Samson! I don't appreciate being used so you can play big shot with some young thing. I don't appreciate being made a fool of!"

By now people were looking in our direction. From the very first time I met her, I had known Frieda Greenglass to have a strange dark streak inside of her, but I'd never seen her like this.

At that moment there was a loud metallic bang outside. It startled me enough to turn around. I looked out the window and saw people staring toward the parking lot. There seemed to be an accident, but I couldn't see. Nevertheless, I decided this would probably be a good time to end the meeting.

"Look," I said, leaning on the table so that I was practically bending over her. "We'll talk about this another time. I'll call you."

She looked up at me, but I didn't want to wait for her to say anything we both might regret. I moved swiftly toward the nearest exit.

People were gathered by the edge of the parking lot, craning their heads to see what was going on. A sausage vendor fired up his grill and laid on a few fresh bratwursts, no doubt in hopes of turning the newly formed crowd into a business opportunity. I asked him what had happened. He said he didn't get a good look, but whatever it was sounded like a real fender bender.

There were too many people blocking the direct path, so I walked to the paved exit that led toward the road. I was about to cross the paved exit in order to reach the grassy expanse that sloped down toward the lot when a black half-ton pickup truck cruised in front of me, not allowing me the right of way. I stepped back, ready to scowl at the driver, only to come face to face with Kelvin Muir, who was sitting in the passenger's side. For a moment the pickup slowed down and Kelvin and Reggie, who was driving, both glowered at me. Then the engine revved and the pickup roared down the path and onto the road, tires squealing as it made the turn.

I tried to ignore this obvious provocation and headed toward the car. It was then that I realized what the loud crash had been. The front of the vehicle was badly dented, with one of the headlights smashed and part of the front bumper sticking out. There was a note stuck in one of the windshield wipers. I unfolded it only to see the word OOPS scrawled across it in a childish hand that looked all too familiar. The writing definitely resembled what I had read in the get-well card Kelvin had left on Aziza's bed. Did this have something to do with me seeing him in Aziza's room? Or maybe acting on Reuben's orders?

After I had surveyed the damage for a second time, trying hopelessly to bend the bumper back into place, I got in the driver's side, only to find Judas sitting in the passenger's seat.

"So, were you here the whole time my car was being smashed into?"

"I want to go to the place in your painting," he said in his gentle and sad manner.

"What place? What painting?"

"In your painting. Where the waters are parting."

"North Cape?" I cried. "Are you nuts? That's a two-hour drive. I should file a report with the cops and have this mess seen to."

"It is important."

"But if the cops stop me on the way..."

"That will not happen," he said simply and folded his hands.

There was a sense of finality in the way he did this as there was in the way he did many things. Never in any authoritative way, but in a way that simply said there was no point in arguing.

I looked at him sitting there, exuding a peaceful aura, patient as a child in a way. I closed my door and buckled myself in, turned the ignition and was relieved to hear the motor turn over immediately. At least there had been no damage there. Then I drove us out of the parking lot and steered the car west.

NEITHER OF US SAID a word for the first thirty minutes. I was still fuming about the car and allowed my imagination to roam willy-nilly. Were Reg'n'Kel under orders from Reuben Arsenault to send me a message? Why would he do that? The synagogue? I doubted it. Maybe for throwing him off guard, especially in front of his family? Who the hell knows? Maybe Reg'n'Kel were acting on their own because I had caught Kelvin leaving the get-well card in Aziza's room. Or maybe because I saw them fighting in the parking lot. But that didn't entirely make sense. Nothing at this point really made sense and now here I was taking a figment of my imagination for a joyride to the other end of the Island.

I looked over at Judas as he stared out the windshield and passenger window. His hat was slightly tilted back and that somehow allowed a vulnerable innocence to soften his weary features. I turned on the radio. The two o'clock newscast was reporting on a statement made by Tourism and Culture Minister, Kerrie-Jo Campbelljohn, about the willingness of the government in general and her department in particular to study the feasibility of Reuben Arsenault's plan to clean up Rossiter's Field. She went on say that the possibility of building Ashlynn's Camp for Kids on the cleaned-up site was a dream close to her heart. The news report was about to go to a public statement made by the camp's Project Director, Chet Affleck, when Judas leaned over and switched the radio off.

"Hey! I was listening to that."

"This is a beautiful place," he said, looking at nothing and everything. "This island."

There was something about the brightness of the day, the solid blue of cloudless sky – open yet impenetrable – that connected one to a bracing edge in the air, even in the confines of a car with all the windows up. Leaves were starting to show their yellows and reds, spreading a familiar claustrophobia that always made me feel the slightly concave loneliness of living on an island.

We were on Highway 2, also known as the Western Road, which goes through Prince County, and passing the turn that would have taken us into Summerside. Instead, we pushed ahead straight toward West Prince. That nagging resentment of having to drive so far at the behest of some imaginary bugaboo in my psyche suddenly blossomed into pinkish-green pinwheels of nostalgia. I could at once recall my first visit to PEI as a recent art school graduate and how I made it my mission to drive across every inch of grey paved artery and red clay back road I could find.

After a brief stop at Compton's, a fresh fruit and vegetable stand, to pick up a dozen corn on the cob, we eventually passed exits leading toward the Mi'kmaw community of Lennox Island First Nation, then Tyne Valley, home of the world-famous oyster festival, and soon Portage, O'Leary (with its Canadian Potato Museum) and Alberton. To pass the time, I taught Judas a song I used to sing out loud in the car on that first visit to the Island. It was a folk song I learned during the only time I ever went to sleep-away camp when I was nine years old. During one of the overnight camping trips, one of the counsellors took out his guitar during the evening campfire and taught us *500 Miles*. It had the mournful refrain, "Lord I'm one, Lord I'm two, Lord I'm three, Lord I'm four, Lord I'm five hundred miles away from home." I sang the verses and Judas soon caught on to the idea and was happily singing out the refrain with me. Although we started mournfully enough, the tenor of the song eventually accelerated into a full-throated hootenanny, replete with handclaps and shouted asides. This lasted well through Tignish until we entered the community of Seacow Pond and saw the field of windmills on the Atlantic Wind Test Site, the rotating blades looking like ghostly-white acrobats cartwheeling in slow motion. At last, we pulled into a parking lot by the Wind and Reef Restaurant that also boasted a sizable gift shop below.

I was happy to finally stretch my legs and feel the brisk ocean breeze against my face. At first, Judas held onto his pork pie hat as he stood beside me, then took it off to let the wind ruffle his long and already unkempt burnt cinnamon hair. There were a few brave souls wandering toward where the shoreline narrowed along the craggy base of the cliffs. Judas pointed to the red rocky strand tapering like a signpost pointing at the rushing tides of the Northumberland Strait and the Gulf of St. Lawrence meeting head-to-head and merging.

"How long had you been contemplating this scene before you decided to paint the parting of these two waters?"

The question took me by surprise, and I laughed to hide the fact that I had no ready answer. I came to this spot on my first visit and was struck by the sight of the two merging waters. That was twenty-two years ago. I've sketched the site many times since then, but I couldn't exactly say when the idea for the painting first came into my head.

"In some ways, I guess, the scene has always been somewhere in my mind," I answered as truthfully as I could. "Why do you ask?"

"Perhaps it would be true to say you have always dreamed of an escape, even when you arrived here?" Although this was posed as a question, it was obvious to me that he meant it as more of a statement. To my ears, there was also a hint of an accusation, which may have been due my naturally thin skin. I breathed deep and allowed the bracing salt air to quell any irrational response welling in my breast.

"I'm not sure what you're getting at," I said as calmly as I could. "Sure, I've been having some doubts about my place here. I'm pretty sure that's what's at the bottom of my creative block. What I still don't understand is why you wanted to come here. I'm sure it wasn't for the scenic view and fresh air."

"I did want to come for those things," he said. "I also wanted you to experience this place again, to remember something pure about your life here."

I had a sense that I was supposed to respond somehow, maybe thank him, but I didn't know what to say.

"Yeshua often liked to walk by the sea," he continued. "Many times, he bade me to join him. Sometimes he would talk about his life, his childhood, knowing even at that young age he was destined for something, although he knew not what. Sometimes he spoke not at all and the two of us enjoyed listening to the murmuring waters."

He stopped and let the sound of the tidal wash emphasize his reminiscence. I thought for a moment about the fact that he was speaking so nonchalantly about someone who was the basis of a whole world religion, particularly one that had so much to answer for. I thought about asking him why he believed everything Yeshua told him. I wondered at the possibility that Yeshua might merely have been a figment of Judas's imagination the way he, Judas, was a figment of mine. The sound of the converging waters grew louder, as if the whole world were merely the hollow whorl of a seashell.

"It was at a place similar to this one, a grassy rising that overlooked the Sea of Galilee, where Yeshua told me my fate. I was going to betray him to the Pharisees, and I would be vilified throughout history as a villain, but that it was necessary so he could fulfill his own destiny and leave his mortal body." Here he stared at his hat and grinned. "Can you believe I argued with him, told him I would not do it? He merely touched my cheek and said I had no choice in the matter."

There was a tenderness in the way he related this story, but something stirred at the back of my neck. I shivered and it was not from the sea breeze. "What are you trying to tell me?"

"You must remember this place, no matter what comes to pass," he said, not as an order or even a suggestion, but more as a plea. "You did not paint it as an escape route on a whim, but more as a reaction to what you knew was coming."

"If you're trying to scare the crap out of me, you're succeeding," I said. Instead of trying to allay my fear, he turned away and started to walk down toward the shore. I thought about following him but knew somehow that I wasn't supposed to. Instead, I watched his shrinking figure make its way to the rocky strand. He stepped gingerly over the stony terrain that tapered toward the merging waters. For a moment I forgot that this was Judas and imagined a lonely Moses, bereft of followers and filled with doubt, wanting to see if he could truly part the Red Sea.

Then he put his yellow porkpie hat on and I was reminded once more that this was the Judas of my own making. I watched his body grow smaller and smaller until it finally disappeared and I was left staring at those tidal waters bearing down on each other – creating a fluid seam that brought to mind this crack that runs through the world – then disappearing into each other. A vortex of no return. I thought about the other two Figs, one railing about Principle and the other espousing Opportunity, and wondered if the part of me Judas sprung from had something to do with Endurance. I certainly had a long and lonely drive home ahead of me to think about it.

When I arrived at the Body Parts, dusk was like a fine carbon-coloured soot descending on the world. I had managed to get home without being stopped by the police for driving with a broken headlight. I'd see to it first thing in the morning. In my apartment, I checked my voicemail. There was a message from Frieda Greenglass. She had set up a meeting for me with the PEI Jewish Collective at their next annual general meeting in November. That gave me two months to figure out how I was going to sell them on this whole synagogue thing.

7

A FEW DAYS INTO the first week of October, the Crazy Diamond was announced as the winner of LovesterFest PEI for their Electric Lobster Acid Zest. Among LovesterFest fanatics, this was seen as something of an upset, as it beat out a few others that were heavily favoured to win, like the Croque-Homard by Café Acadie in the Acadian community of Abrams Village and the Lobster & Bacon Parfait at Skipper's Dairy Bar in Hunter River. There were minor grumblings that the fix was in.

The *Charlottetown Parrot* had a photo of Maggie Beairsto and the creator of the dish, Chef Nathalie Doiron, holding something that looked like a high school diploma they could hang over the bar or in some other prominent spot. They were flanked on either side by Reuben Arsenault and Kerrie-Jo Campbelljohn.

It didn't surprise me that Pius Duffy wasn't in the photo, since he preferred to remain behind the scenes in the Shine Shrine and leave all that dealing with the public stuff to Maggie, not to mention that he'd rather have undergone painful laser surgery to remove all his tattoos than appear in the same photo as Reuben Arsenault. The day the win was announced I happened to run into Pius at the Bertram's Corner Esso. I had just pumped thirty-eight dollars' worth of regular into the Golf and, after paying at the cash inside, came out to see him gassing up his Harley. I congratulated him on his win. He frowned and that unruly chinstrap of a beard drooped in commiseration with his face.

"Ain't nothin' to do with me," he said without taking his eye off the pump's meter as the numbers rolled over. "Nice feather in Nathalie's cap for sure, but I'm staying the frig out of it."

"Come on," I said. "It's going to give a nice boost to business."

"The Diamond does okay, even on a slow night." He removed the nozzle from his gas tank, hung it on the pump and screwed the gas cap on. "Something like this, it might bring in a few more dollars but it can also be a whole lot more trouble than it's worth."

I asked him what kind of trouble and his reply was pretty much as I expected.

"Reuben friggin' Arsenault, what else!" he growled, then punctuated the reply by spitting on the ground. To hear Pius tell it, he wouldn't have been surprised if Reuben had actually rigged the competition somehow for the Crazy Diamond to win so he would have a pretext to make yet another offer to buy into a partnership with them.

"That'd be just like him," said Pius. "Can't help himself from horning in on everybody else's action. 'Specially if he sees you're doing well."

"You have to admit, he's a good businessman," I said. "He's very successful."

"Mags and I don't need a partner who thinks he knows more'n us," he shot back. "We been doing just fine on our own so far."

The pitch this time was that the LovesterFest PEI win, along with a healthy injection of cash from Reuben to fix the place up, could turn the Crazy Diamond into the next culinary hotspot and Mount Russet into a tourist destination.

Pius and Maggie rented the land and building from Tina McCaffrey, a 72-year-old widow whose husband once owned a general store that is now the Crazy Diamond. Tina had long talked about selling everything and moving to Victoria, B.C., to live with her son and his family. Pius and Maggie were trying to save enough money to make the old girl a competitive offer if she ever made good on her chatter. But Reuben was apparently already in talks to possibly buy the land and building from Tina, which would make him Pius and Maggie's landlord. His "magnanimous offer" (his words, according to Pius) was that he would keep the rent the same for a controlling interest in the business.

Pius, fortunately or unfortunately as the case may be, didn't have the opportunity of flatly turning the offer down by flattening Reuben's nose because he only found out about the pitch from Maggie and how it was made directly to her and Nathalie when Reuben took them out for lunch after the photo op. You can be sure Pius went ballistic when he heard about the lunch, threatening bodily harm to Reuben, and was on the verge of losing it again in the retelling until I managed to calm him down.

"Some nerve of that scum bucket," Pius said. "Thinking he could sugar talk Mags and Nat for the price of a fancy lunch. He wouldn't of tried that nonsense with me there."

I had to grin, the way Pius made Maggie and Nathalie, two of the most formidable women I've ever met, and neither of whom I'd ever want to get on the wrong side of, sound like helpless females awestruck by Reuben Arsenault's charms.

"I hope you didn't tell Maggie or Nathalie that."

"You can bet I got an earful." He sighed and shuffled his motorcycle boots like a kid. "Maggie told him straight off we weren't interested. So, then he goes on about how grateful he is that we gave his daughter a job, but he was all worried about her continuing to work there after her accident. Like it was somehow our fault. I could tell that got to Maggie some. Damn sneaky of him trying to lay on that guilt."

I thought it might be better not to mention that I was actually on my way to the hospital to pick up Aziza, who was being released that morning. Her injuries weren't as serious as first suspected, but a recurring headache persuaded them to keep her for observation and a CAT scan. "Maggie's too smart to get sucked in by that," I said.

"Yeah, but I don't want that Arsenault girl coming back to work," said Pius. "Me and Mags had a few words about it. She says we can't fire the girl now, but I think as long as she's there, Arsenault's gonna think he got a foot in the door. Puts us in a bad position."

My first instinct was to stick up for Maggie – and by association, Aziza – but I decided it might be better to take a less partisan stance for the time being. After all, I knew Pius was resentful that I'd brought Aziza to the Crazy

Diamond in the first place. Hoping to smooth things over between us, I tried to assure him that everything was going to work out for the best.

"I don't know," he said. "Mags been acting funny since that girl come to work for us."

"She's probably just worried about Aziza," I said.

He flicked his hand in a half-hearted farewell and trudged off to pay the cashier.

AZIZA'S HOSPITAL STAY was about five days total. Since that initial visit, where I first met her parents, I had gone to see her only one other time. Of course, I was concerned about her and wanted to see how she was doing, but full disclosure, I was also hoping to see Zaina again. Unfortunately, she wasn't there that day and I hoped my face didn't betray how crestfallen I felt.

My disappointment was alleviated by the anticipation of finally being able to talk with Aziza in relative privacy. I'd almost forgotten how much I missed our chats. I told her I had seen Anne Surly's last webcast and was eager to know from where she'd been transmitting. Aziza's tight smile and averted eyes did not bode well, and she told me that it was best if she didn't give the location away. This time, I was less adept at hiding my hurt feelings and she quickly assured me that I hadn't lost her trust, but since the accident she realized that the less people knew about the webcast operation the better for everyone.

Did this mean she thought there was a connection between her accident and the webcasts? She preferred not to jump to any conclusions, which to my mind was a first for her, but lying in a hospital bed gave her a lot of time to think and she decided it was best to be as careful as possible, although she had no intention of stopping her online activities. Just to be more careful about it. I sensed something unspoken in this pronouncement, but decided to push ahead and asked her point blank if she thought Reg'n'Kel were the ones who forced her off the road. From her pained expression I was immediately sorry I'd asked.

I thought about Reuben Arsenault and Reggie Muir arguing in the hospital parking lot and realized implicating Reg'n'Kel in her accident meant a possible link to her father, so I knew enough not to press Aziza on the matter, although I did mention catching Kelvin Muir in her room after she had been sedated, as well as having the front of the Golf smashed by Reggie. She felt bad about that and expressed some guilt about inadvertently dragging me into this.

I assumed that would be that and wondered if it might be best to leave, but she soon launched into some things she had heard before the accident. At this time, it was all innuendo and unsubstantiated whisperings, but she kept hearing Ashlynn's Camp for Kids and The Blue Point Society mentioned in the same breath. She told me that the elite secret club didn't have a specific meeting place and so their monthly get-togethers were held at various locales, including properties owned by Reuben. What happened at these "get-togethers" had never been verified, but the rumours that she had got second-hand, alleged alcohol, drugs and all manner of sexual activity. Aziza's original hunch that the money to build a permanent luxury resort for The Blue Point Society was going to be funnelled through the Ashlynn's Camp for Kids fund was all but substantiated.

I asked her how she even heard these rumours and from whom. She wouldn't give me names, for obvious reasons, but said she had maintained certain contacts from when she used to work for her father. That was why she didn't want to work for him anymore, to distance herself while still maintaining her connections. These were people, she claimed, who were in a variety of low-level positions and knew how to keep their ears open. She kept in touch with them purely on a social level and none of them were aware, as far as she knew, about her online activities.

Without really thinking, I questioned why these things never made their way to the media. Here Aziza actually laughed out loud and I could sense an undercurrent of pity for the naïve schmuck sitting before her. After all, the big news story at the time was Premier Nathan Affleck's recent weight loss. Always on the pudgy side, he had been seen at some public functions looking rather svelte. Public opinion was firmly on the side that the Premier carried his new lean figure rather well, although there was some concern that the weight loss was rather sudden and that he looked tired. Premier Affleck publicly laughed this off by saying his wife had put him on a strict paleo diet and that he had lately been putting in a good deal of overtime regarding some pressing legislative business.

Our chat felt easy and intimate and I didn't want it to end, but I could see Aziza was tired and one of her headaches was coming on. I told her I would get a nurse and decided it was best to cut my visit short.

So, when I found a parking space as close as I could to the hospital entrance, I was looking forward to continuing our discussion and the implications of all these rumours. Little did I expect, as I entered through the sliding glass front doors, to see Zaina pushing her daughter in a wheelchair. My heart sank for a moment then bobbed up again in delight, like a confused buoy cast adrift on choppy waters, at the sight of Zaina in a light blue headscarf and smart navy business jacket and matching skirt with a pearl-grey blouse. I waved at them. Aziza raised her hand with little enthusiasm, obviously unhappy to be in the wheelchair. I smiled and nodded at Zaina, who also nodded and stopped the chair near the cluster of empty wheelchairs inside the front doors.

"Nice to see you," I said to Zaina. "I came to take Aziza back to Mount Russet. But if you're going to drive her..."

"I'm afraid I don't drive," said Zaina. "I came here by taxi. Aziza mentioned you would be taking her home. I wanted to be here to help her."

There was a metal cane balanced on the arms of the wheelchair and Aziza used the cane to help herself out of the wheelchair.

"Are you sure you can go through the parking lot with the cane?" asked Zaina. "Why don't you let me push you to the car."

Aziza was already on her feet. "I'm fine, Ima."

I led mother and daughter to the car. I wasn't sure what was happening and for a moment we all just stood there.

"I still think you should come home, just until you're feeling better," said Zaina.

"I'm better now, Ima," said Aziza. "And I am going home. My home."

"Then I'm coming too," Zaina countered. "At least let me see where you are living."

"Don't you have to go back to work?"

"I went in this morning," Zaina said triumphantly. "I told them I'm taking a half day to take care of my daughter."

"But how are you going to get back home?"

I cleared my throat. "I'd be happy to drive you back home."

They both protested, but I raised my hand.

"Honest. Not a problem. Now, shall we be on our way? You can both ride in the back and I can play chauffeur."

"I'll ride up front if it's all the same," said Aziza, opening the front passenger door before anyone could object, and folding herself in while angling the cane beside her with minimum difficulty. Zaina climbed into the back and thanked me. I closed both of their doors and wondered what the drive back was going to be like.

For the first fifteen minutes nobody spoke and I half-seriously considered breaking the silence with a rousing chorus of *500 Miles*, the way I had with Judas, but I doubted either of them would join in. Now and then I stole a glance at Zaina in my rear-view mirror. In a way, she seemed less real than any of the three Figs, except she was sitting back there quiet and dignified. At one point, when I grew brave enough for another glance in the rear-view mirror, which I was beginning to imagine as a magic portal into a more civilized time, our eyes met then broke away. I could feel my face growing hot and I hoped Aziza would not notice the colour enflaming my cheeks.

"So..." said, Zaina, giving me an excuse to look again into the magic mirror. "How are your plans for the synagogue going?"

"Ima!"

"What?" said Zaina, defensively. "I'm interested."

"I appreciate you asking," I said. "As a matter of fact, I'll be proposing the idea to the PEI Jewish Collective next month."

"Really?" said Aziza. "I mean, that's great and all."

"But?" I asked, waiting for the other shoe to drop.

"Are you going to mention to them that you checked out Rossiter's Field as a possible site?"

"Well, you know," I said. "I did bring it up. As a possibility. To one of the members."

"Why were you even looking there?" asked Aziza.

"Call it an impulse." I fixed my eyes firmly on the road.

"My father thought you were a lunatic."

"Aziza!" said her mother from the back.

"What?" Aziza craned her neck to look at her mother, but it was too much of a strain and she addressed the rear-view mirror. "It's true."

"I'm sure your proposal will get the proper consideration it deserves," said Zaina. "It would be a very good thing for the Jewish community. What have they done all this time without a synagogue?"

I explained to Zaina how the PEI Jewish Collective communicated through an emailed newsletter and organized holidays and other gatherings by holding them in rotation at the homes of various members. For decades, they got on quite well without a synagogue, although the subject must have come up before I came along. I went on to say that I was not observant by any stretch of the imagination but one of the first things that struck me when I moved here was the absence of a synagogue.

I had only attended one Passover seder in Stratford, hosted by a Dr. Eleanor Abramawitz, one of the Collective's founders, the first year I lived on PEI.

"As a kid in Toronto, I used to go to shul every Saturday, but stopped when I became a teenager. I did ask at that seder why there was no temple here. The question was never really answered, except to say they liked things the way they were. Frankly, I'm not sure what I'm going to say to them next month."

"The best thing is to speak from the heart," said Zaina. I glanced in the rear-view mirror, but she was looking out the side window.

AT THE BODY PARTS, I escorted them to Aziza's apartment. I asked if Aziza needed any groceries. She didn't and said to come by in a couple of hours when her mother wanted to go home. Although I had every intention of picking up a few things in town, I stopped off in my apartment for my sketchpad and a few pencils. Then I drove straight for Rossiter's Field.

Sitting on the Golf's hood, I opened my pad and, with a 2B drawing pencil poised above a blank sheet, stared at the accumulation of discarded trash that had been assimilating into wild nature with varying degrees of success for however many decades. Slowly, my pencil sketched out lines and shapes on the clean page: crosshatching here, shading there, following whatever my eyes could discern and allowing that information to follow a circuitous route that led from my brain to the pencil's graphite point, which seemed to move with a mind of its own against the paper. The day was overcast and the murmur of wind-fluttered leaves mingled with the busy chicken scratching of my creative impulses.

Normally, the mere thought of this place caused me to shudder with revulsion and made me feel as if every rusted, broken and tangled remnant of refuse had been heaped on my sagging shoulders. There was the obvious platitude that maintains the nature of all artistic pursuit is to exert control over the chaos roiling within ones intellectual and emotional spheres. I have no doubt that played a part in bringing me back here. There was also the fact that I had barely set pencil to paper or brush to canvas ever since that fateful morning when the Starfish of David washed up on my canvas and into my life.

My impromptu trip to North Cape with Judas kept reminding me of carefree hours sketching one of the few places on PEI for which I felt a deep intimacy. If Rossiter's Field was fated to be the site where the synagogue would be built, then I needed to become intimate with it as well, get inside that mess by studying it with pencil and paper. My mind's ear echoed Zaina's advice to speak from the heart when I made my pitch to the PEI Jewish Collective. I had to open my heart up somehow to what I hoped might be the hidden charms of the place, if such a thing existed in this putrid example of humankind's all-pervading dictum: out of sight, out of mind.

"But that's the thing, innit?" Fagin stood on one side of the car.

"What's the thing?" I asked without stopping what I was doing.

"Forsooth, signor, the existence of what hath been forgotten." Shylock was on the other side of the car. So, it was going to be a tag-team match. Even so, I was well into my drawing by now and determined that neither of them would impede my concentration.

"Being an artist like yourself, my dear, you specialize in creating things what's been long forgotten by others."

"Verily, good cousin, 'tis the bid for immortality guiding thy hand, poised to capture this neglected wasteland."

Immortality? What did this trash heap have to do with immortality? Except for the fact that much of the junk here would most likely outlast those who abandoned it. And yet there was something timeless in the twisted contours and jagged outlines insinuating their way under my unwavering scrutiny. Out of sight, out of mind to some, but I was now a witness (that being the artist's main function), unsentimental, yet not without a modicum of compassion.

"You were bang on, my dear, when you said it put you in the mind of Gehenna. Straight out of the Old Testament, that's where we are now."

"I don't understand," I said.

"'Tis a wilderness that passeth down from generation to generation over the course of these millennia. We Jews wandered our forty years through the desert and yet that very same desert hath ne'er deserted the marrow deep within."

"Ain't that the same hollow wind whistling through our bones whenever they call us Jew to our face?"

"Hath not a Jew grains, fragments, molecules? Hath not a Jew nothingness? If we are cursed, doth such sentiments not echo through the millennia of our being?"

"So, it's all hardwired in the DNA?" I asked. "That still doesn't tell me how I'm supposed to sell this junk heap as a designated holy ground for a future shul to the Collective."

"Even if you were up to turning a sow's ear into a silk purse, my dear, it still wouldn't make it kosher, if you take my meaning."

"'Twere best ye abandon all thy persuasions and effrontery, good cousin, lest ye adopt too stumbling an ardour like an eager swain. One must cast passions to passions and lust to lust in love's ebbing season."

"Speaking from the heart, like your good Moslem lady friend counselled, ain't the same as spilling your guts."

"A finely-tuned temperament is but an instrument, signor, waiting for a sure touch to bow its strings."

"With that, my dear, you may play the pretty refrain of Opportunity."

"And end such with the solemn coda of Principle."

I'm not sure how long they went on like that as I doubled my efforts to maintain my concentration on the task at hand. At some point, I realized Shylock and Fagin had vanished, only to be replaced by the approach of a vehicle, an engine idling behind me then going silent. This was followed by the sound of two car doors opening and slamming shut. Even as I became aware of these I continued sketching, relishing the sensation of being in two minds: feeling safe in the solitude of the creative zone and the unhurried awareness of the presence of others. The approach of footsteps compelled me to lay down my pencil, to look toward the ground and see dark blue trouser cuffs and the rounded toes of shiny black boots. I followed the dark pant leg, with its thin yellow stripe up the side, and recognized a police uniform. A second cop was also there, walking around the Golf, stooping to inspect the back passenger windows.

"Seems like an odd place to find inspiration."

"I'm not breaking any law being here, am I?"

The officer studied my drawing, nodding slightly, which I hoped was to indicate interest or a hint of appreciation rather than a response to my question. He looked up to observe the real Rossiter's Field then looked down at the page once more. His attention to the drawing was beginning to worry me more than any possible legal infringement on my part.

"Who's that supposed to be?" He pointed at a section of the drawing. There, amidst the entangled foliage and garbage stood the image of a person, female, wearing a headscarf. I was surprised that he had noticed this, since the figure looked to be trying to blend in with the surrounding debris. I was a bit embarrassed to have her pointed out to me, not being entirely aware of having drawn her. "Is there someone else here?" he asked and looked around once more.

"No," I managed to say, hoping my embarrassment was not apparent. "Just call it artistic license. A quirk of the imagination."

"I guess artists are expected to have their quirks," he said. "In any case, Drawing 101 has been further suspended in this spot. This area is being closed off to the public."

"Why, what's happening?"

"I guess they want to stop people from dumping here."

A truck arrived and some men wearing orange reflective vests started to put up wooden barriers with the word CLOSED stencilled on them around the dumping ground.

"I'm going to have to ask you to leave now."

I closed my sketchpad and got into the Golf. As I drove away, I could see Rossiter's Field growing smaller in my rear-view mirror. But roadblocks or not, I suspected it would not be the last time I saw this eyesore.

I DECIDED TO PICK UP a few things at the Co-op before heading home and was making a mental list of some staples to get Aziza as well, when something in my peripheral vision broke my train of thought. It was Zaina, standing at the only stop in Mount Russet for the bus to Charlottetown, along with two others. I forgot all about going into the Co-op and pulled up to the stop, lowering the passenger window. "Can I give you a ride?"

At first, Zaina was startled, then embarrassed. I thought she was going to ignore me, but she smiled politely and shook her head. "That's very kind of you," she said, "But I think the bus will be here any minute."

"Yes, but this is door to door service and cheaper than the bus."

"Thanks, but I don't want to trouble you."

I leaned over and opened the passenger door. "No trouble at all."

"Honestly!" she said and looked away to see if the bus was coming.

A woman who was carrying a suitcase said, "If you don't take the ride, I will."

Zaina's composure began to fade and she looked from the woman to me to the bus that was nowhere in sight and then back to me again. She took a step in no particular direction, as if she was trying to make up her mind whether to walk away or not, then, almost in a panic, she opened the back door and got in. The move took me by surprise and I sat there trying to process what was happening.

"Please, if you are going to drive, do it now," she said in a tone that was as brusque as it was pleading.

I reached over to close the passenger door, but the woman with the suitcase obliged and I drove off. Neither of us spoke and I focused on the road, consciously averting my eyes from the rear-view mirror. This was partially out of respect for Zaina's privacy, since I felt a twinge of guilt for coercing her into the car, and partially out of fear, since I was afraid of meeting her reproachful glare, and finally as a discipline, because something about her inspired in me an inclination toward self-restraint.

The distance she had put between us – me in front and her in back – soon widened enough to allow anxious questions to assail my brain. Did she feel safer back there? Did I pose a threat? Had I breached some social etiquette or moral nicety? I wasn't entirely sure how religious she was, but could it possibly be a Muslim thing: the impropriety of her being alone with a strange man? I knew that was the case with many Orthodox Jews. Keeping my eyes straight ahead, as a way of maintaining some sense of decorum, I ventured to chip away at the ice, if not break it entirely.

"I hope you had a good visit with Aziza," I said. "She is lucky to have her mother looking out for her."

"Aziza is old enough to look after herself." It was a statement so firmly impassive that, at once it belied quite the opposite opinion and warned against pursuing the matter any further. I decided on a different approach.

"She's a very intelligent girl. Knows her own mind. You obviously did a very good job bringing her up."

"Thank you."

"I enjoy talking with her very much," I pressed on gamely. "She certainly keeps me on my toes."

"In what way?"

"Sorry?"

"How does she keep you on your toes?"

"Well…" I struggled for the right words that wouldn't lead to a more uncomfortable line of questioning. "She has very definite opinions. Very well informed. Sometimes I feel a bit unworldly next to her."

"Yes, she has a way of making others feel insignificant."

"Oh no," I said. "That's not what I meant. I enjoy our…"

"She often does it without realizing."

I decided a little well-earned silence might be the ticket to smooth out this brief leg of the journey. Despite the contentious timbre of our exchange, I felt a slight bridging of the distance between the front and the back. Driver and passenger were easing the strictures of their assigned roles. The question was, how could I manoeuvre within this newly established wiggle room?

"I'm sorry about the position I put you in earlier," I said with as much good-natured contrition as I could muster. "At the bus stop I mean. I wasn't trying to put you in, you know, an awkward position. Truth is, I'm really happy I got there, you know, before the bus did. I'm really glad to have this chance, you know, to have a chat."

I waited for a response. When it was obvious that there would not be one forthcoming, I started to panic a little. What had I said? Too many *you knows*? My vision shifted to the rear-view mirror. I could see that her attention was elsewhere. She was looking down at something. I dared to take my eyes off the road for a moment to turn around and saw that she had my sketchpad open. I had tossed it in the back seat and forgot about it when I saw her at the bus stop, never even considering that it might catch her attention, let alone arouse her interest. Once I checked the road again, I turned back and noticed she was looking at the drawing of Rossiter's Field. My glance also took in the serious expression on her face, and I suddenly remembered the half-hidden image of the figure in the headscarf that the cop had noticed with relative ease. I could only presume Zaina had seen it as well.

"You drew this?" she asked solemnly.

"I hadn't gone sketching in quite a while you see and..."

"Where is this?"

"Rossiter's Field. That's where I was before..."

"And what about this figure?"

"When I draw, sometimes I go into almost a trance-like state. You know, I just kind of zone out because I'm concentrating so..."

"Please stop the car," she said.

"What?" She closed the sketchpad and set it down as far away from her person as possible. Whatever gap between front and back had been narrowed, it now yawned into an impossible abyss.

"Please," she repeated with tension in her voice. "Stop the car."

We had made the turn onto Highway 7 toward Charlottetown about five minutes earlier. There was nothing but fields and trees on either side of us. If she wanted to get out there would be nowhere to go. What was she going to do, hitchhike the rest of the way? Once more, she repeated her request and there was a catch of exasperation in her voice. I pulled over. Not too far ahead was Luke Gallant's John Deere dealership. I supposed she could walk there to use a telephone. When Zaina let herself out, I also got out, ready to inundate her with profuse apologies. To my surprise, she immediately got in the front passenger seat. Afraid of scaring her off with some too-sudden movement, I leaned against the door and spoke to her through the open window.

"Look, I don't know why I drew that figure. I don't know why I do a lot of things these days."

"It's all right, you don't need to..."

"There was no disrespect meant, I mean, you know, because it's a garbage heap and all. I'm not sure I can explain."

"Please get in the car," she said. "I'm not angry. Truly. You don't have to explain yourself. It's me, yet again, who should apologize to you. I didn't know what to do back there at the bus stop. The truth is I had a big argument with Aziza and so I just wanted to sit alone on the bus."

"That's okay," I said. "I don't always read people that well. I should have seen you were upset."

"That doesn't excuse my rude behaviour," she insisted. "The way I got in the back seat. You were being generous enough to offer me a lift and I... It was nerves, but that's no excuse."

I stopped her there and got back in behind the wheel. Once mobile again, we decided that we had both got off on the wrong foot. The conversation flowed a little more easily and the more Zaina talked it was obvious she had a need to unburden herself. The argument with Aziza had been about something trivial, the way many big blowouts start. It had to do with the sofa in Aziza's apartment, which Zaina thought was very ugly. I had to agree with her there and we bonded momentarily by conceding that it was the ugliest shade of green either of us had ever seen. Miracle of miracles, we even shared a conspiratorial chuckle over how we would like to set fire to the sofa. Then she grew serious again.

"Of course, I didn't say that to her. All I did was offer to have it reupholstered and she took that as a personal criticism of her whole life. As these things always go, one thing led to another. One doesn't realize how far things are going until it's too late. And then I said something I can't ever take back."

She fell silent and the inward gaze moistened, her eyes growing brighter and then darker like stars flickering their last.

I didn't dare ask what she had said but couldn't help wondering how an ugly sofa could lead to words one wished one could take back. Then she revealed a bizarre fact about the sofa's history. Before being installed in Aziza's Charlottetown apartment, it had originally belonged in the outer waiting area of Reuben Arsenault's office. When the waiting area was being redecorated (this was just before Aziza stopped working there), she had moving men deliver the sofa to her apartment.

"She did it as a provocation, of course," said Zaina, referring to the pilfered sofa. "A silly act of rebellion. The irony is that she needed to prove her independence from her father because she had always been a bit of a daddy's girl when she was a child. But once she reached her teens she started to rebel, although not always so easily. It took her a long time to assert herself and, quite frankly, I'm not sure she has totally broken away from him. Stupidly, I accused her of preferring her father over me. That's what we fell out over. She screamed at me to get out. I know now it was a terrible thing to say. Maybe because there is some truth in it."

Here, Zaina started to cry and I reached over and opened the glove compartment, where a packet of tissues presented itself. She apologized and blew her nose and dabbed her eyes. If Zaina was correct about Aziza's conflicted feelings for Reuben, it certainly shed a different light on her activities as Anne Surly. I always assumed that, to some degree, it was meant as a middle finger to her father. If he had seen her webcasts, and Aziza led me to believe he did, then seeing the green sofa in the background would have been meant as a red flag to Reuben, a little extra salt in the wound.

I mentioned how difficult it must have been to raise a child in a mixed household of traditional Christian and Muslim values. I was not prepared for Zaina's laughter and she soon explained that she herself had not been raised as a Muslim. She came from a Christian family as far back as when the Mahmoud's first settled on PEI, around 1910. But she had always heard stories that her great-grandmother was one of the Druze.

"I had heard of them," she said. "A religion that seems to have connections to Christianity, Judaism and Islam, but I knew little else, as do many outside their community. The story in our family was that back in Lebanon she had been courted by the son of a wealthy Christian family and soon emigrated to Canada, where she converted to Christianity. It's not so plausible because the Druze have very strict rules about marrying outside their faith. It's doubtful that she would have been betrothed for money, so the truth has been a family mystery. It's a story that has always intrigued me since I was small."

"So, you have converted back to being one of the Druze?" I asked.

"Not exactly," she said. "After Reuben and I separated, I became very restless and unhappy. I was looking for something but didn't know what. I work as a financial officer for a real estate company and became involved in helping the Muslim community establish the mosque that's just outside of Charlottetown. That was when I decided to investigate Islam and soon went regularly to the mosque. My family were sceptical about it, especially after I started wearing the hijab regularly. They still think it is a rebound reaction of my separation, although some have tried to show support. At the same time, I started to do some research into the Druze. I spoke to our imam about it, but he discouraged me from pursuing it. The Druze are not really considered true Muslims by many." She paused and averted her eyes. "But listen to me blathering. I didn't mean to bore you with all this."

"No," I protested. "Not at all. I find it very interesting. We're not that different really. Me looking to build a synagogue. You searching for your roots."

By this time, we had arrived in Charlottetown and there was a slight lull in our conversation. I drove her to her apartment building, a relatively new condo complex on North River Road. I parked the Golf and we both sat for a moment.

"That drawing in your sketch book."

"It was a preparation for the pitch I have to make to the Collective. I need to convince them that it's the right spot for a synagogue." I grinned sheepishly. "I remembered what you said about speaking from the heart. Maybe that's why I drew that figure. I look at it now and it's like it appeared of its own free will."

"I'm flattered," she said. "But why must the synagogue be there?"

What could I tell her? "I guess you could say there's a voice in my head that insists that's the place. I don't know why. It's become an obsession. I try to resist it but..."

She opened the door. "The Great Prophet, peace be upon him, once said, 'God did not send down the disease without also sending down the cure.'"

She stepped out of the car and walked to the front door and let herself in. I sat there until I was sure she was finally inside her apartment. Then I sat for a while longer.

8

THE NEWS THAT Nathan Affleck was stepping down as premier, as well as resigning his seat (agreeing to stay on until an election could be held), was announced without any warning. Normally some indication would have been either hinted at or leaked, officially or not, but Premier Affleck's abrupt announcement came like the proverbial bolt out of the inscrutable blue, stunning the public as well as political insiders. In a terse written statement, he said only that he would stay on until his party chose a successor, that this was "the right moment to step down" and that he was "confident the transition of power will go smoothly." No specific reason for his departure was given, except the usual platitude of wanting to spend more time with his family.

Media outlets on-air, in print and online all speculated possible reasons for the suddenness of his departure, from unspecified personal or medical problems in connection with his recent weight loss to a possible offer of a senate seat. The general consensus pointed to Kerrie-Jo Campbelljohn as being well positioned to make a bid as party leader and the Island's next premier.

By this time Aziza was back working at the Crazy Diamond. We rarely got in much of a chat these days, except for a quick word during the occasional run-in at the Body Parts, more often than not passing each other in the hallway when one of us would be getting home while the other was heading out. I also saw her at the Crazy Diamond, although she was usually too busy for any socializing. She was fully recovered from her injuries, moving effortlessly from bar to tables. She confided that she still suffered some bad headaches, even though hospital x-rays had found nothing serious.

I hadn't bothered to check in on Anne Surly at all, but when the news broke about Nathan Affleck's resignation, my curiosity regarding her take on the matter got the best of me. It looked like she was still using the same location as the last time I had tuned in and there were still few clues as to where that might be. The only notable change to her presentation was that she had traded in her riding crop for a bamboo cane. It was clear that she was enamoured of this new prop and it's heft by how often she cracked it against her boot and the flashy way she slashed an imaginary S (for Surly, no doubt) in the air – Zorro-style.

According to Anne Surly, the premier's sudden resignation was linked to certain activities of the Blue Point Society. Although she couldn't be specific on details, she assured us that "whatever happens in the Blue Point doesn't necessarily stay in the Blue Point" and repeated the allegations of drug use and sexual exploits she had told me in private. What followed next was a lurid account of a near fatal overdose of a young woman at the last Blue Point party. The woman had been rushed to Queens County Hospital and supposedly was paid off to stay quiet about the incident. The implication was that this incident was somehow connected to Premier Affleck's resignation, although how remained hazy, but it included an allegation that the hush money was taken from the Ashlynn's Camp for Kids fund.

"Let me connect the dots for all you mouth-breathing slag-monkeys out there. The Ashlynn's Camp for Kids project is being headed by radio personality, Chet Affleck, brother to our now ex-premier. Does that mean good old brother Chester green-lighted the funds to shut up Miss OD? One might expect that would be the case, and I'm sure he had a hand in it, until we remember that the camp is supposedly going to be built on the newly road-blocked and soon to be cleaned up Rossiter's Field, which happens to be in the jurisdiction of MLA Reuben Arsenault, whose company, Freeland Corporation, is slated to build the camp, which looks more and more like a front to funnel money into building a state-of-the-art permanent home for the Blue Point Society. This brings us back to that hush money for Miss OD, which in fact was allocated by the camp's project treasurer, none other than – surprise! – Reuben Arsenault. I'd say that kind of political favour is worth the Tourism and Culture post, assuming strange bedfellow Kerrie-Jo Campbelljohn vacates it by grabbing the party leader brass ring. Except now the latest scuttlebutt to reach my privileged ear is that there's trouble in Percale Paradise between Arsenault and Campbelljohn. Could our lovebirds' falling out upset the political applecart? Everybody's eyes are on the prize and we'll all have a ringside seat, so you better tune in next time, my shrivelled little dickybirds. Or else!"

The bamboo cane sliced a closing S in the air with an intimidating hiss and the screen went black right on cue. I sat there, trying to process everything I'd seen and heard, my brain reeling from information overload. How much of this so-called connecting of the dots was credible? That didn't weigh on my mind as much as seeing Anne Surly's slicker presentation.

If anything, the lighting and camerawork had become more professional and now included close-ups and zoom-outs. This wasn't a cheap webcam, more likely a sophisticated video camera, which meant someone else was operating it and possibly at a location that was reasonably safe to store all this equipment. Maybe a studio somewhere? Whoever was behind the camera and wherever they were broadcasting from, I had to assume that Aziza felt very safe in this situation. I also had to assume that it meant she had to take even more precautions about whom she could trust. Apparently, this didn't include me. I suffered an odd hollowness that one might experience on realizing something has ended.

The next evening was the annual general meeting of the PEI Jewish Collective, where I was expected to pitch my idea for building a synagogue and for which I had done next to no preparation and had no idea what I was going to say. The meeting was called for seven o'clock and was taking place in a small boardroom at Prince Edward Island University. The room had been booked for an hour by Stepan Markowitz, a PEIU music professor and one of the Collective's main board members.

I spent most of that morning standing at my kitchen counter with a blank sheet of paper, on which to jot some talking points, and a cheap ballpoint pen, which I mostly chewed on like an adult pacifier. Aside from jotting inane marginal notes, such as *picture everyone naked except for prayer shawls and smile more*, I resigned myself to the fact that I was most likely going to have to wing it.

At six-thirty I found a parking spot by the university's MacLellan Music Building. Once I found Room 327, a few people were already there, milling about and chatting in small groups. A couple of them glanced up to see who the newcomer was, then returned to their conversations, but mostly I was ignored and felt grateful for that when more people opened the door behind me. Frieda Greenglass passed right by me and for a moment I was torn between resentment and relief at maintaining my relative anonymity. After scanning the room, she turned and saw me.

"What are you doing hiding there?" she chided and gave me a hug, the better to whisper in my ear. "So, are you nervous?"

"A little. Public speaking isn't my strong suit."

"Suit shmoot," she said and squeezed my hand. "Everyone here is good people. They'll listen with an open mind. Come, let's sit."

She led me over to where others were already starting to take down chairs that were stacked against the back wall and arranging them in rows facing a long boardroom table. We both pitched in to help a little before seating ourselves on two orange plastic chairs at the end of one row. Professor Markowitz stood in front of the boardroom table where everyone could see him. A twinge of panic tightened in my gut when I realized that I would have to go up there at some point.

"Now that we're all settled in," began Professor Markowitz. "We should probably get down to business as we only have the room for an hour. First, we'll have our secretary Thelma Goldstein read the minutes from the last meeting and then we'll proceed to new business. Go ahead, Thelma."

I can't say for sure where my mind was during Thelma Goldstein's recital of the minutes from the last meeting or whatever new business followed after that. I do recollect something about the upcoming Hanukkah celebration taking place at the professor's house this year. Then Professor Markowitz mentioned the last order of business would be heard and he said my name. Frieda wasted no time in poking me with her elbow.

"Go," she hissed. "You're up."

I got to my feet and made my way toward the boardroom table where Professor Markowitz greeted me with a firm handshake and then stepped off to the side, leaving me to look out at a sea of blank faces ready to hear what I had to say. Right then, my peripheral vision glimpsed a familiar figure sitting at the far end of the front row. The blue ball cap was a dead give-away. When Fagin realized that I had spotted him he made a slight motion with his head, meaning for me to look at the other end of the row. There the coral bucket hat greeted me with Shylock under it, giving me the thumbs up. Then I saw Professor Markowitz looking pointedly at me, his impatient eyebrows arching as a silent signal to get on with it.

I wasted no time in launching into the matter at hand: how PEI's Jewish community had gone without their own spiritual home for too long now, etc, etc. I felt emboldened by the sight of a couple of nodding heads and ventured further by relating how I had been searching for the right location, but to no avail. A certain glimmer in some eyes closest to me was all the evidence I needed they were buying into my spiel. Time for the final pitch that would reel them in.

"And then it hit me," I said, pausing for dramatic effect. "And no, it wasn't a meteor, which some of you might be inclined to think after I tell you."

Another pause for laughter, which was not forthcoming. I decided to take the plunge and dive in where angels fear to do the backstroke.

"When I heard the news that Reuben Arsenault had become MLA for Mount Russet, where I live, and was threatening to make good on his promise to clean up Rossiter's Field, I had what you might call a distinct shiver down the back of my neck. It was as if the good Lord Himself had tapped me on the shoulder to signal His okay that this was the place for Prince Edward Island's first synagogue."

Whatever eye-glimmering that might have been going on before had now devolved into squints of confusion and scowls of doubt.

"You want to build a synagogue on a pile of garbage?" somebody in the middle section asked.

I explained again that Rossiter's Field was being cleaned up and added that I had already briefly discussed the idea with MLA Reuben Arsenault. I barely got that out when hands shot up. I could have predicted the comments in my sleep, which had to do with the land already being designated for a children's camp, how the synagogue should be more central (meaning closer to Charlottetown), who would pay for a synagogue to be built and how much, and so on and so forth. I did my best to answer, or at least speculate on possible solutions to all these questions, but I was quickly running out of steam.

"Flag not, signor, thrust ahead! Use thy tongue as a brush to paint them a picture of a most pious temple with doors flung widely to welcome their hearts and souls."

I glanced at Shylock and scanned the room to see if I was the only one who heard him. All eyes were still trained on me. "After all," I continued gamely. "What our community needs is a home for our hearts and souls."

"We've been doing fine so far," someone called out. "Each of our homes takes turns being open to our hearts and souls, but you might not know that because we've never seen you at any of our High Holiday gatherings."

"He's got a point, my dear," said Fagin. "You ain't exactly been what's called a pillar of the community, have you."

"Forsooth!" said Shylock. "Perhaps thou needst feign an illness. Tell them thou were stricken with the pox. 'Tis a good appeal toward their sympathies."

"Better crank the brain box in gear right quick," Fagin warned in a loud stage whisper. "You're on a pretty perch now, my dear. Things can swing one way or the other, so don't bottle it."

"Thanks," I said without thinking. "You're really no help at all."

Puzzled faces looked at each other and a low murmur buzzed among the audience. The man who had made the remark about not seeing me at any of the gatherings folded his arms and cocked his head in a self-righteous manner. Before I could apologize and clarify that I wasn't talking to him, Professor Markowitz cleared his throat and started to make his way toward the table.

"Well, I think that's all we have time for," he began to say when I put up both my hands to stave off this ignoble end to the evening.

"Wait. Please," I said. "Just five minutes more. That's all."

Professor Markowitz stopped but didn't move back toward the wall. "Very well, go ahead," he said and glared down at his wristwatch to let me know I was now on the clock.

"I want to leave you with two words," I said and paused a microsecond for effect. "Opportunity and Principle."

"Huzzah, good cousin," cried Shylock.

"Well, well," said Fagin. "Looks like some of our hard-won wisdom actually sunk through the lad's thick nut."

I read scepticism on many faces, but at least I had their attention again.

"Getting this synagogue built would be a great opportunity for our Jewish community to become a real part of this island's social and cultural fabric. Not that we haven't been so far, but look at the Muslim community. Having a mosque has really given them a strong presence here and even roused public support when it was vandalized. And the Buddhist monastery holds open houses for outreach to the public as a gesture of goodwill and to demonstrate their culture."

"So, what do you mean by principle?" asked the man in the audience who had spoken before. I was pleased to see he had unfolded his arms.

"What I mean is that, as a matter of principle, we have a right to convene in our own house of worship. Not to have one is not just a loss to us, but also a loss to the diversity of PEI. In principle, we also have a right to exercise our public voice. If we unite as one and tell Reuben Arsenault that Rossiter's Field needs to be the site of our synagogue, I believe he can only respect that."

"And if he doesn't?" called out another voice, which I recognized right away as Frieda's. I thought she was on my side by now and the twinge of betrayal piercing my breast only strengthened my resolve not to back down.

"If he doesn't, then we must exercise our voice in another direction and win over public opinion with the argument I just made: the Island's diversity. If we can make a strong enough case in the local media, and I believe we can, then it would become politically expedient to let us have the site for our synagogue. Once we've accomplished that, everything else will follow naturally. We might even get some government money toward construction costs."

People were now nodding. I couldn't believe I actually managed to swerve this doomed ship away from the iceberg. Professor Markowitz was all smiles when he came up to the table and shook my hand. He called the meeting to an end and people started to restack the chairs. Others came up to shake my hand, offering congratulations and words of encouragement. Frieda edged her way through the crowd to hug me warmly.

"I don't believe you did it, you brilliant *schmendrick*," she whispered in my ear. "I could go for a slice of cake." Her arms lingered around my shoulders and I was uncomfortably aware of her breasts pressing against me for what felt to be a bit longer than necessary.

Some of the others were repairing to Café Istanbul, a small eatery on Grafton Street specializing in Turkish cuisine that was the latest addition in the boom of new restaurants quickly giving PEI a reputation as a foodie paradise. Frieda claimed they served the best baklava she had ever tasted and insisted we join the others. She had taken the bus to PEIU because her Kia was in the shop for a brake overhaul and a new muffler.

"God knows what those *ganefs* at the garage are going to charge me."

"Tell me about it," I said. "I got rear-ended at the Farmers' Market and it cost an arm and a leg to get the front fender and a new headlight replaced."

Although all I wanted at that point was to head home, I couldn't figure out a way to say no. I had done well and maybe it was only right to celebrate with the others and bask in this fleeting moment of glory, as well as reinforce their newly won support with a bit of schmoozing. I offered to drive Frieda to Café Istanbul.

There were about seven or eight of us in all and at the café we pushed a couple of tables together and sat as a group. The conversation flowed easily enough, even for one as socially inept around strangers as myself. We even managed to jot down a few ideas for a campaign to promote the idea of a synagogue. Most everyone ordered food, but I decided to limit my indulgence to a glass of *çay*, a black Turkish tea which I had never tried and found somewhat strong but delicious nonetheless. Despite my protests, Frieda insisted that I try a bite of her baklava. I was never a fan of sweet things and even a small forkful of the honey-drenched confection made my back molars want to extract themselves with a dull spoon.

By the time we paid our bills and people were saying their good-byes to each other on the street, it was clear that I was going to be driving Frieda to her bungalow out on St. Peters Road. It was in the opposite direction to where I was going but I couldn't very well leave her stranded downtown.

She had purchased an extra slice of baklava to take home and put it in the back seat. That was when she saw my sketchpad. She brought it with her into the front seat, asking me to turn on the overhead light while I drove so she could flip through it.

"I haven't seen your artwork in so long. I just want to look quickly, not for the whole drive."

I wasted no time in pulling out of the movie star parking spot I'd found in front of Café Istanbul and maneuvered through downtown traffic. She turned the pages, nodding appreciatively, muttering positive sounds under her breath.

"Wowee," she exclaimed. "Very intricate. You haven't lost your touch."

Then there was a slight pause.

"Hey, what is this?"

"Rossiter's Field," I said.

"Yeah, I guessed that," she said. "I mean, what's this?"

"What's what?"

"This. In your drawing." She held the pad up in front of me. "That's a person. You had someone posing on that garbage heap?"

I pushed the sketchpad away from my face.

"No, I was alone. I just drew it on a whim. To amuse myself."

"It's clearly a woman," Frieda pointed out sourly. "But what's she wearing? I thought at first it was a babushka, but no... that's a headscarf, more like what Muslims wear. What do you call those, hijabs or niqabs?"

"It's just a scarf," I insisted.

"You have a thing for Muslims now? Is this supposed to be that neighbour you mentioned? The one that was in the hospital. She has an Arabic name."

"Aziza. And no, it's not her. She doesn't wear a scarf."

"So, this is what you do when you're not trying to pass yourself off as a good Jew by proposing to build synagogues? Having Muslim fantasies? Feh!"

She tossed the sketchpad into the back seat and we drove the rest of the way in silence. When I arrived at her home, she immediately opened the door, stepped out of the car and retrieved her baklava from the back seat, slamming the door before I could say goodnight.

A WEEK LATER, I received an email from Professor Markowitz saying he had been in touch with the producer of *Good Morning PEI* about the synagogue and they wanted to arrange an interview with me. I already knew that I would be thrust into the role of public spokesperson for this synagogue project, but I was not totally prepared for the reality of it. But like it or lump it, I had made my own bed and I had to lie in it.

I emailed the producer and, after the usual electronic back and forth, we nailed down a date and time. Thankfully it was the next morning at eight o'clock, which meant there would not be too much agonizing beforehand, although any chance of a good night's sleep was slim to none. I spent the rest of the day trying to keep busy as a diversion from my mounting nervousness. After a simple supper to settle the wonkiness in my stomach, I decided a beer at the Crazy Diamond would put things right.

As I perched on my favourite barstool with a pint of IPA in front of me, I watched Aziza hopping from table to table, taking orders, clearing empty glasses, bringing fresh drinks. She nodded to me in passing, which only reminded me of the distance between us. As if to drive the point home, a slightly off-key voice crooned through the speakers something about making "your name like a ghost."

"Man does this song bring back the memories," said Maggie as she sipped a gin and tonic. "*Baby Lemonade* by Syd Barrett. He was Pink Floyd's driving force before he lost his marbles. Too much acid they said. Made some brilliant solo records. This song's my favourite."

The song was both plaintive and hopeful, but it was not doing it for me.

"Aside from the nostalgia for the good old days, what is it that makes this one your favourite?"

"That's what I like about you, Samson, you haven't a sentimental bone in that scrawny body of yours."

She leaned in closer and I could smell the gin on her breath. That and the slightest of slurring in her speech made me wonder how many G and Ts she'd had. Maggie wasn't beyond the occasional tipple during working hours and she certainly knew how to hold her booze, so whatever red flag this raised I decided to let it fly only at half-mast.

"This song happens to hold a lot of memories for me," she continued. "A whole part of my life is inside that song. This was before I met Pius, when I lived in Toronto in the early 70s. I'd split from my family here to see what was going on in the Big Smoke. I was sixteen, although I looked older. Crashing wherever I could, living hand to mouth. I fell in with a group of hippies, all of them musicians, writers, painters. To make a bit of money or a free meal I used to act in what was called underground films. There was some nudity. It wasn't like porn or anything, not too much anyway. Besides, I had a real kickass bod back in the day. These guys were artists. I used to sing this song all the time so everyone called me Baby Lemonade. That became my professional name, the one I used in movies. I was really in demand for a while."

"What happened?"

"I started to really get bitten by the bug, not just acting but everything about making films. Even when I wasn't in a shot I used to hang out and watch them filming. Soon I was helping out with whatever they needed. Running errands, scouting locations, clapperboard girl, holding the boom, I even got to operate the camera. There was one guy who sort of took me under his wing. Matthew. He really seemed to take my interest seriously, even though I knew it was mostly to get laid. I learned a couple of things about lenses and how to cut film, but then I got pregnant. Asshole disappeared when I told him. Gave me a few bucks and I scraped up the rest from friends so I could get it taken care of. A real back-alley butcher. I got sick and came running back home. I even thought about having the kid for about two minutes. Fantasized naming her Lemonade."

"So that was the end of your film making aspirations?"

Maggie looked at me for the longest time then went off to wash some glasses. I continued to nurse my beer.

In all the time I'd known Maggie, she often regaled me with stories of her biker days with Pius, but she'd never disclosed anything as intimate as this. There was something about the telling I couldn't put my finger on. It was all about the nostalgia, but it wasn't wistful or mournful. Most nostalgia is about good times that are long gone or missed chances, but I didn't get that sense of it. I'd almost go so far as to say there was a triumphant note in the way she related the story. Then again, why wouldn't there be? She had a great marriage, as far as I could tell, and she was living out her own dream here at the Crazy Diamond. Not many people could say the same.

I was working on my second pint and jotting some notes on a napkin about what I would say at the interview the next day when I became aware of a commotion at one of the tables. Voices were raised and I looked up to see what was going on. Kelvin Muir was blocking Aziza's way. I couldn't quite make out what was being said, although at one point Kelvin was slurring in a voice amplified by one beer too many.

"C'mon, Zeez. You know we'd never of done nothing on purpose."

I realized then that Reggie Muir was sitting and watching, not getting involved, but clearly enjoying the show by the smirk on his face.

Aziza kept trying to go around Kelvin, but he moved to block her, pleading, "Aw, Zeez, just say you forgive us."

At that point he grabbed the tray out of her hand and set it on the table where he and Reg were sitting, but not before one of the empty steins fell to the floor and broke with an audible smash.

"Never mind that," Kelvin said. "C'mon, girl, let's make it up."

He took her by both shoulders and pulled her to him, knocking Aziza off balance into his arms, where he proceeded to kiss her on the mouth. Aziza managed to turn her head to the side and shouted for him to let go of her. Before anything else could happen, Maggie Beairsto was on the floor brandishing Lorie, her 9-iron.

"You take your friggin' hands off my waitress or you're gonna lose them both along with a couple of other choice parts of your anatomy!"

Kelvin immediately let go of Aziza and Reggie stood up. Then Maggie shoved the business end of the golf club in Kelvin's face and pushed him backward into his brother's arms.

"Get the fuck out of my bar, the two of yez, and don't ever let me see you in here again. I mean it!"

There have only been a few occasions where I've seen Maggie raise her voice and take Lorie out from behind the bar, but only as a warning when somebody got out of line. This was the first time I'd seen her physically charge out on the floor and actually shove the club in someone's face like that. She was only trying to help Aziza, but I really thought she was going to take a swing at Kelvin. In fact, Aziza had to calm her down.

Reggie started laughing and Kelvin suddenly turned angrily to his brother. "What the fuck you laughing at?" he screamed. "You coulda killed her!"

Kelvin took a swing at Reggie, his fist glancing off his older brother's chin.

"Big friggin' mouth on you!" Reggie grabbed his brother in a headlock.

"Get him outta here," yelled Maggie. "Before I crack both your skulls in!"

"Now come along or I'll twist your stupid head off like a beer cap." Reggie said and hauled Kelvin out the door.

Despite the music coming through the speakers, we all heard in quick succession voices shouting in the parking lot, then two doors slamming, an engine revving and tires squealing. A couple of people went outside to look, but Aziza and Maggie headed back to the bar with Maggie's arm draped protectively around Aziza's shoulder.

"BASICALLY, I'LL ASK YOU about the synagogue and its importance to the Jewish community," Chad Peladeau said as I settled into my seat in the *Good Morning PEI* studio and unscrewed the cap from a bottle of water. "Just a free and easy-going conversation."

Behind the glass booth, the engineer was checking our sound levels while music was being broadcast on the air. I nodded at Chad and noticed that Chet Affleck, who was sitting behind another microphone at the large round table where we were all situated, was doing something on his phone.

"Don't mind him," Chad said with a slight laugh. "He's always live-tweeting throughout the whole show."

Chet looked up for a moment and flashed a half-smile at his on-air partner. "Just covering all the bases," he said and quickly nodded at me before returning his attention to his phone.

It started off smoothly enough and I felt I was comporting myself as a suitable spokesperson that would do the Jewish community proud. Chad's questions were easy going, as promised, and I felt he came across as sympathetic, even supportive of adding a synagogue to PEI's "developing cultural diversity", as he put it. In the meantime, Chet Affleck seemed oblivious to what we were saying, rapt as he was with his phone. It felt to me as if the interview was winding down after a mere five minutes, which allowed me to relax and almost enjoy the experience. I felt I had handled myself pretty well. Then Chet raised his head.

"I think we have a bit of time left," he said amiably. "I just wanted to talk about the location where you would like the synagogue to be built. I understand at the last meeting of the PEI Jewish Collective you suggested that the site would be Rossiter's Field."

It's not that I wasn't expecting to talk about Rossiter's Field, but the subject had not been brought up so far and I assumed it wouldn't be. I couldn't help but feel I was being put on the defensive, since the first thing that raced through my mind was the fact that Chet was Project Director for Ashlynn's Camp for Kids, which was also supposed to be built on Rossiter's Field. I wondered if I was being set up somehow in what looked like a case of good-host/bad-host. I quickly composed myself and told Chet and Chad and the rest of the listening audience that I did indeed think Rossiter's Field would be the ideal spot for the synagogue. Rather than leave it at that, I decided to take to heart Vince Lombardi's advice about the best defense being a good offense.

"Now I understand many people believe that Rossiter's Field has already been earmarked for a children's camp," I said as amiably as possible. "I'm not sure if everyone listening knows how large a tract of land we are talking about. I'll go out on a limb and say a hundred acres easy. In fact, when it is cleaned up, and I say when rather than if, because I know that MLA Reuben Arsenault has made cleaning up Rossiter's Field a priority. When it is cleaned up, I think we'll find there are many imaginative ways that it can serve the community."

Chad then took up the interview again, while Chet became once more engrossed in his phone, by asking if the PEI Jewish Collective had already approached Reuben Arsenault about the synagogue, to which I reiterated there had been no official meeting between Mr. Arsenault's office and the Collective, but that he and I had had a very brief and informal discussion. I was sure the interview was about to end when Chet looked up again.

"One last quick question before we wrap up," he said. "You are a painter by occupation, and by that, I mean the artistic kind. I understand that a few years back you created a depiction of *Anne of Green Gables* as a Holocaust survivor, a painting that caused a lot of controversy, but that also brought you a certain amount of fame. There were charges that the depiction was a thinly veiled slur against PEI as being anti-Semitic. How do you think the controversy that arose from the painting impacted the Island's Jewish community and more importantly, how will it affect the community's bid for this synagogue?"

To say this question knocked the wind out my sails would be an understatement. I think even Chad was shocked by it. I could see the producer behind the glass giving us the gesture that time was almost up. There was nothing left to do but square my shoulders and go for broke.

"All I can say about that, Chet, is the intention behind the painting has been greatly misunderstood. I painted it as a reaction to the September 11th attacks, as a way to show a sense of innocence lost, and at no time was I ever levelling any accusation of anti-Semitism at PEI, which I have considered my home for the past eighteen years now. Many people across Canada see PEI as nothing but a rural backwater, but I believe we have come a long way in our cultural maturity, possibly even surpassing other larger urban cities, such as Toronto and Vancouver, in certain ways. I like to think that my painting in some way contributed to that maturity and proved once and for all that Prince Edward Island is a progressive home for the arts and for culture as a whole."

With that, Chad Peladeau thanked me for being there and wished me and the Jewish community the best of luck in our quest before signing off. I shook hands with both of them and walked out of there with my chest puffed out just a little farther for having, in my estimation and hopefully that of anyone listening, hit one out of the park. In the car I found Judas sitting in the passenger seat.

"Were you listening?" I asked.

"Please drive."

Something was eating him and I wasn't in the mood to find out what it was. I drove out of the parking lot and headed east toward St. Peter's Bay. My psyche felt like it had been squeezed through the wringer and there was a nice stretch of shoreline looking out at the bay where I needed to sit to put my head right again.

9

CHET AFFLECK'S AMBUSH questions, as I now thought of them, were out of keeping with *Good Morning PEI*'s casual manner. Sure, every now and then there might be a politician or other guest on the show, someone at the center of a controversial local story, and either Chet or Chad might decide to put on their big boy interviewing pants and throw a few hardball questions. More often than not, it constituted a journalistic version of shooting fish in a barrel, but netted them enough easily won credibility to hold their heads up in public.

What really threw me for a loop was how Chet brought up *Anne of Bergen-Belsen* as if he had scored a moral victory. Was this really about safeguarding his position in the Ashlynn's Camp for Kids project? I expressed all this to Judas as we drove. He listened in silence (at least I think he was listening) but offered no opinion one way or another. In fact, he said nothing at all. I decided not to press him on it. When we got to St. Peter's Bay, I parked the car in the lot of a small picnic area and we walked over to some benches looking out at the water. The sun shone directly above us and a strong breeze beckoned me to zip up my windbreaker and turn up the collar.

"Okay, what's going on?" I asked.

"You acquitted yourself admirably this morning," he said, almost grudgingly.

"You were listening?"

He said nothing, as if this was the stupidest question I could have asked, which, in retrospect, it was.

"There were moments I thought you might need rescuing. I was prepared to assist with a word in your ear. Yet in the end you remained well composed."

"You don't seem too happy about it."

Again, there was silence on his part as he looked out at St. Peter's Bay. I wondered if he was imagining the Sea of Galilee and wishing he was out with Yeshua and some fishermen buddies, putting their trust in fortune and newly mended nets.

"I did not want you to fail, if that is your meaning." He never took his eyes off the water and I could almost see his quiet mind searching for the right words the same way an angler patiently waits for a bite to tug his line. "And yet it is my fear that you do not see the pitfalls in your path."

"What pitfalls?"

"Yeshua was a good man. A wise man. Yet even he stumbled against the growing popularity of his teachings."

"You're not comparing me with..." I couldn't bring myself to finish the thought out loud.

He gave me a sharp look that was just this side of contempt.

"I am saying that your campaign has the potential to capture the public's imagination. This is your strategy. Beware of the drawbacks. Once the public is allowed to imagine something, they are not always easy to control. If you invite them to invest in your quest, do not be taken aback if they reshape it in their own image."

"Why are you telling me this? Do you know something?"

"I was Yeshua's confidant. I offered him my counsel. I saw how, at times, he was swayed by his own influence over others. Sometimes I said so and he listened with a patient ear, to humour me, I sometimes felt. He listened, but he did not always learn."

"Look, all I want is to get this synagogue built so I can get back to my life."

"I do not think you fully grasp what it is you are doing and what path you are walking."

My head was splitting and I rubbed my eyes wildly out of frustration. When I opened them again, I was alone. I had never felt so alone in my whole life. The wind blew off the water and I could feel it whistle through me as if I didn't exist. Or perhaps I really didn't exist and it was only the wind that gave me shape and form. I started to understand that these three figments might always be with me. I would never get rid of them, and in that sense, I would never rid myself of this bone-deep loneliness.

I decided that sitting out here was not what I needed to clear my head. I needed companionship and conversation. Not with the inventions of my obviously sick mind, but with a real live human being. One human being in particular.

I hopped into the car and headed back into Charlottetown. It was almost eleven o'clock and by some miracle I found a parking spot by the northeast corner of the Cradletown Court Mall. I slipped a loonie into the meter and walked along Kent to Great George Street until I found McMurphy Realtors, where Zaina worked. I asked for her at the receptionist's desk and was told to take a seat. In a matter of minutes, Zaina emerged from a corridor. There was a look of surprise on her face that I read as being somewhat pleased. I apologized for showing up out of nowhere like this and mentioned my interview with Chad and Chet. She had heard it and congratulated me on the way I handled myself, especially during that last question which she thought was hostile.

So, it wasn't just me and I felt a rush of gratitude. I explained that I needed to speak to someone about what had happened and wondered if I could take her out to lunch. She agreed, but she had to clear some things off her desk and mentioned that if I could wait for another twenty minutes she would be able to leave for the rest of the day since it was a Friday.

While I waited, I mused on how at one time I would have gone to Aziza to talk. But now, somehow, it seemed more fitting to have Zaina as my confidant, probably because we were closer in age. I assumed, like me, she was in her early forties although I was too much of a gentleman to ask.

After she had cleared her desk, I suggested that we have lunch in Mount Russet, fully prepared for her objection, but she readily agreed. She had been thinking of going there again to try to make things up with Aziza, whom she had not spoken to since their big argument. I mentioned that I had seen her a few times and she was doing fine and busy at work. Of course, I said nothing about the scene I had witnessed the other night. At the mention of Aziza's job, Zaina frowned and shook her head slightly.

"I'm not happy about her working in that place."

"I know it sounds rough, but I go there all the time. Believe me, she really likes it there and the owner, Maggie, really likes her."

"Yes, I met her at the hospital. Maggie. I know I should be grateful because she's the one who found Aziza on the road after she'd been hit. But there's something about the whole thing I don't like."

"What?"

"When we were in her apartment after the hospital. All Aziza would talk about was Maggie this and Maggie that."

"I know Aziza likes working at the Crazy Diamond. I guess they've become close." I considered mentioning how Maggie insisted that Aziza work there against Pius's wishes, but decided it was better not to go there. "I think Maggie feels protective toward her."

Zaina said nothing more and I wondered if she wasn't a little jealous of Maggie. Maybe she felt Aziza had found a surrogate mother in her employer.

"Still," I added. "I'm sure Aziza wants to make up with you as much as you want to with her."

Zaina nodded, more to reassure me that I had suitably comforted her, which I obviously hadn't. The truth was, the remoteness I'd recently been sensing from Aziza suddenly made me feel that much closer to Zaina, as if we were going through the same thing. I recognized immediately how absurd this was, but that somehow only reinforced (in my mind anyway) the connection between us. To temper this irrational feeling, I remembered Shylock's advice, back at Rossiter's Field, to "cast passions to passions and lust to lust."

I decided on Fusion Wok for lunch. We were greeted by proprietor Wayne Mao who led us to a booth by a window that looked out at the hustle and bustle (such as it was) of Orchard Street. He poured us glasses of water and after looking over the menu, ordered the lunch special.

Zaina wanted to know more about the interview with Chet and Chad and I described it as best I could. Even though it all happened less than five hours ago, it felt a bit hazy, as if I had merely dreamt it. What I still couldn't get out of my head was Chet Affleck with his face pretty much buried in his phone, then popping up to deliver these questions that were either meant to trip me up at best, or, at worst, discredit me to the listening audience.

"I keep thinking it all has something to do with him being connected to that camp," I said. "It was almost as if he perceived me as a threat. Or am I being paranoid?"

"What keeps coming back to me was when you came to visit Aziza in the hospital," said Zaina. "When you mentioned the synagogue and Rossiter's Field to Reuben."

"What about it?"

"Reuben is very good at hiding his feelings," she said. "But I lived with him for a long time and I could see how much you threw him off balance."

"I remember you telling me that. To be honest, I threw myself off balance."

"Yes, but Reuben is a man who very much likes to be in control. Being thrown off balance, especially by someone like..." Here she looked a bit embarrassed.

"By a nobody like me?" I said with a self-deprecating laugh to put her at ease.

"That's not what I meant. But... yes."

"You're not saying he perceived me as a threat, are you?"

"I don't know if threat is the right word. He had come out very strongly against your painting and he might think of this, the synagogue and your involvement, as payback for that."

"But it was so long ago."

"Reuben thinks revenge is a dish best served cold, as long as he's the one doing the serving. Let's just say he doesn't like surprises."

"Anyway, what does that have to do with Chet's ambush questions?"

"It's not a very well-kept secret that Reuben is connected to the children's camp. He is the treasurer," Zaina said.

"I didn't realize that," I said, but remembered all too well that Anne Surly had said the same thing in the last webcast I'd seen. Was it my imagination or did Zaina's cheeks redden slightly when she divulged that information?

"You said Chet kept his attention on his phone the whole time," she said. "Supposedly he was live-tweeting. But what if, and I want to stress the if, what if he was being fed those questions by text messages?"

I let Zaina's last question sink in. "Do you mean to say that Reuben was telling Chet what to ask me as a way of torpedoing me on the air?"

"I can't say that for sure," Zaina said. "But you did mention on air that you had an informal meeting with him. To his ears it may have sounded like you were implying that he supported building the synagogue. So, it's possible he decided to, as you say, torpedo you on the air."

I pondered this. The implication that Reuben Arsenault saw me as an enemy took my appetite away. I pushed away my half-eaten lunch. The rest of our conversation was friendly and at one point, Zaina mentioned that she was planning on learning how to drive. When I asked her why she had not learned to drive before this, she admitted that she had enrolled in a driving school right after she married Reuben, before she was pregnant with Aziza. Still with a learner's permit, she sometimes ventured out on her own in Reuben's Buick Century to practice within a small radius close to home. It was during that time that she had an accident. The sun got in her eyes while she was making a turn into a local strip mall's parking lot, resulting in her totalling the front of the Buick against a retaining wall. Aside from the scare it gave her, her learner's permit had been revoked. She became too nervous to get behind the wheel again.

"I'm still nervous," she said. "Hopefully I'll get a good teacher."

I offered to teach her myself. "We can start today, if you want. I promise to be patient."

She accepted my offer. Wayne Mao came by and saw that I had not finished my lunch and brought over a container so I could take the rest home.

Zaina took out her phone and called Aziza. There was no answer and she left a message. Our first driving lesson would take us back to my apartment so I could put my uneaten lunch in the fridge. It was agreed that she would observe from the passenger seat, while I explained everything I was doing. After that, she could get behind the wheel.

As we were approaching Morningstar Crescent, a truck squealed around the corner, barely missing us. I recognized it as Reg'n'Kel's half-ton. My immediate thought was of Aziza, but I said nothing to Zaina. When we entered the Body Parts, the plan in my head was to drop the food off in my apartment and then I'd suggest we knock on Aziza's door, in case she just got home.

I was mentally patting myself on the back for my ingenuity until we reached my landing and I saw that my door was wide open. We both stepped in to see the place had been ransacked. Chairs were turned over, cupboards were opened and plates smashed on the kitchenette floor. Drawers had been pulled out completely and what little cutlery I owned was strewn everywhere. In the studio, paintings were knocked around, some slashed, and my worktable had been upended with paints, palette, brushes and other tools scattered all around.

"You'll have to check if anything is missing," said Zaina, almost officially, despite the distress in her voice, like she was taking control of the situation.

"I'm pretty sure this was no robbery," I said.

"Who would do such a thing?"

I decided to leave the question unanswered, as it might lead to other questions also best left unanswered for the time being. My easel was knocked over, but I could not immediately see the painting that had been sitting on it. The bungee cords looked to have been cut and the drop cloth that had been covering it was crumpled in a corner. I had to search through the mess to find the painting itself and when I did, what I saw shocked me to the core. I held it up. It had not been slashed, as I had feared, but it was not the same painting I had covered up.

"What is that?" asked Zaina, who was standing beside me and staring at the painting with a confused look on her face.

"What do you mean?" I asked, somewhat confused myself.

"Is that supposed to be a starfish?"

I stared at her, more stupefied than I was at the altered painting.

"You can see that?" I asked.

She looked at me as if I was crazy. "Of course, I can see it. I can see it plain as day. I just don't know what it's supposed to be."

I couldn't figure out what was going on. Aziza couldn't see the starfish, which led me to believe I was the only one who could, which in turn convinced me it was a divine sign that meant I should build the synagogue.

But now that Zaina could see it, what did that mean?

"Yes," I finally answered. "It's supposed to be a starfish."

"Then please explain," she said and gave my forearm a light squeeze that asked for assurance rather than affection. "Why does it have ten arms?

PART 3:

A LAND WITHOUT MAN IS NOWHERE

10

CHAD: "So here it is, Chet, the first day of December, and bang! Over eighteen centimetres of the white stuff!"

CHET: "Talk about premature precipitation."

CHAD: "Whoa! Easy there, sunshine. This is still a family show. Kick back with a second cup of coffee and give the snow plows a chance to clear some of the roads."

CHET: "Brace yourself, folks, it's just the beginning of the beginning."

CHAD: "Here to tell us when this beginning might end, taking over from retired weather celeb Boom Boom Burnham, is our new resident meteorologist, Kenny Kilkenny."

CHET: "Oh my God, they killed Kenny!"

CHAD: "Okay, Chet, no more double espressos for you. Why don't we all just take a breath. Kenny, tell us what we can expect over the week."

KENNY: "Well, Chad, if I may paraphrase a popular song from my youth, it's snowing men, hallelujah, it's snowing men."

I turned off the radio. The season of weather porn had begun, and the endless orgy of kvetching that goes with it. Here it was the first day of December and a major dump of snow had everyone in a good old Island tizzy. Also, something was going on with Chet Affleck. Possibly, it was a case of being over-caffeinated, as Chad suggested, but for a while now he sounded on edge, exhibiting a slightly manic behaviour that often verged on the inappropriate.

The weather wasn't the only surprise in store for Islanders. There had been some political fallout that was as unexpected as the fat snowflakes descending ever faster outside my window. I remembered Anne Surly's hint of a rift developing between Kerrie-Jo Campbelljohn and Reuben Arsenault, but I hadn't expected it to manifest so publicly. It all started when Reuben announced his intention to become leader of the Loyalty Party, which he did at a well-attended rally at the Sir John A. MacDonald Civic Auditorium, complete with fiddlers, step dancers and a children's choir singing *The Island Hymn* (which had been declared PEI's official anthem a few years earlier with words, appropriately, by Lucy Maud Montgomery). Obviously, the Tourism and Culture portfolio, supposedly his for the taking (assuming Kerrie-Jo took power) was now deemed small potatoes. The growing scuttlebutt was that Kerrie-Jo didn't have the political clout to become party leader. She and Reuben were now at loggerheads. The camps were evenly divided, with each one having some very vocal supporters. The main objection to Reuben was his lack of political experience. An opinion that was countered by the belief by some that there were worse things in this world than a lack of experience, and that maybe what the province needed was an infusion of new blood and new ideas.

Someone else who was definitely not in Reuben's corner was Tamara Tuplin, leader of the fledgling Great Boat Party, which had been founded a mere two years earlier. The Great Boat Party's policies were aligned with the Mi'kmaq Alliance in pursuing disputes over hunting and fishing rights and land claims.

In one of her first speeches, Tamara displayed a wry sense of humour by describing how she chose the name of her party. First, she explained that it came from an early Mi'kmaw name for PEI, Kjiktú ' lnu or "our great boat" and went on to explain it was only later that the Island was called Epekwit'k (anglicized as Abegweit), which means "lying in the water."

"The Great Boat Party had just the right ring to it, since we are all in the same boat," said Tamara to the crowd, who responded with enthusiastic applause. "Calling it the Lying in the Water Party just didn't have the same pizzazz. Besides, it could be taken the wrong way and we already have enough of that in politics." This was followed by laughter and more applause.

At the beginning of all her speeches Tamara Tuplin made a point of welcoming everyone by reminding them that they were on unceded territory, meaning there was no treaty signing the Island over to the government and that proper consultation with the Mi'kmaq Alliance was needed for any development on the land. One of her most ardent talking points was to have this land acknowledgement, a reminder of being on unceded territory, become an official pronouncement at the beginning of all public functions.

Lately, she was especially outspoken about Reuben's campaign promise to clean up Rossiter's Field (which she said had long been overdue) and to build on it (which she was dead set against, at least not without proper consultation with the Mi'kmaq Alliance). She publicly claimed that Rossiter's Field was long known to be an area of cultural and historical significance to the Mi'kmaq. I wasn't sure what this meant for the synagogue, but it interested me to see that this outright challenge to Reuben's pet project (which he used as an all-purpose platform to drive home various campaign promises of cleaning up the Island, creating new jobs and revitalizing pride in PEI) increased the Great Boat Party's public approval rating by three whole percentage points.

The huge snowfall put any clean-up plans temporarily on hold, which most likely worked in Reuben's favour while he concentrated his efforts on his campaign.

"No doubt he thinks that once he is premier, he will have carte blanche to do whatever he wants," Zaina told me. If she felt any pleasure or amusement at seeing Reuben and Kerrie-Jo become public adversaries, she did not show it outright. "He can be single-minded about getting what he wants, so that every relationship becomes transactional. But he can also have very unrealistic expectations."

Zaina and Aziza were on better terms these days and Zaina often travelled to Mount Russet on the weekend (insisting on taking the bus in from Charlottetown, despite my offers to get her, although she was usually more than happy for a ride back, since that meant a continuation of our driving lessons, which were going well). Sometimes the three of us got together at Sadie's Tearoom. I asked Zaina not to say anything to Aziza, or anybody else, about the painting she had seen in my apartment on the pretext that it was unfinished. I still did not understand why the starfish now had ten arms, but I explained to Zaina that this was something purely experimental on my part and I still was not sure whether I liked the direction I was moving in, which was the truth in more ways than one.

After we discovered the break-in, Zaina insisted I call the police, but I worried that a police investigation might lead them to Aziza's online activities as Anne Surly. Not only did I not want to get her in trouble, but as far as I knew, Zaina had no idea about what her daughter was up to and I didn't want to upset her. I managed to convince Zaina that calling the police would lead nowhere, since they were already regular visitors to the Body Parts and would probably never find out who did this.

Zaina and I enjoyed each other's company. She began taking a keener interest in the synagogue and, having played a part in building the mosque, was keen to offer advice on various aspects of how to make it happen. If my insistence that it be built on Rossiter's Field still mystified many people (although the PEI Jewish Collective were willing to go along with it for the time being), Zaina saw this as a challenge that made the prospect even more interesting. I expressed my concern about the recent revelation of Rossiter's Field being historical Mi'kmaw land. Zaina thought about it for a moment.

"You never know," she said. "It could work to your advantage. After all, you aren't proposing to build a children's camp or amusement park. You want to build a house of worship. Before anything can be built, there will have to be a consultation with the Mi'kmaq Alliance. I'm sure Reuben considers that a minor formality not worth worrying about, if he's even thinking about it at all. It might be a good idea for you to meet with Tamara Tuplin."

"Wouldn't it be better to meet with someone at the Mi'kmaq Alliance?" I asked.

"She has ties to the Alliance. Besides, this would just be an informal chat. Strictly under the radar. A back channel just to get the lay of the land, so to speak. Tamara rents the Great Boat Party headquarters through my company, so I could help you set up the meeting."

I'd be lying if I said I wasn't grateful for the interest Zaina was taking in the synagogue and how proactive she could be with her involvement. The fact that she could see the now ten-armed starfish, made it feel natural she should be involved. But those extra arms, made me curious whether maybe Aziza would be able to see it now. After inviting her to the apartment to look at the painting again, on the pretext of wanting her opinion of how to proceed with it, her only suggestion was to fill up the empty space with more ocean detritus. It was clear that Aziza was still oblivious to the starfish, while Zaina could see it clear as day. The big question for me was, did this mean she had been enlisted by the Supreme One, and if so, was she aware of it?

"Don't be daft, my dear," said Fagin after I managed to conjure up all three Figs in my apartment. "More'n likely the synagogue is a convenient eye-for-an-eye to scupper her old man."

"She's not like that," I argued. "She's not a vindictive person."

"Nay, 'tis not fair and proper to impugn the good character of this daughter of Mohammed," Shylock quickly added. "And yet, good cousin, I wonder if passion's mist hath not clouded thy vision of this comely lady."

"Never mind that," I said. "Is she part of the Supreme One's plan? And if she is, then that means my meeting Aziza, the link to the Anne Surly website that was bookmarked on my computer, even the fact that she moved upstairs from me, which happened the same day you three showed up in my life, all of it is part of some divine scheme, isn't it? All the pieces fit together, but there's more to the puzzle and I need to see it all before I can go any further."

Fagin and Shylock looked gravely at each other then turned to Judas, who was hanging back, probably to observe where this conversation was going. He looked at them both silently and motioned his head ever so slightly. They retreated to the card table and sat quietly. Obviously, it was up to Judas to calm down the petulant mortal. I could feel my body tense up, steeling myself against those mellifluous tones Judas had a way of summoning, like a troubadour plucking soothing music from his lyre.

"Who are you to make demands of the Supreme One?" he snapped, and the pallor of his face flushed deeply with indignation.

I was disturbed to witness the sight of the twisted scar around his throat turning darker. It seemed to be tightening like the very noose that had originally bit into his flesh.

"Do you think it is only the events from these past few months that follow a pattern? Do you think your life before unfolded in a haphazard fashion? If you only knew the intertwining designs that make up the tapestry of all destinies, you would not be puffing up your chest like an ill-tempered child. You have been chosen to carry out a task and that is all you need to know. Being privy to what is to come is not permitted. It is important that you be able to deal with any event, tribulation or obstacle that crosses your path. How you act or proceed has an impact on everybody involved, including us three."

"But I think I have a right to..."

"A right?" He clapped his hands, producing a noise not unlike a crack of thunder. I had never seen him this agitated. "The task you have been given does not come with any rights. The task is a privilege. It is your way to prove yourself to the Supreme One. There are no conditions that give you any rights. We each have our part in this plan and we must carry it out unquestioningly. Trying to piece together the Supreme One's methods like they were pieces of a child's puzzle shows the utmost disrespect and can do nothing but mark you as a fool. If you pursue this line of absurd inquiry I will lose my patience, but worse than that, you might go so far as to anger the Supreme One and then it will be too late."

"Too late? What do you mean? What will happen?"

At this Judas threw up his hands in despair and the other two Figs quickly got up from their chairs to calm him down.

"Peace, good brother Judas," said Shylock. "Methinks thou needst draw deeply the bracing air of tolerance into thy lungs."

"Remember, my dear," said Fagin. "Ours is to be role models as well as guides."

"You're kidding," I said. "Role models? You three? You pop in and out of my life whenever you please, telling me to do this, do that, and never ask how or why. You're going to guide me straight to the funny farm before this is all over."

I expected Judas to direct his wrath at me once more and worried whether the other two might join in, but they didn't hear me. Rather, they got caught up in a heated exchange between themselves, as if I wasn't there.

"You two are of no help whatsoever!" Judas cried at his compatriots. "You are either appealing to his greed or to his vanity. I wonder if either of you are taking this any more seriously than he is? Do none of you understand the importance of what we are here to do?"

"Steady on!" warned Fagin. "Just because you were that glorified carpenter's simpering dogsbody don't give you the moral high ground here."

"Signor, 'tis a great injustice thou cast upon us. Our counsel hath been of the highest quality. Forsooth, the circumstances dictate we must bring our good cousin along with care and sensitive reason."

"We may not have much more time to indulge in care and sensitive reason," warned Judas. "I wonder if you are enjoying yourselves too much and so find cause to dawdle in order to prolong your time here in this lowly realm."

"I'll have you remember it was me who got the bleedin' ball rolling," said Fagin. "He weren't interested no way in this synagogue until I started in with me powers of persuasion. I softened him up for you two."

"'Twas I who partook of foodstuffs with him," Shylock protested. "By this most human of rituals, the sharing of victuals, did I ally my love to good cousin Samson in most effective a manner from either of you."

"While you two have been cajoling him I have been dispensing wisdom," Judas retorted. "He does not understand the dire pitfalls that come with what he is being asked to do."

"Wisdom my bony arse," cried Fagin. "You call reminiscing over your salad days as a lickspittle dispensing wisdom? More like boring the poor geezer with stories about toadying up to the Nazarene."

I kept wanting to jump in to let them know in no uncertain terms that not one of them had any influence on me whatsoever, that I made up my own mind and was master of my free will as much as they were. But it was clear they were so engaged in their bickering I wouldn't have been able to get in a word edgewise.

"It would be best if you watched your tongue," Judas warned in an eerily subdued tone. "What I gave to Yeshua I can never get back."

Fagin grinned. "I s'pose stringing yourself from a tree was your own bid for redemption? You wear that scar round your neck like it were a halo what slipped over your head. Well, I can match you, my dear, I can match you well enough."

With that he undid the topmost buttons of his bright orange sport shirt, which he always kept fastened, revealing a similar red scar around his own throat.

"I swung too, my dear, but I did my swinging the honest way. By the gallows. I don't deny I did many terrible things in my time and I paid for 'em with me neck. But the worst thing I ever did was to cause a girl's death. Poor Nancy! Told Sikes, her old man, she was grassing him up to the coppers and he killed her. Maybe that's what I'm doing here. I'm the only one here who's atoning for something."

I realized the best thing would be to take my leave and let them argue it out. I sidled toward the door, picking up my parka that was draped over one of the folding chairs. Normally, it would be them who appeared and vanished at will. As I slipped out the door, I couldn't help wondering whether they were still figments of my imagination, or if we had switched roles and I had now become a figment of theirs.

IT WAS INEVITABLE that the campaign would move to social media. I didn't go on Twitter myself, but newspaper items and radio reports mostly quoted tweets by both candidates. One item about Team Arsenault carried the hashtag #coughitup. It was alleged that at rallies and public appearances Reuben Arsenault and his campaign manager, Portia MacFadyen, scanned the crowd for people known to have money, who were later targeted for donations. Whenever they saw a likely chump, they alerted each other with the code phrase "cough it up." Later on, the code was shortened by simply covering his or her mouth and pretending to cough. The Twitterverse backlash to this story resulted in GIFs of cats coughing up hairballs and photos of Reuben with the head of Bloom County comic strip character, Bill the Cat, superimposed over his head and the accompanying hashtag #aaackitup. Apparently, Reuben was quite upset about one meme that showed a caricature of himself, red-faced and in the throes of a coughing fit that produced a dollar sign dripping with mucous, while off to the side was a bottle with a label that read Campbelljohn's Cough Syrup.

Kerrie-Jo got nailed by an incident that made her infamous crossing of the legislature floor look like a cakewalk. She had been making a speech to constituents in her riding of Crapaud and by all accounts she was doing a great job of preaching to the choir. During the Q&A, she was asked about Rossiter's

Field and if she still supported the clean-up effort that was the main platform of Reuben Arsenault's campaign. Her answer was politic enough, maintaining that the clean-up was long overdue but casting doubts about what was to be done with the land.

"There are a few hoops to jump through before any real decisions can be made. The first, by necessity, will have to be a consultation with, you know, the Mi'kmaq."

It was at that "you know" where her eyes looked upward. The ensuing Twitter storm that carried the hashtag #eyeroll rained down long and hard. Many, including some members of the Mi'kmaq Alliance and the Great Boat Party, took the opportunity of using the eye roll as a way of branding the government in general for arrogance and pettiness and the overall sense that this agreement of consultation with the Mi'kmaq over land development was an inconvenience.

But it was Kerrie-Jo Campbelljohn's misfortune to be caught on camera expressing it. Eye roll GIFs, from Groucho Marx to Betty Boop – both meant to be symbols of an earlier and less enlightened time – appeared on Twitter feeds everywhere. Campbelljohn eye roll GIFs, accompanied by captions such as "an inconvenient goof" and "with two you get eye roll" (which sparked its own outcry as being offensive to Asians), prevailed. Campbelljohn herself claimed that it wasn't an eye roll at all, but rather, that she had been distracted by the lights above in the auditorium.

When asked to comment on the incident in a radio interview, Tamara Tuplin said, "When are the Honourable Members of this government going to stop acting like a bunch of put-upon children and start taking seriously the process of reconciliation? This is a healing journey that's meant to benefit not just the Mi'kmaq, but potentially all of society. When will the government start to treat this process with the respect and dignity it deserves? We are asking everyone to gather as allies and participants of this reconciliation. The Mi'kmaq are not trying to inconvenience or obstruct your lives. If you can't be supportive, at least be respectful."

After that her approval rating went up another 2½ points.

I began to find one reason or another to drive into Charlottetown and usually popped in at McMurphy Realtors to say hi to Zaina. More often than not, we went to lunch somewhere near her office. Once I brought sandwiches and we ate at her desk. On the afternoon I took her to Café Istanbul, I saw Zaina look up at something behind me. I turned around and there was Frieda Greenglass with a paper bag in her hand.

"Frieda," I said, trying not to look too startled. "Fancy seeing you here. Getting yourself some baklava?"

Her eyes were fixed squarely on Zaina. Frieda smiled and held out her hand and introduced herself. Zaina shook her hand and also introduced herself.

"Yes," I said. "Zaina has been helping me with ideas about the synagogue."

"I see," said Frieda. "I assumed there was a cultural exchange going on."

"Would you care to join us?" asked Zaina.

"Thank you, but I can't stay."

"Zaina works for McMurphy Realtors," I said. "She was instrumental in helping get the mosque built."

"That must have been very satisfying," said Frieda.

"I think it's a wonderful thing for the Jewish community to be getting a synagogue," said Zaina. "Samson is very passionate about it."

"Passionate?" said Frieda. She couldn't keep the smirk from creasing her face. "Yes, he has surprised all of us and become quite the spokesperson for our people. And now I see why."

Zaina looked uncomfortable. "I'm not sure what you mean."

Frieda turned to me and shook her head. "Honestly, Samson, I don't know how long you thought you could string along the Collective with this whole synagogue charade when it's all just an excuse for these intimate little lunches. I think I'm going to have a serious talk with Stepan Markowitz about all this."

"Frieda, why make such a..."

"And you," said Frieda, casting a cold eye on Zaina. "I don't know, much less care what kind of miracle worker you were with the mosque, but the Jewish community does not need your assistance in its affairs, thank you very much."

Before anything more could be said, Frieda Greenglass turned on her heel and exited the restaurant. I apologized profusely to Zaina and suggested that she not take Frieda's words personally.

While walking her back to work, I gave Zaina a condensed history of my friendship with Frieda. I had to own up to the fact that Frieda had seen the sketch I did of Rossiter's Field with the figure in the headscarf in the background and somehow got the wrong idea about it.

"What do you mean *wrong idea?*"

"I'm not sure," I said. "I think she thinks I'm doing all this to impress you."

Zaina's face coloured deeply and I tried to assure her that this was all a misunderstanding on Frieda's part. Before I left her at McMurphy Realtors, I promised Zaina I would have a talk with Frieda and get all of this straightened out. I could see the trace of doubt in Zaina's expression, even as she tried to smile.

"Please believe me," I said. "Your friendship is the only good thing that's happened to me in the last few months. I wouldn't want to do anything to jeopardize that." Zaina nodded, then went inside.

When I returned to where I'd parked the car, I saw there was still five minutes left on the meter. I sat in the car and tried to reassess the situation. How serious was Frieda about going to see Professor Markowitz and what was she going to tell him? Really, what was there to tell, except I was having lunch with someone? As far as I knew, I still had the confidence of the PEI Jewish Collective, yet I couldn't help but feel I was operating on borrowed time.

"Looks like your time's just about run out." My first assumption was one of the Figs was sitting in the back seat, but then I realized the voice was not one of theirs. Still, it wasn't altogether unfamiliar. "On the meter, I mean."

I turned around and saw Kelvin Muir hunkering down on my back seat.

"Geez, boy, don't give me away," he whispered harshly. "Just drive, before you get a ticket"

I did as he said and kept glancing in my rear-view mirror but he kept well down out of my range of vision. It was like talking to an invisible entity. He made the Figs appear more real by comparison.

"What the hell are you doing in my car? How did you break in?"

"Wasn't that hard," he said.

"So, where's Reg?"

"Don't you worry 'bout Reg. Just keep driving and keep your eyes straight ahead,"

"Where are we going?"

"Super-Mart parking lot."

The Maritime Super-Mart was next to a strip mall in the northern end of University Avenue, kitty corner to Prince Edward Island University. I maneuvered through the half-filled parking lot until Kelvin told me to park beside a trolley station. If he had a nefarious plan for me, he'd chosen a fairly public place to carry it out. I invited him to sit up front, but he preferred where he was. He told me not to look behind.

"What are we doing here?" I asked.

"I'm here because of Zeez," he said. "I'm worried 'bout her."

"Is that why you tried to force yourself on her at the Crazy Diamond?"

"That was Reg's idea of a joke, getting me all liquored up and pushing me to kiss her."

"Was it also Reg's idea to run her bike down?"

"That was an accident! We were only s'posed to scare her and things got out of hand. I told Reg he was driving too close!"

"Okay, okay," I said as calmly as I could. "I believe you. But I still don't understand why you're coming to me."

"Look, I like Zeez. I know she thinks I'm just a lowlife, that I'm just Reg's pet monkey, like everyone else thinks. But I really care for her."

The ensuing silence added a certain poignancy to his words, but after a while it was just dead air. "And?"

"You're friends with Zeez, right? She'll listen to you more'n me. I'd go to her directly and tell her the danger she's in, but I don't think she'd listen to me. But she'd probably listen to you, right?"

"Danger? What kind of danger?"

"I don't really know exactly. It's more of a feeling I have. But I know something ain't right with Zeez."

"You're really going to have to do better than that," I said. "What is it you want me to tell Zeez, I mean Aziza?"

"She needs to stop doing all that webcam stuff. It's getting out of hand."

I couldn't argue with him there. Nevertheless, I assured Kelvin that she wouldn't listen to me anyway. She was basically her own person.

"But that's just it," he said. "She's not on her own. She's got some sort of partner."

"Who?"

Kelvin said he didn't know, but he told me about a meeting he and Reggie had with Reuben Arsenault. They knew that Aziza had resumed her webcasting and Reg'n'Kel were expecting Reuben to give them orders to put yet another stop to it. In fact, he told them quite the opposite. He said he happened to know that Aziza had enlisted the help of a partner, someone who was doing the actual filming.

"We asked who it was, but he said we didn't need to know that. He said it was important that all this web stuff she's doing not be disturbed."

"I don't understand."

"Seems like he don't want her to stop doing it. I mean, he's her father and all. He shouldn't want his daughter to be doing all that stuff she's doing and wearing what she's wearing and using all that language. I've watched her, I admit it. But that's not the real Zeez."

"Of course it isn't," I said. "She's playing a part. Like an actor."

"That's not what I'm talking about! We went to school together. She was smart and she never made fun of me like other kids did, those smarter ones. I don't know why she needs to do this online stuff. When Reuben asked me and Reg to put a stop to it I was more than happy to. She's better than all that filth she spews on her webcam. But something's wrong if he wants her to keep doing that stuff. Somebody should warn her."

I told him I'd see what I could do, but I doubted if she would listen to me. I was about ask him if he and Reggie had trashed my place on Reuben's orders, but at that moment something caught Kelvin's eye.

"Shit! What the hell is he doin' here?"

He opened the back door and jumped out of the car if he was on fire. I looked at the parking lot entrance and recognized Reggie's pickup turning in from the road. Kelvin started to run and Reggie's truck sped up toward him. Stupidly, Kelvin wasn't looking where he was going and ran smack into a stray shopping cart and went sprawling on the ground with the truck bearing down on him. Was Reggie really going to run over his own brother? At the last minute, Reggie hit the breaks and stopped mere inches short of flattening his brother for good. Then Reggie jumped out of the truck and grabbed Kelvin by the hair and started yelling at the top of his lungs, calling Kelvin "a little traitor" and warning him that "snitches get stitches." He finally opened the passenger door, still with a handful of Kelvin's greasy curls and shoved him into the truck and kicked the door shut. Once he jumped into the driver's side, the truck roared out of the parking lot, wheels squealing on the road as he barrelled into traffic without stopping.

WHEN REUBEN ARSENAULT won the leadership of the Loyalty Party, Kerrie-Jo Campbelljohn announced her retirement from politics. Asked what she would do next, to her credit, she did not trot out the usual pat response of spending more time with her family. Instead, she said she wanted to "cultivate my creative side", but decided, for the moment, not to elaborate on what that meant. This cliff-hanger did much to feed my already fertile imagination and I speculated a possible exhibition at some local gallery of child-like watercolours of cats and senior citizens à la George Bush or maybe a one-woman show of her political career. *The Kerrie-Jo Campbelljohn Story: It's My Party and I'll Defect If I Want To.*

The only problem with becoming leader, from Reuben's point of view, was that he had inherited a minority ruling party. At the moment, the Retro-Progressives were the opposition and Nathan Affleck was often forced to play nice with them and the Neo-Egalitarians, who were a close third. Reuben had no intention of compromising himself or working within the constraints of a coalition. His only choice was to call a snap election and win by a majority, which he had no doubt he could do.

Reuben wasted no time in launching his campaign to become premier. The surge of support for him was surprisingly strong. His only real competition was Retro-Progressive leader Benedict Fogarty, a man whose name perfectly described the blustering, red-faced, suspender-wearing, patronage-loving, life-long boy's club member that he was. By comparison, Reuben looked younger, sharper and – dare I say it? – more progressive. Trailing far behind both of them, the Neo-Egalitarian Party's Taylor MacPhee was a bright-eyed political neophyte whose family owned a chain of feed stores. The Enviro Party leader, Sandra Fitzroy, wore smart forest green blazers that made her look like a real estate salesperson (which is exactly what she was). Her habit of employing emphatic hand gestures whenever she spoke in public earned her the nickname Semaphore Sandy. As for Tamara Tuplin, the Great Boat Party didn't seem to be on the media's radar.

Amidst the flying rhetoric and candidate signs sprouting on front lawns like unsightly weeds, I noticed something odd. It wasn't something you could put your finger on, but there was a feeling in the air. If I didn't know better, I would have described it as a subtle acceleration (as effective an oxymoron as any). Perhaps it had something to do with the rush election, which was due a couple of weeks into the new year, but there was a sense that things were somehow speeding up, although, as far as I knew, I was the only one who noticed it.

Kelvin Muir's words constantly circled my consciousness and I waffled back and forth on whether I should tell Aziza about my bizarre meeting with him. I still rarely saw her at the Body Parts, so I decided to head over to the Crazy Diamond and take my chances in the late afternoon, when there was a lull just before the dinner rush. If, by some miracle, I found myself able to talk to Aziza, I'd try to broach the subject of Kelvin Muir.

Things looked good when I pulled into their parking lot. Not too many cars. The minute I stepped out of the car, I could hear voices coming from the other side of the building where the Shine Shrine was located. The voices were loud and I wandered toward them without being seen and listened for a minute. They definitely belonged to Pius and Maggie and neither sounded happy.

It was hard to make out everything that was said, but I'm sure I heard Pius shout, "She's got to go! I'm not having any of this here, not in my place of business!" Then I heard Maggie shout, "This is my place of business too and I say she stays! She and I are the ones who close up this place so you don't have to worry your fat head about anything!" I decided not to wait around to listen to any more. If they were outside then Aziza was most likely holding down the bar.

I entered and, sure enough, there she was. She was surprised to see me coming in so early, but smiled and waved, curbing any thoughts I had that she was trying to avoid me.

There were a few customers scattered at the tables and Aziza was pouring ingredients into a shaker. The Pink Floyd song coming through the speakers was one I'd heard many times and featured a plummy British voice reminding me that there was "no other day" and advised to "try it another way", which emboldened me to raise the Kelvin subject with Aziza.

She interrupted what she had been doing to pour my pint of IPA before my backside settled on my usual stool. I took a tentative sip while she returned to the shaker. Small talk ensued and then I told her about my meeting with Kelvin and what he had said. Her expression soured. She said she didn't want to talk about Kelvin or Reggie.

"But what did he mean about wanting to warn you?" I asked. "Is there something going on? I just heard Pius and Maggie arguing outside. It sounded like they might be arguing about you."

Aziza poured the contents of the shaker into two glasses and told me in no uncertain terms to mind my own business. "Whatever nonsense Kelvin Muir is spouting about me is all in his head."

"But he admitted that it was him and Reggie who ran you down on Mount Russet Road. They obviously did it on your father's orders. And now Kelvin is saying your father wants you to keep on doing your Anne Surly broadcasts. What's going on?"

"What's going on is that you're letting yourself get sucked in by a very disturbed and infatuated boy," she snapped. "As for my father, he confessed about getting those two mental midgets to scare me. He's heartsick about how badly it went. He blames himself. And for your information, not that it's any of your business, he begged my forgiveness. He'd do anything to take it all back. Of course, I forgave him. My father loves me. Don't you ever forget that."

"Then what's this about you doing the webcasts with a partner?" I asked. "Who is it?"

"None of your damn business!" she said. "And I suggest you forget Rossiter's Field for your synagogue. You don't want to antagonize my father and make yourself a target."

She picked up the tray of drinks and went off to serve her customers. Maggie entered from the kitchen. She wasn't in the greatest mood at first but put on a braver face when she saw me.

"You'll lose your mind..." warned the voice over the speakers. I took that warning to heart and silently drank the rest of my pint while Maggie set about washing glasses.

LATER THAT NIGHT, I decided to check in on Anne Surly. As expected, she went on at length about how Reuben looked to be a shoo-in as the next premier. She went so far as to call it a coronation and said that PEI was about to become yet another Crown Corporation. She laughed mirthlessly at her own pun and I realized there was something more ominous and less playful about her forecast. She ended the webcast by saying she had heard some confidential scuttlebutt about an operation in the works that Reuben had going. It was top secret and she had no real details as yet. But the operation did have a code name of sorts. Project Friendly Occupation. Something Kelvin said came to mind: "Seems like he don't want her to stop doing it. I mean, he's her father and all."

I had no idea what he was talking about at the time, but then I noticed something different about her prop. The bamboo cane was gone. Instead, she carried a golf club and it looked very familiar. I could have sworn it was Lorie, the prize 9-iron that Maggie Beairsto kept behind the bar.

11

THE GREAT BOAT PARTY headquarters was on the second floor of a commercial warehouse on Richmond Street in Charlottetown. The layout was open spaced with five desks on which were bulky computer terminals and telephones. Two young women, a young man (who was no more than a teenager) and an older man sporting gray pigtails sat behind their desks, either typing on computers or talking on phones. The fifth desk was Tamara Tuplin's.

On this day, movers were carrying in two more desks. A telephone repairman was installing new phone outlets and an IT tech was setting up the computers. The space was also furnished with a Xerox machine, a fax machine, a flat screen TV and three large metal filing cabinets.

Tamara Tuplin apologized for the mess and noise, explaining that they were in the middle of expanding their operation. Having been told by Zaina that I was an artist, she led me around the space to show me some framed posters adorning the walls. I recognized a Norval Morrisseau print and another by Jane Ash Poitras. Behind Tamara's desk hung a good-sized quillwork design of an eight-pointed Mi'kmaw star in traditional black, white, yellow and red. It was an elaborate work of art on framed birch bark that brought to mind the ten-armed starfish, which made the back of my neck tingle and gave me an unsettling sensation, as if this space was being watched over.

She sat at her desk and I sat opposite her in a comfortable old armchair. There was a plate of what looked like mini pizzas. She offered me one. "Bannock

Bruschetta," she explained, holding out the plate toward me. "My son made them. He recently graduated from the Island School of Culinary Arts. Try one."

I bit into one. It was delicious. She explained that the bannock was made with maize and the olive oil was infused with a mixture of jalapeño peppers and blackberries that her son had created himself.

"When we had a *wi'kipaltimk*, an honouring ceremony when he graduated, he catered the feast with the help of two of his classmates. They eventually went into business together in a food truck specializing in Indigenous-inspired food called The Bannock Wagon."

"I've heard good things about it, but I haven't had a chance to try the food," I said. "I didn't realize that's your son. You must be proud of him."

"Absolutely," she said. "In that ceremony all our family and friends and neighbours were invited. But first the elders ate while Eli watched. Let me tell you, he was the one beaming with pride, seeing how much they loved his food. He has his whole heritage to build a future on, one that goes back tens of thousands of years, maybe even longer. We Mi'kmaq were stripped of our identities, our history, our humanity. We have had to relearn who we are, and in many ways, reinvent ourselves. It's the younger people like Eli who are leading the way."

I thanked her for the food and for taking the time to see me. Zaina had set up the meeting with the explanation that I was representing the Jewish community regarding the possible building of a synagogue on Rossiter's Field. I was surprised to learn that Tamara Tuplin had heard my interview on *Good Morning PEI*. I hastened to add that I hoped she would consider this an informal meeting, merely to discuss the Mi'kmaw claim on that land. She sat back in her office chair, swivelling slightly from side to side. She was in her fifties with short dark, grey-flecked hair, cut bluntly with bangs almost reaching her eyebrows. Her bulky cable-knit sweater was designed with a pattern of wide-eyed owls.

I already knew that any final decisions about Rossiter's Field would first have to go through a consultation with the Mi'kmaq Alliance. Tamara Tuplin made it very clear from the start that she had no influence over those decisions. The Great Boat Party was not part of that process and remained a separate entity, although partisan to an obvious degree, but she did have a sense of how things were done and how decisions were made. More intriguing to her was why the Jewish community was interested in Rossiter's Field in the first place.

"They aren't," I said. "But I am."

"I thought you represented them."

"I do," I said. "I'm the one who is pushing this project along and the PEIJC has allowed me to be their spokesman, in regards to the proposed synagogue."

"So why are you interested in Rossiter's Field?"

I thought about the arguments I had used when pitching the idea to the Collective, Fagin's and Shylock's arguments of Opportunity and Principle, which I had repurposed by the seat of my pants at the PEIJC annual meeting. I considered rehashing all that for Tamara Tuplin and I might have done it convincingly, except for the fact that they would have fallen flat in this instance.

"The synagogue can't be built anywhere else."

"Why not?"

"The Supreme One decrees it."

The sound of a drill droned in the background and her expression of confusion was followed by a half grin that quickly inverted into a disbelieving frown.

"Say that again?"

"The Supreme One has decreed that the synagogue must be built on Rossiter's Field."

"Who is the Supreme One?" she asked. "I've heard of rabbis and cantors, but not that."

"I'm not talking about a rabbi. It's not a person."

"Okay." She tried to remain dispassionate. "So, when you say the Supreme One, you mean..." Her eyes glanced upward.

I nodded. "Yeah, I mean..." I repeated her upward glance.

"And this Supreme One told you that the synagogue has to be built on Rossiter's Field?"

"Not directly," I admitted with an open-handed gesture that implied therein lies a tale.

"Can you elaborate on that?"

I knew it was now or never and decided to dive in headfirst, hoping what I was about to say seemed not too far-fetched, or at least not to make myself look too much like an escapee from the local booby hatch. I then launched into an abridged account of my history with the three Figs while still hitting all the salient points: them being sent by the Supreme One, the plan to make PEI the new Promised Land, the whole schmear.

Tamara listened patiently. If I wasn't mistaken, there were traces of amusement amidst the expressions of dismay, shock and disbelief that flitted across her moon-shaped face. I could tell when what she was hearing affected her by the intensity with which she swivelled back and forth in her chair. When I was done, she stopped swivelling and fixed me with an unwavering stare.

"Is this a joke?"

"Sometimes I'm not so sure it isn't," I said. "Other times I wish to hell it was."

"Zaina didn't mention any of this to me," said Tamara Tuplin. "I'm not sure what I would've thought if she did."

"Same thing you think now," I said. "That I'm some kind of fruitcake."

"You're some kind of something, that's for sure."

"In any case, don't blame Zaina. She doesn't know any of this. You're the only one I've told so far."

As much as Tamara tried to keep a straight face, I could see a trace of fear in her eyes.

"Why me?" she asked.

This was a good question and I had to admit to myself that I didn't have an immediate answer. The only thing I knew was that it felt unspeakably good to finally tell somebody. I actually felt myself physically relax, slumping comfortably in what was already a comfortable chair.

"To be honest, I hadn't planned on it," I said. "Please don't take this the wrong way, but I guess a part of me thought..."

"Thought what?"

"I don't know," I said. "I hoped maybe an Indigenous person might be more open-minded about such a story. After all, how different is the Supreme One from the Creator?"

"I see," she said. "Well, speaking as an *Indigenous person* I'm not actually privy to that sort of information."

"I'm sorry," I said. "I didn't mean to offend. I'll leave if you want me to."

I was halfway standing when Tamara Tuplin raised her hand for me to stop and motioned for me to sit again.

"Don't get your *gatkes* in a twist. I'm screwing with you a *bissel.* But just a bissel."

"You know Yiddish?"

"I'm not what you'd call fluent, but you wouldn't believe what you can pick up here and there."

"So, you believe me then?"

"Let's not go overboard," she said. "I don't know what to make of any of this, but you don't seem particularly dangerous. You came here to find out about Rossiter's Field, so I'll tell you as much as I know."

Tamara quickly outlined how stories passed down through countless decades told of a fertile area where many plants and herbs grew wild. In certain warmer months, it was a place to hunt small game, and in the winter its many maple trees yielded sap. Eventually, it became the site for an annual *Mawi'omi* of spiritual importance, a place to give thanks for the bounty that nature provided year-round.

Much later, the area became the site for a few different enterprises by white settlers. First there was a dairy farm, which seemed ideal because the cleared area made for a fine pasture until the cows mysteriously got sick and dried up. No reason could ever be found for this and the land was sold to become a couple of other ventures that Tamara couldn't remember, except that they failed. In the Mi'kmaw community, there spread the belief that the area was cursed for anyone who built on it because the land was not being used for its intended purpose. Nevertheless, it was finally sold cheap (due to the rumours of bad luck) to a man named Abner Rossiter who built a granary there.

Contrary to the area's history of bad luck, the granary prospered for a number of years before it too finally succumbed to misfortune and burnt to the ground. I had heard this story in various forms, that the mystery of the fire had something to do with money or a love affair gone bad. The version Tamara told me combined the two and added something new.

Supposedly, in the course of expanding the business, Abner Rossiter incurred enormous debts. At the same time his wife, a younger woman he'd brought over from England, was known to be having numerous extramarital affairs. It was rumoured that her latest in a long string of lovers was a Mi'kmaw fisherman. The way Tamara told it, many believed that Abner himself was responsible for setting the fire in order to use the insurance to pay off his debts. Unfortunately, his wife died in the fire and so what might have been a simple case of arson became a matter of manslaughter and possibly murder. There was some suspicion that Abner was killing two birds with one stone (so to speak), not only to recoup the insurance but also to punish his wife for her infidelities.

Somehow, he managed to make it look like her alleged lover, the Mi'kmaw fisherman, had done the crime as retribution for Abner breaking up his affair with Mrs. Rossiter. With the prevailing prejudice at the time, it wasn't hard to make that far-fetched charge stick and the fisherman was convicted, jailed and ultimately hanged.

"The fisherman's name was Ned Tuplin," Tamara said. "He was a great-great-uncle of mine. The rumours of bad luck began again, having a restless ghost wandering through the area. When I was active in the Enviro Party some entrepreneur from Montreal bought up the land. He had all these big ideas about turning the area into some kind of eco-tourist theme park or something like that and wanted the party's help with getting building permits. Turns out, he was trying to build time-share vacation homes and already had some interest from investors who'd given him money. When the PEI Regulation Appeals Committee started to investigate him, he suddenly took off and no one knows where he is. Some holding company then took ownership, but they just sat on their hands while the vegetation grew wild over the decades and eventually it just became a convenient dumping ground."

Tamara's image of "a hungry ghost wandering through the area" reminded me of the spectral figure lurking in my sketch of Rossiter's Field, the image of Zaina that I had drawn even when I wasn't aware of it. Again, I wondered why

I chose to reveal my secret to Tamara Tuplin when it was Zaina who could see the ten-armed starfish. Logic would dictate that I should tell her about the three Figs and the Supreme One before I told anyone else. But logic (as I know it anyway) had no place in whatever was going on. In some way, I may have been hedging my bets in telling Tamara Tuplin. Maybe I was somehow trying to sabotage this whole thing by telling her. Or maybe I needed to test the veracity of these delusions by unburdening myself to a complete stranger.

"A man without land is nobody," she said.

"What?"

"It's a line from that book by Mordecai Richler."

"*The Apprenticeship of Duddy Kravitz*," I said, remembering that this is what Duddy's zaide tells him, which Duddy later recalls as, a man without land is nothing. A subtle distinction that may say a lot about Duddy's psychology. Possibly mine too. "What about it?"

"All that trash is sitting on sacred ground, you know," she said. "And now you're saying... how did you put it? The Supreme One? Told you to build a synagogue there?"

"Didn't tell me directly."

"Right, right, these figments of your imagination." She rubbed her chin for a moment. "I couldn't help thinking of that book. Duddy's desperation for that land, to impress his grandfather, to build on and make something of himself."

"That's not what this is about," I said, unable to keep the edge out of my voice, since her remark seemed to echo Frieda's accusation that I was building the synagogue merely to impress Zaina. "I'm not trying to impress anyone. To be truthful, I think the whole thing should stay a garbage dump."

"It's a very Jewish theme is all I'm saying," she said, motioning for me to calm down. "The search for a homeland. It's a universal theme. But if Richler had been an Indian, he might have written it the other way around. A land without man is nowhere."

"I don't understand."

"The sacredness of Rossiter's Field, or at least what it was many years ago, was all about teaching us our connection to the earth. A land without people has no purpose until we are there to learn how to live on it, how to grow food and use its gifts. How to respect it and, in turn, respect ourselves. The land is here to nurture the sacred part of ourselves. The land cultivates us the same way we learn to cultivate it."

I let that buzz around my brain for a moment. "Could that include building a synagogue on it?"

"It wouldn't necessarily exclude it," she said.

"So where does that leave us?"

"It depends on what you're bringing to the table," she said without taking her eyes off me.

I wasn't sure at first what she meant, but it was clear that the spiritual, historical and philosophical parts of this meeting were over. It was now down to some plain old quid pro quo. I spoke about how a synagogue would galvanize the Jewish community, explaining further that a synagogue on Rossiter's Field could be seen as a potent symbol of the sacredness that the area once represented. I added that I noticed how the Great Boat Party's approval rating was slowly climbing in the polls, partly due to her outspokenness against Reuben Arsenault and his plan to build a children's camp there. If she publicly lent her support for a synagogue to be built on Rossiter's Field it could very well result in votes from the Jewish community at the upcoming election. I said I would speak to members of the PEI Jewish Collective on her behalf.

Tamara indicated that this sounded reasonable. To seal the deal, she offered me one of the last two Bannock Bruschettas on the plate. I took it gratefully. If all her son's food was this good, I predicted great success in his future.

"This is nothing," she said. "You should try his smoked eel sliders."

SHYLOCK, FAGIN AND JUDAS were waiting for me at home. The last time I'd seen them, they were at each other's throats, but judging by the looks on their faces they had found a common enemy to unite against.

"Have you gone flippin' barmy?" Fagin growled before I had a chance to get my parka off. "You made a right bollocks of it this time!"

"What did I do?"

"You stuck it to us good. Tipped our hand. Let the barkin' cat out of the bag."

"You mean I told someone about you three? What about it?"

"It weren't just us you shopped, my dear," Fagin said.

"Thou uttered the Supreme One's name and divulged the ultimate objective to make this ruby isle the new Promised Land." Shylock added.

"And? What's the problem?"

"Thou opened thyself to a posture most disadvantaged."

"I'm pretty sure she didn't believe me."

"All the more, good cousin, 'twas an unwise decision."

"I don't see why."

"Our presence was s'posed to be for your eyes and ears only," cried Fagin.

"Make not a pointing finger the rule of thumb, lest best laid plans to ruin succumb."

"A pithy verse, good cousin," I said in my best plummy accent. "But in this case, I'd say, loose lips good risk. Sorry, I'm not much of a poet but you get the idea."

I waited for the third voice to chime in and glanced over to see Judas's back. He was standing in front of my easel, studying the ten-armed starfish, which I no longer bothered to keep hidden. Just when I assumed I was going to escape any reproach from him, he turned to me and stood aside so I had a clear view of the starfish. If he was just going to stand there like a pencil salesperson on a street corner, I saw no reason to entertain his silence. I turned to leave just as he cleared his throat.

"Can a risk ever be good when one does not understand the deeper consequences?" he asked. I looked from him to the starfish, whose ten arms now took on a more sinister depiction of those unknown consequences. "Had it occurred to you that this risk you took will push you in many different directions? For every action there may be more than one reaction in a universe that is constantly in motion."

Indignation coursed through my veins and made my blood boil like liquid in a laboratory's glass tube network. "In the world where I live, you can only go in one direction at a time and considering what I have had to deal with, I'd say that I've been pushing forward against all odds. And if any of you don't like the job I've been doing, you are welcome to take over instead of just criticizing from the sidelines."

The three of them merely looked at each other with puzzled expressions. I wasn't sure if my outburst had taken them by surprise. Perhaps they didn't expect me to demonstrate that I actually had a spine. After a moment, I concluded that they were considering what to do next. Judas pressed his hands prayer-style against his lips before speaking again.

"Did you not stop to think why this lowly creature has grown these extra appendages?"

He gestured toward the starfish.

"And did you not wonder why your Mohammedan ally was suddenly able to see it, when you thought no one else could?"

"Umm, yes," I said. "I just didn't..."

"Didn't what?" snapped Fagin. "Didn't think it mattered a tick so you could go blundering ahead?"

"What Fagin struggles so valiantly to express, signor, is that these twin phenomena hath been made apparent to you as guideposts."

"Guideposts to what?" I shouted. "To the deteriorating state of my mental health?"

"Just the opposite," said Judas. "Think of these extra appendages as proof that your mission does not merely impact the Jewish community, but has much wider implications. And the reason your Moham..."

"Zaina!" I interrupted. "Her name is Zaina."

"Of course," Judas said in a deferential tone. "The reason Zaina was allowed to see the creature was indeed to assure you that you were not losing your mental faculties. But you must understand that it is the Supreme One who makes these decisions. These things must be done with great delicacy, rather than divulging them thoughtlessly."

I had to admit his explanation was doing its intended job of mollifying me until that last sentence. Something in me resented its patronizing tone. I resented being kept in line when my methods, slapdash as they may have been, were actually getting the job done so far. "I may not be delicate," I said. "But apparently I'm all you've got."

THE CAMPAIGN HEATED up as Christmas approached. Party leaders gave speeches and held rallies, often mixing in holiday messages with political promises. They spoke at charity drives, pancake breakfasts and bowl-a-thons for literacy. Reuben Arsenault served lunch at a local soup kitchen, handing out plates of turkey and mashed potatoes with sleeves rolled and a handshake for everyone in line. In speeches, he praised the Island's "mosaic of cultures" and declared what united all was "the right and privilege of wishing each other Merry Christmas" while still acknowledging diverse beliefs and traditions. The remark was quoted in both the *Charlottetown Parrot* and the *Summerside Echo*. There followed a number of letters to the editor, some criticizing the remark as chauvinistic and pandering. But there were far more letters of support, claiming that Reuben's sentiments represented the true spirit of Island life and its Christian values.

I had received an invitation to a Hanukkah celebration that was being held this year at the home of Professor Stepan Markowitz. Since all holidays celebrated by the PEI Jewish Collective were by nature potlucks, I was encouraged to bring something. Normally I might have turned to Frieda Greenglass for some help, but I hadn't been in touch with her since she confronted Zaina and me at Café Istanbul. It had been a little over a month and I was nervous about seeing her at the Hanukkah celebration but hoped it might prove to be an occasion to get back into her good graces. That's why I was grateful yet reluctant when Zaina offered to come to my rescue by volunteering to make hummus from her mother's recipe. If Frieda found out that Zaina had made my contribution, there could be a scene, which I was most eager to avoid. As a compromise, Zaina said she would teach me how to make it and therefore I could honestly say I had made it with my own hands. I considered just buying some hummus, but Zaina's withering look quickly put the kibosh on that notion.

It was my first time in her apartment. The furnishings were sparse but elegant, the main focus of the living room being a beautiful Lebanese tapestry – a peacock fanning out into shades of turquoise and ruby and lavender – that took up almost a full wall. Zaina explained that it was a wedding present from her parents and the only thing she insisted on taking when she separated from Reuben. While the apartment itself was not that spacious, it did boast a beautiful hardwood floor and a real kitchen from which a starchy, but not entirely unpleasant smell wafted. These were the dry chickpeas that had been soaking overnight then brought to a boil with a teaspoon of baking soda and were now simmering. The kitchen was almost the same size as the rest of the apartment with plenty of counter space, over which copper pots and pans hung rustically, and medium oak cabinets with brushed metal handles. She said it was the kitchen that sold her on the apartment.

I was feeling self-conscious and tried to cover it with idle chit-chat about my meeting with Tamara Tuplin, most of which I had already gone over with Zaina, except of course for the whole part about the Figs and the Supreme One. Since Zaina had originally set up the meeting, I'd been worried that Tamara told her everything I had said. But Zaina made no mention of anything to me, so I assumed everything in the meeting remained confidential.

"I only hope I can convince everyone at the party tonight that Tamara is on our side."

As she listened politely, I pondered the possibility of telling her everything. The weird thing was that, as easily as it was to spill the beans to Tamara Tuplin and as relieved as I felt afterward about baring my secret, the idea of telling Zaina filled me with terror.

Having thought about it for a couple of days, I rationalized that telling Tamara was a calculated risk, a way to make her listen to me. It was all business-like in its own wonky way. The worst she could have done was throw me out of her office, in which case I could have laughed it all off and claimed that I was making a joke to break the ice. Telling Zaina was a different matter altogether. I liked her and I wanted her to like me. I was afraid of scaring her off.

"Samson, don't worry about the party," she said in a soothing, albeit slightly bored tone. "They are already on your side. Your meeting with Tamara went well. That's all they need to know and you can build on that."

Her hastiness to reassure me seemed to be a polite way of changing the subject, or at least to get me to stop sounding like a broken record. Zaina had been busy herself the past few days. She did volunteer work with the Island

Welcoming Society, an organization that helped people who chose to make PEI their home, mostly those from different countries and cultures, settle into life here. Through some connections with Canadian Immigration Services, she had heard about a Druze family in Lebanon who wanted to settle here and she decided to get personally involved in securing a place for them to live. The family was a husband, wife, two girls, who were young teens, and a ten-year old boy.

My initial reaction (and I'm not proud to admit this) was to feel slightly crestfallen. She had been so supportive about the synagogue and had given me such encouragement that I was sorry to see her so enthusiastic about something else. In the split second it took me to recognize how selfish I was being, I did everything I could to reciprocate all that support and enthusiasm. Still, what little I knew of the Druze, specifically that they were a tightly knit community, compelled me to raise some obvious questions.

"Wouldn't it be difficult for them here?" I asked. "Do we have any Druze on PEI?"

"Of course, I've thought of that," Zaina answered, sharply at first. Her voice softened as she continued. "I realize that PEI might just be an entry point for them. There are Druze communities in larger cities and they will want to ultimately be with their own kind. On the other hand, maybe they could be the start of a Druze community here. If they stayed, maybe more would come."

I merely nodded and grinned thoughtfully, all the while wishing I could take her in my arms and make her feel safe.

"It would be difficult for them to be so isolated from their community," she said. "But I could help them."

"And they could help you?" I said, trying to keep the softness in my voice so it wouldn't sound critical.

"I know I'm being a bit selfish."

"No, not at all," I insisted. "You're the least selfish person I know."

There was a moment of awkward silence and it occurred to me that if this were a film or a play, now would be the moment for me to take her hand or put my arm around her or some kind of gesture of physical intimacy. Zaina was obviously aware of it too, because she abruptly stood. The timer beeped and she said the chickpeas were ready. "Time to make hummus," she announced with sudden cheerfulness. She wasn't able to totally cover the relief in her voice and I admit, far from regretting a missed opportunity, I also experienced a wave of relief.

AFTER THE BOMBARDMENT of snow and plummeting temperatures that had marked the beginning of December, we were later rewarded with some milder weather and drizzle that melted the snow into grayish patches where dead brown grass and slushy pavement were now visible. A sky drained of colour struggled to exude signs of watery sunlight as if being strained through cheesecloth. After leaving Zaina's place I returned home to have a nap that did little to refresh me. After a shower I put on a denim shirt, a plum-coloured woolen knit tie, tan corduroys and navy blazer (an outfit I had worn only on a handful of occasions in all my eighteen years on PEI). Soon I was back in the car and motoring my way to Stepan Markowitz's home in Cornwall with a Rubbermaid container filled with hummus as well as another smaller container of sliced carrots, celery, broccoli and cucumber sitting in the back seat.

I'd been thinking about the Druze family that Zaina was trying to bring over and the whole question of self-interest in what essentially was an act of kindness. PEI was not an easy place to make a living and the odds of this family settling here were 50/50 at best. I myself had been managing to eke a frugal living off the dwindling interest from my cashed-in Israel bonds, an inheritance from my father's will and the odd commission through connections I'd made after winning the NovaBank Art Award. I hadn't sold a painting in over a year, but my rent at the Body Parts remained reasonable enough and thankfully, I only had myself to worry about. I couldn't imagine what it would be like to raise a family, especially in a strange place where you didn't speak the language.

If the Druze family eventually left the Island to live in Toronto or Montreal, what would that do to Zaina? I knew she had a good enough heart to wish them the best and move on with her life. But I knew the idea that they might stay and start a Druze community on PEI was close to her heart, which forced me to look at my own evolving feelings about getting this synagogue built.

For the most part, it felt like a burden foisted upon me, something that needed to get done quickly so I could get back to my regular life. At the same time, it seemed a task so insurmountable as to make Sisyphus's uphill boulder struggle look like a frolic in the park. Yet, with each small inroad I made, such as winning over the PEI Jewish Collective, handling Chet Affleck's gotcha questions during my radio interview and striking up an association with Tamara Tuplin, the synagogue became more like a point of pride. At first it felt as if it was sucking up all of my creative energy, but lately it was feeding it.

Sometimes I wondered if I would ever paint again and was more than a tad startled to discover that I didn't care, as if all the canvasses that were strewn all around my apartment existed in a parallel world of the distant past that I could see but was beyond my concern. Even the unfinished painting that still sat on my easel and was dominated by the image of a ten-armed starfish captured my state of mind (a frenetic yet energized feeling of going in all directions at once) and lately offered a strange sensation of comfort, allowing me to feel reconciled (dare I say happily?) with my lot in life.

It was 4:00 when I walked with the containers of hummus and crudité cradled in both arms along Warwick Lane, situated in an upscale residential part of Cornwall lined with red maples and white birches. There was no sidewalk, but the road was clear enough. The sky was starting to darken and the air was clean and crisp. Each breath emitted a slightly bluish-grey spectre of steam. I could see a porch light shining in the distance, but I took my time and savoured this brief period of personal quiet before the practicalities and politesse of the evening's socializing began.

Stepan Markowitz and his wife Ilana, a handbag designer with her own line on Etsy, lived in a charming modern bungalow with rustic plank-styled siding painted a mustard yellow that was common to many Island homes. It was topped by a slanted aluminum roof that allowed accumulated snow to slide off effortlessly when it became soft and wet, which sometimes resulted in mini avalanches that Stepan complained sounded like the real thing. A long walkway of tessellated grey and coral sandstone led to the porch. I was greeted at the door by their teenage daughter Judith, who relieved me of my contribution to the Hanukkah edibles. I took off my paint-spattered shoes and added them to the other galoshes, boots and outdoor footwear jostling for position on a row of plastic mats in the foyer. Judith quickly returned and led me to the master bedroom where I took off my parka and laid it on the mound of coats already growing on the queen-sized bed. I soon found my hosts in the kitchen, where an array of dishes brought by the other guests was laid out on a long table. Ilana gave me a plate and said to help myself. I piled my plate with latkes, cold cuts, beet salad, eggplant tagine, cabbage rolls and fresh challah. There were also plenty of traditional desserts, including *sufganiyot* (jelly-filled donuts), rugelach (rolled up pastry with apricot and raspberry fruit filling) and sugar cookies. There was a small line-up of people holding bowls by the stove where Frieda Greenglass was ladling out soup with her own homemade gluten-free potato-based matzo balls (an item which I'd heard was becoming a big seller at her Latke Lady stall at the Farmers' Market). I tried to catch her eye, but she was too engrossed in her ladling duties to notice.

I wandered into the living room where blue and silver streamers with paper Stars of David, menorahs and dreidels were festooned around the walls and ceiling. Every inch of couch and chair space was already taken. Many people were standing and I managed to find a portion of wall by the large picture window looking out at the now streetlamp-lit road. Most people had clustered into small groups, so I was resigned to eating my food peacefully while others engaged in conversations. Much to my surprise, some of the guests, many of whom I recognized from the AGM, quickly gravitated toward me and soon I was holding court within my own group. Many had heard the radio interview and congratulated me on how well I handled myself. Soon more people, including Stepan and Ilana Markowitz, gathered round and this presented itself to be an opportune time to talk about my meeting with Tamara Tuplin.

I tried to paint a positive picture of the importance of the Mi'kmaw claims on Rossiter's Field and having Tamara as an ally. When someone suggested that if the Mi'kmaq don't want a synagogue built on their land then we could just build elsewhere, I quickly countered that there was still a cultural advantage to having our house of worship there. The Jewish community would be seen as being culturally sensitive, assuming we got the Mi'kmaq Alliance's okay. That was why my meeting with Tamara Tuplin was an important step, I went on to explain, and why a show of support for The Great Boat Party, which had candidates in Cornwall and Stratford as well as a couple of other ridings with significant Jewish populations, could make all the difference. Hearing myself glibly rattle off this line of reasoning gave me the odd sensation of detachment, as if I was operating on automatic pilot. The old Samson, who, during almost any social situation, could be found hiding off in a corner somewhere, watched me with a mixture of wonder, envy and mild disdain.

"But Reuben Arsenault is the one who is promising to clean up Rossiter's Field in the first place," said a familiar voice in the back of the room. "Doesn't it stand to reason that he should get our vote?"

Everyone turned and I could see it was Frieda Greenglass who spoke. She stood at the living room entrance with soup ladle still in hand.

"Except he hasn't shown any support for building a synagogue there," I countered. "So far anyway. The Mi'kmaq have been making significant inroads with their land claims. I'd say we would be in a better position to align ourselves with them."

"But will the Jewish vote for The Great Boat Party ensure that support?" asked Ilana Markowitz.

I paused theatrically and rubbed my chin thoughtfully (while the old me looked on, as if from the vantage point of an out-of-body experience, and tried not to retch with disgust). "There are no guarantees," I said. "But between Jews voting for a progressive grass roots Mi'kmaw party or a conservative mainstream businessman, which would you say might play better in the media?"

I was worried that I was pushing it too hard, but luckily there was laughter. Stepan good-naturedly reminded us that this was not a political rally and that it was time to light the first Hanukkah candle. Everyone's attention turned to a beautiful frosted glass menorah sitting on a bookshelf. It was very modern looking, made up of basic geometrical shapes. The base was a half-circle set on a rectangle and each of the nine candle holders were triangles. Ilana fit a candle in the centre holder, which was set higher than the other holders This candle was the *shamash*, or attendant candle, which was used solely to light the other candles over the course of the eight nights. Then she set a candle in the far-left holder, which of course represented this first night of Hanukkah. She lit the shamash and Stepan took it in his hand and said the prayer for the first night in both Hebrew and English.

"Blessed are You, O Lord our God, Ruler of the Universe, Who has sanctified us with Your commandments and commanded us to kindle the lights of Hanukkah.

"Blessed are you, O Lord our God, Ruler of the Universe, Who made miracles for our forefathers at this time.

"Blessed are you, O Lord our God, Ruler of the Universe, Who has kept us alive, sustained us and brought us to this season."

When the first candle was lit, we all repaired to the kitchen to replenish our plates. Stepan opened some bottles of wine and glasses were filled. Traditional songs, such as *The Dreidl Song* and *Ner Li (I Have a Candle)* were being sung. Not having a taste for wine or singing, I filled my plate with some sweet treats and mingled with the others. At some point in the evening, I felt a hand on my shoulder and a voice close to my ear saying, "You have all the answers, don't you." I turned to see Frieda Greenglass holding a glass of wine. The hand on my shoulder was there solely to steady herself. Obviously, this was not her first glass.

"Answers? Me?" I feigned an innocent look. "I'm still trying to figure out the questions."

"You don't fool me for a minute," she said. "This whole synagogue crusade. You're up to something."

"Have you eaten anything?" I asked. "Too much wine on an empty stomach..."

"Don't worry about me," she said. "I'm not driving tonight anyway."

"Kia on the fritz again?"

"That hunk of junk is ready for the scrapyard," she sighed and downed the rest of her wine. "I had to shlep over here with all my food in a taxi."

"Don't worry," I said. "I'd be happy to give you a ride home."

She made a face as if she was deigning to consider my offer. "In that case," she said. "Another glass of wine is definitely in order."

"Is that really a good idea?"

"I'm going to find out your secret, Samson. Believe you me... me... you." She tried to look me in the eye, but it was obvious her vision was starting to lose its ability to focus. "You know what they say, *in vino veritas*. And since you're not drinking, then it's all up to me."

I couldn't hold Frieda's suspicious nature against her. In her place I'd probably be thinking the same thing. This whole synagogue crusade. Is that what it was? To what end? After it was built would I start actually attending this synagogue with all these good people? Or would I leave them all behind and go back to being my same old reclusive non-observant self? For someone who supposedly had all the answers it was clear to me that I didn't have a clue as to what I was doing or where I was going.

Stepan Markowitz noticed I wasn't drinking. He went to the fridge and produced a bottle of Beirsto's IPA. Being told I didn't care for wine (by who? Frieda Greenglass maybe?), he had bought a case of twelve. I took the beer gratefully and happily imbibed. I figured one bottle couldn't hurt. He insisted that I help myself and what I didn't drink that evening I could take home, since he wasn't much of a beer drinker himself. I thanked him, took a swig from the bottle and decided to enjoy the rest of the evening.

I don't have a clear recollection of how the rest of the evening went. I remembered getting involved in a few conversations. There was more singing and I'm pretty sure some dancing. I do recall helping to move furniture aside to make some space in the living room where we managed to dance the Hora in two concentric circles moving in opposite directions. After dancing clockwise, then counter-clockwise for a while, I definitely needed to get my bearings and decided it was time to leave. I packed the containers I brought, as well as what Frieda had *schlepped* over in the taxi, not to mention the rest of the Beairsto's IPAs. I'd had a couple of beers but was relatively confident I could get us to her house in one piece.

The next morning, opening my eyes was a bit of a chore and my tongue felt like it had spent the night in one of those fruit dehydrators that are always being hawked on infomercials. I knew the best thing would be to try and sleep for a while longer, except for a strange sound close by. I couldn't quite figure out what it was at first and I sat up groggily to have a look around. Slowly, I began to recognize the unfamiliarity of where I was. This definitely wasn't my room. And that noise was coming from a shape under the blanket beside me. Suddenly there was movement and the figure rolled over. There beside me was Frieda Greenglass snoring loud enough to put a buzz saw to shame.

12

"WE SHOULDN'T BE doing this. We shouldn't." These words were the clearest memory I had of what happened the previous night. That they were spoken by Frieda Greenglass was a given at first, although my own voice easily replaced hers as the words came back to me, often unbidden, during the next couple of days. There were even times I'm sure we said them together, their cautionary tone morphing into something more titillating and gaining in urgency (or am I making that up?) as things moved beyond the point of no return. Her voice whispering, "We shouldn't be doing this." And mine answering, "We shouldn't."

Sure, alcohol played a role, but only as a lubricant for the cogs of a deeper and more intricate mechanism. As I carefully snuck out of Frieda Greenglass's bed that morning, I wanted to believe that I was actually making a getaway. Gathering up my clothes strewn across her bedroom floor in a breadcrumb trail that led to her living room, where a half-empty (such was my state of mind) bottle of Beairsto's IPA sat on her coffee table like a lone bowling pin waiting to be knocked down, I dressed quickly and quietly as possible. I half-expected Frieda to catch me at the last minute and demand to know where the hell I thought I was going. Or would she have been as embarrassed as I was? Could she even have been feigning sleep until I had hightailed it out of there? Were we going to have to face each other sooner or later or was this some drunken episode that would best be forgotten between us? When I finally made it inside the Golf, I took one last look and swore I could see the drapes behind her front window rustling slightly before turning the ignition and making the long drive back to Mount Russet.

"'Tis a strange turn of events, good cousin, wouldst thou agree?" Shylock grinned in the passenger's seat. "Or in good faith, might this amorous junction be following an inevitable course?"

"What do you mean inevitable?"

"Wouldst thou not admit, even in thy most intimate ruminations, a constant cloud hath cast the shadow of incomplete circumstance between thee and this lady?"

Me and Frieda destined to make the beast with two backs? My kneejerk reaction was to snub the idea as a matter of principle. But the funny thing about ideas that are ridiculous at the outset, they have a way of burrowing into one's consciousness, thus giving them the last laugh.

"Forsooth, the question of a shared dark history can play fancily on whims of desire."

A flash of memory came back to me at that moment. We hadn't left the Markowitz home yet. I think I went into the master bedroom to get my parka from the pile of coats on the bed. I'd only had a couple of Beairsto's IPAs by that time. Suddenly Frieda was in the bedroom too, also looking for her coat. She kept talking about the way I looked at her sometimes, how she could see the fear in my eyes, how she knew we shared something dark in both of us. What she called intergenerational trauma, which I'd heard of but knew little about. I understood she was referring to her father and my zaide, our relationships with them and how we, not only experienced, but inherited their suffering in our own different ways.

Then she confessed that when she was a teenager, she used to cut herself. This was still the 1960s, when that sort of thing wasn't spoken of the way it was later. She told me that once her father caught her and flew into a rage. He rolled up his sleeve to show her the tattooed numbers on his left arm. Then he took the blade from her and threatened to cut those same numbers into her arm. He'd grabbed her and made like he was about to do it. Her wailing had alerted her mother, who intervened. The story shocked me and at that moment I wanted to take her in my arms, even though the idea of doing so shamed me somehow.

"Whether her father was somehow responsible for sending my grandfather to Auschwitz is moot at best," I said to Shylock. "Who knows what hopeless situation Rabbi Greenglass was in? When it comes to Nazis, your back is always against the wall, either being forced to collude or facing a firing squad. Zaide Jakob was in a transit camp. He was heading somewhere, one way or another, with or without Frieda's father's involvement."

"Thou couldst not conjure a better portrait of reasonable justification if thou hadst brush and paint at hand," Shylock said in a manner too obsequious for me not to hear the underlying mockery. "Yet something quelled passion's flames lo that eve long past. Doused and yet not drowned enow to extinguish a secret ember, glittering with muted tenderness ere lust's liquors aroused its heat."

I cast my mind back to that first and last date with Frieda so many years ago. Once the spectre of whether her father was somehow responsible for sending my grandfather to Auschwitz was raised in my mind, I knew the seemingly inevitable conclusion to that evening was off the table. But if I was to be brutally honest with myself, it wasn't that I had lost any carnal interest in Frieda Greenglass. If anything, the rawness of the situation aroused me, even as I was simultaneously repulsed by it. I shuddered to think how it could have gone one way or another, like a flipped coin landing on its edge waiting for any wind blowing ill or good to cast the deciding vote. In the end I gave into fear more than disgust, or rather the disgust was with myself. So was the fear. I didn't hate Frieda Greenglass for being a product of a history she had no hand in. Truth be told, and I could never quite own up to it until this moment in the car with Shylock, I was inundated with self-loathing for having wanted to ravage Frieda then and there as an act of revenge for what her father might have done to my zaide.

Was this what had happened last night? And even if it was Frieda who had initiated things, it didn't change the ugliness of this self-revelation. I was stunned by a glimpse of vengeful cruelty in my own character and it shook me to my inner core to such a degree that I shut the revelation down as fast as I could.

It was at this point that I had to pull over onto the shoulder of Highway 7, my vision having been suddenly impaired by a foggy, moist heat. I leaned against the steering wheel while my tear ducts considered whether they were going to well over or not. I had fulfilled my carnal retribution on Frieda Greenglass, although I could barely remember a moment of it. My body started to heave. In whatever way a dish best served vengeance might be, cold, hot or lukewarm, it now threatened to come up unceremoniously like bad chicken salad.

"Cousin? Prithee, breathe softly and let thy lungs be like wings upon which thou sweetly may be borne to peace and equanimity."

His advice, and the genuine concern with which he solicited it, was enough to let me get my bearings and stem the flow of hot salty liquid from my eyes, not to mention whatever frothy bile was currently burning my oesophagus. I inhaled steadily through my nose, exhaling through gently puckered lips. I noticed that Shylock was staring past me, his attention caught by something through my driver's side window. I turned to whatever had caught his eye and saw a police car positioned by the barrier blocking Rossiter's Way. I decided it was probably best not to linger but Shylock stopped my hand from turning the ignition key. He wasn't so much staring at the cop car as listening to something. "Hark," he said in a half whisper. I listened but could not hear whatever he was attuned to. I opened my door and eventually my ears detected something in the distance. The sound of machinery,

"That sounds like it might be coming from Rossiter's Field," I said. "Could they really have started the clean up? Who authorized it? Where did the money come from?"

"And yet a most pervasive phenomenon is afoot, signor."

"What do you mean?"

"Canst thou not sense it?" Shylock opened the passenger door and stepped outside. I followed suit.

"What is it?" I asked.

"A change, good cousin, a permutation of the atmosphere. Those rumblings in the distance are but a mere symptom of some grander hastening taking place. Hast thou not felt it deep in thy bone and sinew?"

"Come to think of it, I did feel something strange."

At that moment I could hear a car slowly approaching, driving up Rossiter's Way. A police officer got out of the cruiser and moved the barrier so the car could pass through. As it made its turn onto the highway, I glimpsed the driver's face and recognized him as a reporter for the *Charlottetown Parrot*. There was another man in the passenger's seat, but I couldn't get a good look before they sped up. The policeman returned the barrier to its place and stood looking at us before returning to the cruiser. When he started writing something in his notebook, I took it as a cue to continue the drive back to the Body Parts.

ON THE FRONT PAGE of the next day's edition of the *Charlottetown Parrot* was a photo of men in hard hats and orange vests, along with some heavy machinery, hard at work on Rossiter's Field with the headline: *Cleanup Crew*. When asked to comment, the leaders of the other opposition parties denounced the clean-up, in their own ways, as an unabashed campaign stunt by the Arsenault-led Loyalist government that would shut down after the election was over. The insinuated assumption was that the cost for the full clean-up would either never make it to the next provincial budget or that Rossiter's Field would be long forgotten, as it had been so many times in the past, once its political usefulness came to an end. Reuben Arsenault argued that this initial start to the clean-up, far from being a campaign stunt, was a genuine show of commitment on his part to see his campaign promise through. He vowed to finish the job, whether he became premier or not, and if he didn't accomplish anything else in his political career he would "Clean Up the Island", he pronounced, echoing his campaign slogan. The photo op did much to strengthen Reuben's electoral base, giving him the reputation of a maverick who gets things done.

In the meantime, I had been trying to contact Frieda Greenglass since our drunken Hanukkah tryst and for the first few days succeeded in only getting her voicemail at home and on her cell. When I started to worry and wondered whether I needed to go to her home or contact the authorities, she did answer in person. The conversation veered around the awkwardness of that night, but we both finally conceded that meeting in person would be the best thing so that we could discuss the situation like rational adults. I assumed we would meet somewhere in public, but Frieda suggested we spend New Year's Eve together at her place.

"Are you sure that's such a good idea?' I asked.

"What are you afraid of, Samson?" she said with feigned exasperation in her voice. "You think I'm trying to entrap you into a repeat performance?"

"No!" I insisted, a bit too emphatically. "It just feels like a weird time to hash this thing out."

"If you have other plans, I understand," she said.

"I prefer to dodge all that Auld Lang Syne hokum," I said. "I usually stay home and go to bed early."

"Me too," she said. "So, if you think about it, this is the perfect time to have this discussion. A way to clear the air for the coming new year."

I couldn't argue with her logic, so I agreed to be at her place around seven o'clock.

Christmas has always been a non-event for me and I ended up doing the usual Jewish Christmas thing and had dinner at Fusion Wok, accompanied at the last minute by Zaina and Aziza. Since that episode in the Crazy Diamond, where Aziza told me to stay out of her beeswax, we had more or less made up and resumed our friendship, although not with the same closeness that it once had.

It was a low-key, but not entirely sombre Christmas evening. I think what struck me most was the easy, almost girlish, rapport between mother and daughter, resembling nothing of the strained distance I usually witnessed between them. Aziza, in particular, was more relaxed than I'd seen her in months and I had to wonder what had changed. I mostly listened as they spoke wistfully about Aziza's childhood. It almost felt like I was eavesdropping, but I found it fascinating to get this perspective. Interestingly, or at least I felt so, Reuben was rarely mentioned and when he was it was as a peripheral character. I tried to imagine the three of them as a happy family but couldn't conjure up the image. As has often happened, it felt as if Zaina had read my mind and decided to rectify Reuben's exclusion by telling me about Aziza's first birthday.

"This was a very important occasion for us, Samson. We made a very festive party with members of both our families in attendance and our birthday girl of honour feeling right at home as the centre of attention."

Aziza shook her head. "I've heard this story so many times I feel like I actually remember the party."

Zaina continued, "We played all kinds of party games and opened presents and everybody took turns taking pictures with Aziza and each other and there was much food and drink. It was fantastic how well the two families, the Arsenaults and the Mahmouds, got along. Reuben played the proud papa and it was no act. I think it was a new experience for him and he wanted to make the most of it."

I tried to picture Reuben changing Aziza's diapers, but my usually vivid imagination came up blank.

"Of course, what is a birthday party without a cake?" Zaina laughed and so did Aziza. I got the sense we were getting to the story's main event. "I made a beautiful three-layer white angel food cake from scratch and covered it with a very thick dark chocolate butter cream frosting. There was a single candle on top and, my word of honour, Aziza blew it out all on her own."

"Even then I was full of hot air," Aziza added with a sly grin.

"After the cake was cut Aziza got her own piece and immediately picked it up and started to eat it. Very soon her face was covered in chocolate and everybody laughed and started taking pictures. I'm pretty sure this only encouraged her to smear more chocolate on her face."

From the corner of my eye, I could see Aziza's sheepish grin and the way she started to shake her head.

"Then Reuben decided to play the dutiful father and crouched down in front of Aziza's highchair with a cloth and started to clean her face. Again, everyone started to ooh and aah and take pictures. I could see that he was pleased to have people record this domestic side of him."

I couldn't help thinking that Reuben was never shy about photo ops that put him in a good light, but wisely said nothing.

"I don't know if it was to thank him or maybe he looked hungry." Zaina started laughing and for a moment I wasn't sure if she would be able to finish the story. "Anyway, Aziza took her piece of cake and tried to feed it to him. Instead, she pushed the cake into his face and got chocolate all over his face.

I think she did it quickly, because it took him by surprise. Suddenly everybody is laughing and taking photos of Reuben with chocolate all over his face. I expected, I think all of us expected him to laugh it off, but in fact he became quite angry and stormed out of the room to clean up. He was conspicuously absent from the party after that. I think he only came out to say goodbye to the guests when they were leaving."

That was the end of the story and there followed a brief but pointed silence at the table. Zaina pushed food around on her plate, all the while maintaining her smile. Aziza checked her phone. I got the sense that the story made her uncomfortable and she was relieved that it was over.

At some point during that uneventful period between Christmas and New Year, I set my laptop on my kitchenette counter to watch Anne Surly. The screen showed a light green PEI tartan and the lowercase words *please be patient...* with the ellipses lighting up and dimming while the stream was buffering. When it dissolved, I was looking at an image of Anne Surly in her usual straw hat, pigtails, opaque half mask and dominatrix bustier and boots. She was standing absolutely still in a military-like stance with legs slightly apart and her hands behind her back. I wasn't entirely sure whether I was looking at a still photograph until she finally spoke. At the top right corner of the screen, I glimpsed yesterday's date.

"Greetings to all my little dickybirds. As you can see, I am now pre-taping my little chats. This has become an increasingly necessary security measure as we move ever closer to the election in the coming new year. There are more of you out there watching and it's no secret that some of you would like to shut me up. Good luck with that. We have a lot of ground to cover, so all you bicycle seat sniffers better keep your hands where I can see them and hold tight because it's going to be a bumpy ride."

The patter hadn't changed, but her delivery was slower, more deliberate. Ever since I first started watching her, I was keenly aware of the steady honing of this Anne Surly persona. How self-assured she had become. Dispassionate, but in a way that was most compelling to watch. She still hadn't moved, and that impressed me too – the stillness she had cultivated that one sees only in consummate actors. She was definitely coming into her own as a commanding presence. I also noticed the locale had changed, although there were no clues as to where this recording was made. The vaguely rustic background was gone only to be replaced by an unadorned dark blue wall.

Then she moved her hands from behind her back to reveal a golf club, which she held with one hand and, in one swift movement, tucked under her armpit in a militaristic fashion, like a commandant's swagger stick. I remembered the club from another time I had watched her. It was definitely Lorie, the 9-iron Maggie Beairsto kept behind the bar at the Crazy Diamond. Did Maggie know about this? I thought about the story Maggie had told me of her younger days in Toronto making underground films. Was Maggie Aziza's secret webcasting partner, the one behind the camera?

It all started to make sense. And yet it made no sense at all.

"Where to start? "asked Anne Surly as she thoughtfully tapped her chin with a leather-gloved forefinger, which she then raised, pointing it upward like an exclamation mark. "I know. How about that exquisite bit of political theatre at Rossiter's Field, care of Reuben Arsenault. Of course, the sixty-four-thousand-dollar question is where did the sixty-four- thousand dollars, or however much it took to get this clean-up started, come from in the first place?"

The stance, the finger, these were new gestures, new body language, more measured and economic, displaying a maturity that, at first, was at odds with the child-like straw hat and pigtails and even the more adult bodice, gloves and boots. And yet, such was the confidence with which she controlled her body and movements that she gave the garish costume a newfound authority. I kept trying to picture Aziza under there, the easygoing person with whom I'd had dinner only a few nights before, but I couldn't see her, so completely was she hidden in this character.

"Anyone wanting to examine campaign finances or political contributions is going to be sorely disappointed. No doubt the official books are clean as a whistle. The official party line is that the cost for this start of the clean-up came out of Reuben's pocket. He claims to have the bank records and receipts to prove it and I have no doubt he can produce them if he has to. But like any sly dog, he's got bones buried in a number of different backyards and my sources say payments to one account are connected to Project Friendly

Occupation. Those of you with a grey cell or two might remember that name from my last webcast."

Chalk one up to whatever grey cells I still possessed, because I did remember. Where the grey cells got a bit more of a workout was trying to follow everything that came after, but I'll do my best to lay it out as coherently as possible. Whatever Project Friendly Occupation entailed could not be verified by Anne Surly as there was a fair bit of covert financial zigging and zagging. But it looked as if part of the financial trail was moving through Ashlynn's Camp for Kids, which was also supposed to be a cover for the state-of-the-art resort for the Blue Point Society. Except now, it had been announced that a resort, intended for the campers' visiting parents, was part of the overall plan. What could be verified, and indeed had apparently been reported in the media, was the purchase of Rossitor's Field and a good part of the surrounding area that included much of the outskirts of Mount Russet, all of which came directly from Ashlynn's Camp for Kids funds.

Funny, I'm not what you'd call a news junkie, but I don't recall reading about the added-on resort for parents or the sale of Rossiter's Field. Most likely these were not front-page items. Possibly they were buried in the back pages of the *Charlottetown Parrot* and the *Summerside Echo*, both of which I skim whenever I'm in Sadie's Tearoom. Anne Surly's revelation – not so publicly known and not entirely verified by her sources – that controlling shares of both newspapers had been bought by ShoreWire Inc., a media company whose owner sat on the board of directors of Freeland Corporation (of which the CEO was none other than Reuben Arsenault) shed at least a sliver of light, circumstantial as it was, on the matter.

The other media shoe that Anne Surly unceremoniously dropped was that Chet Affleck had stepped down as co-host of *Good Morning PEI* to become the radio station's News Editor. I had noticed for the past week that Chad Peladeau had been doing the show solo, saying that Chet was on temporary leave. I assumed that it had something to do with his growing erratic on-air behaviour. He was definitely under some strain, culminating in an impromptu rant on the price of Christmas cards as further evidence of the war on Christmas.

This time Anne Surly reported that the water cooler talk among her sources was that Chet Affleck's strange on-air behaviour had something to do with stress, related to the Blue Point Society hush-hush scandal where a young woman had OD'd and was paid off with money from Ashlynn's Camp for Kids, of which Chet was Project Director, and had now "stepped down" from that volunteer position. Anne Surly was short on the details there, but could report that Reuben Arsenault somehow, possibly through connections with the radio station's management (some of whom were purported to be members of the Blue Point Society), orchestrated Chet's move from on-air personality to the News Editor position. Perhaps that was why those particular newsworthy items, the added-on resort and the sale of Rossiter's Field, were nowhere to be heard on the daily radio news reports.

My head was starting to reel from trying to follow these squirrel droppings of information when, in summation, she returned to how Reuben was getting his ducks in a row to fulfill his campaign promise to clean up Rossiter's Field, which would clear the way to building Ashlynn's Camp for Kids and the state-of-the-art resort, which would net him a substantial financial windfall, when she added, out of nowhere:

"The only wildcard that could get in the way of Rotten Reuben's plans is reclusive artist, Samson Grief, and his proposal to have a synagogue built on Rossiter's Field, which is being supported by the PEI Jewish Collective. Could this David have the magic slingshot to knock our Goliath down to size?"

Stunned as I was to hear my name being uttered on this webcast of unsubstantiated chatter and questionable innuendo, I couldn't be sure how long I stared at the blank screen after Anne Surly signed off. What the hell was Aziza doing bringing my name into this? Did she think she was doing me a favour, giving my bid for the synagogue a bit of a push? Or was she trying to get under her father's skin? Was I being used as just another piece of cake to smush into his face?

As much as I dreaded any kind of confrontation, I was going to have to have it out with her about this. It was late and I knew she wasn't home, so, rather than waiting up for her and getting more agitated, I decided to go to bed and leave it until the morning when, hopefully after a proper night's sleep, I could speak to her more calmly. Sleep came fitfully, but the next morning I trudged up the hallway stairs to the next floor carrying a tray laden with a pot of Earl Grey and two cups, just to remind myself to keep things friendly. The door was answered by an unshaven older man in a bathrobe, who eyed the tray and its contents with some suspicion while explaining that he had moved in just the day before. Funny that I had not noticed any movers coming in and out of the building. I managed a glance into the apartment and saw the ugly green sofa still in the living room. When I questioned him about it, he grew outwardly impatient at my nosiness.

"Not that it's any of your business, but the apartment was advertised as fully furnished. Now you can bugger off to Wonderland with your little tea party," he concluded and unceremoniously slammed the door in my face.

What was going on? I'd only had dinner with Aziza not that long ago. She mentioned nothing about moving. Zaina hadn't said anything to me either. Surely, she would have known?

When I drove to the Crazy Diamond later that afternoon, fully expecting to find Aziza there, I was met with my second surprise that day: a sign on the door that read CLOSED FOR RENOVATIONS. There were no other cars in the parking lot. I wandered around, trying to look through the windows, but they were covered up from the inside with newspaper. The place looked more like it had been condemned rather than closed for renovations. Around the back I saw Pius's half-ton truck. He was sitting in the driver's seat talking on his cell phone. He didn't notice me at first. I waved but he didn't acknowledge me. I stood there, not sure of what to do. I was on the verge of walking back to the car, when he raised a finger. He still wasn't looking at me, so I wasn't sure what was going on, but he kept the finger raised so I decided that he was telling me to wait. The day was crisp and the snow on the ground patchy and gray. I shoved my hands into the pockets of my parka just as he put the cell down and got out of the truck.

"What's going on, Pius?"

"Did you see the sign on the door?" he said with a weary gruffness. "We're closed."

"The Shine Shrine too?" I asked.

"No, that's still open. It's just the front that's being done over."

"But tomorrow's New Year's Eve. You've never been closed for New Year's Eve. Why did you pick now to renovate?"

"I didn't pick nothing," he said. "None of this is my choice. It's all him that's running the show now."

"Him?" I scratched my head and thought for a moment. "Who are you talking about?"

"Reuben Arsenault, who else?"

I could see he was about to walk past me to enter into the Shine Shrine, so I stood in his way. He was surprised to see me blocking his path and his mouth tightened into a scowl. Suddenly aware of Pius's size and girth, not to mention his temper, I stepped back to keep things less aggressive and asked what the hell was going on.

"When he bought up that dumping ground at the end of Rossiter's Way, he also bought up the land we're standing on."

"Are you telling me he owns the Crazy Diamond?"

"If he owns the land then he owns what's on it," said Pius and punctuated his disgust by spitting into a patch of slush.

When Reuben let Maggie and Pius know he was now their new landlord, he made good his promise of not evicting them or raising their rent in exchange for a controlling share of the Crazy Diamond and insisted on sinking money into renovations to improve the look of the Crazy Diamond, just to show his good faith.

"I don't have to tell you, Samson, I was dead set against it," said Pius. "I told Mags I'd rather close up all together and see if we could set up shop somewhere else, start from scratch. She wouldn't have none of it. That was the last straw between us."

"What do you mean, the last straw?"

Pius kicked some snow with his work boot and dug his hands into his overall pockets.

"Thought you woulda heard by now," he said, almost under his breath so I could barely hear him. "We're separated."

"I don't understand."

"What's to understand?" he growled. "She moved out."

"Where is she?"

"Some house on the Blue Shank Road, outside of Summerside. She got the Arsenault girl living with her."

"Aziza?"

"Always knew it was a mistake hiring that one. She got Mags mixed up in all kinds of nonsense."

"What kinds of nonsense?"

Pius flung his hands out of his pockets and made a gesture of frustration, grabbing at the air where there was nothing to grab.

"Some video-taping thing they were doing. They were using the Shrine, Samson! I don't know what the hell Mags was thinking of."

"The Shrine?" I had never been inside the Shrine, no one had outside of Pius, his brothers and Maggie. And now Aziza. That must have been the rustic background from her webcasts. And this last recorded video must have been made in the house they were in now.

"I ain't got no time for jawing with you, Samson," Pius snarled. "Somebody's got to do some work around here. It's all I got to keep me from going crazy."

With that, he rushed past me, the force of his bulk like a sudden gust of wind knocking me off balance. It was all I could do not to fall ass over teakettle as I watched him enter the Shine Shrine and slam the door behind him.

Now that I knew irrefutably that Maggie was the cameraperson behind Anne Surly's later videos, probably the reason they were of better quality than Aziza's earlier self-shot webcam broadcasts, I began to wonder more about Anne Surly's preference for Lorie, the golf club, over the bamboo cane and riding crop she used to use. In past webcasts, Aziza made sure to feature the ugly green sofa, which she had taken from her father's office. It was a signal to him, since she knew he saw her webcasts. Was it purely meant as a middle finger to him or did it have some other significance? The fact that she left the sofa behind when she moved out of the Body Parts indicated that she had moved on from something. The sofa, and its significance, had outworn its usefulness. But now there was the golf club. Was it meant as a signal to me? Is that why she included my name in her rant? Was she merely using it as a provocation or did it mean something else?

And now that Reuben owned Rossiter's Field, what did that mean for the synagogue? There was no way he'd agree to it. And if the Supreme One had been pulling the strings to make him an MLA, then surely the same strings had been pulled to make him premier. What was going on? When were some strings going to be pulled for me? Instead, it was one roadblock after another.

AT FOUR O'CLOCK in the afternoon on New Year's Eve I sat in the tub with the take-out menu of Currying Flavour, Frieda Greenglass's favourite Indian restaurant on Queen Street in Charlottetown. I had promised to pick up some nibbles for our New Year's Eve supper.

"Ain't you afraid of them exotic spices getting the old girl worked up?" Fagin was sitting on my toilet seat lid, which was close enough to the tub that he could peruse the menu over my shoulder.

"Do you mind?" I said, vainly trying to obscure his view of my private personage with the fanned-out menu. "I thought even figments would be respectful of a person's privacy."

"Aw, don't be boohooing like some naff old dowager," he said. "There's nothing bobbing in your bath water that I got no interest in. Besides, ain't we chosen blokes all snipped the same under our kecks?"

A shiver ran through me at the word "snipped" and the bath water went cold. "If you're going to sit there, could you at least turn the other way?"

"Crikey," he said with an exasperated groan. "As your Majesty wishes."

He shifted himself to face the bathroom door.

"Seems your friend with the ginger braids has superadded the pressure on you," he said, half turning his head toward me so he spoke from the side of his mouth. "I'd wager a bob and a magpie she was stirring the pot as a provocation to get some reaction out of you."

"What kind of reaction?"

Fagin fiddled with the peak of his baseball cap.

"My conjecture is she's trying to expedite matters somewhat."

"Expedite?" I pondered this for a moment. "What for?"

"You got to admit things is pushing ahead and you're happy enough to lollygag here and watch others run the show."

"What do you expect me to do?"

"Me?" he exclaimed with unconvincing innocence, "I ain't got no expectations. I'm merely making an observation. You have to admit you been a tad slack when it comes to pushing ahead with our agenda."

I rattled the menu pointedly. "Well, excuse me for exercising a bit of caution. Besides, you know what they say, slow and steady..."

"You know what else they say, my dear. He who hesitates..."

"They also say fools rush in..."

I could see this trade-off of unfinished clichés was getting us nowhere.

"Besides, what can I do before Rossiter's Field is cleaned up?

"You has to show some bottle," he said. "Be more aggressive-like."

"But Judas says..."

"Never mind that holier-than-shite geezer," he snarled. "You got to stake your claim and keep the idea of the synagogue in the public's mind. That's what the girl was reminding you. Her whole David and Goliath spiel. You're the underdog in this situation, my dear. That's the position you got to use to gain the upper hand."

"That's all very well," I said. "But what's my course of action?"

The moment the question popped out of my mouth I knew instinctively there would be no answer. I turned and he was gone. I was starting to develop a second sense about the Figs' entrances and exits, as if I was getting a feel for their rhythms. As familiar as their presence was, I knew I would never altogether get used to having them in my life.

FRIEDA GREENGLASS answered the door in baggy olive-green sweats and her hair tied back in a bun. I'm not sure if she was deliberately trying to dress down for my benefit, but it was clear she was prepared for an evening of no expectations. She relieved the large paper bag of Indian food from my burdened arms.

"Did you remember the papadums?"

"Present and accounted for," I said with a salute.

As I unpacked the food on her kitchen table, Frieda laid out plates, cutlery and put the kettle on. She had bought some Darjeeling especially for this evening. She was complimentary of my choices, and I have to admit hearing compliments from Frieda made me somewhat wary, but I said nothing. Small talk accompanied the meal, but eventually we found ourselves moving inevitably into the main topic of discussion.

"I have to say, I don't remember a whole lot about that night," I admitted.

"Frankly, since we last talked, I've been thinking. Maybe we don't need to go into all this," she said. "I mean, if neither of us really remembers that much..."

"So, you don't remember either? I thought we were going to clear the air here."

"Consider it cleared."

"Why do I feel there's something you're not telling me?"

"Samson, we're having a nice little meal." Frieda's smile was a wry mixture of regret and relief as she slowly shook her head. "Maybe we should leave well enough alone."

"Okay, what aren't you telling me?"

"To be honest, it's all still a bit hazy."

"But something happened that night. What I mean to say is, we... you know?" I asked, unsure of whether I really wanted to know.

"Well, let's just say we were off to a promising start. Not that you didn't give it the old college try."

I looked down at the food on my plate without any trace of an appetite. Was my male pride affronted? Maybe a smidge. While Frieda patiently ate, I silently tried to sort through the tangle of emotions unravelling in the pit of my stomach.

"You're not eating?" she said, finally looking up at me. "It's okay, you can take some home."

I tried to cast my mind back to that night. I couldn't shake off the feeling there was still something that Frieda wasn't telling me. "How did things end?"

"Why can't you just leave well enough alone?"

"Tell me," I demanded.

Frieda pushed her plate away and proceeded to describe, as best as she could recollect, how we started making out in her living room and eventually stumbled toward the bedroom, stopping to grope in various stages of undress along the way. By the time we collapsed on her bed we had got down to the nitty-gritty, as they used to say (I think), and it looked like what had been postponed for all these years was now getting underway.

"And then... you know." To illustrate her point, she held up a green bean from the container of vegetable curry. It drooped between her thumb and forefinger. "To be fair, you had a lot of beer that night."

"Did I apologize at least?" I asked.

"Not exactly," she said, popping the limp green bean in her mouth. Apparently, the look on my face caused her to go on the defensive. "What? I touched it. I couldn't very well put it back in the container."

"Just tell me what happened."

After some obligatory hemming and hawing, she went on to tell me that, at first, I refused to give up so easily and kept trying to fulfill the act, even though my physicality refused to respond in kind. After various ministrations on Frieda's part failed to do the trick, I quickly worked myself into a frenzy of frustration until, in the end, when I knew beyond a shadow of a doubt that I could not seal the deal, I threw myself on top of her and broke down weeping, all the while calling out to my zaide over and over for forgiveness until I finally passed out in her arms.

After an indeterminate silence, I spoke. "You know, Zaide Jakob used to tell me stories about being in the camp. Little things that happened, people he met, those who lived, those who died. He said something once about the true will to survive being that moment when you can give yourself over to the idea of death. I must have been about eight or nine. I didn't understand what he meant at the time. I've thought about it every now and then over the years. There were times I thought he might have been talking about God. Not necessarily a belief in God. Even though he remained observant all his life, going to synagogue every Saturday, his faith had been shaken. I think he went to synagogue as an act of defiance, daring God to show His face. I think he felt going to synagogue might even have been a show of triumph. Not over the Nazis, but over God. God had tried him sorely, but He hadn't broken him."

"Many people lost their faith."

"Did your father?"

"Faith is the least of what my father lost."

"Do you think they met?" I asked. "You know... in Westerbork."

She searched my face. "Why? Do you?"

"I don't know," I said. "I've thought about it. After what you told me, about the newspaper story about your father."

"That story was never proven," she said.

"I know, but... it got me to thinking."

"Thinking? About what?"

"Forget it," I said. "I'm sorry I brought it up."

"No, Samson, go ahead and say it."

"Frieda, let's not..."

"You really think my father sent your zaide to Auschwitz, don't you?"

I stared at all the food that was spread out on the table between me and Frieda Greenglass. Such an excess, such a waste, such a cynical display of self-indulgence it all was when I thought of the countless people who starved throughout history and today and who will keep on starving well into the future.

"Who the hell knows what happened back there in Westerbork a million years ago?" I said. "I don't care anymore. I know now that my zaide had a will to survive because he was ready to die. And every day he went to synagogue he was saying to God: I'm still ready so where are you?"

I began to obsessively pile food on my plate the way Richard Dreyfuss piled up mashed potatoes in *Close Encounters of the Third Kind*. I started with a base of papadums then tore off strips of naan, placing those in a lattice-like pattern, and stacked beef and potato samosas on top and pakoras on top of them. All the while, Frieda looked on wide-eyed.

"What the hell are you doing?" she said.

"You know why I was begging my zaide's forgiveness?" I continued labouring without looking up at her. "Because I wasn't able to avenge him by shtupping the daughter of the man who may have sent him to Auschwitz."

She let out a low whistle. "Oy, I knew there was something twisted beneath that nebbishy look of yours, I just didn't know how twisted."

I doubled down on my efforts by spooning curry-soaked rice as mortar around my culinary edifice to keep the thing from collapsing.

"But this synagogue, the one that's going to be built on Rossiter's Field if it's the last thing I do. That is how I'm going to avenge my zaide. That is how his years of observance and waiting will be redeemed. If I build it, then God or the Supreme One or whatever He/She/It calls Himself or Herself or Itself... When that shul opens its doors, God better damn well show His face, because you know what? That son of a bitch has a lot to answer for."

13

THE ELECTION WAS HELD three weeks into the new year, while everyone was still, more or less, getting over their hangovers and trying to remember to write a new date on their cheques. Even with the foreseeable sweep by the Loyalty Party, Reuben Arsenault's victory as premier of PEI was uncharitably being described in loud whispers (within certain circles) as a coronation, echoing a sentiment by Anne Surly during one of her webcasts. It was alleged that a demarcation in riding boundaries that happened in late December was tantamount to gerrymandering. The loudest voices (and not even pretending to whisper at this point) alleging unfair electoral practices, resulting in some voter registration cards being sent to the wrong addresses, belonged to the PEI Coalition for Electoral Equality. This was a grassroots movement pushing to change the electoral system to proportionally favour all voters. Although the use of the word "coalition" implied that it included supporters of all political parties, it basically meant everyone except for the Loyalty and the Retro-Progressive parties.

Most members of the Neo-Egalitarian and Enviro parties, as well as their supporters, publicly endorsed electoral change, but by far the most vocal proponent among the smaller independent parties was Tamara Tuplin, leader of the Great Boat Party. After a government-ordered plebiscite the previous year, where the vote for electoral reform came in at 52 percent, she openly shared the stage with members of the PEI Coalition for Electoral Equality at many of her Great Boat Party rallies. The results of the plebiscite were immediately dismissed by then premier, Nathan Affleck, as "a mere testing of the waters, but did not reflect the true will of the people as only 37 percent of Islanders actually voted." After that, Tamara Tuplin always ended her speeches with the cry that was adopted by supporters of the PEICEE: "Respect the Electorate!"

The Loyalty Party won with 67 percent, giving Reuben Arsenault a solid grip on the premiership for the next several years. The Retro-Progressives became the official opposition, while the Neo-Egalitarians barely managed to hold onto enough seats to keep them in the game. The most surprising outcome of the election was Tamara Tuplin winning a seat in the legislature, which meant the Great Boat Party now had a place at the table.

As per our meeting, I had rallied many members of the PEI Jewish Collective to go to Tamara Tuplin's campaign rallies and, true to her word, she spoke supportively about having a synagogue built on Rossiter's Field, as long as there was a proper consultation with the Mi'kmaq Alliance. Many in the Collective were impressed by her, nevertheless, I had my doubts about how many of them would actually vote for the Great Boat Party. And yet, in her victory speech, Tamara Tuplin acknowledged "the many who showed us great support. Mazel tov to us all."

That sound bite came through the Golf's radio as I sat in the passenger's seat while giving Zaina her final driving lesson. We had started in the fall of the previous year and she insisted on continuing into the winter because she said if she could learn then, she would become that much better a driver during seasons when the road conditions were easier. She was a very eager and serious student, often chiding me for not being stricter with her when it came to following certain rules.

"Why didn't you tell me to check my side mirror when I made that turn?" she would say.

"But it looked like you were doing it."

"So? You're the teacher. You still should have said something."

I probably learned more from her during our lessons than she did from me.

The day was relatively mild, a balmy minus 2, and the sky's grey patches could not deter the hazy glimmer of sunshine. We normally practiced on the Mount Russet Road where there was not that much traffic. She was doing well on this particular day, but when I expected her to turn back toward town,

Zaina kept going onto Highway 7 and proceeded to head west. When I asked where we were going, she smiled and said something about testing her sense of direction. I smiled back nervously, but the further she drove with no sign of turning around the less there was to smile about. Then she made the turn on the roundabout that led onto Highway 2 (aka the Western Road) toward Summerside.

"You need to go back," I said. "I doubt your learner's permit allows for this."

"But you're here. How will I know how to drive on the highway if I don't try?"

"Where are we going?"

"I want to see Aziza."

So that was it. The real impetus for learning to drive. Now that Aziza was living in a house near Summerside with Maggie Beairsto, Zaina was determined more than ever not to lose contact with her only child. But how did she know where the house was?

"After you told me she moved, I was livid she hadn't said anything to me."

"Yes, I remember."

"I kept calling her cell and getting her voicemail. I kept leaving messages every hour until she eventually called me back."

"So, we're going to Summerside?"

"She's living in Wilmot Valley, just outside Summerside. It's a bungalow on the Blue Shank Road. I know it because Reuben and I lived there briefly when we first got married. He bought it and held onto it after we moved. I'm sure he used it as an out-of-the-way place to conduct his affairs."

"The house belongs to Reuben?" I tried to hide the astonishment in my voice. "He's renting it to them?"

"I can't believe Aziza would live there," said Zaina. "And with that woman from the bar. I asked Aziza what was going on and she said Reuben was helping her out because she wanted to get out of her apartment. And this Maggie woman's left her husband, so he's helping her too. I don't understand any of this."

"And does she know we're dropping by?"

Zaina didn't bother to answer, which I presumed meant no. I mulled over all this new information. Kelvin Muir's warning during our brief meeting came to mind: "Seems like he don't want her to stop doing it." Was this Reuben's real reason for renting to them, supplying Aziza and Maggie with a safe haven from which they could continue making the Anne Surly videos? If so, why?

When we got to the house in question, Zaina pulled up to an asphalt driveway, stopping short of a garage door. Snow covered the lawn out front, but the walkway leading to the front door was shovelled. Zaina rang the bell and peered into the pebbled glass oval ornamenting the front door. Part of me hoped nobody was home and the longer we waited the more hopeful I became. I was about to suggest to Zaina that we leave when footsteps behind the door became apparent and the pebbled glass oval went dark. The door opened and Maggie Beairsto's mildly surprised expression greeted us.

"My apologies for not calling first," said Zaina quickly. "But we were out for my driving lesson and we happened to be in the neighbourhood."

"Nice to see you again, Mrs. Arsenault," said Maggie, hoping to recover from her surprise with a friendly grin. "Come in."

Maggie ushered us through a narrow foyer, past a stairway leading down to what I assumed was a basement. I glimpsed a light switch at the top of the darkened stairs and could not help wondering if this basement was where the Anne Surly webcasts were being made. Maggie placed her hand on the small of my back and guided me to a spacious kitchen, where we sat on large country-style chairs at a matching round blonde oak table. Maggie called up toward a stairway to Aziza and announced our presence then immediately set about making tea.

"She'll be down in a minute," said Maggie. "How are the driving lessons going?"

"I got us here in one piece," said Zaina, who was looking around the kitchen. No doubt, being here was bringing back more than a few memories.

"When do you think the Crazy Diamond will be open again?" I asked.

"Should be less than a week," Maggie said. "There'll be a big gala opening. Hope to see you there, Samson. You too, Zaina."

The small talk flowed steadily between the three of us, with an underlying fear that any slight pause or moment of silence might grow into a gap too big to fill, until Aziza skipped down the stairway. She kissed her mother and joined us at the table.

"I want to apologize again for dropping by unexpectedly," said Zaina. "But I felt it was important that we all meet together."

"Look, Ima," said Aziza. "I know you're upset that I didn't let you know where I moved to."

"Don't interrupt, Zizi," she calmly replied. "The point I'm trying to make is that I know what's going on. Here, in this house."

No one said anything. Everyone looked at each other and when I feared the silence might go on indefinitely Zaina continued.

"These ridiculous speeches you give on the Internet wearing that absurd get-up. I tried to tell myself that this was some, I don't know what, a phase or rebellion or whatever. Then you had the accident and I thought that would have cured you."

So, Zaina knew about Anne Surly? How did she find out? I doubted Aziza told her. Maybe Reuben? Obviously, she believed Aziza's accident was connected to the webcasts. I thought back to her looking at Reuben and Reggie Muir arguing in the Queens County Hospital parking lot. Had she suspected that they were arguing about Aziza's accident?

"Ima, I don't want to talk about this," said Aziza, trying hard to stay calm. "This is my business."

"And now I have to make it mine," said Zaina. "You're not a child anymore, Zizi, but you are still my daughter. I have always tried to give you the freedom to express yourself in your own way, even if I didn't agree with..."

"Ima, this is not the time or place!"

"I'm afraid it is, Zizi."

Zaina now turned her attention to Maggie. To her credit, Maggie did not look away and I could not read what lay under Zaina's poker face.

"I do not understand how you came to be involved in this, Ms. Beairsto."

"Ima, why are you doing this?" Aziza crossed her arms. "You're embarrassing yourself."

Zaina ignored her daughter and continued to look at Maggie. "I have not forgotten how you helped Aziza during her accident. How you contacted me and drove me to the hospital. How you felt you were responsible. I want you to know I am still grateful to you for all that. So, you will forgive me if

I ask, why are you involving yourself with Aziza in this way? What are you getting out of it?"

At this point, Aziza rose from her seat and raised her hands in exasperation. "You have no right to come into this house and interrogate us like this."

Maggie motioned to Aziza to sit down. "It's okay. I want to answer."

Rather than sit, Aziza stood behind her chair and kept her hands on the back of it as a way of staying in control of herself.

"First of all, you can call me Maggie and I hope it's okay to use your first name."

There was a slight pause before Zaina nodded.

"Thank you," said Maggie. "I know we don't know each other that well, Zaina. If I were you, I'd be suspicious of me too. I guess it started when I was telling Aziza about some of the stuff I used to get up to when I was her age."

I remembered Maggie's story about doing underground movies in Toronto back in the day. I'm pretty sure Zaina would not have been impressed by it, so I said nothing and let Maggie continue.

"Anyway, that led her to showing me one of the rants she was doing on the web, before her camera was busted. To be honest, my reaction was just about the same as yours. I felt embarrassed." Here she turned toward Aziza. "I even told you that, right?"

Aziza rolled her eyes and couldn't suppress a sheepish grin.

"I didn't get it at first," continued Maggie. "But all the same, I recognized something in what she was doing. The passion of it, I guess. It just started as helpful tips. I tried to give her my own viewpoint, just to show her what I thought she could do differently. I had this video camera, something I bought years ago. I only used it a couple of times and put it away. Once I picked it up again... anyway it just felt right. I don't know what to tell you. Sometimes I think maybe I'm trying to relive my youth or something, but there's something about doing this. I don't know. It feels like I'm part of something."

"Well, whatever you think you're a part of, I'm afraid it has to stop," said Zaina. "Zizi, I want you to pack your things and come with me. You can live with me until you find a place of your own."

"You have no right to come here and order me around. In fact, I think you should leave."

"I'm not going anywhere without you."

"Well, I'm not coming with you. And if you aren't going to leave, then I will."

Aziza stormed out of the kitchen and stomped up the stairs. A door slammed and it was clear that we had worn out our welcome.

Outside, I insisted that I drive Zaina back home. She made no protest and I took my place behind the wheel. Back on the road, I commiserated that she and Aziza had fallen out again. Zaina didn't acknowledge me, lost as she was in her own thoughts. Concern wrinkled the corners of her mouth. I knew enough not to say anything more and we drove the rest of the way in silence.

A NEW OPENNESS blossomed between Zaina and I since she revealed she was aware of Anne Surly. That I knew about it came as no surprise to her, although when I related the circumstances under which Aziza and I first came to know each other, Zaina looked visibly shaken.

"I remember that night, when those two masked thugs broke in," she recounted. "That was the first time I watched this web show she does. I had no idea whether this was part of the show or if something really happened. It didn't matter, it scared me to death."

She had first found out about the webcasts after Aziza moved from Charlottetown to Mount Russet. An anonymous note, folded twice, had been left in her mailbox. It was typed and simply read: *Look what your daughter has been up to* and the URL for the Anne Surly website. Zaina admitted that, at first, she thought it was from Reuben, since she couldn't imagine anyone else who would send her such a thing.

"He denied it, of course. Said he didn't know what I was talking about. When he admitted that he knew what Aziza was up to, I started to believe he didn't know about the note. That was when I realized it was Aziza herself who sent the note. She admitted it after we brought her home from the hospital. That was part of the fight we had. It started because I recognized the sofa on the webcast. That was why she didn't want me to go to her apartment. I really did offer to have it reupholstered. I really did accuse her of preferring her father to me."

REUBEN WASTED NO time in rejigging his cabinet and it received some unexpected publicity. Reuben and the other cabinet members were posing for a photograph on the steps of the legislature building. That morning it had snowed and the steps looked like the tiers of a cake topped with vanilla icing. The atmosphere appeared both chaste and celebratory. The photographer had just positioned them and ordered everyone to smile. At that moment, a passerby, possibly a member or supporter of the PEI Coalition for Electoral Equality, yelled out, "Respect the electorate!"

In a knee-jerk response, Reuben's new Finance Minister, Ralph Tweel, yelled back, "We did!" all the while grinning for the camera. As if punctuating the statement, his middle finger shot up at the passerby when the photographer clicked the shutter.

A copy of this photo – which showed Justice Minister Stewart Munt, who was standing behind Tweel on the step above, tossing back his head in wide-mouthed laughter, looking not unlike a braying ass – found its way on the front page of the *Charlottetown Parrot*. In the accompanying article, Reuben Arsenault brushed off the incident, saying that the gesture was not made in a "mean-spirited way" but rather "in the spirit of over enthusiasm for this new chapter of PEI governance." All the same, Ralph Tweel was forced to make a public apology, but the matter wasn't laid to rest before an editorial cartoon in the *Charlottetown Parrot* showed a caricature of Ralph Tweel as a giant middle finger with the caption: "We're No. 1!"

It was around this time that Reuben charged his freshman Finance Minister with his first legislative duty, which Reuben dubbed the Fair Dissemination of Public Information Act. The gist of the act would be to put a cap on the amount of money that any special interest group could spend, regarding spreading their message. I didn't put two and two together until Anne Surly pointed out that this proposed legislation seemed to specifically target the PEI Coalition for Electoral Equality and was meant to quash any free expression aimed toward reforming the current voting system.

For many of those newly named cabinet ministers, such as Ralph Tweel, this was their first portfolio. One of the more suspect appointments was Mortimer MacFadyen, husband to Reuben Arsenault's former campaign manager Portia

MacFadyen. Mortimer was the MLA for Belfast-Murray River and had used his position mostly to promote his blueberry u-pick and his restaurant, Mortimer's Family Diner. He had been named Minister of Agriculture and Fisheries.

In her latest webcast, Anne Surly hinted that Reuben and Portia had been engaging in a not-so-secret affair during the campaign when she found out she was, what our British cousins euphemistically call, *up the duff*. Supposedly, Portia had an abortion posthaste at a clinic in Bathurst, New Brunswick, which was complicated but necessary, since she and Mortimer were vocal supporters of a pro-life group called The Sacred Gift. Portia's connection with them had yielded many votes for Reuben. Anne Surly went on to allege that Mortimer had threatened to divorce Portia and go public with the pregnancy and abortion, but Reuben managed to keep him in check by promising him the plum portfolio.

One other new, but not so surprising, appointment was naming former CEO of the PEI Board of Health, Dr. Humphrey Becker as Minister of Health. Becker had done so much public ass smooching during Reuben's campaign you didn't need a crystal ball to see that appointment coming a mile off. What was surprising was the retooling of the portfolio itself. For years, Tourism and Culture had been paired together in a way that trivialized the latter to benefit the former, which resulted in growing criticism from certain sectors of the arts community. So now, in an effort to show he was all about change, Reuben married Tourism to Economic Development, which was sensible enough, but in what felt like a counter-intuitive move at best, threw Health and Culture into bed together. The reaction was unsurprisingly mixed, with many calling the pairing "absurd," while Reuben's supporters dubbed this "a bold and visionary move."

When asked what plans he had for Island culture, Dr. Becker said: "There are a lot of interesting and, in my learned opinion, innovative initiatives in the pipeline to integrate the arts into healthcare."

When February rolled around, Zaina passed her driving test and got her license. I drove her to Monty Tweel's Toyota near the Charlottetown Airport to buy a car. She opted for a used 2015 Camry. I thought it was a good choice and she beamed with pride when the three of us took it for a quick spin before repairing back to Monty's office to sign the papers.

At first Monty took me to be Zaina's husband and directed his sales spiel to me. But Zaina, in her own direct way, soon set him straight and fired a few questions at him while I looked on in admiring silence. In Monty's office, I was surprised to see the *Charlottetown Parrot*'s editorial cartoon of his cousin, Ralph Tweel, as a walking middle finger emblazoned with "We're Number 1!" tacked to the corkboard on the wall behind his desk. When Monty noticed my interest in the cartoon, he chuckled. "Old Ralph got quite a start to public life. Always had a strong personality, but I don't think he was expecting this kind of publicity so soon out of the gate."

"I guess the Premier wasn't too pleased with him," I said.

"That's an interesting thing," Monty said. "After this cartoon came out, I called him up to give him a bit of a ribbing and asked if he was in hot water with the boss and he said it was just the opposite. Oh sure, Reuben made all the right noises about being more careful in the future and whatever, but he also told Ralph that this wasn't the worst way to show everyone that this government means business and plans to do things their way."

Subsequent newspaper photos always showed Ralph Tweel with something in his hands – important looking folders or a briefcase or, in one instance, a chicken leg during some fundraising dinner – possibly to keep his hair trigger middle finger in check, or so rumour had it.

Yet, as far as doing things his way, Reuben Arsenault was right on track. Despite the cold weather and some heavy snowfall, the clean-up at Rossiter's Field continued. Reuben invited the press to the clean-up site for photo ops and made public appearances at local auditoriums and meeting halls, where he talked about the clean-up being ahead of schedule and added that plans to build Ashlynn's Camp for Kids and the holiday resort were being put together.

Of course, now that he owned Rossiter's Field and the surrounding land, he made it clear that all of this was being done with private money. And yet, the tone with which he spoke about this often gave the impression that this was his government in action, an uncomfortable mixing of personal and public affairs that did not sit well with the opposition parties in the legislature or the media. Some went so far as to remark that this unprecedented blurring of boundaries gave off a vague stink of autocracy.

Rather than trying to mollify this blowback, he doubled-down by declaring: "And this is just the beginning. Once this project has been completed it will usher in a new era of prosperity for PEI. I'm not just talking about an increase in tourism, but rather a whole new makeover for our Gentle Island."

Even though he would not go into detail about the "makeover" – or maybe because of the lack of details – these appearances were met with mixed reactions. Political foes criticized him for flogging the clean-up as if he was still campaigning and using these public platforms outside the legislature to create a safe bubble for himself where there were no dissenting opinions. But his usual vocal supporters thought these public appearances made Reuben more accessible to the public and set him apart from past premiers.

In her legislative capacity as the lone member of the Great Boat Party, Tamara Tuplin repeated her support for the clean-up, but hammered home, any chance she could, the importance of honouring the duty to consult with the Mi'kmaq Alliance before any building could be done. For her pains, she was sometimes shouted down by the other ministers or criticized by Reuben himself for wanting to stand in the way of progress and deny PEI its destiny for greatness, despite its small size.

In the meantime, Anne Surly ranted on about Reuben, but there was something different in her message. Referring to the Ralph Tweel debacle by calling him "the middle finger that walks like a man", she warned that Reuben and "his cadre of hand-picked neophytes" who made up his cabinet were not the bumbling clowns the media sometimes made them out to be.

"There is a sense of purpose propelling this government," she said. "For all their lack of political experience, or maybe because of it, they are taking this island down a certain path that not many are expecting."

I couldn't entirely tell whether this prediction didn't carry as much a sliver of grudging admiration as it did caution. She also dropped more tidbits about the operation known as Project Friendly Occupation, which she had mentioned in past webcasts. Apparently, it had something to do with the ongoing negotiations with a foreign investor (either American, Chinese or from the U.K., depending on who she spoke to) who expressed interest in the untapped potential of our small island. I was intrigued when the name of former premier, Nathan Affleck, cropped up as an emissary or liaison involved with the hush-hush negotiations.

Whenever she brought up the subject of Rossiter's Field, I was less intrigued to hear Anne Surly continue to invoke my name and the proposed synagogue, wondering why I hadn't been heard from lately, as if she was goading me into action. I remembered Aziza's warning to me to forget having a synagogue on Rossiter's Field lest I make myself "a target." She was like two different people and their mixed messaging was enough to make my head spin.

To make matters worse, I received a phone call from Professor Markowitz, saying that he had spoken to some members of the PEI Jewish Collective. The consensus was that they were cooling on the idea of Rossiter's Field as a site for the synagogue.

"But the clean-up is underway," I said. "Now isn't the time to give up on this."

"We all still want the synagogue," Professor Markowitz assured me. "But we'd rather find another site for it. I hear there's a vacant lot in Brighton that would be perfect."

"Who did you hear that from?" I asked, trying not to sound too suspicious.

"Actually, it was from Premier Arsenault himself," said Professor Markowitz cheerfully. "He was speaking at the university and we got to talking afterward. I was surprised he knew who I was and the PEIJC and the synagogue. Your name came up, actually. Anyway, the premier was quite supportive of the synagogue. He knows the owner of the lot in Brighton and said maybe something could be worked out."

"I'll bet he did. But we can't back down. It's either Rossiter's Field or nothing."

Professor Markowitz couldn't understand why I was being so obstinate about this and I couldn't elaborate any further than I dared to. He said whatever reason I had for insisting on Rossiter's Field as the site for the synagogue wasn't in the interest of the PEIJC or the Jewish community in general.

I kept expecting Fagin, Shylock or Judas, either individually or en masse, to appear with advice on what to do next, but they were nowhere to be found. Could I dare hope that I was rid of them for good? If so, then maybe it really didn't matter where this synagogue ended up or even if it would be built at all. Despite the prospect of putting this whole affair behind me, I knew in my heart of hearts that I couldn't give up on the synagogue now. If I was on my own, then good riddance to those three thorns in my side, I would deal with this in my own way.

As during other times when the Figs seemed to have disappeared for good, I struggled to reconcile my mixed feelings of relief and abandonment.

When the opening of the newly refurbished Crazy Diamond was announced, I knew I had to go, if only to see how my favourite watering hole had changed. I was stunned when Zaina said she wanted to go too and offered to be my designated driver. When I asked why, she explained that she had always been curious about where Aziza worked. It was also clear to me, without her having to say so, that, like the visit to the house in Wilmot Valley, this was Zaina's way of letting her daughter know that mother was not going to give up on her so easily. I gladly accepted her offer.

The grand opening was scheduled to begin at 7 o'clock sharp. The change in my old haunt was apparent the moment we pulled up to the parking lot. Judging by how many cars were there, others were also curious. For a relatively new driver, Zaina was quite adept at maneuvering her way through the lot and backing into one of the few vacant spaces. What used to be a ramshackle façade with a hand-painted sign (created by a local artisan featuring 3D-like psychedelic lettering) was now expensive metallic blue siding sporting CRAZY DIAMOND in a glittering ornamental script. Trust Reuben Arsenault to suck all the personality out of what was essentially a PEI institution. I couldn't believe that Maggie had gone along with this, although I could only imagine what Pius thought of it. I was prepared to leave then and there and said as much to Zaina, but she convinced me to go in since we were already there.

Inside it didn't get much better. Gone were the rare Pink Floyd album covers and the mural depicting the back of the *Ummagumma* album that covered one wall, the whole Maritime psychedelic vibe of lobster traps and buoys hanging from the ceiling (the fishing nets were still there). The lava lamps on the tables were replaced by tea candles in glass vases of various colours. The tables were now covered with café-styled checked tablecloths and the chrome-bodied chairs had leatherette padding on the seats and backs. The old splintery bar had been replaced by something that looked like faux granite and the new stools were chrome and leatherette to match the chairs.

Aside from the fishing nets, the only other holdover from the previous incarnation was the Wurlitzer jukebox that still played Pink Floyd, but at a noticeably lower volume than before. I assumed Maggie had put her foot down about that. She was behind the bar, chatting up customers and making drinks just like always. Rather than the usual tight tee shirt, she was wearing a low-cut white blouse and a tightly buttoned dark vest that showed off her *zaftig* figure as much as ever.

Zaina and I made our way to the bar. There was only one stool free and I gallantly offered it to her, while I stood beside her at the far end of the bar. Maggie noticed us and signalled that she'd be with us shortly. I noticed something else that was very much out of place. One of the few empty tables had a *Reserved* sign on it. To my knowledge nobody ever reserved a table in the Crazy Diamond and I'm sure they would have been laughed at (or even cursed at) if they tried.

"Do you see Aziza?" Zaina asked.

I scanned the room, but she was nowhere in sight. I checked the opening behind the bar. She wasn't in the kitchen either.

Maggie approached us with a pint of Beairsto's IPA. "Glad you could both make it," she said. "What can I get you, Zaina?"

"Soda water, please."

Maggie opened a bottle and poured it into a glass with ice and a wedge of lime and set it down on a coaster before Zaina. "So, what do you think?"

"It is very elegant but warm as well," Zaina said, taking in the surroundings. "I gather from Samson that it looks very different from the way it was before."

Maggie laughed. "Yeah, we made a few changes." She looked at me expectantly. "I take it you don't approve, Samson?"

"I'm a bit surprised that you do," I said.

"I know you think I made a deal with the devil," she said. "You aren't the only one. But I still run this place, or at least half of it, and I know what's best for my end. I'm a pretty good businesswoman to have kept this place going for as long as I have. This was an opportunity I couldn't say no to. Things can't stay the same if you want to move ahead. You gotta move with the times or else get bulldozed over"

I conceded to Maggie's wisdom and raised my glass to the Crazy Diamond's continued success in whatever guise it may take. After all, what did I know about running a business? When I asked how things stood with Pius, she tried to keep up her philosophical and professional demeanour, but it was clear I had touched on a sore spot, for which I apologized.

"That's okay," she said. "In a way, it's like nothing has changed. He stays where he's most comfortable, in the Shine Shrine, and I rule this side of the roost. Other than that, there isn't much in the way of middle ground. Or none that we can see at this time anyway. But the Crazy Diamond is our baby, so we'll have to wait and see what happens."

Zaina asked after Aziza and Maggie explained that she had some personal business to take care of and would be along shortly. It wasn't long before she walked through the door. Maggie waved her over and she was soon hugging her mother and apologizing for the way she had acted at the house in Wilmot Valley. Her grin was tight-lipped and contrite enough. I couldn't help but be moved by its sincerity, and yet the way she touched my arm conveyed a subtle sense of foreboding, or at least that's how I interpreted the uneasy shiver somewhere between my sternum and my belly. Aziza excused herself and soon she reappeared in a uniform like Maggie's and was moving among the tables with a tray of free opening night nibbles.

"I had heard so many bad things about this place," Zaina said. "How rough it was and the lowlife people who came here. But maybe Reuben has done them a favour with this makeover. Maybe he..."

She didn't finish her thought when she noticed my attention was elsewhere. It was as if the mere mention of his name was enough to conjure the man himself, who was now stepping through the door, trailing an entourage of four or five others in his wake. A few customers who first noticed him were treated to a personal greeting followed by chitchat and glad-handing. Soon everyone knew he had arrived and there were smiles and hand waving all around. They must have been expected because the entourage made themselves comfortable at the empty table with the Reserved sign on it. Reuben went to the bar and kissed Maggie on the cheek.

"The place looks great," he said. "I think you're going to see business grow to a whole new level."

"You've been some generous," said Maggie. "What are you drinking?"

He ordered a glass of Irish whiskey. Zaina and I were trying to keep a low profile, but as soon as he got his drink, he came over. He stood there, appraising us. The slight smile was trying to make sense of the two of us together, computing all the possibilities of what that might mean. I remembered that the last time, actually the only time the three of us were in the same room was when Aziza was in the hospital. Quite possibly, he was thinking the same thing.

"I didn't expect to see you here tonight," he finally said to Zaina, not exactly ignoring me. If anything, I was included by my mere proximity as if I was an old fixture, part of the furnishings that surprisingly didn't get discarded in the makeover.

"I want our daughter to know that her mother also takes an interest in her life." Zaina took a sip of her soda water and added, "Without the need to control it."

Reuben laughed. "I'll admit that part of the reason I paid for this makeover was for her. If she has to work in this place, it may as well have some class."

"And the house in Wilmot Valley?"

"She needed a place to live," Reuben said. "Better than where she was before."

I noticed a quick glance over Zaina's shoulder at me.

"And Maggie?"

"That's something you'll have to take up with Aziza. Maggie's going through her own difficulties and Aziza's just trying to help her out. I understand you already paid them a visit. Did being at the house bring back some memories? Good ones I hope?"

Up until that point, if I didn't know better, I would have said his attitude toward Zaina was on the flirtatious side, possibly for my benefit as he relegated me to the background. But now he actually raised his glass at me.

"Hello again, Mr. Grief. I hope you approve of the changes in your old haunt. Just a matter of getting rid of a few cobwebs. But then again, you artists have a natural affinity for squalor, don't you."

"What I personally lack in class, I try to make up for with the company I keep." I said and wondered if I put Zaina in an awkward position, but she immediately raised her glass, turned toward me and clinked my pint. "By the way, I'm impressed you're keeping your initial promise, cleaning up Rossiter's Field. Classy move, buying up the whole thing."

He was about to excuse himself to join his entourage at their table, but I managed to detain him, ignoring the red light flashing in the back of my brain that warned I could be about to stick my foot in my mouth.

"My only question is about what will happen to the land once you've cleaned it up."

"I can promise you we plan to put the land to good use," he said.

"Oh right, the children's camp and resort. I'm sure that will create a few jobs."

"That's the idea," he said cheerfully. "I take it you have no objection to people actually working for a living."

I took that to be a dig at my being an artist. "Not at all, but I also have no objection to people having a place to worship. You already know I think Rossiter's Field should be the site to build a synagogue for the Island's Jewish community."

"According to what I've heard, the Jewish community doesn't necessarily agree with you. I already had the pleasure of speaking with Professor Markowitz. By the way, your name came up. In a good way, I assure you. In any case, the Professor and I both see eye to eye on where the synagogue should be."

"The professor told me," I said. "But it's my understanding there's been no actual agreement, only a suggestion. What you haven't taken into consideration is that a synagogue would be a needed cultural addition to Mount Russet."

"Needed?" he said. "I'm not sure the good citizens of Mount Russet would see the benefit."

Something told me my mouth had better limber up to accommodate a size 9½ Blundstone.

"How do you know?" I blurted out. "Have you asked them?"

He slowly drained his glass and pondered something. I wondered if I had actually cornered him when he set his empty glass on the bar and signalled Maggie for another.

"As a matter of fact, Mr. Grief, I have not asked them," he said finally. "I suppose I could, since I'm scheduled to speak at the Bertram Civic Center tomorrow night." Maggie brought him his whiskey and he stared at it, his eyes lighting up as if discovering a sudden flash of inspiration from its amber hue. "But I have a better idea. Why don't you come and ask them yourself? I will give my talk and then you can come up to the podium and make your case in person. I think that would be more than fair."

I didn't know what to say. The offer was totally unexpected. I looked at Zaina. Her wary expression told me to be careful. Reuben sipped his drink, obviously enjoying the fact that he had caught me off guard. I couldn't afford to hesitate much longer and readily agreed to appear at the Bertram Civic Centre.

"Excellent," he said. "I look forward to hearing you make your case."

And with that he went off to join his entourage.

I stared at the beer in my pint glass. It was somewhat murkier than the liquid gold Reuben took guidance from in his own glass. So much was not in my favour. I was pretty much the only Jew in Mount Russet. And although I'd rarely come across any kind of anti-Semitism here, and that mostly from drunks in the old Crazy Diamond, a synagogue might arouse a whole new wave of anti-Jewish sentiment. Possibly more than Maggie could fend off with a golf club.

Through the speakers, I recognized a Pink Floyd song I had heard many times over the years I'd been coming here. Industrial whooshes and a ringing acoustic guitar accompanied the singer whose haunting voice explained that I'd "been in the pipeline, filling in time."

"Hmm," I mused aloud. "That didn't go the way I thought it would."

"How did you think it would go?" Zaina asked.

"I don't know, but I feel like I've stepped into something that I can't quite get out of."

"You can be very persuasive when you want to be," said Zaina. "Look how you won over the Jewish community and how you handled yourself on the radio."

I thanked her and felt grateful for how much better she made me feel. And maybe she was right. After all, the land was big enough for three projects. I'd just have to state my case reasonably.

On a whim, I took her hand and planted a gentle kiss on her knuckles. She made no reaction except to use the hand to pick up her glass and take a sip of her soda water. I glanced over at the table where Reuben and his entourage were sitting to see if he saw what I had done, but he was too preoccupied by something he was saying to Aziza.

It was she who then looked in my direction then quickly looked away when I noticed. In the dim lighting I found it hard to read what she might have been thinking. Through the speakers the singer conceded that I was "nobody's fool" before welcoming me "to the machine."

14

WHEN I ARRIVED at the Bertram Civic Center, I tried to read the crowd who were chatting among themselves and slowly finding seats. The Civic Center was mostly used for concerts and hockey games and held about 250 seats. A wooden floor covered the rink and a stage with two microphones was situated in the middle, with chairs set up to its left and right for Reuben's aides and flunkies, while everyone else would be sitting in the stands. It looked like it would be a packed house. There was a seat on the floor with my name on it. I decided to walk around, hoping to work off a bit of nervousness and marshal my forces.

I saw a few familiar faces, some local residents such as Sadie Phinney from Sadie's Tearoom and her business and life partner, Bonnie Weinberger, who was also in the PEI Jewish Collective. Wayne Mao, the owner of Fusion Wok, waved at me and gave me the thumbs up. Other members of the PEIJC, including Professor Markowitz with his wife and daughter as well as Frieda Greenglass, were there. I also recognized Tamara Tuplin (who nodded at me when I caught her eye) and some of her staff, as well as Chief Darren Sark from Lennox Island First Nation and Chief Lucy Paul from Abegweit First Nation (consisting of three reserves: Morel, Rocky Point and Scotchfort). There were also some members of the Mi'kmaq Alliance. Obviously, word of my appearance tonight had gotten around. Zaina waved at me from her seat. To my surprise, sitting beside her, was Aziza whose attention was on her phone, perhaps as a way of avoiding me. I felt both heartened and anxious by the turnout. I saw Professor Markowitz making his way toward me.

"Just wanted to wish you good luck," he said, shaking my hand. "It should make for a lively debate."

Debate? What debate? I smiled and thanked him. As far as I knew Reuben was going to speak and then I would be allowed to come up and say a few words. I had not prepared anything, since that worked well enough for me when I spoke at the PEI Jewish Collective's meeting. But an actual debate was a different animal altogether. I kept trying to convince myself that Zaina was right. I could be persuasive. I had a knack for thinking on my feet. Sure, this was a much bigger group of people, but I had pulled off the same trick in my *Good Morning PEI* interview and thousands had been listening then. Of course, I couldn't see them, but this was no time to nitpick. It was all a matter of channeling my nervousness to get energized. I tried to convince myself that I could handle whatever Reuben threw at me.

Once everyone was settled in, I took my seat and waited for things to commence. I noticed that on the stage there were two microphones on stands. The lights dimmed and Robbie Bulger, the mayor of Mount Russet, took the stage. He went into a rambling introduction that detailed Reuben Arsenault's long and sometimes controversial career as an entrepreneur, his supposed community-mindedness and his short but meteoric rise in Island politics. One couldn't help but suspect that Reuben might have written the intro himself, the way he waited patiently off to the side of the stage, listening with head slightly bowed in an affectation of humility, but more likely mentally making sure that the mayor didn't miss anything. Bulger must have spoken for over fifteen minutes before he finally got around to introducing our new premier, who bounded onto the stage as the mayor beat a hasty exit.

"Thank you, Mayor Bulger, for that lavish introduction. What you lack in brevity you more than make up for in generosity," he said. Then as an aside to the audience, "Better not introduce me to your speechwriter, I may just steal him – *or her* – away from you." This drew a smattering of laughter from those on the floor and a few in the stands, to which Reuben (ever a man of the people) added his own *aren't-I-incorrigible* chuckle.

He went on to speak about equality and the Loyalty Party's commitment to level the playing field for all special interest groups so that certain points of view would not have a disproportionate advantage over others. This was obviously a reference to the Fair Dissemination of Public Information Act, which was about to receive its second reading in the legislature.

As widely reported (and commented on by Anne Surly), it would curtail the amount of money a group could spend in the course of getting out its message, with heavy fines for those who spent above the allotted limit. There was a contingency to apply for extra funds (up to $10,000), but the application process entailed support letters from three separate financial institutions in order to prove monetary destitution and a detailed twenty-five-page form to fill out.

"Critics of this bill are calling it nothing short of censorship and I'm here to tell you that nothing – and I mean nothing – could be further from the truth," he said with well-practiced sincerity, giving the last part of his statement an undercurrent of indignation by applying a slight catch in his throat. "As a matter of fact, this bill is a declaration against censorship. It has been carefully drafted to ensure that everyone has an equal say and can get across all points of view in a fair and democratic fashion."

He stepped back from the microphone and looked around at the audience, allowing those last few words to sink into their collective consciousness. Fair and democratic. What could be simpler? I looked around at those seated on the floor and up at the stands, searching for any sign that at least one other person was aware of the elephant in the room.

What many of the bill's critics, including Anne Surly, were saying was that the Fair Dissemination of Public Information Act was created to specifically target the PEI Coalition for Electoral Equality because of the growing support they were receiving. The Coalition's leader, Tina Chelmsford, had written an op-ed in the *Charlottetown Parrot* complaining that if the bill was passed their ability to get the word out about electoral reform would essentially be hog tied and the Coalition would most likely have to disband.

"Of course, we have to be realistic," Reuben continued, gesturing with arms open wide to emphasize the inclusivity of what he was about to say. "The complex process of ensuring a level playing field for all special interests requires that certain rights must fall by the wayside."

I thought I heard a slight intake of breath among the audience, followed by a low murmur.

"There's nothing draconian about that," he said with as much sincerity as he could muster.

Interesting word, I thought. Draconian.

"Free speech is a God-given right in every democracy," he pressed on. "And yet we do not, and should not, tolerate hate speech under any circumstances. We can ensure the integrity of free speech by curtailing its most egregious manifestation."

There was applause, not resounding, but enough for Reuben to join in and accept it as support for what he'd just said.

Was I the only one who heard his underlying message: equating electoral reform with hate speech? That meant if you were against the current system then anything you said that criticized this system, or any activity or organization you were involved with to change this system, would be considered hateful. He seemed to be demonizing the idea of a fairer electoral system. Suddenly the vague stink of autocracy was taking on a more pronounced stench.

Then he quickly moved on to Rossiter's Field. His message was clear and the same drum he had been beating throughout his campaign, going back to when he was running for MLA of Mount Russet: clean up the Island and create jobs. He strode the stage like a rock star belting out his greatest hit. Now that he owned Rossiter's Field and the surrounding land, the dream come true known as Ashlynn's Camp for Kids would be a symbol of hope, not just for youngsters, but a symbol for all Islanders that a new time of prosperity, the likes of which they had never seen before, would soon come for everyone. He invoked the name of Ashlynn MacKenzie, the little girl who died of leukemia whose wish to go to summer camp had inspired the building project, as if uttering the name of a saint.

"Unfortunately, Ashlynn won't see her dream come true. I spoke to her parents and they assured me that among her last words, she said that knowing the camp would be built made the burden of her disease that little bit easier to bear."

The odd sob here and there could be heard in the stands. I couldn't help wondering if there was a Kleenex concession somewhere in the auditorium, along with the cold drinks and fries with the works, and whether Reuben was pocketing a percentage of that choice chunk of coin.

While that rather uncharitable notion was coursing through the darker regions of my cerebral cortex, I heard him opining on the fairness of hearing all points of view. Before I knew it, I heard him call my name. The audience broke out in applause, led by Reuben who, all the while, motioned for me to come up on the stage. The applause was enthusiastic and this encouraged me to leap up from my seat and make my way along the floor to the steps at the side of the stage.

The applause slowly ebbed when I reached the stage. Reuben stayed behind his microphone and motioned for me to stand in front of the one that had been provided for me. Right away I noticed that it pointed directly at my forehead. After a momentary breath to get my bearings, I adjusted the stand and lowered it so the mic was at mouth level. I thanked the Premier for graciously sharing his stage with me and for giving me the opportunity to put across my point of view.

I revisited the argument I first made at the PEIJC's annual meeting, about how a synagogue on Rossiter's Field would reinforce Mount Russet in particular, and PEI in general, with the identity of being a more diverse community. I was about to elaborate on the benefits of diversity in any community when Reuben politely interrupted me. He said that he, in fact, agreed with me about diversity and said that he had found a very nice plot of land in Brighton that would be perfect for the synagogue.

"Do you know who owns that land?" I asked. "One of your cronies maybe?"

"As a matter of fact, a good friend of mine does own it," he answered with a nod that feigned admiration I had done my homework. "Which is why I would be in a good position of suggesting he make the PEIJC a reasonable offer for building on it." Seeing I had no rejoinder, he continued. "Besides, I assume Brighton would equally benefit from being identified as a diverse community." He addressed this more to the audience than to me, to which they responded with resounding applause. "Furthermore, who's to say that Ashlynn's Camp for Kids won't be a diverse enterprise? As a matter of fact, we are conferring with the Island Welcoming Society and the various ethnic communities connected to them on how to make the camp more inclusive to the different cultures that now make up the Island's citizenry."

More applause greeted this last statement. When it died down, Reuben apologized for interrupting what I was saying and beckoned me to continue. For the next ten minutes I struggled to get back my train of thought but failed to come up with any compelling arguments for building the synagogue on Rossiter's Field. The audience was silent and Reuben thanked me for giving my point of view and implored the audience to "show our artistic friend some good old PEI generosity."

The applause was indeed generous and I knew that this was my cue to get off the stage and return to my seat, and yet I found that I could not let go of the microphone.

"Excuse me, Premier," I said with some trepidation in my voice. "But I haven't told you or these good people the real reason why Rossiter's Field must be the site for the new synagogue."

I knew what I had to do, but opted for a dramatic pause while I scanned the faces on the floor and in the stands. There were alternating expressions of doubt, impatience and anticipation. I noticed Tamara Tuplin sitting forward in her seat, possibly remembering what I had told her at our meeting and wondering if I would make such a declaration here.

"The fact is, Rossiter's Field was never my first choice as a site for the synagogue. In fact, I would have chosen pretty much anywhere else. So, you're probably asking yourself why I've been so insistent that the synagogue be built there. The reason is that it was decreed by... the *Supreme One*."

There was a moment of silence and many looks of confusion. Reuben too looked puzzled but managed a grin.

"I don't understand," he said. "Who or what is the... *Supreme One*, is it?"

How was I going to explain? A flash of regret that I had ever chosen to go down this road made me drop my head, hitting the mic and resulting in a screech of feedback.

Suddenly, a large collective intake of breath, filled the auditorium, along with a few gasps and a couple of outright cries of surprise, followed by a general murmuring among the audience. I assumed they, like myself, had been startled by the feedback.

But when I lifted my head, there were Judas, Shylock and Fagin standing in the middle of the stage, apparently having appeared out of nowhere. Rather than the tourist outfits of loud shirts and, what I came to think of as their signature headgear, they wore clothing more in keeping with their true identities. Judas wore a robe of roughly woven material and crude sandals of thick rope. Shylock was garbed in a heavy cloak that was opened part way to reveal a white blouse and a light brown doublet. He wore knee-length breeches and white stockings with simple leather footwear. On his head was a floppy red hat that looked not unlike a flattened mushroom cap. Fagin, looking for all the world like some raggedy villain, was clad in a shapeless black coat that reached his knees, baggy shapeless trousers and black boots. A black wide-brimmed hat that had seen much wear and tear was scrunched on his narrow head.

Reuben himself was taken aback, his wide eyes and gaping mouth momentarily bordering on panic. He took a few involuntary steps backwards and was saved from falling off the stage by an alert sound technician.

"What the hell is going on?" he demanded once he found his bearings. "Who are they? What kind of cheap theatrics are you trying to pull, Grief?"

Managing to extricate my hands from the microphone, I threw them in the air in a show of bewilderment. I was about to proclaim my innocence when Judas stepped forward in front of my microphone. He introduced himself and the two others in a voice that rang out clearly.

"I assure you we are not conjurers nor is our sudden appearance a theatrical trick. We were previously emanations known only to this person, Samson Grief, having originated from the deep recesses of his intellect. As a demonstration of our independent willpower, we now make ourselves manifest to all of you."

"Well, I happen to be the premier of this province and I say we are not going to be taken in by three hucksters."

Shylock looked at his comrades then at Reuben then took his place at the microphone.

"Verily thou hath cast such a base aspersion on we three messengers, yet as well upon the honest head of our good cousin, Samson. The Supreme One hath sent us here to compel him to build the temple on this red jewel of an island and so a new era might commence in the lives of them who dwell here."

"The Supreme One," said Reuben with suspicion. "Who or what is that?"

"The Supreme One ain't a who or a what, my dear," said Fagin, edging Shylock out of the way so he could get in front of the mic. He pointed a talon-like finger upwards. "The Supreme One gives and takes away as pleases the Supreme One. We ain't but messengers sent to do the Supreme One's bidding and right now the Supreme One bids that a synagogue be built on the hallowed ground of what is known here as Rossiter's Field."

"I'll give you three credit," said Reuben. "You sure know how to sell it. And you too, Grief, for concocting this whole bit of theatre, assuming you're the mastermind behind this impressive show of smoke and mirrors. I don't know who you're all working for, but I'll tell you right now that, impressive as this all is, it's not going to pull the wool over my eyes or the eyes of our good citizens."

"Our purpose is not to cover your eyes, but to open them," said Judas. "I must confess to you that we do not do this lightly. The moment Samson Grief spoke the name of the Supreme One in public, he compelled us to reveal ourselves, but we do it in protest and at great risk of displeasing the Supreme One."

"Forsooth," chimed in Shylock. "'Twas of the utmost significance for this plan of building the temple to proceed without revealing the Supreme One's invisible hand, thus might this isle evolve into a Promised Land."

"But even now, my dear, the Supreme One's wrath is brewing in the skies," warned Fagin. "It will make itself felt across this island in the form of a raging storm."

"Nonsense," scoffed Reuben. "There have been no storm warnings. In fact, quite the opposite. Only this morning the weather report called for mild temperatures and sunny skies. There was even a chance of an early thaw this year."

"The debate can be swiftly concluded by venturing beyond this great hall to see for yourself," said Judas. "If what we say is shown to be true then you must agree that our presence here is more than just theatrics and trickery."

Reuben considered this for a minute then snapped his fingers at an aide who ran out of the building and returned to report that a storm was indeed brewing. But nobody was prepared for the tempest that in less than a minute had people scurrying out of their seats and to their cars, causing major congestion on the roads. Reuben was quickly escorted out of a side door. I saw Frieda and Stepan Markowitz and his family elbowing their way toward the aisle and Aziza and Zaina being swept along by the crowd at the front exit. The Figs did their usual vanishing act. I managed to make my way off the stage and followed a group of people toward the washrooms and soon found a rear exit that led to an alley behind the civic centre. I had to walk clear around the building to get to my car, just as the skies had darkened.

By late the next day the devastation resulted in Island-wide power outages, fallen trees, battered buildings and smashed windows and countless road accidents. The most alarming development that occurred was the destruction of the Confederation Bridge when the raging gale caused it to buckle and plunge into the freezing waters of the Northumberland Strait.

PART 4:

SAMSON EX MACHINA

15

IN THE FOLLOWING WEEKS, reports came in detailing the extent of the damage from what was now being called Hurricane X, since it appeared out of nowhere and was not designated with a name by any of the weather bureaus. It was estimated to be a Category 5, although destroying the bridge suggested something more powerful and incalculable. No part of PEI had been spared. Many houses, barns, silos and shacks in all three counties were either razed to the ground or had sustained serious structural damage. Fishing boats and pleasure yachts were tossed and broke loose from their moorings. Most either smashed into each other or capsized and sank. Seaside boardwalks and sand dunes were washed away and many lighthouses were battered by violent winds and towering waves. Sudden drops in temperature froze pipes, which then cracked and flooded basements. Many inland roads were also flooded due to surges that broke through the ice of nearby rivers and bays.

Hailstones that ranged in size between golf balls and grapefruit were hurled through windows and left huge dents in concrete and steel. Ice and snow were plastered over almost every surface. Many lampposts, street signs and traffic lights had been uprooted and propelled like missiles, smashing into the sides of buildings or through windows or sometimes impaling whatever was in their paths. Trees toppled onto power lines and crashed down on roofs and porches and totalled many vehicles.

By some miracle – or more to the point, the infinite mercy of the Supreme One, for which I was most grateful, seeing as I had a hand in bringing about this devastation – not a single life was lost.

The most critical development was the rapid depletion of food, evident by the all-but-bare shelves in the Maritime Super-Mart and other grocery stores. By swiftly addressing this pressing crisis, Premier Reuben Arsenault asserted himself as a decisive leader, surprising many of his severest critics (including me) and even some of his most ardent supporters. A state of emergency was declared. There was no bridge to the mainland and the ferry terminal at Wood Islands had been pretty much washed away. The burden fell mainly on Charlottetown's tiny airport – once radio frequencies in the control tower were re-established and runways made available with the cancellation of all commercial flights – to make room for shipments of food to be flown in. The airfield at Slemon Park near Summerside was slated as the landing point for air force and army aircraft to land, with reservists enlisted to help with food and medical transport, as well as other rescue operations. After the Premier declared a state of emergency, the federal government responded with a $7.5 million assistance package, with Prime Minister Selfridge vowing that Ottawa would do everything in its power to bring the birthplace of Confederation back to normality. Reuben, almost as a response to the P.M., appeared on television and radio to assure the public that he had the situation well in hand. Canadians across the nation held donation drives and humanitarian organizations such as the Red Cross, set up relief stations in Charlottetown, Summerside and various smaller towns across the Island.

Internationally, the reaction was supportive of Canada's smallest province's plight, but much more coverage was allotted to the unsubstantiated reports of a public meeting where three strange figures appeared before the storm hit. Although there were press and a couple of photographers present at the Bertram Civic Centre, everyone was too stunned by the sudden appearance of the Figs to take pictures. The photos that were circulating, both from the press and the phones of those in the audience, were taken after the fact, and showed three men on stage who seemed to be dressed for some costume party.

The BBC speculated that it was some kind of elaborate hoax, while *Le Monde* and *Der Spiegel* likened it to some kind of cult worshipping.

In the United States, CNN, MSNBC and Fox News convened their talking heads to sum up the situation as a "cultural phenomenon," "political theatre," and "a socialist nightmare." The evangelical right-wing movement held prayer vigils and President McRonald praised this segment of religious America, who made up the majority of his base, by tweeting that they were "our country's best hope."

Back on PEI, clean-up crews, first responders and East Coast Utility linesmen were stretched to the limit. Makeshift emergency shelters were established in town halls, fire stations, school gymnasiums and even some private homes. In the meantime, medicine, supplies and volunteer assistance were also flown in to deal with the overwhelming situation. A percentage of the aid was domestic, meaning it came from other parts of Canada, mostly from Nova Scotia and New Brunswick as well as Quebec and Ontario and as far west as Saskatchewan. The rest of the volunteers originated from international areas, the United States and parts of Europe. Even technical crews from China and Taiwan showed up. The repeated phrase by most local officials echoed Reuben's own assertion that "we have been blessed with many friends."

When the storm first began to rage, I managed to get to the car in the Bertram Civic Centre parking lot, but I could only drive it halfway through Mount Russet, before abandoning it in the middle of downtown. Luckily, I was able to take refuge in Sadie's Tearoom, where the staff ushered a group of us down into their basement storeroom. By next morning, when the worst of the storm was over, I managed to locate the Golf. It had been flipped over a few times by the swirling windstorm until the front windshield, as well as the side and back windows, cracked and buckled under the force of being tossed around like a rubber ball. The roof crumpled into useless metal. My trusty Golf was a write-off. So, I made it on foot back to the Body Parts. The building had sustained extensive damage and my own windows were shattered, resulting in chaos in the studio itself ten times worse than any damage Reg'n'Kel could ever have hoped to wreak. Paintings were destroyed and all my paints, brushes and other implements scattered everywhere. Miraculously, the unfinished painting of North Cape, which was all but obscured by the ten-armed starfish, survived. Possibly, a testament to the divine protection surrounding that mutant creature.

Having taped cardboard over the smashed windows and cleaned up as best I could before despair got the best of me, I couldn't bear to spend one more minute in what was once my humble yet beloved sanctuary. I felt strangely frozen in a time and place that seemed more and more like some form of man-made hell.

Not knowing who else to turn to, I managed to find a working payphone at a nearby gas station (my own landline still being out of order) and put a call in to Zaina, who was working from home. This was about a week after the storm and most power lines and cell phone towers had only recently been restored and communication systems were slowly getting back to some semblance of normal.

Although Zaina's building had its share of damage, her apartment was barely touched. Miraculously, her windows stayed intact. Even her Toyota Camry remained relatively unscathed, suffering only a smashed left headlight and some dents on the passenger door and front hood. It made me wonder if the Supreme One was specifically looking out for her. I offered up silent thanks.

During our phone call, Zaina worried that I did not sound well. "I want you to pack a bag. I'm coming over there to take you back to my place. My sofa folds out into a bed."

My instant refusal to her offer was not merely out of politeness but carried with it an irrational fear of her seeing me at my worst. I argued that her apartment was small and that we were bound to get in each other's way, but she countered that we would deal with all that as it came. To be honest, I probably could have put up more resistance, but a sudden fatigue overpowered the fear and I acquiesced, self-pitying but grateful. When she showed up at the Body Parts to fetch me, I was all packed and ready to go. I felt like a castaway, setting eyes on the first ship I'd seen in years. Zaina cast a sombre eye around the hastily straightened disarray in my dimly lit studio and gently chastised me for not calling her sooner.

Back in her Camry, we barely spoke until we reached her building. Once she unlocked her door, I hesitated at the threshold with my suitcase like a nervous bride until Zaina ushered me in. I had a fleeting vision of her carrying me through the doorway newlywed-style, but quickly banished it from my mind. I chalked this up to suffering from a post-hurricane mental aftershock and worried that I would have to be extra vigilant while I was her guest.

She found some extra hangers and made room in her hall closet for my things, which I dutifully hung up. Near the sofa there was a side table with a couple of empty drawers into which I stuffed rolled-up underwear, socks and tee shirts. Finally, we were sitting in her kitchen together, all out of small talk but staring at the elephant in the room that had never lagged far behind since we first set eyes on each other. Now the tenacious pachyderm had finally caught up with us and made itself at home in her kitchen, seated precariously between us.

"Those three... whatever they were, those three, um, those men at the rally..." she said, leaving the obvious question hanging in the air for a moment.

"The figments?" I said, hoping to be helpful. Her puzzled expression told me I wasn't helping matters. "Figments of my imagination, I mean."

"How could they be?" She crossed her arms on the table and leaned forward, like that would somehow add weight to her incredulity. "We could all see them."

"I'm just as confused as you are," I confessed. "I think they were trying to help me in some way. Or they could very well have given up on me."

This last statement had been weighing on my mind since the rally because I had not seen nor heard from Judas, Shylock or Fagin since their dramatic appearance on the stage at the Bertram Civic Centre. I had gone through periods of not seeing or hearing from them before, often during which I hoped and feared, in equal measures, that they had abandoned me for good. But this time felt different somehow.

They had warned me about speaking of the Supreme One to anyone after my meeting with Tamara Tuplin. As I understood it, my invoking the deity on stage was the last straw, that I had somehow forced their hand, leaving them no choice but to reveal themselves, which in turn inflamed the Supreme One's fury, thus setting in motion the super hurricane that had all but destroyed the Island. Even when radio and television broadcasts had resumed, I barely tuned in and stayed away from the print media altogether, too nervous to find out what was being said, certain that I'd been implicated. I did try to log on to Anne Surly – using the Wi-Fi at Sadie's Tearoom since my own had yet to be restored – but the website was dark.

"Why didn't you tell me about them?" asked Zaina. "These figments."

"I would have thought that was obvious," I answered, with probably a touch too much condescension in my voice, judging by the offended furrow on her brow. I wasted no time in trying to remedy this perception. "You have to understand, throughout the whole time this has been going on, since that day I met you at Queens County Hospital, you were the only person that I ever felt was wholly on my side. I couldn't risk losing that by telling you some cockamamie story about figments of my imagination. Please tell me you understand."

Her features softened, but her voice retained a trace of hurt feelings. "It's just that..."

"What? Please tell me."

"You told Tamara Tuplin," she said. "You told her everything."

"Who told you that?" I cried and realized that I was now standing up.

"Tamara did, who else."

I suddenly felt stupid standing there with my hands on the table, all the better to lean over her. I must have looked as menacing and ridiculous as a cartoon vulture. I sat again.

"She called me after you went to see her and told me everything you'd said. She wanted to know if I knew anything about it."

"Didn't you think I was crazy after she called you?"

"Maybe, a little," she conceded. "Okay, a lot. But I wanted to hear it from you. Tamara even said that she thought you might tell me, since you told her. I was waiting for you to bring it up."

"How come you never told me? That she called you. That you knew."

"I don't know," she said and her body slumped slightly as if a great weight had been lifted from her shoulders. "I think, if you told her then you probably believed it. She was convinced you did. I mean, who would make up something like that? I kept telling myself that I was going to confront you about it, but every time an opportunity came up, I found some reason not to. I think, in some way, I didn't want to know. I didn't want to confront the possibility."

"What possibility?"

Her head tilted slightly forward in a feeble attempt to obscure her face, or at least not to have to look at me head on. "That you were, you know..." She pointed at her temple and made a circular motion with her forefinger. "Coo-coo for Cocoa Puffs."

I could see her facial muscles gamely struggling before a tight-lipped grin stretched uncontrollably across her face and we were both suddenly laughing like idiots. It took a few minutes and a couple of impromptu bursts of renewed laughter before we found our composure.

"And now you know, beyond a shadow of a doubt, that I'm nutso for Nutella."

"You mean gaga for Grape Nuts."

"Freaky for Frosted Flakes."

"Bonkers for Raising Bran."

"*Meshuggah* for Sugar Crisp," I said with a self-satisfied grin.

"I think maybe we have exhausted this silliness."

We succumbed to another brief spate of laughter that soon dissipated. Zaina's eyes met mine. It was a moment that seemed like it might veer toward intimacy. But the moment quickly passed when I saw she wasn't smiling.

"If you're crazy," she said soberly. "Then I guess all of us are also crazy now."

Over the next couple of weeks, we fell into a routine of sorts. I was fastidious in how neatly I kept my section of her apartment, waking early enough to fold up my bed to once more become her sofa, then shower, shave and clean the bathroom before she emerged from her room. That usually gave me enough time to dash into the kitchen and make tea. After her morning prayer, she made her own oatmeal, since I couldn't stand the stuff. I learned quickly that morning conversation didn't fit in to her waking up schedule. She had the kitchen to herself while I sat in the living room with my tea and surfed the Internet on my laptop or leafed through a selection from her bookshelf.

Her taste was eclectic, ranging from fiction bestsellers to pop psychology to books on religion. These mostly dealt with Islam, including the Quran, but also a King James Bible, the I-Ching and a book about Kabbalah. There were also a couple of books on the Druze culture. Once she had washed, dressed and eaten, she either joined me in the living room or I would venture back to the kitchen where, after proper good mornings, we had a second cup of tea together.

Not once did I ever see her without her hijab, nor did I want to. At least that's what I told myself. If, in fact, I did have some deep desire to see her bared head, I dared not delve so far down into my psyche to admit it. But I was pretty sure she was violating some Islamic rule about being alone with a man by letting me stay there. There were times I wanted to ask her about that, but I had a feeling such intimate questioning about her adopted religion might embarrass her. Living together under the same roof in such close proximity made me hypersensitive to the delicate balance of our situation.

During this time, she started to go into the office again. More often than not, I took a ride with her downtown where she could park for free behind McMurphy Realtors in a lot the company owned. Alternatively, I could walk the two blocks from Zaina's apartment building to catch the bus that would let me off in front of the Cradletown Arts Centre. I sometimes did this if I needed some alone time or sensed that Zaina needed the same. Aside from needing to get out of the apartment, I felt compelled to see the extent of the hurricane's damage.

But when we were together, she often questioned me about the three Figs. What were they like? Was I ever scared of them? I explained that from the beginning, when they first confronted me in my apartment (which did in fact scare the bejeezus out of me), they claimed to have free will and would appear and disappear on a whim. But this ability to show themselves to everyone had thrown me for a loop. In a way, I felt that I was truly losing my marbles, more so than when I was the only one who could see them.

Zaina's own perception of them at the rally was unclear because she assumed, like everyone else, that they were actors and their appearance was some kind of stunt. When the storm was quickly brewing and people were scrambling to get back to their homes, she began to consider they might actually be the real article and that I was possibly not a prime candidate for the funny farm.

I wondered what Tamara Tuplin was thinking when she saw Judas, Shylock and Fagin make their appearance at the rally and realizing that everything

I had told her during our meeting was true. I asked Zaina if she had spoken to Tamara at all since then. She hadn't.

In Charlottetown, I would wander around with my sketchpad and a few drawing pencils. What I could see of the devastation that the city had endured hollowed out something in me, a part connected to identity and place, a part that I felt could never be recovered in the same way the city would never be what it once was. For the first few days, I just wandered around in a daze, staring stupidly at rows of boarded up windows, whole corners of buildings gouged away, the skeletal metal frames of missing store signs, trees sprawled out across footpaths in parks or leaning precariously against other felled trees (holding each other up like drunken comrades). I walked past the corner of Queen Street and Victoria Row where the bench with the seated statue of Sir John A. MacDonald was missing altogether, as if the statue had miraculously come to life and fled to seek shelter, carrying the bench with him. East of Great George Street and well past Prince Street, roofs with missing shingles lined the narrow side roads of Sydney Street, Dorchester Street and King Street. Much of the waterfront was still cordoned off by yellow police tape. From what I could see buildings, piers and boats looked as if they were remnants of a war zone.

All I could do to process what I was seeing was to choose my preferred 4B pencil and record everything I witnessed on my sketchpad. But unlike drawing the dumping ground of Rossiter's Field, which allowed me to look deeper into the heap of trash with some intimacy, all that I sketched in our crumbling capital city, the process of zeroing in on detail after detail, had the opposite effect. I wasn't able to penetrate the initial shock of what I saw and, instead, the concentration of my labour detached me from my surroundings. At first, I found this frustrating, but soon I realized it was part of coping with the traumatic effects of immersing myself so relentlessly. I stood and balanced my pad on one forearm, holding it steady with my hand and allowed the pencil in my other hand to record what I saw with a certain amount of dispassion.

I showed the sketches to Zaina. She suggested that I send them to the *Charlottetown Parrot*. It seemed like a strange suggestion at the time and when I asked why the newspaper, she said the galleries were still closed and the *Parrot* had recently resumed publishing. It made more sense when she explained it and I took them to the newspaper's office. An editor from their art department looked over the drawings and agreed to feature them in a spread for their weekend edition. I was paid a lump sum of $75. When it came out, I flipped through the Entertainment section and found four drawings on the last two pages. Over the following week there were letters to the paper praising the sketches and a small exhibition was soon arranged at the Cradletown Art Gallery, which had sustained a few broken windows and needed something to put in one of their upper spaces. The aftermath of this calamity that had befallen our beloved island now became the catalyst for a resurgence of my artistic career.

The downside of this resurgence was that I was now aware that I had become a person of interest, as I discovered from hearing my name mentioned on Pole Star, our local evening news program. Now that recovery efforts, particularly in Charlottetown and Summerside, were on the upswing with concentrated infrastructural improvements on roads and bridges, questions stemming from the Figs' appearance at the Bertram Civic Centre began to resurge as well. I had been wondering why I hadn't heard from the cops. But now apparently, they were looking for me, having paid visits to the Body Parts, as well as the offices of the *Charlottetown Parrot* and the Cradletown Art Gallery. The news reports also mentioned that the RCMP and possibly CSIS might want to speak to me as well.

I hadn't told anyone that I was now staying with Zaina, so we were both gobsmacked, while watching the news on her TV in the kitchen, to realize that I was ostensibly hiding out at her place. We had a brief discussion about whether I should turn myself in, with Zaina taking the pro side and me decisively taking the con.

"They're going to find you sooner or later," she reasoned. "You might as well get it over with. After all, it's all out in the open. What else do you have to hide?"

"I have nothing to hide," I argued. "But that's never stopped the police before. If they like you for something they have ways of making it stick."

"I think you've been watching too many TV shows."

She may have been right. So right, that now I began to secretly worry that Zaina might take it upon herself to give the cops a heads-up as to where they could find me. Not that I thought she had Crime Stoppers on speed dial or anything, but maybe she was worried that she would be implicated in some kind of wrong-doing by harbouring a fugitive. Then she received a voicemail from an aide at the Premier's office asking for her to contact them if she knew where to find me. Apparently Reuben was also anxious to have a word with me and obviously remembered seeing us together at the Crazy Diamond opening. When I asked Zaina whether she was going to call them, she insisted on deleting the voicemail then and there in front of me.

"You got no worries, Scarface," she said mirthlessly. "I ain't gonna rat you out."

IT WAS ZAINA who first mentioned that there was something strange in the atmosphere, a sense that things were moving in a certain way, somehow quicker, a suspicion that time had passed without one's realizing it. I had felt this a couple of times before, this sense of acceleration, most recently around autumn of the previous year when I was in the car with Shylock and we first heard the machines beginning the clean-up at Rossiter's Field. After that I thought no more about it. Whether things had slowed down or I had merely become inured to the sensation, I couldn't say. But it was only when Zaina mentioned it that I became newly aware of it. And with this new awareness, I realized there was something different from what I felt that time with Shylock.

"It might be an aftereffect from the storm," I said to Zaina.

"Maybe," she conceded. "It's certainly not like anything I've ever felt before. It feels like the air is somehow in flux. Every breath seems to be moving through me, but also carrying me along. Almost against my will."

This description interested me, as it was different from my own sensation. For me, it was a feeling of something, an energy moving around quite separate from me. Zaina was more immersed in it.

I also remembered something the Figs told me when I first encountered them. How what passes for centuries in this world is but a moment where the

Supreme One dwells. Could this sense of acceleration somehow signify the presence or proximity of the Supreme One? A sign that divine intervention had a hand in whatever was going on?

Despite our distinctly different experiences of whatever was happening, Zaina and I both felt a similar twinge when it was announced that Premier Reuben Arsenault would make a special address on television. The announcement was expected to affect the future of the Island and everyone on it. Speculation was rife that efforts to ship in supplies and workers had hit a snag and new drastic cost-cutting measures were going to be enforced. There was no evidence that this was really the case, so it was difficult to know how these rumours were started.

On the night of the broadcast, Zaina and I settled in at her kitchen table to watch the 12-inch TV screen that faced us from her kitchen counter. Cozy as it was to be sitting there, we shared a chill of anxiety as we waited for the broadcast to begin.

Reuben had made a few television appearances since the storm, but immediately we could see that this one was different. He stood behind a podium with a single microphone attached to a stand. He was only in his shirtsleeves, which were rolled part way up his forearms. He was rarely, if ever, seen in public without a jacket. His shirt collar was unbuttoned and his signature bolo tie (one I hadn't seen before, shaped like a sapphire blue oyster shell) was loosened. He looked like an auctioneer at a county fair and I half-expected him to start spewing a rapid-fire sales patter. He took the mic from the stand and walked around from behind the podium and planted himself firmly in front of it. Everything in his body language, from his squared shoulders to his unwavering gaze into the camera, exuded the demeanour of a man of the people who is ready to take action. This expectation was reinforced when he began to speak.

"Friends, citizens, Islanders. The past months have been a testament to the fortitude of the people of Prince Edward Island. It is times like these, in the face of devastation, that we are tested as a people. We are burdened with the question of what it means to survive. As we try to rebuild our homes, our farms, our businesses and our communities we cannot help but ask ourselves

– why? Why did this happen to us? Why were we targeted by the wrath of this merciless storm? Who do we turn to for answers? Where can we find a glimpse of the truth?"

Zaina and I briefly looked at each other with puzzled expressions. Reuben was giving a sermon rather than a political address. He continued briefly in this vein then began to talk about the Bertram Civic Centre, how the evening began with great promise but soon became "the turning point in our collective fortunes." When I heard him say my name, I felt tiny pinpricks trickling down my spine to the small of my back.

"When I allowed Samson Grief to take the stage at the Bertram Civic Centre, little did I know what was to befall our unsuspecting island," Reuben said as if he was a lawyer assuring a jury of the Island's innocence during his final argument. I couldn't help but feel I was the one on trial in a Kafkaesque nightmare. "And when those three mysterious figures suddenly appeared on the stage, who among us did not suspect some theatrical trickery was taking place? There are those of you who might still hold that opinion. For a long time, I did not know what to think. I have not had the opportunity to speak with Mr. Grief since that night, so I must draw my own conclusions. But I am nothing if not flexible in my outlook on the world. When confronted with things that cannot be easily explained away, I do not close my eyes and cover my ears. I open my heart and, more importantly, I open my faith and let it take me where it will. I am here now to ask you to follow me, to trust my judgement and consider my conclusions. I am here to ask you to take that leap of faith with me. You see, I had hoped Samson Grief might be able to conjure those three figures, as he did at the Bertram Civic Centre, so we could get some answers. But when my attempts to contact Mr. Grief were unsuccessful, I knew I had no choice except to turn to prayer."

He fell silent, bowed his head and clasped his hands together. Three figures behind him stepped forward from the dimly lit background. Zaina and I stared at the TV screen as Judas, Shylock and Fagin took their places beside Reuben. They wore the same outfits as when they appeared at the Bertram Civic Centre, their native garb, so to speak, the outfits that our collective consciousness imagines them wearing. They had no more use for their tourist disguises, although, to tell the truth, I missed the loud shirts and goofy hats. I didn't recognize Shylock without his bucket hat or Fagin without the ball cap. Most of all, I missed Judas's yellow porkpie hat and the way he pushed it forward, not in some hipster's cooler-than-thou posture, but almost apologetically, as if he was trying to hide behind it.

Now the three of them – Fagin and Shylock standing on one side of Reuben and Judas standing alone on the other side – appeared somewhat stupefied by their surroundings, the lights and cameras pointing at them. There was restless murmuring off camera that most likely came from the technical crew, since the broadcast was in a studio with no live audience. Reuben lifted his head and motioned for calm and quiet.

"No, my friends, this is not a trick. Nor is it cheap theatrics. These are the three figures who appeared at the Bertram Civic Centre that fateful night. The two on my left are Shylock and Fagin. This gentleman on my right is Judas. Yes, that one. Judas Iscariot. Amazing as it may seem, through prayer I have asked them to join me tonight, and they have graciously accepted my invitation, so that their presence might support what I have to say to you. I bring you the message of a bold new future for our island, our home, and yes, our sanctuary."

Reuben wasted no more time in putting his message across while Judas, Shylock and Fagin looked on. The message was simply this: the hurricane that had all but decimated PEI was not an accident or a freak of nature. It was an act of God, or rather, as Reuben bluntly stated, "It was an act of the Supreme One, as my friends up here will attest." The three Figs nodded solemnly.

"But don't just take my word for it," he said and pointed his microphone in front of each Fig, looking not unlike Phil Donahue or Jerry Springer encouraging his guests to tell their stories.

"You can be sure, my dear, that this was the Supreme One's fury raging across this poor red jewel of an island," said Fagin.

"Verily," said Shylock when the microphone was pointing at him. "'Twas more than a paltry expression of vexation. The Supreme One hath executed the emergence of a larger scheme."

Then Reuben turned and aimed the mic at Judas, who merely stared at it with some suspicion. "My friends speak truthfully, yet with limited knowledge.

There are none of us who can know what is in the infinite mind of the Supreme One. Yet I can verify some of what they have already stated and add to that. The Supreme One's will shall be done in one fashion or another."

Reuben's eyes lit up and he raised an index finger, like a lawyer stating his case or a clergyman in mid-sermon, as if to emphasize a universal truth. "And isn't it true that the Supreme One's will, the reason the three of you have been sent to us, is to refashion this island as the new Promised Land?"

"'Struth!" chimed in Shylock. "'Twas toward such an end as we enlisted our good cousin Samson."

"It were the synagogue," added Fagin. "The painter was tasked with building it as was the Supreme One's command."

"Yea, my brethren are giving you but the main facts," interrupted Judas. "This was our original mission and the main motive, among others, of why we have revealed ourselves."

Judas paused, taking a moment to formulate a thought in order to say something further, but Reuben wasted no time in thanking them and stepping toward the camera, leaving Judas, Shylock and Fagin behind to linger in the background. The three of them looked uncertainly at each other before the camera zoomed in on a close-up of Reuben, cutting the three Figs out of the shot.

"There you have it," said Reuben.

Despite Judas's earlier advice against second-guessing what might be in the Supreme One's "infinite mind", Reuben asserted that Hurricane X had not wreaked disaster so much as it had embarked on a cleansing, wiping the slate clean for a new beginning.

"The path of what seems to us like destruction is actually the gateway to a new tomorrow. That tomorrow is now upon us in a dawning of independence. I am hereby declaring that Prince Edward Island, in accordance with its status as the new Promised Land, is now a sovereign nation unto itself. And I know what many of you are thinking. How can he do this? This is a coup d'etat! That's just not how things are done here. But it is not me doing this alone. I did have a meeting with my cabinet to share my vision and I can tell you they have offered their full support. But most importantly, I am acting through divine intervention. My fellow Islanders, you can see with your own eyes that life as we knew it has changed unalterably. I am asking you to put your trust in me, as I have put my faith in the three messengers who have brought us tidings of a new era where Prince Edward Island is at the forefront. Because, as of this moment, we are taking the reins of our destiny firmly in our own hands. Not only will we steer our own course, we will break the ground that opens the road to new fortune and prosperity."

After Reuben assured us that more details would emerge in the coming days and weeks, the broadcast was abruptly over. Zaina turned off the TV before the usual panel of talking heads could get started with their analyses of this bewildering declaration. Zaina and I regarded each other, silently allowing our own thoughts to turn over at their leisure.

Where did one begin? There was nothing vague about this stink. Even the more pronounced stench of the Fair Dissemination of Public Information Act smelled daisy fresh compared to this out-and-out embracing of authoritarianism.

"He can't do this," I said. "And what was all that about our status as the new Promised Land? There's no status. PEI doesn't have any status as any kind of Promised Land. Not until there's a synagogue on Rossiter's Field. That's how I got dragged into this mess."

"Allow me to rectify thy statement, good cousin. Thou weren't dragged, but rather, thou hath been favoured to turn as a blessed cog within the cosmic wheel of golden providence."

Zaina gave a sharp gasp and I jumped up from my seat to see Shylock standing directly behind my chair. Seeing the effect he had on us, Shylock bowed and clasped his hands in a show of penitence.

"A thousand pardons to the fair lady. Prithee, be not alarmed at my intrusion on the sacred privacy of thy modest abode."

"Forget that," I said. "What were the three of you doing with Reuben Arsenault? And why didn't any of you set him straight about the synagogue and Rossiter's Field and this Promised Land business?"

"Put yourself in our shoes, my dear." Fagin stood beside the refrigerator. This too startled Zaina, but she took it in stride far more quickly than I ever did. "We wasn't what you'd call in our element, was we, what with all them big metal contraptions aimed at us and the lights blinding us. We could barely put two thoughts together afore it was all over."

"To be fair, they were on Reuben's turf," Zaina interjected. "He tends to have the upper hand when the cameras are on him and he controls the conditions."

Zaina had a point, but I still wasn't satisfied. "You three never had any problem running circles around me. Now all of a sudden you don't know your right foot from your left? Give me a break. The real question is what were you doing with him on this broadcast in the first place? It looked like you were endorsing this plan about PEI becoming independent."

There was a momentary pause while I waited for the triumvirate to be completed. It was a pregnant pause, but sure enough it finally gave birth as Judas materialized at the kitchen's entrance. He smiled and nodded at Zaina, then adopted a more doleful countenance when addressing me.

"We had no choice but to appear with Reuben Arsenault when it became clear that he needed our assistance to state his case," he said. "In short, we were there because of what you had set in motion by invoking the Supreme One's name."

"You mean the hurricane."

He lowered his eyelids and nodded.

"I know I overstepped my bounds," I said. "But why punish the whole island? Why not just me?"

"Verily, good cousin, 'twas punishment directed at thee to bear the onus of witnessing thine adopted home laid to waste," said Shylock.

I turned to Judas. "I can't say you didn't try to warn me. But what's to be done? Or is it all over now?"

"All I can say is it was the will of the Supreme One that we appeared first at the public hall and then again with Reuben Arsenault. It is now the will of the Supreme One that we avail ourselves to further the providential path of this island. And if that is the will of the Supreme One, then it is our will too, as well as yours."

"Whatever happened to free will?"

Fagin jumped in. "What indeed, my dear? The best this life has to offer is free and yet it all comes at a cost. That is the secret proviso of Opportunity."

"Ne'er stumble into the error of confounding 'freedom' and 'duty' as detached entities," Shylock said. "They both entwine securely and shall not be extricated from t'other. Thus, is Principle securely knotted."

"Spare me the homespun platitudes!" I said, losing patience. "What about the synagogue and Rossiter's Field?"

"They have not been forgotten," said Judas. "But I must admit, all that has befallen will not make your task easier."

"Oh, I see, this is still my task."

"Surrender thyself to reason, signor," said Shylock sternly. "Circumstances may yet alter, but our initial quest changeth not."

"That depends," interjected Zaina, almost to herself. She was suddenly aware that she spoke aloud and had our attention. "What I mean is goals, or the way to achieve them, change all the time. You just have to know how to read the signs."

"What signs?" I said.

"I don't know," she said. "But I think I know someone who does."

With that, she left the kitchen and soon returned with her laptop. She sat at the kitchen table and opened the computer, quickly typing on the keyboard while the Figs and I gathered round. The Anne Surly website soon appeared on the screen. Then we were looking at Anne Surly herself. The only recognizable things about her were the trademark straw hat, orange pigtails and the half mask. Gone was the dominatrix bustier, only to be replaced by a dark jacket with a Nehru-like collar and broad shoulders, which gave her upper body an angular V-shape. The jacket was matched by a dark pair of jodhpurs and polished knee-high riding boots. She looked strangely like a militaristic schoolgirl. Instead of elbow-length leather gloves, she wore pale cotton gloves that were virginal in contrast to the severity of her outfit. She forsook the riding crop and golf club or any other prop and kept her hands folded in front of her.

It's hard to fully convey how this change in Anne Surly affected me, except to say I felt a vague foreboding, mixed in with a sharper sense of loss. Perhaps I was remembering how Aziza had once confessed to me, during our first proper talk together, that she had been influenced by my painting *Anne of Bergen-Belsen*, from which I understood she meant by its subversive temperament. Although one could argue that her current mode of dress was in its own way subversive, it was still a far cry from the outlandish rebelliousness of her dominatrix image. In its stead was a more puritanical persona. Along with the change of costume, also gone was the husky, profanity-laced manner of speaking.

"Thank you for watching," she said in a measured, almost melodious voice that had lost none of its confidence. "Although I may look different than before, I can guarantee what has not changed is that I will continue to speak truth to power."

She paused to let that phrase sink in. Truth to power? What was the truth and who held the power? What followed didn't illuminate matters any.

"Our premier has not been telling us everything. In past webcasts I mentioned something called Project Friendly Occupation. I haven't been able to convey the full breadth and scope of this operation. I've only been able to piece together some innuendo here or some insinuation there. Until now, that is."

What followed was a methodical, if intricate roadmap, where she attempted to describe a series of communication backchannels, as well as a few side channels and even one or two up front channels, all of which had culminated in meetings between an array of businessmen, lawyers, attachés and some characters whose backgrounds were a touch shadier. A couple of names were familiar, the most recognizable being, Nathan Affleck (who had been mentioned in a past webcast and who was apparently a major player), but many names were new to me and the mental scorecard I was keeping quickly became inundated and almost impossible to follow. The meetings involved a number of different representatives from various foreign powers, the most prominent being the United States, which always had someone on the scene who was representing its interests.

Where things took a more bizarre turn, which nevertheless shook me awake from the stupor of trying to keep track of all the names Anne Surly had been spewing, was when she mentioned the whole Bertram Civic Centre thing with me, the three Figs and the ensuing Hurricane X.

"In its original form, Project Friendly Occupation would have taken much longer to implement, maybe a few years. But the hurricane expedited matters. As it was, Prince Edward Island was slowly gaining minor footholds in international partnerships and trade. It took major destruction from a hurricane to raze the Island to practically nothing so that, ironically, it could be built up that much faster. As an independent entity, PEI will be able to become a home away from home for our American friends as well as those abroad. In the past, we relied on the vagaries of tourism. Project Friendly Occupation and our new sovereign independence will give us the economic security of being an offshore tax haven, since there are no plans to rebuild the Confederation Bridge or the Wood Islands ferry terminal. PEI will now be a place where our friends can safely invest their money and resources, all the while feeling confident that we are all building a future together. That is all I can tell you for the time being. In the meantime, have faith in our Premier's plans and in his ability to guide us. The better tomorrow we have always wanted is here today."

The screen went black. Zaina closed her laptop. We stared at each other in stunned silence.

"I don't understand," I said. "Have faith? Better tomorrow? When did she become Reuben's cheerleader? How is that truth to power"

"She was always her father's daughter," said Zaina. The response was automatic, a familiar trope to fall back on. I could tell her mind was on something else.

She looked pale. I wanted to ask if she was okay, but I could feel it too. That sense of acceleration or temporal shifting or whatever you want to call it. Existential contractions somewhere between tendons and blood vessels. An arrhythmic shudder deep in the marrow. I struggled to formulate a question but Zaina spoke first.

"Explain something to me," she said turning to Judas, Shylock and Fagin, who much to my surprise were still there with us. "You originated in Samson's mind. Figments of his imagination. Yes?"

"'Twould be most simplistic to verify that hypothesis, good lady," said Shylock. "And yet those complex channels within the mind may leadeth to greater spheres of continuity."

Zaina pondered this for a moment. "So now that we can all see you, does that mean you are a figment of all our imaginations? A collective hallucination or a form of mass hypnotism?"

"If you reckon this is all a waking dream of a sort, my dear, you may not be too far off," answered Fagin. "But even dreams have their own logic that won't answer all your questions."

"Besides, they would be the wrong questions," said Judas. "Yet I can tell you this. What you call hallucination is a culmination of distortions. What you call hypnosis can be better described as an ongoing prognosis. A mutation that moves in circular courses and adopts familiar strains of experience like half-remembered echoes."

And then they were gone. Who wouldn't want to disappear after those convoluted explications? I tried to explain to Zaina the comings and goings of the three Figs, but she wasn't as discomfited by their disappearance as I often was. I wanted to talk more about Anne Surly's webcast, but it was clear that Zaina was tired. She said we could talk in the morning.

WHEN I MADE A CALL to Darcy, the super at the Body Parts, he said the damage in my apartment had been fixed and my windows replaced. I wasted no time moving back. The daylight streaming into my studio did much to improve it.

As happy as I was to return to my old refuge, I soon became keenly aware of an odd sense of emptiness. I realized that a part of me missed being at Zaina's. Her place was definitely too small for two people, but while I was there, I felt like I was cocooned in an in-between life, similar to what one feels when staying in a hotel. But there was one difference. In a hotel one feels a disconnection from one's identity and sense of order that can be liberating in a strange way. You can do what you want, leave your bed unmade or throw wet towels on the bathroom floor, knowing someone else will deal with it.

At Zaina's, it was exactly the opposite. I was very aware of being in someone else's space, aware that I had to be on my best behaviour and not wear out my welcome. I had lived alone for so long I forgot what it felt like to have another person present in the same place. In one way, it was nerve-wracking and I could never fully relax. But in another way, the limitations imposed on me felt safe. I became acutely aware of how lonely I had been all these years and how protected I felt from all that loneliness, if only for that brief period with Zaina.

But once I settled back into my apartment, the loneliness returned, like a phantom roommate having shown up unannounced. It would not bother to be as considerate as I had strived to be with Zaina. It would make its presence felt by leaving its clothes strewn on the floor and dirty dishes in the sink for me to deal with.

As might be expected, Reuben's announcement of PEI as a sovereign nation became instant news, not only nationally but also internationally. Whether Reuben had the constitutional right to make such a decision was fiercely debated in parliament, written about in the press and trended across all social media platforms for the next few weeks.

At the outset, it seemed like a rash decision that was sprung on us. So many questions remained unanswered. What about all the benefits we enjoyed as Canadians? What currency would we use? Would we still have a parliamentary government? What would relations with the rest of Canada be like?

On PEI, there were demonstrations for and against independence. Sometimes there were violent clashes. A pro-independence group, calling themselves Island Strong, held a rally at a public park in Borden-Carleton to celebrate one month since the destruction of the Confederation Bridge, calling it an act of emancipation for all Islanders. The rally was soon interrupted by a pro-federalist group called The Confederation Nation. What started as a shouting match turned to a physical confrontation with rocks, bats and fists. When police, made up of a hastily assembled group of reserve trainees, showed up, neither group showed any inclination to back down. At the end, there were two dead and many injured, including three police trainees. And after the Mi'kmaq Alliance made an official statement that any form of Island independence would not be legitimate until their land claims were honoured first, somebody shot out the windows of their main office.

Throughout it all, Reuben insisted that he was not acting autocratically, but rather that he was merely conceding to the Supreme One's decree of a new Promised Land as a way of ensuring PEI's best interests and leading it into a new era of prosperity.

I thought it best to keep a low profile and toyed with the idea of going away, maybe permanently. But some part of me rejected that idea. After stocking up on provisions, mostly frozen premade meals, a few staples and boxes of tea, I hunkered down in my apartment in order to think things through and plan my next move before the cops came knocking on my door, which I expected to happen at any minute. When the knock never came, rather than feeling relieved, I was even more on edge. That could only mean something else, and probably worse, was around the corner.

16

IT DIDN'T TAKE LONG before the prospect of eating another frozen dinner filled me with an existential dread the likes of which has not been known since Sartre declared Hell is other people. To that I would add: and they are condemned to a diet of Swanson, Stouffers and Birds Eye. The plan was to hole myself up in the apartment for an indefinite amount of time, partially because I was feeling paranoid about having my name publicly associated with the three Figs, the Supreme One and Hurricane X. Even while I was buying all those frozen provisions at the Co-op in Mount Russet, I was sure people were looking at me and whispering to themselves. I needed time to think and stay out of sight (and hopefully out of mind) for as long as it took for things to get back to some semblance of normalcy. I doubt I lasted a full week in the apartment. The final straw that broke the camel's back (and my will to live) came during a moment of delirium, possibly brought on by malnutrition, when I peeled back the corner of the opaque plastic cover of yet another prepackaged tray only to be confronted by what appeared to be cryogenically frozen entrails but in reality, was fettuccine carbonara. Or at least that's what was advertised on the box.

Although I couldn't figure out how to escape this self-imposed exile, it at least had afforded me a few minor insights about what drove me into exile in the first place. These insights mostly had to do with Anne Surly, or more precisely, Aziza Arsenault. I couldn't get Anne Surly's sudden change in look and attitude out of my mind, particularly her unexpected allegiance to Reuben Arsenault. I thought back to Aziza's behaviour before my appearance at the Bertram Civic Centre.

I could trace how she began to distance herself from me way back to the period following her release from Queens County Hospital after her bike accident. I put it down to her wanting to be more careful about revealing the new location of her webcasts, which it turned out later was in the Shine Shrine behind the Crazy Diamond with Maggie Beairsto as her cameraperson. According to Kelvin Muir (when he spoke to me confidentially from the back seat of the car), at some point Reuben knew where she was broadcasting from and gave explicit orders to let her keep doing so. Anne Surly's webcasts still had a distinct anti-Reuben bias back then. Or was that for show? Did the slow revolution toward her recent about-face actually start back then?

When Anne Surly started to mention my name during her rants, I sensed something more suspicious was afoot, even if I couldn't put my finger on what it was. Later she warned me about forgetting Rossiter's Field as a site for the synagogue, lest I make myself a target. That word "target" always stuck in the back of my mind. Then I remembered her at the newly refurbished Crazy Diamond, the way she lingered at Reuben's table and could barely make eye contact with me. This was after I had accepted Reuben's invitation to appear at the Bertram Civic Centre.

Was that why Anne Surly kept mentioning my name on her webcasts, trying to portray me as the David against Reuben's Goliath, goading me to take action? Was it all really a set up to get me to agree to Reuben's suggestion and appear at the rally so he could humiliate me publicly? And he'd been succeeding masterfully until things took a sudden left turn when the three Figs showed up and then Hurricane X struck from out of nowhere. The possibility that Aziza had been in cahoots with her father all that time – incredulous as it was – sent my paranoia spiralling.

During my time in the apartment, I hadn't been totally cut off from the outside, occasionally tuning in to *Good Morning, PEI.* Although Chad Peladeau could hold his own as a solo host, he had recently been joined by a female co-host, Janella Chatterjee, a perky-voiced millennial, obviously recruited to infuse some fresh blood into the show. On the surface their banter maintained the usual cheerful inanities of morning radio, but where the dynamic between Chet and Chad was a hermetic aging frat boy zaniness, Janella introduced an air of buoyant femininity and savvy intellect to Chad's old dog grudgingly trying to learn a new trick or two.

CHAD: "So, now that PEI is an independent country or a sovereign entity or whatever Premier Arsenault is calling us this week..."

JANELLA: "A self-determining theocracy, I believe, is the term he used in the last speech he gave."

CHAD: "He's just making this stuff up as he goes along, isn't he."

JANELLA: "I'd say 'theocracy' is stretching it a bit, since that usually implies that religious leaders of some form are in control.

CHAD: "But his whole argument is that PEI has been singled out to be some kind of Promised Land by, and I'll never be able to wrap my head around this, the Supreme One."

JANELLA: "Although, if I remember correctly, that would entail building a synagogue."

CHAD: "And that's the other thing. Wasn't that the whole bugaboo with the artist, Samson Grief? Building this synagogue on Rossiter's Field? When I interviewed him last year, he was all gung-ho for it."

JANELLA: "I remember hearing that interview. At first many thought Grief was nothing but a crackpot, but after the interview he seemed to gather a swell of public support. And yet, we haven't heard much from him since he appeared at the Bertram Civic Centre in Mount Russet. And now it seems it's Premier Arsenault himself who has picked up the mantle. In his last speech, the premier vowed that he would indeed build the synagogue. Where it's going to be is another question."

CHAD: "I'd say in the larger scheme of things that's probably the least of his problems."

That was about as much as I could stand and turned off the radio. Self-determining theocracy? Reuben seemed to be flying by the seat of his pants in his efforts to define his vision of independence. And now he was actually going to build the synagogue? That really was news.

Still, building a synagogue anywhere but on Rossiter's Field was not going to put him or this newly-independent free-standing land mass in the Supreme One's good graces. On the other hand, Chad was spot-on when he implied that our Reuben definitely had his hands full when it came to getting PEI on its transitional feet. Setting up a governing infrastructure presented one speed bump after another. Reuben's cabinet were not much more than wide-eyed neophytes when it came to governance. That was their charm early on, but none of them were prepared for Reuben's autocratic parlour trick of declaring the Island as sovereign, despite his claim that he had full support from a legislative majority.

The most ludicrous scheme was something called the Creative Wellness Act, concocted by Health and Culture Minister Dr. Henry Becker. Doctors were encouraged to prescribe different arts and crafts for their patients as supplemental forms of therapy. At the same time, local artists and artisans were called upon to set up instructional workshops for their various disciplines: painting, writing, theatre, basket-making, etc. For every patient doctors sent to a so-called therapeutic workshop, they received a kick-back, from the workshop instructors, who, in turn, were subsidized by a private arts organization for the initial setting up of their workshops. On paper, the idea seemed far-fetched at best, receiving much criticism from the media. But in practice, the whole scheme spiralled into chaos when patients complained long and loud about being sent to workshops that had no beneficial value for their ailments. What's more, there were cases of patients being nickel-and-dimed for arts and crafts supplies.

At first, Reuben was forced to defend his Health and Culture Minister, but finally he had to disavow himself from the ill-conceived legislation and repeal the act. Dr. Henry Becker had to resign and Health and Culture (the pairing of which was Reuben's idea in the first place) were given their own separate portfolios. Other headaches, such as setting up a taxation system, some form of public pension plan, creating courts and a police force, all of which were slowly being privatized, subjected Reuben to further media criticism. A plebiscite proposing a lottery-style form of pension scheme (dubbed the Island Ponzi Plan by the media), where percentages of the top cash prize would somehow trickle down to all participants to be paid out annually, was met with such disdain, nobody bothered to cast any votes whatsoever. For that, Finance Minister Ralph Tweel (he of the infamous hair-trigger middle finger) was forced to resign immediately, while Reuben had no choice but to leave the portfolio unrepresented until he could find a suitable replacement.

In the case of Justice Minister Stewart Munt, his initiative to start up a program recruiting felons who had served their time – often for violent offenses – to be correctional officers, armed security guards in court houses and other governmental buildings, and police trainees, painted Reuben in a corner because he couldn't afford to lose another minister. So, in the face of growing criticism, Reuben had to double down on his support for Munt, calling the criticism "a backlash of woke hand-wringing" and declaring that everyone deserved a second chance to be a contributing member of society. In retaliation, public safety groups spread a meme with a pair of wringing hands and the caption "Woke Is Me." Meanwhile, the increasing social instability led to many protests and an escalation of violent confrontations between divided factions, stretching the trainee reserves that still made up the existing police force to a breaking point.

More and more, Reuben publicly invoked the name of Project Friendly Occupation without offering too many details, except to say that an infusion of foreign funds through carefully-planned deals were going to change the Island's fortunes in a way that federal handouts never could. He ended every televised speech with a moment of prayer, during which he pleaded to the Supreme One to "see our blessed Island through this transitional trial."

THE PROSPECT OF almost half a freezer full of frozen dinners waiting to be nuked, was enough to push me out the front door of the Body Parts and into the sun-streaked glare of a new day.

The warmer spring weather felt incongruent alongside the boarded-up storefronts, bent street signs, dilapidated buildings and major road damage due to flooding along Orchard Street. It was a grim reminder that, like Mount Russet, many other small towns and communities across PEI were still behind in the efforts to rebuild, compared to that of Charlottetown and Summerside, despite Anne Surly's assertion that restoration across the Island would happen at a much faster rate. The divide between rural PEI, which was (in terms of land mass) basically ninety-five percent of the Island, and the two larger cities (such as they were) was wider than ever.

I was glad to see Sadie's Tearoom had a few customers, but even happier that my favourite table by the window was vacant. It was one of the few businesses with a front window, which made it all the more welcoming although the view of our rundown main drag left something to be desired. While still immersed in the relief of being anywhere but my apartment, I realized somebody was speaking my name. I looked up and there was Tamara Tuplin standing at my table. My peripheral vision caught three members of her staff, whom I remembered from when I was at the Great Boat Party headquarters, sitting at a nearby table. They were all looking at Tamara Tuplin. A vacant seat was pulled out and waiting for her.

"Sorry to bother you," she said. "I didn't expect to see you here."

"Hello there," I said, my thoughts still on the view through the window. "What are you doing here? In Mount Russet, I mean."

"Kind of an unofficial visit," she said and cast a quick glance to her party settling in at their table. "I wonder, would you mind if I joined you for a moment?"

"Make your yourself at home," I said and noticed someone from the next table, an older man whom I remembered for his silver-grey pigtails, push the chair they were holding out for her closer to the table.

She came right to the point. "My staff and I are in Mount Russet because we wanted to see what was happening at Rossiter's Field," she said. "But there's a blockade with flashing lights and some uniforms barring the road."

"Cops?"

"What police force we have is mostly reserve trainees and are stretched to the limit as it is," she said. "No, looked more like guards-for-hire. Nobody's allowed to enter without a special pass."

"Well, it is private property."

"Yes, except Reuben keeps mixing it up with public policy."

"What did you expect to see?"

"Just whatever's going on over there. There've been no reports about any progress for the clean-up."

"It's not like I want to make any excuses for Arsenault," I said. "But his plate has been kind of full since the hurricane."

"I'm sure it has." Tamara Tuplin nodded, although the gaze she fixed on me contradicted that gesture of agreement. "Still, nobody put a gun to his head and forced him to make PEI a sovereign nation. There's some kind of special project going on at Rossiter's Field. But I don't think it's this children's camp. He keeps talking about Project Friendly Occupation, like it's public policy, but because Rossiter's Field is private property, he doesn't feel obligated to give many details."

I assumed she would get back to her staff. Instead, she changed the subject to our first meeting last year at the Great Boat Party headquarters. Her manner became oddly deferential, saying how courageous I was to confide in her about the three Figs and the Supreme One, knowing the risk I was taking. She felt honoured that I trusted her enough to confide in her. If she was having me on, she was doing a good job of it with the way she managed to keep a straight face. I tried to play it cool and see where this was going. That didn't last long.

"How courageous did you paint me out to be when you called Zaina to tell her what I told you?" I said, louder than I intended. "Nice way to thank me for my trust in you. I assume you wanted to take her to task or warn her that she had sent a lunatic to you."

From the corner of my eye, I could see her staff at the next table turn their heads in our direction.

"First of all, what else was I going to do?" she said without a trace of defensiveness. "She referred you to me. I thought she had a right to know. In the second place, whether you were a lunatic or not, I didn't think you were dangerous. Or else I would have called the police. But third, and most importantly, you seemed to have a genuine respect for the spirit of reconciliation in general and specifically the importance of consultation with the Mi'kmaq Alliance when it came to building your synagogue on Rossiter's Field. That showed you were serious. So really, how bad could you be?"

I couldn't argue with that logic and, to be truthful, felt a bit ashamed at my outburst. Without missing a beat, she brought up what happened at the Bertram Civic Centre. Like everyone else, she didn't know what to think at first when Judas, Shylock and Fagin appeared on the stage, but it didn't take long for her to believe that what was happening was real rather than some staged hoax.

"I can't say exactly what convinced me. I was more focused on you than them. Your reaction to them. I guess if it had been something staged or planned you would have looked, I don't know, proud maybe. Or gloating, or something. But I could see by the look on your face. You weren't just taken aback. There was a deflation in your whole body language. You looked defeated. I could see you weren't expecting it. I knew it had to be real."

I'd be lying if I said I wasn't impressed by her powers of observation at that moment. I can't say I was aware of exactly what I was feeling back then – it felt like a lot of things swirling inside me all at once – but when she described it to me, I knew, without a doubt, that she had nailed exactly what I was going through emotionally. Maybe it was the sympathetic note she struck that caught me off guard, but I had no problem confessing that the sense of defeat hadn't quite left me. She wondered if I had been in touch with the three Figs since the rally and when I admitted that I had, she leaned in. The appearance of compassion in her dark searching eyes tapered into something more conspiratorial. She lightly rubbed her palms. She wanted to know what the Figs were doing at Reuben's broadcast. Were they agents of the government now?

"I don't think so," I said. "It's a bit more complicated than that, I think."

"What's your relationship with them?"

"It's the same," I said, not entirely sure what that meant. "They come and go whenever they please. To be honest, I'm never quite sure where I am with them."

Then she wanted to know if I had a way of contacting them.

"Not really," I said. "Why?"

"What better way to find out what's going on at Rossiter's Field." she said. "They wouldn't have to worry about barriers and guards. Just tell them to pop in and pop out. Easy as gooseberry turnovers."

"Gooseberry turnovers? Is that another one of your son's specialties?"

"You gotta try one," she said and rubbed her hands gleefully. "To die for."

I tried to explain to her that the Figs were more about telling me what to do rather than taking orders. Besides, chances were they already knew the state of things at Rossiter's Field. They tended to know far more than they liked to let on. She insisted that anything I could find out could be helpful and let on that Rossiter's Field was possibly one in a series of illegal land purchases that had been going on for the last two years. She had been to a few meetings of the PEI Lands Protection League, a group of Islanders from different backgrounds who were trying to raise awareness of issues surrounding PEI's land rights. One of the more pressing issues was the violation of the Landholding Act, which specified certain rules of ownership. Most serious was the mounting allegation that certain corporations and groups and even private individuals were circumventing the rule of how much land could be bought and owned. At first it looked like Reuben, or rather his company, the Freeland Corporation (from which he had supposedly divested himself after taking power, as proscribed by law) stayed within the legal limit of ownership when it bought Rossiter's Field (which was part of Mount Russet) and the land where the Crazy Diamond stood. Still, there was a suspicion that the Freeland Corporation used several individuals to buy surrounding land that went beyond the limits. For what purpose was unclear, but Tamara Tuplin surmised that the idea was to extend beyond the original plan to build a resort that was supposed to be part of a children's summer camp.

"I hate to say it, but that hurricane came along at a very convenient time for certain interested parties. So many small farms were wiped out and all that land was suddenly just there for the picking." She went on to say that the most prominent name implicated in skirting the Landholding Act was the Devlins, referring to one of the wealthiest oil and gas dynasties in Eastern Canada. Devlin Service Stations were dotted all across Newfoundland, Nova Scotia, PEI and New Brunswick, like mushrooms in a boggy marsh.

"No doubt they still have interests in PEI, independent or not. Too much money for the Premier to ignore. Their big involvement is industrial farming that's been a source of polluted runoff into our lakes and rivers. Meanwhile, a lot of land has become sites for construction projects."

"How long has all this been going on?" I asked.

"Violations of the Landholding Act have been suspected but not proven for the past two or three years now, but there's been a spike in land transactions recently. It's starting to look like the hurricane and this plan to make us a sovereign nation are connected to that spike."

If everything she was saying was true, add to that what Anne Surly said about PEI becoming an offshore tax haven for American and other foreign interests, then rebuilding the Island was merely a smokescreen for something bigger in the works, more along the lines of an economic and political restructuring. Friendly Occupation indeed.

But the more pressing question, as far as I was concerned, was: how did the three Figs, or the Supreme One for that matter, fit into all this? Adding to the mystery was a phone call I received from Aziza a few days later.

"And to what do I owe this pleasure," I said, trying only for a hint of sarcasm. Rather than take the bait, she cut to the chase.

"My father would like to have a meeting with you."

"What, he doesn't have a secretary to set these things up?"

"This isn't exactly official," she said. "He wants to keep it under the radar."

"I see," I said. "So, not in an auditorium or anything."

"I don't blame you for being suspicious," she said in a bluntly dismissive manner. "Or bitter."

"Wow, next you'll say you tried to warn me," I shot back, only to remember that in fact she had when she warned me about making myself a "target."

"We need to get past all that. My father's making a sincere effort to reach out."

"Sweet. I'll bring my guitar and we can sing *Kumbaya*," I said. "What does he want anyway?"

"He wants to talk to you about building the synagogue."

"I heard he's planning to greenlight that. But why talk to me? I assumed he'd want all the publicity for himself."

"You couldn't be more wrong," she said. "He very much wants to share the credit with you."

Before I could ask her to explain, she gave me an address in Charlottetown to go to and told me to be there the next morning at 10:00. Then, without any further niceties, she hung up.

AFTER GETTING A MEASLY fifty bucks for the Golf at Leo Murray's Scrap Yard, I had purchased a used Civic from the Honda dealership in downtown Mount Russet. I headed out from the Body Parts the next morning and turned onto the Mount Russet Road to Highway 7 toward Charlottetown. Great tracts of rust coloured soil that were usually being cultivated at this time of year by tractors, sprayers, harvesters and the like were now being excavated by industrial diggers. Cement mixers and dump trucks piled high with mounds of gravel could be seen near a billboard announcing something I could only assume was a development project. All it had were the bold letters BAUC on a sky-blue background with white clouds. I had no idea what BAUC was. Maybe a corporate acronym?

Farther along, the blockade in front of Rossiter's Way did indeed have flashing lights now, as Tamara Tuplin had described. The presence of no more than three black official-looking SUVs added to the appearance of a crime scene or site of an accident. Low key it was not. There were also a few men in dark quasi-military uniforms: ball caps and bulky vests with blue shell-shaped insignias over one breast. Loose trousers were tucked into laced-up hobnail boots. Some of the men were armed with holsters and pistols, as well as being strapped with radio packs attached to high-tech single earphone clips and curved flexible mouthpieces. Two of them stood at either side of the blockade in stiff at-ease poses and another two, holding take-out coffee cups, conferred with each other.

One lone unarmed guard stood near the road and as I passed. I recognized him as Kelvin Muir. I briefly slowed down and scanned the other guards' faces and saw that one of them having coffee was his brother Reggie. It was obvious that Kelvin was supposed to be waving the cars by as if to say nothing to see here, despite the conspicuousness of it all. Instead, he just stood there looking for all the world as if he wished he were anywhere else except here.

I stopped to watch when Reggie broke away from the guard he was talking to and went over to Kelvin and said something to him. Words were exchanged and then Kelvin took off his cap and threw it on the ground and screamed something. Reggie pointed at the cap and it seemed that he was telling Kelvin to pick it up. Instead, Kelvin kicked it at Reggie, which also brought up a cloud of dust from the dirty ground. Reggie merely screamed louder, but when he unholstered his pistol, the other guard he had been talking to, went over to calm Reggie down. By this time cars behind me had also stopped to watch, which caused other cars further behind to start honking their horns. Reggie, hearing this and seeing us all rubbernecking at the confrontation between him and Kelvin, started to shout and frantically waved at us to keep moving. Whether he recognized me or not was unclear, but before driving on, I noticed that on the doors of the SUVs was the same blue shell-shaped insignia as on the vests and the words BLUE POINT SECURITY. My mind flashed back to the bolo tie Premier Reuben Arsenault wore on his TV appearance after the hurricane. It was the same shape and colour as the insignia.

I ARRIVED AT THE ADDRESS Aziza had given me with barely a minute to spare. It was a house in a quiet neighbourhood on the outskirts of Charlottetown. An SUV with a Blue Point Security logo on the side door was parked in the driveway. I parked the Civic on the street and rang the bell. A Blue Point guard opened the door and ushered me in, leading me to what seemed to be a sparsely furnished den. Reuben Arsenault sat in an easy chair. A flat screen television showed a news program. He invited me to sit on a small sofa and told the guard to wait outside and close the door. Reuben watched the news program briefly, then picked up the remote and turned the show off. The screen went blank.

"Would you like something to drink?" he asked and pointed to a wet bar with a small fridge. "We have soft drinks and juice. Or if you prefer, something with more of a kick."

"I'm good, thanks," I said. "The word is you're all gung-ho to build the synagogue. Not converting or anything, are you?"

"Let's just say things have gotten off to a bumpy start."

"No kidding, you're getting your *tuchus* handed to you out there."

"Be that as it may, building the synagogue could be a way of buying some good will until the road gets smoother."

"In other words, a diversion from the shit storm we're currently in," I said. "So, what am I doing here?"

He stood and made his way to the bar, produced a bottle of double malt and poured himself two fingers.

"Sure, you won't join me?"

"A little early in the day for me," I said, barely able to mask my alarm at the way he knocked back his drink. "Look, as long as you're planning to build the synagogue on Rossiter's Field, as stipulated by the Supreme One, you're home free."

He remained at the bar, looking a bit shaky. I thought he might pour himself another, but he merely surveyed his empty glass.

"Unfortunately, that isn't going to be possible. That tract of land, as sizeable as it is, has already been ear-marked for a specific project that is already in the works. A house of worship just wouldn't fit in the scheme of things."

"Something to do with Project Friendly Occupation? This off-shore tax haven thing?"

"Let's say it's an extension of that," he said and returned to his easy chair, suddenly looking more refreshed. "But I'm not at liberty to go into details at the moment."

"I hate to break it to you but building the synagogue anywhere else but on Rossiter's Field just ain't going to cut the mustard with the Supreme One."

"And you know this how?"

"Same as you, Premier, the three Figs."

"So, you've never actually communicated directly with the Supreme One?"

"The Figs are my go-betweens," I said. "Look, where are we going with all this? What exactly do you want from me?"

"I want to offer you the opportunity to be the official spokesman for the synagogue."

"I don't understand."

"Many believe that the Supreme One has decided our Island is to be the new Promised Land. But that can only happen when the synagogue is built."

"On Rossiter's Field," I reiterated.

"Which cannot happen, as I've already stated," he said. "Let's be reasonable. All you have to do is make a few public statements saying that the Supreme

One is satisfied with having the synagogue built wherever. A show of good faith, let's say. I can get some of my people to get the wording right. If you endorse the synagogue on the Supreme One's behalf and ensure everyone that we are well on our way to becoming the new Promised Land, that should buy us enough time for Project Friendly Occupation to kick in. After that we will be well on our way to a new prosperity."

After taking all that in, I was suddenly ready for that shot of whiskey, if only to clear my head.

"You can't be serious about this," I said.

His impassive countenance assured me that he indeed was serious.

"Let me get this straight," I continued. "All this self-determining theocracy mumbo-jumbo, based on the Supreme One blessing this Island and bowing your head in prayer after your speeches, it's just a lot of snake oil chin music. You don't believe in the Supreme One or the Promised Land, do you."

"On the contrary, Mr. Grief. Something unexplained caused that hurricane. If we can give it a name, such as the Supreme One, well then why not? But after that, it's up to us, the mere mortals, to create the opportunities that have been laid out before us. Isn't that what your Fagin is always going on about? Opportunity?"

"But you're forgetting Shylock and his whole schtick about Principle. Where's the principle in trying to skirt around the Supreme One's decree? Opportunity and Principle. You can't have one without the other."

"I couldn't agree more," he said with a curt nod. "Except you see, opportunity is my principle. It's so much more convenient that way. A much neater package without all that ethical red tape. If you do this now, who knows what it might lead to? I'm still looking for someone to be Minister of Culture."

"Wouldn't I need to become an MLA first?"

"A mere formality. But first, I need you to endorse the synagogue."

"I don't think all that glad-handing and baby-kissing is my bowl of borscht. You'd do a lot better enlisting the Figs to endorse the synagogue rather than me. They're the Supreme One's messengers. I notice they're not above appearing with you on TV. You got them to help you sell this whole scam of an independent PEI to the public. I'm sure they'd do you another solid."

A small sigh escaped him. "You would think so. But when I presented this idea to them, they refused. Apparently, they don't have the same efficient concept of Opportunity and Principle as I have. I mean, a synagogue is a synagogue no matter where it is. I'm meeting the Supreme One halfway, aren't I? You know, for the principle of it. In any case, that leaves you. What do you say?"

"I think your idea of half way is probably not the Supreme One's idea of halfway. I've already angered the Supreme One once, and you saw what happened. If I sanction a synagogue anywhere but on Rossiter's Field who knows what the Supreme One might do. Possibly sink this whole *farshtunken* island to rot at the bottom of the Atlantic with the Titanic and Davy Jones' Locker. I don't want to take that chance. And neither should you."

"I don't take chances, I take calculated risks," he said. "But what about the chance you're taking if you don't take up my offer?"

I stood up. "Is that a threat?"

"What would be the point of threatening you, Mr. Grief?" He was now standing as well. "If you haven't realized already, circumstances have put you in quite a precarious position as it is. Do you really want to tip the scales against yourself?"

When I made it clear that I could not be his Jew-for-Hire, he declared the meeting over and opened the door. The Blue Point guard escorted me out of the house. As I drove away in the Civic, I couldn't help wondering, if this was the frying pan what would the fire look like?

17

THE NEWS THAT THE MANGLED body of a young woman, recently found on the rocky shore of a remote cove around North Cape and identified as Krystal Wedge, a server from Charlottetown, had set the Island abuzz. The body had apparently been washed onto the cove. It was bloated, due to many days in the water, and identified only later through dental records. But a preliminary forensic report later ruled out an accident or even suicide, due to traces of ligature marks on the wrists and ankles, indicating that the hands and feet had been bound at some point.

It was only when I tuned in to *The Anne Surly Cyber-Report* (as her webcast was now called) that I found out Krystal Wedge was the same girl who had suffered a drug overdose during a private party with the Blue Point Society and was rushed to Queens County Hospital. She was later paid off for her silence with money purportedly from the Ashlynn's Camp for Kids fund. In an earlier webcast, Anne Surly made no bones about linking Reuben Arsenault to the Blue Point Society and Ashlynn's Camp For Kids. But now she reminded her viewers that, at the time, it was Chet Affleck who'd been the Program Director of the kid's camp organization and would have been the one who requisitioned the funds for that hush payment. I remembered from her earlier webcast that she named Reuben as the camp's treasurer, but in this new explanation she claimed that Reuben had been misled by Chet Affleck about what the funds were for, which supposedly was office supplies. The amount of the cheque was for five thousand dollars, so unless they were painting the walls with Liquid Paper, something was seriously amiss.

Was it me, or was her spiel becoming more defamatory? Was she pushing the envelope because she had her father's protection? How long could that kind of immunity go on? All I knew was, a couple of days later, when it was reported that Chet Affleck was being questioned by the reservist police about Krystal Wedge's death, I didn't know what to think. So far, events were nothing more than a bewildering series of intrigues. But things had suddenly taken a far more serious turn, now that murder had entered the picture.

In the meantime, I was waiting for whatever shit storm Reuben Arsenault had in store for me to start raining down. Was it too much to hope that the Supreme One might look kindly on me for sticking with the celestial plan and maybe help deflect any tribulations to come? Still, even if I had to fend for myself, as I usually did, I had no regrets about refusing to become Reuben's synagogue poster boy and enraging the Supreme One even further. Given the choice, I'll take man-made comeuppance over divine retribution any day.

To take my mind off things, I decided to accept an invitation, via email early that morning, to visit the poet, Nelson Chiasson, who was a friend of mine. Best known in the Acadian community for his collection *Les Diamants Verts*, a cycle of poems that ruminated on the entwined themes of romantic desire and the madness of jealousy as told from the perspective of Gabriel as he searched for his elusive Évangéline over the years. Reviews praised the collection for its fresh and erotically edgy slant on the well-known story. It won the Governor General's Award for Poetry in the French language division and was later translated into English, Italian and German.

But Nelson reached an even wider English audience with his children's book, *We All Freak Out for Fricot* (referring to the traditional Acadian stew). Local PEI publisher, Sapling Books, had suggested the idea to him and enlisted his wife Thérèse, a talented watercolourist, to supply the illustrations. It was widely lauded across Canada, as well as parts of the U.S. and the U.K., for popularizing Acadian culture among kids and parents alike.

After ending a five-year stint as PEI's Lieutenant Governor last year, he was elected as the Loyalty Party MLA for Evangeline-Miscouche. Personally, I always found it odd that Nelson was a card-carrying Loyal, since his political temperament leaned decidedly to the left and seemed (in my opinion) more suited to the Enviros or Neo-Egalitarians. But his family had voted Loyalty Party going back as long as he could remember and, as is often the case on PEI, one's political affiliation was a matter of family tradition.

I drove to his home in Egmont Bay, a predominantly Acadian community in the Évangéline region of central Prince County. Egmont Bay had been hit especially hard by Hurricane X. Landlines and Internet service had only recently been restored to the community. There were many reports that other rural communities, particularly the smaller ones, were in similar situations and some of the more remote areas were still without power. The fact that most cell phones were restored before landlines, brought Atlantic Telecom under fire from their customers and the media alike. Constituents complained to their MLAs, including Nelson. Reuben Arsenault assured the public that an enquiry would soon be underway, but as yet no action had been taken. A rumour was spreading that this was part of a plan to start phasing out landlines in favour of cell phones, which would disadvantage many elderly citizens who relied on their landlines as their only means of communication.

Possibly the rumour resulted from a similar question about our dependence on the Internet since the emergency recording for many services, such as Atlantic Telecom and East Coast Utility, suggested that their websites be consulted even when the power was out. Nelson assured his constituents, particularly the elderly ones, that he would do all he could to look into the situation.

When I drove up the lane to Nelson's property bright and early, I saw many fallen trees in his adjacent woods, mostly white birches stripped of bark from hurricane winds and some fallen white spruce leaning against other dead trees. I found Nelson behind his small cottage, wielding a chainsaw to a huge maple that had decimated the back porch and also took down a good chunk of the roof. I noticed a couple of the windows were still covered with cardboard and sections of the broken eaves trough were scattered on the ground, along with stones from the hand-built chimney.

Nelson was geared up in orange protective chaps and vest, heavy padded gloves and a hardhat with full visor covering his face. He looked like a warrior who had recently done battle with a wooden behemoth and was now in the process of finishing off the beast. The chainsaw's incessant roar assaulted my ears as I watched Nelson cutting up the trunk and took care to stay well away from flying wood chips. The maple had been uprooted by relentless gusts and the tree's unearthed base was exposed to the bright day, all dangling roots and tendrils and clumpy dark soil. When the maple was cut up, I helped Nelson move the sections to a pile. The cleanly shorn ends revealed pale wood, looking like white cured meat encircled by a rind of coarse greyish-brown bark.

After Nelson stripped off his safety gear, he fetched us a couple of cold beers and we walked along the wooded perimeter of his property toward the open shore of Egmont Bay. The water shone blue with ethereal crystalline shards reflecting off the sun's white burning eye. The beer was cold and the day was warm. The setting was perfect for some silent communing with nature, but Nelson got to the point of why he asked me to come. He had been notified by Reuben Arsenault's office a few days earlier that his name was being put forward as a candidate for Minister of Culture.

It hadn't taken long for Reuben to find someone else, after dangling that particular carrot in front of me, although I was never entirely sure how serious he was. I assumed that the proviso of shilling for the synagogue was not part of the offer to a good Catholic boy like Nelson. In any case, I decided not to mention that I had passed on the plum portfolio and why.

"Congratulations, mon ami," I said. "I can't think of anyone more suited to the job. It's good to know that Reuben's taste in cabinet members has improved, considering the clown show that followed him into office."

"Actually, it's between me and someone else," he said. "I don't know who. Before they actually offer it to me, if they do, I wanted to talk to you first."

"Why me? Politics is not exactly my area of expertise."

"It's just all these crazy things that are going on. The hurricane and these three weird guys and now the Island becoming independent by some kind of divine decree. I can't make head or tail of it. And frankly, Samson, you seem to be at the centre of everything. I was hoping you could help me make some sense of it, so I'd know what I was getting into if they do offer me the job."

While I appreciated the good faith and trust he showed in coming to me, I didn't know what to tell him. An uneasiness sat squarely in the pit of my stomach and I asked what he meant exactly by "the centre of everything."

"The op-ed in today's *Charlottetown Parrot*. You haven't seen it?"

"Um, I've been trying to cut back on my information overload these days."

"I don't blame you," he said. "Anyway, it's calling for an official inquiry as to your involvement in what happened at the civic centre in Mount Russet. There was a suggestion that CSIS and the RCMP might be interested in questioning you, since that event took place before PEI went sovereign, and that PEI should extradite you to the Canadian authorities. It even said Interpol might be interested."

On the one hand, I couldn't believe what I was hearing, and yet there was a weirdly familiar sense of inevitability about it all, as if this was somehow happening to some other poor schmuck named Samson Grief, someone who I remembered from somewhere, a vaguely familiar passing acquaintance, until in one momentous shock of lucidity, like a sudden jolt of electricity being pumped into my cerebral cortex, I realized with heart-stopping clarity that poor schmuck of a passing acquaintance was in fact me. As I was wrapping my head around this realization, Nelson continued.

"The weirdest part is that the op-ed brought up the whole controversy about your painting."

"*Anne of Bergen-Belsen*?"

"Yeah. I didn't get how it figures into all this. That part of the op-ed bordered on the sensational. She seemed to mention it for no reason except to open up an old scab."

"She?" I couldn't imagine who he could be referring to, although I admit Aziza immediately popped into my head. "Who wrote it?"

"That's another weird thing," said Nelson. "It was written by Kerrie-Jo Campbelljohn. Hadn't heard anything from her since she lost the party leadership. Don't know how this bee got in her bonnet."

Reuben Arsenault, that's how, although I kept that particular nugget of information to myself. The bigger question was how and why Kerrie-Jo had resurrected herself from ex-lover and political opponent status to collaborator in, what seemed to be, the start of Reuben's campaign of revenge. For what? Just because I wouldn't endorse his synagogue?

"I wish I could help you make sense of it all, Nelson, but I've been struggling with that myself since day one. I guess I am at the centre of this, but how or why I got here I can't say. The more I think about it, the best I can come up with is that the Supreme One and Hurricane X and the fact that everyone can now see the three Figs and this whole vortex of craziness that the Island has been sucked into… the only conclusion that keeps returning to me is that all of it exists in my deteriorating mind. Even this conversation I'm having with you. All of it seems to be a mere figment of… or in some way manufactured by my fractured imagination. My worst nightmare is that the world as I know it is in reality some kind of simulation that exists only in my noggin. All I can say with any certainty is that beneath this seemingly stable outer demeanour, I'm just barely hanging on by my bitten-to-the-nub fingernails."

Nelson listened patiently and, fixing me with a wary eye, nodded his huge melon of a head.

"Sorry to lay all that on you," I said. "I hope I didn't freak you out too much."

"I'd be lying if I said I wasn't worried about you, Samson."

"Moi aussi, buddy boy. But I appreciate your concern. You've always been a mensch of the first order. And since I've come all this way, if you still want my advice, for what it's worth, I say you should take on the Culture portfolio if it's offered to you. We need a voice of sanity right about now in the leadership. And it looks like your number might very well be called up. You're a great poet, Nelson. That's no small thing. If you get the call, it'll be to go straight into the belly of the beast. Auden, or someone like that, said poetry changes nothing. But he never said anything about poets. In fact, despite my frazzled mental state, the only glimmer of hope I have to hold onto is that, if anyone is going to save us at this point it's going to be the poets. I mean it. All we have is our culture, our voice and our sense of self. Once we lose those, we're fucked."

Draining the last of my beer, I let the bottle's neck dangle loosely between my fingers, keeping time like a silent pendulum. I observed Nelson (pondering how real or mentally manufactured he might be) as he stared far off into the deeper silhouettes between dappled pine needles and layered shades of dishevelled greenery that made up his thick woods. Following his line of vision, I shifted my focus to where dangerously crosshatched twigs and branches jutted off in all directions – not unlike the ten-armed starfish – pointing toward false trails and dead ends.

DESPITE WHAT I'D SAID to Nelson about curbing my info intake, I checked in on Anne Surly when I got home. Now that she didn't have to keep her activities secret, she maintained her own version of banker's hours. It was early afternoon and there was a newly-uploaded webcast. I expected, her main topic to be Kerrie-Jo Campbelljohn's op-ed from that morning's *Charlottetown Parrot*, but she immediately zeroed in on one aspect of it.

"I would like to delve a bit deeper into something that this morning's op-ed only touched on briefly. And that is the painting known as *Anne of Bergen-Belsen*. This painting created much controversy when it first was displayed in public. Some took offense and claimed that it cast unsavoury aspersions on the people of this Island. Samson Grief himself has gone on record to say that it represents, and I quote him now from a radio interview, 'the delusion of our collective innocence.' An interesting phrase, that. What exactly does it mean? That we're all deluded? That we're all guilty? It seems to be an indictment of some kind. If any of you have ever seen the painting, you are struck by the way it stares at the viewer. But not only staring. It judges the viewer. And not favourably. It finds the viewer guilty. But of what crime? Merely the crime of being a viewer. Of being a witness. It condemns those who view this painting for presuming that they are innocent. Is that how Samson Grief himself sees us? Is he condemning us, the good people of this island, for believing we are innocent? When in fact, we have been the victims of the fury that he brought upon us. Our only crime has been to soldier on bravely in order to prove ourselves to the Supreme One. And the Supreme One is seeing fit to bless us with the prosperity that is our true destiny. The fury that Samson Grief has wrought unto us, will, at some point, find its way back to him. He has much to answer for."

What the hell was that? Some kind of sermon, by the sound of it. But with a specifically anti-Samson spin. And not only did she paint me in some villainous light, but she dragged the very painting – the one that she once confessed to me was an inspiration to her! – through the mud along with its creator. Well, if I had much to answer for, then so did she!

Now that the smear campaign was charging full speed ahead, I couldn't risk showing myself out in public. I'd need a disguise. The manic state I was in, thanks to Anne Surly's venomous sermon ringing in my ears, propelled me to scramble around my apartment for any way I could cover up my identity. I definitely wasn't thinking too clearly, because I found myself rummaging around my studio and happened upon some leftover red dye that I had once experimented with, in lieu of my usual acrylic paint. The next thing I knew I had used the stuff on my hair. When I looked in the mirror, I was horrified to see that my hair had turned a demonic shade of cerise. I looked like a haunted version of Howdy Doody gone to seed. I couldn't go out like this. I rummaged through my closet and found an old jungle green Tilley hat I had once bought on a lark. I jammed the shapeless canvas hat onto my head. Then I quickly donned a floral Aloha shirt, found it too ostentatious and covered it up with a corduroy safari-style jacket. I finished off the look with a pair of mirrored aviator sunglasses. Surveying myself in the mirror once more, I was shocked to discover that I had transformed myself into something that could easily pass as one of the Figs. This is what things had come to. I was now a figment of my own imagination.

Once in the Civic, I sped west toward Summerside until I arrived in Wilmot Valley and the house on the Blue Shank Road. I didn't bother to phone first, with the hope that I would catch Aziza at home. Maggie Beairsto answered the door. I was too upset to notice the look of alarm on her face.

"Where's Aziza?" I demanded.

"Samson?" said Maggie. "What the hell happened to you?"

"Never mind that. Where's Aziza? I need to speak to her now."

"Aziza's not home," she said. "She went to see her mother. She has the SUV and I'm waiting for her to get back so I can run in to Summerside for some things. But maybe you could drive me and we can discuss whatever's bothering you."

I took a deep breath and, allowing a cooler head to prevail, decided that Maggie might be a bit more straightforward with me than Aziza. In about twenty minutes we were tooling along Water Street.

I hadn't been in Summerside for almost six months and I was surprised by the changes since Hurricane X. Compared to Mount Russet and its still frail and failing infrastructure, Summerside was looking robust and thriving beyond what I'd previously seen. It had become more pedestrian-friendly with new sidewalks put in and flashing crosswalks every couple of blocks. We also passed two or three construction sites. "New condos," Maggie explained. "Waterfront properties are taking top dollar and the word is all the units are sold. The development money supposedly comes from Ukraine. Word is it's a money-laundering scheme by some Russian-connected oligarch."

"You seem well informed," I said.

"You know me, Samson. I like to keep my ear to the ground."

I wasted no time in getting down to brass tacks. "Then maybe you can shed a little light for me on what the hell is going on with Aziza? It looks like I'm being played for a patsy."

Maggie stared at my dashboard's glove compartment like she was contemplating opening it up and crawling inside. "I don't know what to tell you, Samson. If I were you, I'd wait for it all to blow over. You just have to lay low for a bit."

I tried to lay out everything I knew, from the time Aziza first started to keep me at arm's length to when she began to mention my name in her webcasts and linked it all to my fateful appearance at the Bertram Civic Centre. I spoke slowly, hoping it sounded reasonable and not some paranoid lunatic's ravings until I finally couldn't help myself. "And now Anne Surly has become a propagandist for Reuben Arsenault. And you're behind the camera playing Leni Riefenstahl for all of this. What the hell is going on?"

As soon as the words left my mouth their accusatory tone came echoing back, so I tried to prepare myself for Maggie's defensive onslaught, having witnessed firsthand what happened to others who found themselves on the business end of the famous Beairsto temper. What I didn't expect to hear was the earnestness in her justification of Aziza's and, by extension, Anne Surly's online conduct.

"You don't understand, Samson. I've watched Aziza develop Anne Surly from a crude caricature playing to the ugly nature of whatever audience tuned in, all just to get her message across. And I was part of it, that development. I helped her grow into something more sophisticated, someone with real authority. Aziza has worked hard to get respect and she has it now. Her audience has more than tripled since she changed her image."

As worrying as that was, the idea of Anne Surly's more than tripled audience hearing my name being scapegoated, what worried me even more was Maggie's fawning idolization of Aziza. It was almost like hearing a teenager defending the integrity of some personal hero or pop icon. I remembered Maggie's explanation to Zaina about how she got involved with videotaping Anne Surly's rants, how it somehow gave Maggie a sense of purpose and brought back a part of her youth. Suddenly the sycophantic tone, as troubling as it was, made more sense. Before I could think of how to respond, she continued.

"And you're wrong, Samson. She... we... we're not part of any propaganda. Anne Surly still speaks truth to power. Yes, Aziza supports her father now. He's the premier, after all. Back when the old Anne Surly was taking it out on him and the rest of the establishment, she was just getting in her own way. It was self-defeating. Aziza understands that now. She's taken control of her message by aligning herself with him and the changes he's bringing about."

"So, you're pro-independence?"

"I grew up here, Samson. PEI has been the poor relation in Canada's history for too long. We sold ourselves cheap by playing up our country bumpkin image for the tourist dollar, like Anne Surly said. But now we have respect because we're standing up for ourselves. Quebec and Alberta are all just talk. We actually did it."

It would've been easy enough to poke my finger into all the holes in her argument, but I thought better of it. At this point, Maggie was still an ally, even though she was affiliating herself with a system that had it in for me. I didn't want to risk alienating myself by antagonizing her. She was obviously convinced that she was on the right side of things. I decided a different approach was needed and asked her how she and Pius were getting along.

"He calls me almost every day," she said. "The Crazy Diamond took a major hit in that hurricane and the Shine Shrine is pretty much gone."

She paused and gave me a look that was hard to read. Even though she didn't come right out and say it, I could tell she was laying some of the responsibility on me for the hurricane that killed Pius Duffy's pride and joy. Or maybe I was just projecting my own burden of guilt in her enigmatic stare.

"You know Pius," she continued. "He puts on a brave face. Says he'll rebuild somewhere else. He's got offers from Freeland Corporation to set him up again.

They could do it in a minute but he refuses because it's Reuben's company. I told him Reuben doesn't make those deals for Freeland anymore because he's premier now."

"You really believe that?" I challenged. "You think Reuben has really divested himself from Freeland?"

Maggie's shrug grudgingly conceded that I might have a point. "I just want Pius to get back on his feet again."

"But what about the two of you?" I asked. "Any chance of getting back together?" I wanted to add how much Pius needed her at this low point in his life, but I was already tiptoeing in a minefield and I didn't want to overstep.

"It's complicated, Samson," was all she would say and I retreated from the subject. I wished I could have consoled myself with the knowledge that I had put a bug in her ear, but the truth was I probably only exacerbated whatever inner conflict she was going through. The best I could say was that she hadn't abandoned Pius altogether, which made me wonder about the Crazy Diamond. Running that place meant everything to her. Being behind the bar was her second home, or possibly her first. With the Crazy Diamond out of commission I wondered how she and Aziza were getting by. Maggie wouldn't exactly confirm or deny that she and Aziza were on Reuben's payroll (not that I expected her to), but she did say, without giving up any specifics, that she would resume her place behind the bar in the not-too-distant future and she would let me know when it happened. I decided to leave it at that and we continued with Maggie's errands.

Much of our conversation was conducted while picking up groceries at the Maritime Super-Mart at one end of the Granville Mall, some women's hygiene products at Chevrier's Pharmacy and then across the street to Denholm's Electronics to pick up some cables for their video set-up. Our last stop was on the other side of town, near the outskirts in St. Eleanor's, where I got to manoeuver around Summerside's newest roundabout and barely missed rear-ending a Maserati, of all things. Don't see many of those in Summerside, where it's hatchbacks, sedans or big-ass pickups. It looked like a new breed of vehicle was making its presence felt in the Little Town That Could, but I was yet to be surprised further when we arrived at the Four Seasons Garden Centre, where Maggie wanted to get some seeds, bulbs and various implements so that she and Aziza could start a garden in their backyard.

The garden centre's parking lot was half taken up by a phalanx of black Cadillac Escalades. Naturally I assumed that either the mob was getting into the gardening business (possibly as a way of laundering drug money) or some suburban rapper and his entourage had descended to make a lawn-care music video (possibly as a way of laundering drug money).

Inside the centre I was amazed to see young Asian men in mustard-coloured robes wandering around with shopping trolleys filled with all manner of gardening paraphernalia. A small line of them were checking their wares at the cash register. As each one emptied his trolley, an elderly man, also in robes, held a wad of cash that would have made any wise guy green with envy and he paid for each purchase followed by a respectful bow to the bemused cashier. Maggie noticed my own look of bemusement.

"They're members of something called the BAUC: the Benevolent Association of Universal Cultivation," she whispered in my ear. "Aziza has been hearing a lot about them. They're a spiritual organization based in Taiwan. They already have a temple in Kings County and a new one being built in Queens County. They have a lot of farm land and grow food for community outreach programs. There's another temple planned for Prince County."

"And by Universal Cultivation they mean cultivation as in agriculture?" I asked Maggie sotto voce.

"It has to do with their spiritual practice. Cultivating their characters to reach high levels of enlightenment. Rich families from Taiwan and China pay big bucks to send their sons to these temples. They're all over the world."

"I see," I said. "Putting the cult in cultivation."

Maggie playfully elbowed me in the ribs and I followed her around the gardening centre, pushing a shopping trolley. I remembered seeing a construction project with a billboard that said BAUC on the way to my meeting with Reuben in Charlottetown. I also remembered what Tamara Tuplin had said about industrial farming and a rise in construction projects being connected to certain organizations skirting the Landholding Act. I mentioned this to Maggie.

"The BAUC has come up in connection to all that," she said. "Aziza tells me there are some conspiracy theories that the outreach work they do is to launder their brand and cover up how much land they're buying up."

"But why here?"

"I probably shouldn't be telling you this, since Aziza's gonna talk about it on the next webcast." Here Maggie looked around in that exaggerated manner film or TV characters have before they give up a big secret. "Supposedly the BAUC are being settled here as part of Project Friendly Occupation. It's a quid pro quo for the McRonald administration bankrolling our independence. The BAUC are big McRonald supporters because of his hardline stand against China. The BAUC has been persecuted by the Chinese government for years and its practitioners jailed as political enemies because of the movement's rising popularity."

"I didn't realize the Island's independence came with conditions," I said.

"What doesn't?" said Maggie. She tousled my hair with a sarcastic look that said, *aw aren't you precious.*

HAVING SEEN AN AD in the latest monthly edition of *The Drone* for Frieda Greenglass's newest venture, a Latke Lady food truck, I headed into Charlottetown to check it out. It was parked on Kent Street in an empty lot between the Bon Voyage Travel Agency, and (coincidentally enough, if there is such a thing) the Bong Voyage Head Shop. There were no other customers yet when Frieda Greenglass stared down from the window. She didn't recognize me at first, still decked out as I was in my newly acquired disguise, which I was starting to feel at home in. I ordered my usual Frieda's Dozen.

"Samson?" she said. "It's a little early for Halloween, isn't it?"

"Nice to see you too," I said.

"What's with the get-up?"

"I'm in disguise," I explained. "Trying to keep a low profile."

"You've certainly hit some kind of new low."

"How's business?"

"Pretty good. It gets busier around lunch time. This is a choice spot and you know what they say: location, location, location."

"How long have you been back in business?"

"It's only been a couple of weeks."

"Ah, good cousin Samson. 'Tis but curious chance, yet none too unexpected methinks, to find you here at this dear lady's ambulatory emporium."

I spun around to see Shylock's imposing girth. Before I could stop him, he whipped the Tilley hat off my head.

"*Oy vey iz mir!*" cried Frieda. "What the hell did you do to your hair?"

"Good cousin, these crimson locks doth become thee," said Shylock. "If only Fagin and Judas were present to witness this most miraculous of transformations."

I grabbed the hat back and jammed it on my head.

"How nice to see you again, Mr. Shylock," Frieda said with what looked like, if my eyes weren't playing tricks on me, a youthful blush rising in her cheeks. "Your usual?"

"Usual?" I said and turned to Shylock. "What's your usual?"

Frieda piped up from her service window. "Why the Frieda's Dozen of course."

"But that's my usual!" I protested.

"Now now, it doesn't have to be a competition," Frieda said, clearly relishing the idea of Shylock and I vying for her latkes. "Besides, Mr. Shylock is one of my best customers."

"And I have none to thank but thee, good cousin, for initiating my teeth and tongue to the foodstuffs conjured by this one and only enchantress, the divine Frieda."

Frieda giggled (my hand on a stack of Bibles, she *giggled*). "Mr. Shylock you're going to spoil me."

"As thou spoileth me, and so shall we ever consider ourselves equal to our faults as to our acclaims." With that, he bowed as low as his prodigious paunch would allow.

"Could you stop calling him Mr. Shylock?" I said. "How did you two meet anyway?"

As it turned out, Mr. Shylock was Frieda's first customer when the truck opened for business. Apparently, he cut a dashing figure in his classical Venetian garb, which is how Frieda recognized him, from the time she saw him at the Bertram Civic Centre rally and later on Reuben Arsenault's televised broadcast. They hit it off from the start and he began to show up every day, often twice a day. It was becoming clear that their relationship soon escalated from that of mere proprietor and customer to something chummier.

This was too much for me to get my head around. Having to accept that the general public could now see these figments who originally sprang from my feverish imagination – *my Figs!* – took some time. But now that someone I knew (and almost Biblically too!) had entered into a relationship with one of them, the situation went strictly beyond the pale.

"Excuse me for saying the obvious, but it sounds like somebody's jealous," said Frieda Greenglass. "Anyway, it's not like you didn't have your chance."

"Never mind that," I said. "Don't you understand that our Shakespearean friend here exists only in the dishevelled interior of my noodle?"

Frieda folded her arms and fixed me with what used to be known in the last century as the stink eye. "Well, he seemed real enough in my bed last night."

"That's insane! You and he… I mean him and you… making the *chaye* with two backs?" My voice rose an octave or two. "What are you, a figment floozy?"

Frieda leaned out of the food truck window. "You're plenty lucky I have latkes to watch over or else I'd come down there and give you a real what for."

Suddenly Shylock was towering over me. "Signor," he intoned quietly. "I wouldst have thee know thou art disparaging the fair lady to whom I am betrothed."

The earth beneath me was spinning one way while the sky above rotated in the opposite direction. I staggered over to one of the picnic tables that were arranged in rows at either side of the food truck. I sat and took a few breaths until I was seeing straight again.

"You two can't get married," I uttered weakly, almost under my breath.

"Tell it to the rabbi when he asks if anyone objects," said Frieda, who was now at the table with our latkes. "Or better yet, why not just forever hold your peace."

Frieda set my latkes in front of me. Then she joined Shylock on the other side of the picnic table while he dug into his Frieda's Dozen.

"I love a man with a good appetite," she said and dreamily watched Shylock slather his latkes with sour cream before taking healthy bites, savouring each mouthful. Then she looked over at me. "Samson, why aren't you eating?"

I stared down at the lid of the container covering my Frieda's Dozen. Even through the thick compostable material, the latkes' heavenly aroma wafted up to my nostrils yet failed to trigger the saliva glands or whet my appetite in any other way. To some extent, Frieda was right. I was jealous. Was it the image of a naked Frieda Greenglass straddling Shylock's hairy and pale bulk that was now burned into my mind's eye as if by a red-hot branding iron? To some degree. Was it that said image conjured my own brewer's droop of a failure with Frieda, or more to the point, my failure to exact revenge for the perfidy her rabbi father may or may not have inflicted on my zaide? Now we were getting closer to the centre of the chasm that was only beginning to yawn within me.

And now it looked like I couldn't even build the synagogue that was going to somehow set everything right again. Yet I could not articulate any of this to Shylock and Frieda. All I could think to say was: "Everything's slipping away."

"Despair not, signor," said Shylock with a mouthful of latke. Frieda wiped some excess sour cream from the corner of his mouth with a napkin. "Sanity hath e'er been gripped by thee to mingle with the very marrow 'neath thy fingernails. I beseech thee to hold fast."

"But I don't know where to go or what to do," I complained. "All avenues have closed themselves off to me."

"Oy, such a whiner," said Frieda. "Eat something, you'll feel better."

"Disavow not this wintry lady's true wisdom," Shylock laughed and crammed a whole latke into his mouth.

"Hey!" Frieda said and lightly punched Shylock's burly shoulder. "Who you calling wintry?" Then she buried her hands in his carrot-coloured beard and planted her thick lips on his sour cream smeared still-chewing mouth in a long lusty kiss.

"Please, don't let me get in the way of you two lovebirds, I mean just because the walls are closing in on me."

My grievance went unnoticed for a few more minutes before they managed to break off from each other and Shylock finished masticating and swallowed his food.

"When the world engirds our existence by walls e'er encroaching, 'tis within yon oppressive towers freedom doth embraceth us most."

"But it's becoming too much for me to deal with!" I protested. "I thought I had you and Fagin and Judas to back me up. I thought I had the Supreme One to help me."

"We hath not abandoned thee, valiant cousin. Our presence lingers to bolster thy efforts, yet it may not be in the mould of thine expectancies. 'Tis as the immortal bard penned so sagely in centuries of yore, thus the world is but a stage and the inhabitants players assigned their roles. In those glorious theatrical extravaganzas of ancient Greece, the day was oft rescued by that contraption known as *deus ex machina.* Let that be thy model, sweet warrior, to kick against these encroaching shadows plaguing thy faculties. Stand tall, signor, swathed in a mighty guise of thine own! A newly structured identity! Present thyself to combat so nightmarish a swirl of events and embark as the nemesis heretofore known by such designation as Samson *Ex Machina.*"

18

ME FROM A MACHINE? Me as a plot device? Me flying in at the last minute to save the day? None of these were very likely, although I could picture myself dangling helplessly in a cable-strung harness from the top of a crane-like contraption with arms and legs flailing in midair. That kind of helplessness pretty well described my state of mind these days. Beach weather was upon us, although if anyone felt much like basking in the sand or splashing in the Atlantic it was to escape the general malaise of their everyday lives in the bumpy-as-ever transition to Island autonomy.

Canada's federal government waged an all-out crusade, employing all of its political clout and threatening legal action to force Prince Edward Island back into confederation's fold. They did their best to court the allegiance of "all good Islanders" by casting them in the dramatic role of hostages that Canada was fighting to rescue.

Relations between Canada and the U.S. as well as other European allies were strained, to say the least, with Prime Minister Selfridge (still apple-cheeked beneath the faux gravitas of his newly grown beard) testing the limits of his rhetoric in diplomatic statements that, nevertheless, excoriated these countries for political interference disguised as emergency aid in PEI's time of crisis. Selfridge vowed that investigations into such interference would soon be underway.

Along with trying to hammer out a coalition agreement with the other parties for his newly re-elected federal minority government, Selfridge was also dealing with the double-barrelled headache of having the premiers of Quebec and Alberta loudly voicing their indignation that PEI, the runt of the national litter, was getting all this attention. Premiers Gélinas and Whitehead were only too happy to raise the twin spectres of their own bids for independence (political cudgels they'd been brandishing separately for the past fifty years) if Ottawa didn't pay some attention to them. In political cartoons, op-eds and satirical television shows Quebec and Alberta were depicted as the wicked stepsisters jealously railing against PEI's Cinderella when her dainty foot fit effortlessly into President Charming's glass slipper: an image (apt for its transparency) of coveted Yankee-funded independence.

A second body, this one male, had been found washed up onto a cove in the North Cape area, not too far from where Krystal Wedge's body had been found. My insides went cold when local news identified him as Kelvin Muir. Ligature marks were evident around his wrists and ankles, similar to those found on Krystal Wedge. And like Krystal's, his body was bloated from overexposure in the water.

"Apparently, there was a connection between Kelvin Muir and Krystal Wedge," reported Anne Surly. "According to eyewitness accounts, Kelvin had sought out Krystal and was trying to convince her to go public about her overdose at the Blue Point Society party. Why he wanted her to do this is not known. The speculation is that Kelvin may have had something against Chet Affleck, who seemed to be trying to cover up her overdose with that hush money from the kids' camp fund. So far, while Chet has been questioned about Krystal Wedge, he has not been connected to Kelvin Muir's death, but an investigation is underway. I will be keeping all of you informed with any new developments in this story."

Trying to unpack this was akin to opening a deceptively simple suitcase only to find one locked secret compartment after another. Casting my mind back to last year, I distinctly remembered from one of Anne Surly's earlier webcasts, her assertion that it was ex-premier Nathan Affleck who had been connected to Krystal's overdose. It was our favourite pigtailed dominatrix's assertion that this barely contained scandal was what led to Nathan Affleck's sudden stepping down from his lofty position as the province's top political leader. And, Anne Surly went on, it was then MLA Reuben Arsenault who curried political favour with the retiring premier by getting his director of Ashlynn's Camp for Kids, Chet Affleck, to requisition a hush money cheque to pay off Krystal as a way to keep the ex-premier's name out of the news, and also to cover Reuben's tracks, since Reuben was the treasurer who controlled the purse strings. There had been, of course, not a shred of evidence to back these claims up.

The mere effort of dredging up this whole tangled mess from memory brought on the beginning of a migraine that I could feel rumbling in my back molars.

So, if Anne Surly was right about Kelvin Muir trying to convince Krystal Wedge to go public about the overdose, was it to incriminate ex-Premier Nathan Affleck? Was that why Chet Affleck killed Kelvin and Krystal (if in fact he did)? To protect his brother's name?

The other possibility – knowing Kelvin Muir's affection for Aziza Arsenault and his resentment toward Reuben Arsenault for encouraging her to keep up the Anne Surly persona – was that maybe Reuben was Kelvin's target. Did that mean Reuben was involved with Kelvin and Krystal's deaths? That would explain Anne Surly's spin, a way of shielding her father by focusing all the attention on Chet Affleck.

The only thing I could be sure of was Anne Surly's growing expertise at taking the raw material of whatever information was at her disposal – factual or fictive or some combination thereof – and repurposing it into a narrative that became her own unique brand of "truth to power", as Maggie would have had me believe.

In a visual sense, it occurred to me that the straw hat and ginger pigtails stood for truth, while the militaristic jacket and jodhpurs stood for power. In an odd way, this gave her incongruent look a newfound unity.

But whether or not this narrative she was pushing provided enough heave-ho to throw Chet Affleck under somebody's bus, it was still anybody's guess as to who was sitting pretty in the catbird seat behind the wheel.

Whatever pangs of sympathy I had been able to muster for Chet, despite the fact he had ambushed me during my radio interview (most likely at the behest of Reuben Arsenault), soon waned when I received some devastating news, all the more so because I didn't see it coming and, to make matters worse, it concerned Zaina.

At this time my name kept cropping up in newspaper editorials and commentaries on radio and television in connection to Hurricane X. I was on edge, waiting for the police to come knocking on my door, and in need of a sympathetic ear and some encouraging words, so I made a lunch date with Zaina. Normally, we would have gone to one of our favourite eateries, but she said over the phone that it might be better to meet somewhere more private. In retrospect, that should have raised a red flag for me, but I was too grateful for the invitation to have supper at her apartment to think twice.

There was no mistaking that something was going on when Zaina answered her door. I was still sporting my Fig-style disguise and we both stood with our mouths agape, staring at each other. While she burst out laughing at me, I, on the other hand, only managed to close my gaping mouth in time to catch the saliva pooling around my tongue before it spilled down my chin. Gone was her hijab, revealing short black hair that might have looked like a boy's, except for its stylish sweep across her forehead and curved sides, like the bottom halves of black crescent moons accentuating her fine seashell ears.

After I explained the purpose of my outlandish garb and let her have a gander at my red locks, at which she let loose a renewed gale of laughter, it was my turn to react to her new look.

"Wow," I said, for want of anything more eloquent. "Look at you."

"Do I look that bad?" she said with a sad smile.

I stammered an apology and assured her that she looked perfectly fine. The fact was she looked stunning and I could feel a sweet anguish rippling through my insides. I struggled to keep my reaction muted so as not to sound like the love-struck fool I feared I might betray myself to be. Zaina ushered me in and I happily took a seat at her kitchen table to ease some of the strain off my trembling knees. There was a bowl of freshly made hummus at the table's centre with a plate of crudités on one side and another plate of pita triangles on the other side. The table was set for two and the delicious aroma of *yakhni*, a traditional Lebanese stew, was emanating from a pot on the stove.

"So, when did this happen?" I asked and immediately regretted the flippant tone of the question, chalking it up to my attempt to act nonchalant. "Sorry,

I mean when did you decide to do this? And why?"

I smiled openly and she smiled back and continued to speak slowly with quiet purpose.

"The thing is, Samson, I'm going away."

"What? Where? Why?"

"I'm sorry to spring this on you," she said. "Let me explain."

Since last year, she'd been corresponding with the Druze family whom she was trying to bring from Lebanon to PEI through the Island Welcoming Society. The Haddads lived in Chouf, the heartland of the Lebanese Druze community, southeast of Beirut. The Druze community is very close-knit, which made travelling to Canada a difficult decision for the Haddads, yet slowly but surely, visas, passports and other documents were being gathered and things were starting to fall into place. A home was found in the Charlottetown-Parkdale area, which happened to be Tamara Tuplin's riding. She lent her support by rallying the community to accept the Haddads. Household items as well as good winter clothes were donated to welcome their arrival. All that was left to do was finalize their travel arrangements. For a husband and wife with two teenage daughters and a young son, this was not a cheap undertaking, but the money was eventually raised through generous donations to GlobalGiving, a crowd funding website. When Hurricane X hit PEI, all travel plans were put on hold and the money was frozen. Further complications arose when Reuben Arsenault declared PEI to be a sovereign nation.

"Suddenly the Haddads were not going to be allowed into PEI," said Zaina. "I went to my imam, but all he did was try to dissuade me from my efforts. Because the Druze are not necessarily seen as pure Muslims, he said, the mosque could not get involved."

I wanted to ask if this was why she wasn't wearing her hijab, if she had turned her back on Islam, but I sensed this might not be the right time. Instead, I asked: "Why didn't you go directly to Reuben?"

"I made some calls but he conveniently never got back to me. As a last resort, I spoke to Aziza to see if she knew anything. You know, through her contacts. We hadn't seen a lot of each other since that time we went to the Crazy Diamond. She drove to my office in Maggie's truck."

I realized that was the same day I had taken Maggie to Summerside.

"We had a nice long lunch and I have to admit it was wonderful to have some time alone together. For some reason, I thought she was going to throw it in my face."

"Throw what in your face?" I asked.

Zaina looked down at her barely touched stew. "That I was coming to her for information. I mean, because this is the kind of information she uses in her broadcasts and she knows I disapprove of them. Yet now I needed her. Mothers and daughters, you know? It can get so tangled sometimes. But she knows how important the Haddads are to me. She was able to tell me that the government's policy on immigration was in a state of flux. She had heard talk of a quieter policy that was being put in place, but without any publicity, influenced by whoever is pumping the money into the Island's independence effort."

"The Americans?"

"Probably, but there may be others involved. Aziza said something about the credit unions being taken over and amalgamated into a single bank to create offshore accounts for foreign money. There have been some reports in the media but mostly it has been kept quiet. So, this infusion of foreign cash that's being invested into the Island economy comes with policy strings, like the one for our immigration that is keeping people like the Haddads out."

And yet we were letting in practitioners of the Benevolent Association of Universal Cultivation that Maggie had been telling me about. Why were the members of a spiritual organization from China and Taiwan being allowed to settle on PEI when other immigrants were being kept out? True, they were here before the hurricane and they have money.

In her webcast that reported on the BAUC, Anne Surly asserted that the organization's vocal support for the U.S. president, mainly through their free newspaper *The Enlightenment Gazette* (which was now being published by ShoreWire Inc.), was part of the message that accompanied their food outreach efforts into communities on the Island. With every food basket came a copy of the paper. It was a convenient way to spread pro-American right-wing propaganda, although Anne Surly's spin on it was more as a way to promote the U.S. support for the newly independent PEI. But that still didn't answer why the U.S. would risk offending Canada by interfering like this.

Unbidden, almost like a visitation, I suddenly remembered the words of Tamara Tuplin at our first meeting when she quoted the dictum by Duddy Kravitz's *zaide*, "a man without land is nobody", and flipped it around as "a land without man is nowhere", her interpretation being that "the land cultivates us the same way we learn to cultivate it." It personified a healthy relationship of reciprocity.

But now here was a different relationship, not so much reciprocity as a Kafkaesque metamorphosis, involving cultivation of a different sort. This group, the BAUC, whose members apparently practiced cultivating their characters with the goal of spiritual enlightenment, was itself being cultivated by the American government as a tool for political fealty. The duty to enlightenment waking up from restless dreams to find itself trapped in the carapace of authoritarian ideology.

It was enough to send Gregor Samsa scurrying back under his bed for good.

I wanted to ask Zaina more about her lunch with Aziza and whether she thought her daughter was in a dangerous position as a propagandist for the Arsenault government, but I knew Zaina must be mightily disappointed in having to give up on the Haddads.

"So, what are you going to do now?" I asked.

Zaina looked at me for a moment without saying anything. There was a strange expression in her eyes, almost like pity. It made me very uneasy and I wished she would say something.

"Well, the good news," she began and that could only mean there was bad news to follow. "The good news is that the GlobalGiving money was unfrozen and airline tickets for the Haddads were purchased. The PEI Welcoming Society was able to network with another newcomer group in Ontario. They found a house for the Haddads. They land in Toronto next week and then go on to Hamilton."

"That's great news," I enthused even as I was waiting for the other shoe to drop. "You can always visit them there. Oh, I see. That's where you're going?"

Zaina nodded. Her smile carried no happiness. "I plan to go to Toronto to meet their plane. Then I will go with them to Hamilton and help them get settled in."

So far so good. "That sounds great. How long are you going to be there?"

This time she tried to infuse her smile with something hopeful, although it looked more like she was trying to bolster her courage. The silence went on just that little bit longer until her unspoken reply dawned on me with the clarity of a sunrise through prison bars on a day of execution.

"You're staying there?" I managed to croak, only because I didn't think I could bear to hear her say it. "For good?"

"I'm sorry, Samson. I hope you can understand."

For a moment I felt a sinking motion inside me and I worried that the half bowl of stew I'd eaten might come up without warning. I braced my hands on my knees and steadied my breathing. "Yes," was all I could get out of my throat with any confidence. The silence continued and when that was starting to become unbearable, I searched my mind for something else to say. I wondered if I should just wish her luck and leave.

"I still don't understand why you took off your hijab," I said, mostly for something to say, trying to inject any attempt at getting back to a normal meal together. "I know you are disappointed in your imam. But maybe it would help the Haddads to see you wearing it?"

In lieu of an answer, Zaina reached over and placed her hand over one of mine, which was still bracing a knee. The next thing I knew her face was looming closer to me. I wasn't sure what I should do. I was going to lean back in my chair but I merely stayed still until she was out of her chair. Then her mouth was pressing against my mouth. Somehow, we both stood without bumping into each other. It was oddly clumsy and then it wasn't. Our arms were around each other. Her shoulders were slender and I could feel the fine bones beneath her light cotton blouse. We were kissing, not in any hurried way. The passion was in the savouring. Part of me anticipated her breaking away at any moment. But that didn't happen. Our bodies nestled into each other and for some reason the ridiculousness of doing this in her kitchen didn't feel at all ridiculous. When we stopped kissing our foreheads were still touching and she asked me if I wanted to stay with her that night.

We made love and on that I'll say no more, except it had been a while since the last time I did that to any satisfaction (and on this particular night it was very satisfying). I might have expected a deep dreamless sleep. Not a chance. I don't normally remember dreams, which is perfectly all right with me, but this was one of those dreams one remembers long after one wakes up.

What I remember most clearly was that I was a machine. I wasn't made of metal or anything like that. I wasn't a robot or an android like in some science fiction story. But I was a machine. I had this knowledge in the way of dreams when it's simply something you know. Everyone else knew it too. I felt different from everyone. I knew that my insides were made up of gears and pulleys. I lived with a vague fear of winding down, coming to a standstill. I didn't know how to keep myself wound. I stood naked in a room that had a mirror where I could examine myself and searched my human-looking body for the slot or hole where a key could fit in. I didn't actually have a key, but I knew that if I could find the opening or aperture then I would come into possession of a key. I could hear the Jewish lo-fi blues poet singing his song *Anthem*, but instead of singing the part about there being a crack in everything for the light to get in, he sang: "Except for the tuchus crack, Lenny, 'cause that's where the sun don't shine."

Then, in the way that these things happen in dreams, I was walking through the woods and came upon a clearing that was the shoreline of a river. In the distance was a man fishing in a boat. I waved to him but he either didn't see me or decided to ignore me. I realized that this man was Ned Tuplin, the great-great-uncle of Tamara Tuplin, who had been wrongly hung for the murder of Abner Rossiter's wife. I had the urge to swim to him. Then I realized that if I got in the water all my gears would rust and I would drown. The last part of the dream was Ned Tuplin rowing away while I walked along the shoreline trying to follow him. Then I woke up.

The blinds in the bedroom were down but I could see sunlight peeking through the slats. I realized I was in a strange bed then remembered whose it was. Zaina was not beside me. I lay there thinking about the dream. What little I knew about dreams was that the key to their meaning often lay in how one felt upon waking. If one felt hopeful or maybe at peace, it most likely meant something good. If one felt sad or troubled, then it probably meant something bad. Another theory about dreams was that their meaning was related to something one lacked or was hoping for. The best way I could describe my current feelings was that something felt unfinished, which wasn't particularly helpful in understanding what my dream meant.

I thought back to key elements in the dream. I was a machine, which brought to mind Shylock's advice about becoming Samson *ex Machina*. It was more the idea of being a machine than any real evidence of being one. The residual feeling for this, now that I was awake, was isolation. Then there was the image of Ned Tuplin, someone I only heard about that first time I met Tamara Tuplin. It was hard to imagine what he represented, except for the fact that he was connected to Abner Rossiter and thus to Rossiter's Field, which was supposed to be the site of the synagogue. The only thing that it brought to mind was unfinished business. And the image of Ned Tuplin rowing away while I tried to follow him along the shore left me feeling like I was going nowhere.

I decided the best thing now was to get up. Still naked, I opened the bedroom door a crack and softly called out for Zaina.

"I'm in the kitchen," she called back. "I've already showered and dressed. I thought I should let you sleep. The bathroom is all yours."

I quickly showered and dressed and joined her in the kitchen. She was sitting at the table, sipping tea. She poured me a cup from the teapot. She was wearing her hijab.

"Thanks for letting me sleep in."

"I woke up early, a little after four. You had your arm around me, so I lay there for a while."

"You should have woken me up."

"No, it was nice. Watching you sleep. You looked so peaceful. I never really saw you like that."

"You mean not fretting and moaning."

"Just peaceful. Content." She waited until our eyes met once more. "That is how I want to remember you."

There were so many things I wanted to say. Unnecessary things. Things I knew the answer to. So, we sat there and drank our tea. We could have been any couple enjoying a quiet morning together before the start of a busy day. We could have been any couple who would meet up later on. Maybe go out for dinner. See a movie or a play or just go for a walk beneath the moon and stars. And then home to bed. Together. It was nice to sip my tea and smile at her and hold that possibility, even momentarily, in my head. An image of an alternate reality that I could stash away, like an old photograph, and take out to look at whenever the mood struck me.

FOR THE NEXT WEEK or so, I stumbled aimlessly through a funk of separation anxiety, trying not to think of Zaina. She promised to stay in touch, keep me apprised of her new life, even suggested I might want to visit her in Hamilton sometime in the future when she was settled in. It was clear that her priority was the Haddads and helping them adjust to their new home and they, in turn, would provide an intimate Druze community through which she could connect to her roots.

Zaina knew that her great-grandmother also came from Chouf and that the region was historically a site for clashes between Christians and the Druze. The story passed down through the broken telephone of family lore postulated that the great-grandmother had somehow been taken by a Christian family as retribution during one of these clashes and was betrothed to a son, who then spirited her off to Canada, possibly landing in Toronto, Montreal or Halifax (depending on who you spoke to) but finally settling on Prince Edward Island. Another version of the story had the great-grandmother and the Christian son in a secret relationship, sparking a clash between their families after they were found out, upon which the lovers eloped to Canada. For Zaina, connecting with the Haddads was a way of coming full circle. They represented something ageless that carried a hidden key to her identity.

On the day Zaina's flight was leaving, I toyed with the idea of showing up at the Charlottetown airport. To do what? Stage a dramatic parting I had worked out perfectly in my head? It kept splitting off into dual narratives of either me convincing Zaina to stay or me purchasing a last-minute ticket to join her. I could never settle on one or the other because it was too tempting to live out both possibilities in my imagination, although I took the second scenario a bit further when I imagined part of the plane would be separated by a curtain with a private section that held a double bed for us, where our cries of ecstasy could be drowned out by the roaring engines. Creating our own turbulence, so to speak.

That particular director's cut looped through the Moviola in my brain until the evening when I knew her plane had taken off. Nothing made sense to me at that point. I remembered when she and I discovered my apartment had been ransacked and she saw the ten-armed starfish. That was when I knew she and I were destined to be together. The Supreme One had allowed her to see the starfish so she could help me build the synagogue and together we would usher in a new era of the Promised Land. I could not understand what happened. What had I done to have this last hope taken away from me?

While I assumed her plane had landed safely in Toronto, I experienced my own inner crash landing, a plunge into despair so severe the only thing I could think of was to tune in to Anne Surly, knowing Zaina's daughter was under the mask and costume, and watch it as a form of methadone treatment to help wean me off magical thinking with the dismal hope of healing my broken heart.

I'd recently discovered that one of the reasons *The Anne Surly Cyber-Report* had increased its viewership, as Maggie Beairsto informed me, was because her webcasts were now on *Vox Populi*, a website onto which anyone could upload their videos that covered a myriad of subjects and interests. Due to a glut of homemade videos featuring people ranting about whatever was bothering them, the site was nicknamed *Vex Populi* by detractors and supporters alike.

Anne Surly had her own channel on *Vox Populi*, which also served as an archival platform for some of her earlier webcasts when she was still in her dominatrix outfit. It was these earlier archived webcasts (which had their own cult following if the comments were anything to go by) that I binge watched during my post-Zaina depression.

What struck me after a while was that, despite Anne Surly's raw delivery and in-your-face persona of these earlier webcasts, Aziza actually was, in her own way, auditioning for her father. Perhaps this was the only way she could get his attention. And even though she came across as critical of him in particular and the Island establishment in general, this was her way of proving that she was the only one who could effectively take charge of his image. Even putting him at number 1 on her Island Enemies list was her way of making him her priority. By tearing him down, she built him up in the public's eye, much in the same way that *Vox Populi* pushed the Vex Populi nickname on their unsuspecting users. By casting Reuben as her adversary – she herself being a lone voice on the fringes – she ensured that there would be others in the mainstream who would see him as an ally.

Reuben must have also recognized this at some point, probably when he discovered that Maggie Beairsto was behind the camera and the quality of the webcasts was improving. That must be when he ensconced them both in the house on the Blue Shank Road and gave them free rein. I wondered if he had any input into this new Anne Surly persona, the idea being to get her out of that bustier. And yet I suspected the militaristic garb was a natural progression that sprung directly from Aziza's own imagination. Maybe it was at this point that speaking truth to power morphed into the alternate reality of doctoring facts into loyalty.

There was never much else that interested me on *Vox Populi*, although I occasionally scanned the thumbnails and captions of some of the news videos to see if anything caught my eye. That was how I saw the news clip of Judas speaking at a press conference for something called Ceilidhlujah. When sounded out, it was obviously a clumsy portmanteau of ceilidh and hallelujah, pronounced kay-lee-loo-ya. On a platform stood Premier Reuben Arsenault and Kerrie-Jo Campbelljohn. The absurdity of the name Ceilidhlujah actually made more sense now, coming from the branding geniuses who gave us Lovesterfest PEI.

Reuben introduced Kerri-Jo Campbelljohn as the new Minister of Culture. This didn't surprise me as Nelson Chiasson had let me know that he didn't get the offer, or rather, had flatly refused to write up an op-ed about me as Kerrie-Jo had written. Apparently, the op-ed was a kind of audition for the portfolio, to see who could do a better job of taking me down as part of Reuben's vengeance campaign. Nelson had been asked to write one up only after our meeting. Since he refused, Kerrie-Jo became Culture Minister by default. And as far as I knew, she had not become an MLA, so apparently that "formality" (as Reuben had referred to it in our meeting) was more easily taken care of than I had imagined possible.

Reuben was changing the rules as he needed to. This was achieved more easily when he struck a deal to merge the Loyalty Party and the Retro-Progressives into the New Judgement Party, thus gaining a super-majority. This conveniently diminished any kind of opposition, since the Neo-Egalitarians and the Enviros had too few seats to make any real difference, even if they merged, of which there was some talk. In the face of what was ostensibly a one-party system and quantum leap toward authoritarian rule, Tamara Tuplin, to her credit, hung in there in her one seat, making her voice heard as much as possible with the shrewd ability to know when to pick her battles.

After Reuben introduced her in the press conference video, Kerrie-Jo spoke briefly about how Ceilidhlujah was going to be a new cultural experience steeped in the Prince Edward Island tradition of intimate kitchen parties where stories were told and music played, but with a spiritual and moral emphasis that would be the foundation of the Island's independent status. To talk a little more about the divine origin of PEI's sovereignty, Reuben brought out Judas, who emerged from somewhere behind, sans his two cohorts, and made his way to the front of the platform with the others.

Once again, Reuben questioned Judas on the Supreme One's decree that PEI was designated to be the next Promised Land, which Judas confirmed. But unlike the last time he was before the cameras, when Reuben first announced PEI's sovereignty, Judas added that the prophecy would not come to pass until a synagogue was built.

REUBEN: "Is it true that before you appeared to all of us you could only be seen by Samson Grief?"

JUDAS: "Yes that is true. The Supreme One chose Samson Grief to build the synagogue."

REUBEN: "Why him? Why Samson Grief? Why a painter?"

JUDAS: "It was my understanding that this choice was made because the Supreme One's attention was captured by one of his paintings."

REUBEN: "Which painting?"

JUDAS: "The image of the young red-haired waif in rags. The one called *Anne of Bergen-Belsen*."

REUBEN: "The Supreme One liked this painting?"

JUDAS: "All I know is that this painting caught the Supreme One's attention. There was something about the painting. The appearance of deep suffering in this girl affected the Supreme One."

REUBEN: "Can you tell us why it was only Samson Grief who could see you at first, but now all of us can see you?"

JUDAS: "The Supreme One prefers to work in secret, hidden from all humans. Myself and the other two, Shylock and Fagin, were enlisted to be messengers so that Samson Grief would do the Supreme One's bidding. It was through us that the Supreme One entrusted Samson Grief. In reply to your question, when Samson Grief spoke of the Supreme One out loud at your gathering, the Supreme One grew vexed. Shylock, Fagin and myself were obliged to reveal ourselves with the hope it might help appease the Supreme One's temper."

REUBEN: "And did it?"

JUDAS: "No. As a punishment the Supreme One created a storm that raged throughout this small island."

REUBEN: "A punishment? Who was the Supreme One punishing by creating the hurricane that almost destroyed all of us?"

JUDAS: "The punishment was for Samson Grief. Because he angered and betrayed the Supreme One's trust."

REUBEN: "All that destruction and misery was because of Samson Grief? The man who insulted Islanders with his painting of a suffering Anne. That man and his immoral painting caused the hurricane that nearly destroyed all of Prince Edward Island?"

Judas hesitated and looked away, staring either into the crowd or at nothing in particular. For a moment he glanced into the camera, looking right at me. I tried to read his face and waited for him to answer.

Then the video ended.

What the hell was that? Surely Judas was going to defend me and make it clear the hurricane was not my fault. Surely, he was going to say that *Anne of Bergen-Belsen* wasn't meant to insult Islanders. He would explain that it wasn't an immoral painting, that it was its inner truth that caught the Supreme One's attention. That's why I was chosen to build the synagogue.

Reuben knew what questions to ask Judas in a way that made it look bad for me, not to mention how the video was edited. But the real question that kept nagging my gray matter was how much did Judas let himself be used? Or was he in on this smear job? Was it part of some sick cosmic joke that the most infamous traitor in history was being used to take me down? I saw that the video had almost 50,000 views and it was posted only a day earlier.

Almost overnight there were reporters and camera crews staking out the Body Parts. PEI is a small place so it wasn't like swarms of them, but there were enough to render me a virtual prisoner, which felt a lot different from the self-imposed exile I chose to end after only a few days. The phone kept ringing and I had to unplug it. Emails were coming in faster than I could delete them. I was feeling caged in with no relief. Annoyance turned to resentment until that gave way to anger and then desperation.

After another day in my apartment the walls were beginning to conveniently close in, encouraging my hope that being crushed to death might end this whole ordeal faster than expected, when Fagin and Shylock appeared with take-out cartons of latkes from Frieda Greenglass. The revitalizing aroma of fried potato and onion pancakes seemed to solidify, expand and push back at the impending walls, neutralizing them for the moment.

"Blimey," exclaimed Fagin when he saw me.

"Did I tell thee not that our good cousin was a sight to behold?"

"You weren't half joking when you said his mop looked like the bleeding fires of the underworld."

"Okay," I said. "That's enough of that."

"Take not offense at Fagin's jest," said Shylock. "Rejoice, sirrah, you are one of our kinsmen now. Yet one more ginger Hebrew to add to literary history's fabled roster."

The three of us sat around the card table, devouring our Frieda's Dozens with an exaggerated murmur of chewing, gulping and lip smacking as if we were engaging in a wordless debate on whose appetite was keenest. Our gluttony soon ground to a halt with no clear winner. Fagin let out an appreciative belch.

"To be sure, my dear, humanity has found some delectable compensations for that miserable existence known as mortality."

"Nay, signor! Misery hath been banished not recompensed, by such means as the lowly potato hath been elevated to crisp goldenness by my blessed Frieda's blissful alchemy."

"So, I take it the honeymoon continues," I said.

"Our nuptial celebration is not for another fortnight, yet 'tis true our honeymoon long preceded that glorious day and, I doubt not, shalt continue evermore afterward."

Fagin leaned over and gave Shylock's beard a playful tug. "You are well lucky, my dear, to find a mistress who knows the way to her man's stomach as well as below it."

I didn't want to be a party pooper but I had to point out that we were one merrymaker short. Shylock and Fagin merely nodded noncommittally, hoping, as far as I could ascertain, that the subject would pass and we could get on with our belching and laughter. But they should have known better that I would not let it go that easily. Shylock and Fagin had always been forthcoming about what they individually stood for, the former being Principle and the latter being Opportunity.

But what was Judas's watchword, the thing he stood for? For all the advice he'd given me and stories he told me about his time as Yeshua's right hand and confidant and positioning himself as unofficial leader of this fabricated triumvirate, he'd never been able to distill what he was all about in a single word. Was that supposed to make him complex or multi-layered or mercurial, thus being somehow all the more credible or enigmatic? The thing he was best known for was betraying his good friend to the authorities, despite his assurances that it was all Yeshua's idea and he had been saddled with the rap throughout history. I tried to give him the benefit of the doubt by ascribing to him the possible attributes of Selflessness or Forbearance as his personal shibboleth, rather than the obvious one of Betrayal.

Still, the obvious was what I kept coming back to. I showed Shylock and Fagin the video of his interview with Reuben Arsenault on *Vox Populi* and asked them point blank whether or not he was selling me out.

"I know our Judas can be a bit overbearing and holier-than-thou," said Fagin. "But I don't think this moving picture would hold up in a court of law. It ain't what you'd call a hanging offense, if you take my thrust."

"Verily, good cousin Samson, Judas is a brother and hath taken you close to his bosom," Shylock was quick to add. "The eyes will see guilt or innocence as is the brain's predisposition."

"Of course, it ain't beyond old Iscariot to shop a mate. He's known for that sort of thing."

"I grant thee the nub of the thing, Fagin my outspoken *landsman*, even the most sterling of souls shimmers only as its least crease deepens."

What was I to think? With friends like these...

A sound by the door distracted me from my waffling lunch companions and I saw a copy of the *Red Island Clarion* being slipped under my door. The *Red Island Clarion* was new in PEI print media: a convenient merger of the *Charlottetown Parrot* and the *Summerside Echo* concocted by ShoreWire Inc. since one paper essentially rehashed the stories from the other. Not being a home delivery subscriber, I rushed out into the hallway to see who this furtive newsie might be and only heard footsteps stomping down the stairway and then the front door opening and slamming shut. There was no point in following to see who it was.

The front headline was a mere two words in bold type: *Painting Confiscated* and below it a photograph of *Anne of Bergen-Belsen*. For a moment, the picture turned blurry, until I realized everything around me had lost definition. My insides seemed to crumple and I struggled to take a breath. I staggered back to the card table where Shylock and Fagin were picking their teeth and continuing the argument on the merits and faults of their compatriot.

"I mean, there's times he's got the bottle to be pushing his weight around with us and all," Fagin railed. "Who does he think he is?"

Shylock merely shrugged. "Yet for the sake of fairness, our good brother hath a most critical mien toward his own conduct."

I showed them the front page and, my vision's clarity having been restored, read the article to them out loud. Essentially, three uniformed men, two of them armed with automatic weapons, entered Manson's Art Gallery the day before and identified themselves to proprietor, Angus Manson as being with Blue Point Security. One of them presented Angus with an official document stating that they had the legal right to confiscate the painting known as *Anne of*

Bergen-Belsen. Although Angus knew better than to resist, he did ask why the police weren't doing this and was told that Blue Point Security had been hired by the government to carry out this court order as it had been classified as high priority. When they left with the painting, Angus contacted the newspaper with the story.

I stood there disbelieving what I was reading. Both Shylock and Fagin took me by both arms and helped me to my chair. All I could think was that this had Reuben Arsenault's fingerprints all over it. Why else send Blue Point Security? But for what reason? What did he want with the painting? I remembered the vehemence of his op-ed against the painting all those years ago. As disturbing as it had been, I'd never really taken his outrage that seriously.

Then it struck me. Ever since I had returned to the Body Parts, the cops never showed up at my door. And for the Body Parts that was odd enough. After Reuben declared PEI independent and the RCMP was gone, police presence was greatly diminished, with only a meagre amount of reserve trainees to fill the gap. That would provide ample opportunity for Reuben to set up Blue Point Security as his own privatized police force, loyal only to him. Why would he send them to me, when he could just get them to confiscate *Anne of Bergen-Belsen*? As long as he had her, it didn't matter what happened to me.

Or would the confiscation of *Anne of Bergen-Belsen* offend the Supreme One enough to have some pity for this lowly-but-chosen servant and intervene on my behalf?

As the old showbiz adage had it, the only bad publicity is your obit. That had already proved to be false, judging by my own recent experience. But this new turn of events took things to a different level altogether. Like the dark foreboding of a police state. A vision of some *Entartete Kunst* type of exhibition (as had been masterminded by the Nazis against artists such as Ernst, Kandinsky, Klee and many others) bore a hole into my skull. As bad as that was, I couldn't help assuming something worse to come, although I had no idea what it might be.

19

FOR THE NEXT FEW DAYS, Shylock and Fagin barely left my side. This was both comforting and annoying. I tried calling Angus at the Manson Gallery but kept getting his voicemail. After the fifth message the recording informed me that the inbox was full and I could not leave a message. Shylock volunteered to check the gallery only to report back that the door was locked with a CLOSED sign hanging in front.

At each level of frustration, my constant companions offered pearls of, if not wisdom then something akin to good intentions. And we know which road is paved with those.

"Torture thyself not, good cousin. Thou must giveth over to merciful Providence for thy creation to wend a pretty path that circles higgledy-piggledy until once more she is safely restored to her proper circumstance."

"Think of Jonah, my dear, finding hisself up to the earlobes in the leviathan's innards. That pitiful waif in your painting need only sit tight until the natural course of events either spouts, vomits or defecates her from the bowels of the justice system."

"Reassuring," I deadpanned. "Such compassion from the two of you makes my cup upchucketh over."

I couldn't just sit and do nothing, but there didn't seem to be any alternative. Shylock and Fagin did their level best to keep me distracted with latkes and what I considered to be an unhealthy preoccupation with the word game Boggle, at which Shylock proved to be irritatingly adept. Aside from seriously considering going full Van Gogh on both my ears if I had to endure that abrasive clattering of dice in the covered tray one more time, I decided I'd had enough when he somehow conjured the word *clotpole* (apparently a grinning idiot) from a zigzagging pattern in the grid of random letters.

Advertisements for Ceilidhlujah – billed as "an Island cultural extravaganza" – were starting to appear as the opening night, which was scheduled to be produced on an outdoor stage still being built near the Water Street Quay, loomed ever nearer. Kerrie-Jo Campbelljohn was doing interviews to promote the show and I remembered that after she lost the election to become Loyalty Party leader, she had made some cryptic statements about exploring her creative side. I didn't think much of it at the time, I doubt anyone did, but this was the result and it sounded impressive. As the name implied, the show took the idea of the ceilidh, an old-fashioned kitchen party with songs and stories, and expanded it into a big stage variety show where Kerrie-Jo herself was the evening's hostess and would be singing (who knew?) as well as telling stories and introducing the other acts.

A rundown of those other acts included a six-piece bluegrass band called Sonny Milligan and his Goose Grease Go-Getters; community choir, The Happy Clappy Clan; the ecumenical comic stylings of Winston Smale; nine-year-old champion oyster shucker, Kyle DeBlois; identical twin step dancers, the Aberdeen Sisters; seventy-seven-year old Island historian, Lois Handrahan; blind fiddling prodigy Alvin MacKay; the Heritage Academy Pipers; magician and monologist Wilfred Hardy; the Abegweit Spirit Drumming Circle; and finally, Acadian spoon-playing sensation Dorothée Thériault.

"If you ask me, my dear, it'd do you a world of good to take your mind off your troubles for an hour or two," said Fagin.

"I concur, good cousin," Shylock joined in, a little too quickly I thought. "An evening's amusement may well allay that which bedevils us in sun-drench'd day and dispel all manner of sin and sorrow awaiting to greet us in the morrow."

Word was the show had been sold out, but Fagin, reverting back to his tourist disguise, managed to snag three of the few remaining tickets for us. Shylock advised that it would be wise for me to don my Tilley hat, aloha shirt and aviator shades, and, in a show of solidarity, he in turn reverted back to his own tourist garb. Seeing them decked out that way filled me with an odd nostalgia, and the three of us together looked to me, for all the world, like three figments in search of some sucker whose imagination needed goosing.

The weather offered up a warm evening. Being an outdoor event, there was no seating and people brought blankets to spread out on the grass and beach chairs to sit on. Concession stands sold ice cream, fast food and soft drinks. It was a decidedly non-alcoholic event that was strictly enforced by searches at the entrance, carried out by Blue Point Security guards who also positioned themselves by the stage and at strategic points on the grounds. Fagin, Shylock and myself staked out some space on the grass further back among the crowd, but still had a good view of the stage.

The set was made up to look like a kitchen with a real smoking wood stove, an old-fashioned icebox, pots and pans hanging on a backboard and a long kitchen table with chairs around it. At either side of the stage were two large screens, both emblazoned with the show's name and what looked like a coat of arms featuring an oyster shell that resembled the Blue Point Security symbol. As performers silently took their places, some sat at the table while others, such as the bluegrass band and members of the choir, stood on stage. Finally, Kerrie-Jo Campbelljohn walked to centre stage and the lights came up to thunderous applause. Sonny Milligan and his Goose Grease Go-Getters began to play a soft melody as she welcomed the audience and promised us a full evening of wholesome entertainment. When she announced that there would be a special message from Premier Arsenault, Reuben's face suddenly loomed large on the two screens at either side of the stage and he spoke as the Goose Grease Go-Getters continued playing.

"I know everyone is impatient to get on with the evening's entertainment, so I won't take up any more of your time than I have to. But today has been an auspicious day for us. The show you are about to see is not meant to be any old distraction, but rather a statement about who we are as an independent nation. The name of the show has been carefully chosen to represent a heritage that has kept us strong all these years as well as a spiritual fortitude steeped in moral purity that is the cornerstone of that heritage. We feel the name says so much that I can now announce a legislative bill has been drawn up and passed by a majority vote that officially changes this island's name from Prince Edward Island to Ceilidhlujah."

There was a moment of stunned silence into which Kerrie-Jo Campbelljohn beseeched the audience to rise for the new national anthem. Slowly, people got to their feet as the music began to swell. Not everyone stood but most did and then some of the ones still sitting saw that many around them were up and so they too got to their feet. The choir hummed softly as Kerrie-Jo Campbelljohn began to sing. I couldn't believe my ears when I recognized the first strains of the melody as L. Cohen's classic song, *Hallelujah,* but with very different lyrics that I'm sure would have made the Jewish lo-fi blues poet choke on his Montreal bagel and cream cheese.

"In the aftermath of the hurricane
the sacred rose from the profane
and with the sacred came a great renewal.
From the Supreme One's mighty Hand
we have our very own Promised Land
this shining island we call Ceilidhlujah
Ceilidhlujah... Ceilidhlujah...
Ceilidhlujah... Ceilidhluuu-u-u-u-ujah..."

I found that I too was standing, as were Shylock and Fagin, although not due to any patriotic fervour (at least not on my part). I scanned the audience and saw that many were singing along with the refrain while others were still scratching their heads. There had been nothing in the news about this bill as far as I could tell. With the New Judgement Party holding almost all the seats I had no doubt that the bill passed easily. Such is the way of any one-party system. This name change was being freshly sprung on us and this anthem was their way of spoon-feeding the idea before we had too much time to think. As if on cue for that very purpose, the music modulated to a higher key and Kerrie-Jo Campbelljohn gave it all she had in full-throated, heart-stopping, belt-it-out-to-the-nosebleeds delivery.

"The Hand that smites and the Hand that soothes
are one and the same and it only proves
that might is right and nothing less can rule you.
Have faith, have faith, that's all we need
in our Government and in our Creed
the mustard seed that bloomed into Ceilidhlujah.
Ceilidhlujah... Ceilidhlujah...
Ceilidhlujah... Ceilidhluuu-u-u-u-ujah..."

Soon more and more people were joining in the refrain and I could feel something in me go cold. When the anthem was over, a great cheer arose and the Goose Grease Go-Getters broke into a banjo-picking and fiddle-sawing tune to which the whole crowd clapped along. The show that followed was fast-paced and by turns corny, sentimental, humble and patriotic, the last being no mean feat considering the Island's new national identity was only this evening being born. Kerrie-Jo Campbelljohn and her cohorts were, as the showbiz term goes, really selling it with all they had. State-sanctioned down-home hand-on-heart propaganda in all its glory. Winston Smale was up first and I admitted to myself a morbid curiosity as to what was meant by "ecumenical comic stylings."

"There's really not much crime on our good Island, is there," he began. "You can tell by the TV shows set here. There's a new one called CSI: Miscouche, Special Tomfoolery Unit. In the first episode this one fella gets arrested for spray painting lewd pictures on the side of a church. The judge says, 'Let the punishment fit the crime. For defacing a church I'm sentencing you to twenty whacks with the jawbone of an ass.' So, the fella grins back like the cat that ate the canary and says, 'Jawbone of an ass, eh? Well that really is some fitting, your Honour, seeing I just been sentenced by one.'"

That surprisingly got a huge laugh, as did much of his twenty-minute set. Then Kyle DeBlois exhibited his oyster-shucking prowess and, to be honest, he was pretty impressive, shucking thirty-two oysters in under a minute. There was also a vague odour of something baking and much to the audience's delight fresh biscuits were taken from the wood stove, which I had assumed was only supposed to be a stage prop. Soon oysters on the half-shell and biscuits slathered with butter and molasses were being set on trays and brought out by volunteers to the audience of roughly 300, possibly more, accompanied by the Heritage Academy Pipers. I couldn't help but wonder if oysters and biscuits were supposed to be an updated Ceilidhlujah version of loaves and fishes. After the pipers, Alvin MacKay and Dorothée Thériault duetted on fiddle and spoons respectively while the Aberdeen Sisters step danced a lively reel. In between acts Kerrie-Jo Campbelljohn praised the newly dubbed Ceilidhlujah and the life of independent governance and prosperity that it guaranteed.

Almost two hours had passed, interspersed with historical anecdotes from Lois Handrahan, which she skilfully connected to the ultimate inevitability of the Island's current sovereign status.

The Abegweit Drumming Circle performed a ceremonial Mi'kmaw song, which felt to me like a brief respite from all the jingoism being shoved down our throats. From what I could see by scanning the crowd, there were a smattering of Mi'kmaqs in attendance. No doubt, the drumming circle were added as a token bid for diversity, but I was nonetheless thankful for their presence. I sensed from them a genuine display of resilience in the face of settlers staking yet another new claim to their land. It felt like a moment of sanity to hear the heartbeat of their drumming (as opposed to patriotic chest-thumping) and the emotion in their song (as opposed to rewriting the lyrics to one of my favourite tunes with a message of out and out religious right-wing chauvinism).

After the Abegweit Spirit Drumming Circle finished their song and exited the stage, the aw-shucks propaganda spectacle returned with a vengeance in the form of Wilfred Hardy, whose "magic" was essentially card tricks one might see at any house party while he spoke at length about his misspent youth and how lucky he felt to be alive at this historic moment of nationhood. The Happy Clappy Clan sang hymns and folksongs, accompanied by the Goose Grease Go-Getters. I sensed the evening was soon coming to a close when Kerrie-Jo Campbelljohn took centre stage once more.

"We've been having the time of our lives up here and I hope it's been the same for you." The crowd answered her with cheers, whoops and hollers. "But we've come to a moment of this historic night when I have to speak seriously to all loyal citizens of Ceilidhlujah. I speak to you of how we came to this great moment in our history and in our present-day lives. We are a chosen nation and a chosen people and that is an awesome and a solemn distinction to live up to. We have been through a lot, what with a super hurricane testing our resolve. That's right, we were tested by the almighty wrath of God – or rather the benevolent fury of the Supreme One – and it was our faith and fortitude that saw us through. We passed the test to become the Promised Land that has always been our destiny."

Promised Land? Had the synagogue been built while I was noshing on latkes and playing Boggle with Fagin and Shylock? Not to my knowledge. And somehow, I had the sneaking suspicion that little "formality" was also being dispensed with. So how was Reuben Arsenault going to appease the Supreme One, if indeed he felt the need to theologically hedge his bets? The answer was coming sooner than I expected. Minister of Culture Kerrie-Jo Campbelljohn continued.

"But what incurred the Supreme One's wrath in the first place? The answer is simple. A painting. In fact, it was this painting."

At that moment two Blue Point Security guards came to the front of the stage, one carrying *Anne of Bergen-Belsen* and the other carrying a metal easel. The painting was set on the easel. I tried to get to my feet but Shylock and Fagin held me back.

"Hey!" I said. "Let go. They have my painting."

"Peace, good cousin," said Shylock sotto voce. "'Tis best for all if thou keep thy wits sharp and humour intact."

"A deep breath and all, my dear, is what you need," advised Fagin. "Bringing attention to yourself at this juncture could well prove to land you in a sticky wicket."

With heart racing and temples throbbing, I had no choice but to wait and see what was going to happen.

"This painting," Kerrie-Jo continued, as the image of *Anne of Bergen-Belsen* appeared on the two screens on either side of the stage for those too far back to see properly. "This painting angered the Supreme One so that a super hurricane came to destroy us. But we proved to the Supreme One that we were made of sterner stuff and we persevered and rebuilt our tiny island and proved ourselves worthy of the Supreme One's love. We proved ourselves worthy of being the new Promised Land and that is exactly what we have become. To be sure, the temple that has been stipulated by the Supreme One is still on Premier Arsenault's agenda. But now the time has come when we must pay homage to the Supreme One for gracing us with the test that proved our worthiness. The time has come to extend a sacrifice. A burnt offering of reverence and gratitude."

A small jerry can was brought to the front of the stage and one of the guards splashed the painting with its liquid contents as the pipers began to play. The other guard produced a Zippo from his jacket pocket and lit a corner of the painting. It was soon engulfed by orange dancing flames with an emaciated Anne, in her sewn-on yellow star and tattooed forearm, staring out helplessly as the Goose Grease Go-Getters played along with the pipers and the Happy Clappy Clan and Kerrie-Jo Campbelljohn once more sang with patriotic gusto the Ceilidhlujah national anthem.

"In our future we find our past,
a heritage we know will last,
a destiny that has the force to pull you.
Our hearts will cast a fiery glow
so that the whole wide world will know
this blood-red clay known as Ceilidhlujah.
Ceilidhlujah... Ceilidhlujah....
Ceilidhlujah... Ceilidhluuu-u-u-u-ujah..."

FOR THE NEXT DAY or so Shylock and Fagin kept a close eye on me as if on suicide watch. Offing myself was not foremost in my mind, mostly because there was no room for anything in there except the horrifying image of my immolated work of art being reduced to cinders before my eyes. I doubted whether I would be able to unsee that heartbreaking sight ever again. To add insult to injury, there was that revisionist dreck of how the Supreme One was angered by my painting and brought down Hurricane X as a test. I suppose I should have been thankful that Shylock and Fagin got me out of there before anyone recognized me. They might very well have strung me up on the spot.

"This is how nations are created," I railed. "Twisting and spinning a story until it becomes a convenient mythology, an out-and-out lie for everyone to pledge allegiance to. The new Promised Land my ass! How can your beloved Supreme One let this atrocity happen in His/Her/Their/Its/My/Yours/Our/Whoever's name? I mean, was I ever really supposed to build a synagogue in the first place? Or was the whole thing just a cosmic ruse, a karmic zetz, an elaborate punishment leading up to this?"

For once Shylock and Fagin didn't have any snappy retort, no Shakespearean couplet or Dickensian quip to fall back on. They merely sat at the card table, unable to look me in the eye. That just set me off further.

"And the ironic cherry on top of this whole shitball heap of a sundae was playing a melody from the Jewish lo-fi blues poet's most popular song! During the public burning of a painting! Of a Holocaust prisoner! Created by the grandson of a survivor yet! So, you can take the last tree on this dying island and stuff it up the hole in your culture before you trundle off to build your little house deep in the desert. One way or another, they're gonna find you. The world always has, always will. So, remember that before you think you can go clear. Sincerely, L Motherfucking Cohen."

The burning of the painting was all over the news and the usual barrage of emails and phone messages from the media assailed my inboxes. Reporters camped outside the Body Parts. There was no way I'd be able to leave my apartment. Maybe ever. The phone rang yet again and in a fit of anger, without thinking I picked it up. Maybe I should make a statement to the press. I was half thinking of what I would say with the phone pressed to my ear. I didn't say anything at first and then I heard a familiar voice on the other end.

"Hello? Samson? Are you there?" It was Maggie Beairsto.

"Maggie? Why are you calling?"

"I didn't think you would answer," she said shakily. "I heard what happened. I don't know what to say. You must be..."

"I don't know what I am," I said. "Screwed sideways most likely."

"I was expecting to leave a message," she said. "I'm sorry I'm in a bit of a rush. I just called to tell you to watch the webcast that was uploaded today. It's important."

"Why? What's going on?"

"I can't get into it right now. Just watch."

I could hear voices in the background. "Where are you calling from?"

"I'm at the airport. Me and Pius."

"Pius?" I said. "So does that mean you two...?"

"Pretty much," she said and I could hear something in her voice, an inhalation common in the speech of most Maritime natives. But there was something else I couldn't quite place. Possibly relief with an undercurrent of sadness.

"What happened? With Aziza I mean. Is she okay?"

"I think she will be. It's complicated. We both had to face some hard truths. She's just trying to figure things out. Me too." There was a pause and I could hear a muffled voice over a loudspeaker. "They're calling our flight."

"Where are you going?"

"We're flying to Halifax. Pius has a cousin with a microbrewery in Lawrencetown. He wants to start making shine and Pius is going into business with him. Once that gets underway, we're going to try to set up the Crazy Diamond 2.0."

"Save me a seat at the bar," I said.

"You bet. I'll get in touch once we're settled."

"Good luck, Maggie. I hope Pius knows how lucky he is."

"I'm sorry, I have to go. Our plane is boarding." There was a moment's silence before she added, "I love you, Samson. Stay strong."

Then the line went dead.

An eerie sense of finality in those last words stayed with me as I waited for *The Anne Surly Cyber-Report* to load on my laptop. I only realized at that moment that Shylock and Fagin were gone. Not even a fare thee well, good cousin or cheerio, my dear. I resigned myself to watching on my own. Anne Surly appeared on the screen and immediately launched into the burning of *Anne of Bergen-Belsen*.

"I was not present at what has been described in the mainstream media as 'an unsettling display of the direction where our island is heading' and in a statement by Culture Minister Kerrie-Jo Campbelljohn as, 'a cleansing that signifies a return to the cultural wellbeing of our young nation.' Much has been made of the talking point that the painting was directly linked to

Hurricane X and that this sacrificial offering was to appease the Supreme One. While this has begun to take on the patina of official doctrine in the history of Ceilidhlujah that is now being written, a new development may shed some light on a different motivation for destroying *Anne of Bergen-Belsen*.

"Yesterday, members of the media and certain government officials were invited to a sneak preview of the construction project that has been going on at Rossiter's Field for a few months now. Those of you who have been long-time followers of this webcast will remember that Rossiter's Field was an unofficial dumping ground for a number of decades. After promising to have it cleaned up during his campaign, Premier Arsenault originally earmarked the land to be a children's camp, while Samson Grief wanted it to be the site for a synagogue, which he claimed was decreed by the Supreme One. Yesterday, those who attended this sneak preview of the construction site got a much clearer picture of what is actually being built."

The image of Anne Surly was replaced with still photos of a construction site comprised of tall girders, cranes, trucks and other machinery. Anne Surly's voice continued behind the photos.

"These photos are of the ongoing construction of what will be the Blue Point Detention Centre, a private state-of-the-art prison that is slated to be completed by next year. As the name implies it has some connection to Blue Point Security, which has been more and more visible in the past few months. Despite being a privately owned company, Blue Point Security is being groomed to become the main source of law enforcement on Ceilidhlujah.

"The cost of building the Blue Point Detention Centre is unknown but is unofficially estimated to be in the tens of millions. The source of the funding is not specifically known, but is widely believed to involve foreign money, most likely American, with some other investors, and is suspected to be part of the larger deal that turned this island into an offshore tax haven, which allowed us to become a sovereign nation. Similar to Blue Point Security, the question of who actually owns the Blue Point Detention Centre cannot be traced to one specific source, although Freeland Corporation, Premier Arsenault's own development company, is known to be a partner. And, most importantly, who will be imprisoned in this facility is not officially known, but it has been alleged that 'undesirables' from the U.S. and possibly other countries will be incarcerated here. Whether that means this facility is being set up as another Guantanamo Bay remains to be seen."

What the hell was she talking about? Gitmo? Here? On this red mote of an island that doesn't even have a federal prison? This pipsqueak of an ex-province where everyone calls the main jail Sleepy Hollow, like the warden was Ichabod Crane or something?

The photos disappeared and Anne Surly once more appeared on the screen.

"The painting *Anne of Bergen-Belsen* showed Anne Shirley, the protagonist of the novel *Anne of Green Gables*, depicted as a holocaust victim, a prisoner in a concentration camp. It was painted shortly after the 9/11 Twin Tower attacks and was meant to be a comment on how the western world was fundamentally changed by that event. As its creator, Samson Grief, stated in a radio interview, it represented 'the delusion of our collective innocence.' At the time, Reuben Arsenault wrote an op-ed that called for the public burning of *Anne of Bergen-Belsen*. And now it has been burned in public, this image of our Island as an imaginary prison camp, to make way for an actual prison. The artistic rendering of one man's nightmare of the imagination had to be destroyed to make that nightmare a reality. As long as that painting existed for all to see, it was an indictment of what we are becoming.

"In my opinion, the creator of *Anne of Bergen-Belsen*, Samson Grief, was ahead of his time. While most people think that's meant as a compliment, it's also another way society has of trying to absolve itself of any guilt by laying the blame back on the artist. A way of deflecting any responsibility by arguing that we didn't know what he was trying to say, he was simply ahead of his time. This painting had personal significance for me. It had a hand in creating me. And I, in turn, had a hand in destroying it. It's for that reason, among others, that this webcast is Anne Surly's last."

I expected the screen to go black. Instead, Anne Surly took off her straw hat, and with it, the attached red pigtails. Then she removed the half mask to reveal the face of Aziza Arsenault beneath it. For a moment she stared into the camera and I could feel her eyes piercing through the screen, making direct contact with mine.

“Forgive me,” she said before the screen went black.

I picked up my phone and ignored the pulsating beeps that told me there were unheard messages in my voicemail and dialed the number for the house in Wilmot Valley. It rang three times before the voicemail message came on. The recording was Aziza’s voice: “Please do not bother to leave a message. We are not here anymore. There is no forwarding number.” Then I heard beeps and another automated voice informing me that the inbox was full.

Somehow that was as apt a metaphor as any for the place we had come to. Inboxes crammed to the limit with unheard messages, emitting beeps to get the attention of a world that alternated between being cold and uncaring to being scared and unwilling.

I returned the receiver to its cradle. Judas appeared wearing a loose robe and rope sandals, looking like he had just stepped out of the pages of an illustrated edition of the New Testament.

“What are you doing here?” I said.

“It was left to me to inform you that this mission is over,” said Judas.

“What mission?”

“The same one we were always on.” Judas smiled kindly, as if to someone slow-witted. “To build a synagogue on Rossiter’s Field.”

“So that’s it?” I said, suddenly feeling the anger rise within me. “They win? Do you know what’s being built there? A monstrosity of a prison! Instead of a synagogue! And you have the bloody nerve to just shrug and say we’re giving up? Why do you get to call the shots? How dare you rope me into this whole *mishegas* and then say oh well, it’s over now. Who the hell do you think you are, you goddam traitor, you snake, you turncoat. You… you… you Judas!”

I waited to see what effect that would have on him, but he barely flinched.

“Why did you do that to me?” I screamed. “Why did you let everyone think the hurricane was linked to my painting? Thanks to you, they destroyed my painting. My poor beautiful suffering Anne! And with her they destroyed me. You destroyed me!”

Judas merely stood there. Part of his robe had slipped open and I could see the brutish scar around his throat where the rope had bit into the flesh when he lynched himself. Fagin had once derisively referred to it as a halo that had slipped over his head and that's exactly what he looked like, a fallen angel whose halo had lost the ability to float and could no more act as a crown, having grown too heavy, only to become a millstone around his neck.

"I know you always wondered what I represented," he said in a voice that betrayed no emotion. "What was my connection to you, what did I symbolize? Fagin was proud to identify himself as a promoter of Opportunity, while Shylock openly espoused the belief in his beloved Principle. And you wondered what I represented. At first, you assumed I might represent the obvious: Betrayal. Then you were charitable enough to consider that I might possibly represent Sacrifice or Forbearance."

"And now I see I was right the first time."

"Even though I have had to live down the title of Traitor, even as my own name Judas, as you demonstrated, has become synonymous with that vile attribute, and yet I preferred this demonization to the terrible truth."

"And what's that?"

"Yeshua told me that I would be vilified through the ages as the one who betrayed him. Yet he wanted to give me some comfort and said that treachery was not my true nature. He declared by a whisper in my ear that my true nature was indeed... Obedience. Not Friendship. Not Love. Not Trust. Not even Service. But Obedience. Like I was an underling. I could not believe my own ears. Yeshua thought he was giving me succour. He believed he was paying me a compliment. He expected I would be grateful to hear such a thing. Little did he know to what degree he had injured me. How he was betraying me by confessing what disregard he had for me. Obedience. It wounded me ten times more than the kiss I bestowed on his cheek to signal the centurions in Gethsemane."

"You didn't say anything to him?"

"I held my tongue," said Judas wearily. "In the end, I understood all I could do was resign myself to my designated nature."

"I guess you're saying I also have to be obedient?" I turned my back to him and crossed my arms to show I meant business. "Well, I may be a schmuck, but I'm not a stupid schmuck."

"Obedience is my designation, not yours," he said. "Things can only be set into motion if one of us plays the servant and the other the master."

"Master?" I turned to face him. "You mean me? But you spent your whole time here bossing me around."

"We were merely sent here to guide you," he argued. "Until you could find your own way toward building the synagogue. Yet we have done all we can. That is why Fagin and Shylock are not here."

I thought for a moment. "But isn't Shylock supposed to get married to Frieda Greenglass?"

"I do not see how that can happen now."

I ignored him. A plan was starting to formulate in my mind. Far-fetched, yes. But it was my only hope and I'd be damned if some Fig was going to get in my way.

"If you're the servant and I'm the master..."

"Perhaps master is too strong a word," said Judas.

"Whatever. You said you stood for Obedience, then obey this: I want to speak to the Supreme One."

Without a word, Judas went to my easel where the unfinished painting of North Cape was now entirely obscured by the ten-armed starfish. I hadn't looked at the painting in a while and immediately noticed that a number of new arms had been added. I had no inclination to count exactly how many. It looked like my doppelgänger, the one that existed in whatever alternate dimension where he first painted the original Starfish of David, had been busy.

"That other version of you who created this creature has added these extra arms as a way of marking time until the mission has been accomplished."

"And you're telling me this because..."

"You asked to speak to the Supreme One."

"This is the Supreme One?" I said.

"The Supreme One has no form incarnate," Judas explained. "This crude depiction is as near as you need be to say your piece."

"Just speak to the painting?"

Judas moved aside and motioned for me to step forward. I wasn't sure how to start and decided to spell out my idea plain and simple. I waited for a response, not exactly sure what to expect. I remembered Judas had once said the Supreme One's voice was an all-pervading silence. While there was indeed silence, I wasn't receiving any message. Then the mutant starfish slowly began to shrink and, as it shrank, the painting I could not finish was visible once again. When the starfish became, once more, part of the detritus I had painted on the ocean floor, I saw the majestic rise of the waters of North Cape that were meant to mimic the parting Red Sea. What at one time seemed like an unfinished painting, I now saw as the Supreme One's way of green lighting my plan. The parting waters, the stretch of ocean floor, it all beckoned me to take on the role of, if not Moses setting his people free, then at the very least my own interpretation of what Shylock had dubbed as Samson *ex Machina*.

"What happens next?" I asked Judas.

"It is your plan, Samson," he said. "I am but your obedient servant."

GRADUALLY I BECAME aware that we were in the open air.

"What the hell just happened?" I asked.

"You said we had to go to Rossiter's Field," said Judas. "That is where we are."

"Just like that?"

"You said there was no time to waste," he said. "This way is much faster than your vehicle."

"Be that as it may," I said, trying to acclimatize myself to my surroundings. "A little heads-up would have been nice."

The warm night carried a slightly sweet acridity, like tar and the chalkiness of dust. The sky was made that much deeper and darker by a full moon emitting a slightly pinkish tinge. In the pervading glow, my vision soon became used to my surroundings. I started to make out a shadowy grid of scaffolding and a cement mixer tipped toward a metal trough. I could make out the contour of a wheelbarrow and beside it a pile of rebar. Behind me, steel girders and sheet metal rose from the darkness to form the beginning of a soon-to-be impenetrable exterior. This was the construction site for the Blue Point Detention Centre. There was nothing here to remind me of what used to be the foliage-entangled junk of Rossiter's Field.

"What happens now?" asked Judas, and I wanted to pinch myself when I realized it was me calling the shots for once.

"Well, we can't do this with just the two of us," I said. "We need a bride, a groom and a best man. Can you handle that?"

Shylock and Fagin appeared. They were no longer wearing their tourist get-ups and had returned to sporting their regular attire: Fagin in a dark and beat up wide-brimmed hat and long dark coat; Shylock in his floppy red hat and doublet. With them was Frieda Greenglass. She was still wearing her Latke Lady apron over a simple dress.

"Oh my God!" she exclaimed looking about her. "What the hell happened? One minute I'm fixing a late-night snack for these two and the next we're in... whatever this place is."

"We're on Rossiter's Field," I said. "Where the synagogue should have been built."

"So, tell me, how did we get here?"

"'Twas simple, my love," said Shylock. "And yet I can offer no explanation that would suffice. So let us happily say, carried were we 'pon the wings of love." He took Frieda in his arms and the two engaged in an unabashed display of tonsil hockey.

"Cor, these two have been at it all night while I was waiting for me grub," moaned Fagin. "My belly was laying ten-to-one odds my throat had been cut."

As much as I wanted to turn away, at least for propriety's sake, I found myself gawking at them like a voyeur at a peep show.

"I think we get the idea," I said, but they continued sucking face. "Excuse me, but hath not a Jew a bedroom to do that in?"

They continued to devour each other for a few seconds more until Frieda broke off, turned to me and said, "Prude."

"Save it for after," I said.

"After what?" said Frieda. "I have two freshly toasted bagels with lox and cream cheese sitting on my kitchen counter. What am I doing here?"

"You and Shylock are going to get married."

"What? Here? Now? I'm wearing an apron for God's sake."

"I know it sounds crazy, but bear with me," I said. "If we can't actually build a synagogue on Rossiter's Field, then the next best thing is to use whatever is here as a makeshift synagogue. And what better way to do that than have a Jewish wedding? Ostensibly, all of this scaffolding and these bare girders will be functioning as a synagogue. We have to put our faith in the power of the ritual. Then once the ceremony is complete, it will kick start whatever cosmic wheels need to be set in motion to transform PEI or Ceilidhlujah or whatever it's going to ultimately be called into the new Promised Land. Or that's my theory anyway. Seeing as we're here and things are going to plan so far, I'm feeling relatively confident that we have the Supreme One's blessing."

"Well, it looks like we won't be having a DJ or a swan made out of chopped liver," said Frieda. "Although if I'd been given a little bit of notice... But how am I going to get married without a *chuppah*?"

Of course, her reference was to the ceremonial canopy that is *de rigeur* at all Jewish weddings and I couldn't resist such an easy set up. "You know what they say, no chuppah, no shtuppah."

"Too late for that I'm afraid," she said with a knowing smirk toward her husband-to-be.

"Behold," said Judas, looking up. Where there had only been blackness made even more foreboding by the moon's eerie glow, the sky was now shimmering with thousands of stars.

"For none else but thee, my own Frieda," crooned Shylock. "A marriage canopy as vast as all Heaven and glitt'ring as thine emerald orbs that looketh on me with fond yearning."

"I ain't supposing somebody packed a ring on them," said Fagin. "Luckily, I found this in my waistcoat. A little souvenir from the Dodger during one of his outings in London's bustle." He produced a simple gold band from his pocket and offered his services as Shylock's best man, which was readily agreed to.

Frieda broke away from Shylock to tug at my elbow. "I don't mean to pour cold water over your sudden career change into wedding planner, but is anybody here an ordained rabbi? If I'm not mistaken, you need one of those for an honest-to-goodness Jewish wedding. If anyone had bothered to give me a bit of a heads-up, we could have flown in my brother Avi from Moncton."

"That would have been nice," I admitted. "I hope what we have is just as good."

I could see by the puzzled look on her face she was waiting for me to elaborate. That's when I knew I was in trouble. I probably should have said "Let me be entirely honest with you" rather than what popped out of my mouth. She obviously inferred that I had somebody specific already lined up, when what I meant was, I had no idea who was going to perform this ceremony, but I hoped he or she would be just as good as having Rabbi Avi Greenglass do it.

You see, when I was laying out my plan to the Supreme One, or rather the mutant starfish depicted on my canvas, I was a little short on the details, although I have to say I was totally upfront about it. The two elements that I knew were needed to have this event considered an honest-to-you-know-who Jewish wedding were the chuppah and the rabbi. In true sucking-up fashion, I said I would leave it to the Supreme One's all-encompassing wisdom and merciful benevolence, not to mention better judgment, to supply both items. I was a little worried whether the Supreme One would come through and breathed a small sigh of relief to see the star-filled night magically appear as our celestial chuppah. I was still trying to figure out how to explain to Frieda that I didn't know who would be officiating the ceremony, when I saw her attention diverted elsewhere. Her face was overcome with great emotion.

I turned to where she was looking and saw a figure walk in from the darkest outreach of Rossiter's field. An older man in a dark suit no longer in fashion and a felt fedora. He was thin and serious with small round rimless glasses and a full beard which made his narrow face look even more cadaverous. The satchel he was carrying made him look not unlike a doctor from a Gothic novel.

"Pa?" said Frieda in a tremulous voice.

"That's your father?" I asked. "That's Rabbi Greenglass?"

"How did you make this happen?" Frieda asked and clutched my arm.

"I had some help," I answered as truthfully as I could.

"Is he a ghost?"

"That would be my guess," I said, noting the rabbi's ashen complexion.

"You know the circumstances surrounding his death," she said, and I remembered she told me he had been hit by a bus, but there was some question whether it was an accident or if he had purposely stepped in front of it. "Because nothing could be proved, we were allowed to bury him in a Jewish cemetery."

I understood what she was getting at. "Then I'm sure the fact that he was summoned here as a rabbi to perform this holy ceremony means there is no black mark on his death."

"So much I want to say to him," I could see she was fighting back tears.

"I'm sorry Frieda, but we really don't have the time," I said and put my arm around her shoulders. "We have to get started now."

"What about after?"

"We'll see what we can do." Frankly, I had no idea what the ground rules were here. Were there limits in our interactions with the dead? I assumed there would be enough leeway to allow Rabbi Greenglass to perform the ceremony, but beyond that we'd have to wait and see.

Judas, in his role as assistant wedding planner, gathered us all in a clearing at the perimeter of the construction site. For once I was thankful for his take-charge attitude as I was feeling susceptible to Frieda's show of emotion. There were things I also wanted to say to Rabbi Greenglass and I was trying to formulate in my mind exactly what words I would use and wondering if I would get the chance. Judas's focus on getting the ceremony started reminded me I needed to get my head back in the game.

As we were taking our places – Shylock and Frieda side by side, Fagin standing next to Shylock, me and Judas standing behind them – Rabbi Greenglass opened his satchel and took out a *talith* and draped it over his shoulders. At that moment, he raised his hand and waved at Frieda. She waved back.

"Pa," she called.

He nodded to her, a thin smile playing on his lips, then took out a Bible. The ceremony commenced and I noticed Frieda's shoulders trembling slightly. I had to use all my powers of concentration not to lose it myself. All was going well. Then I became aware of three figures standing off to the side.

I recognized the first one as Ned Tuplin, Tamara Tuplin's great-great-uncle, whom I had seen in a dream when I spent the night with Zaina. Speaking of whom, the second figure was an older woman wearing a headscarf. I gradually recognized the resemblance this woman had to Zaina. Could this be her

Druze great-grandmother? I sensed a pattern emerging here and presumed if the Supreme One was going to produce one dead ancestor, why not go all out? I felt a pang of regret for the absence of Tamara Tuplin and Zaina, both of whom would no doubt have loved to meet such important ancestors from their family histories.

But it was the third figure that made me lose all concentration on the ceremony at hand. It was my own zaide, Jakob Grief. I stared at him for a long time, but he, Ned Tuplin and the Druze great-grandmother were respectfully watching Fagin give the gold ring to Shylock, who in turn slipped it on Frieda's finger. Rabbi Greenglass spoke the vows that Shylock and Frieda dutifully repeated.

"Repeat after me," instructed the rabbi. "I, Shylock, take you Frieda to be my lawfully wedded wife."

Shylock complied.

"And I Frieda," said the rabbi, looking tenderly at his daughter. "Take you Shylock to be my lawfully wedded husband."

After a deep breath, Frieda repeated her father's words.

"I now pronounce you man and wife," concluded the rabbi. "You may kiss the bride."

Once the married couple sealed the moment with a long, but tender kiss, Rabbi Greenglass sang the Hebrew song, *Im Eshkakech Yerushalayim* or *If I Forget You, Jerusalem.* When the song was over, Judas produced a small wine glass, which he had taken from my cupboard at home, wrapped it in a handkerchief and set it by Shylock's foot. He brought his heel down hard on the swathed glass and the ceremony was complete. Shylock then embraced his bride and they kissed again as we all cheered.

I glanced over at Rabbi Greenglass and saw him quickly look to the side, where Zaide Jakob caught his eye. The two men simply looked at each other for a moment, then Zaide Jakob nodded and Rabbi Greenglass nodded back. Whether this acknowledgement constituted recognition of each other or was mere politeness between two strangers I couldn't tell. I wasn't even sure if it mattered. Had Rabbi Greenglass, in his alleged capacity as unwilling stationmaster for the Nazis at Westerbork, chosen my zaide to be put on the train to Auschwitz rather than some other death camp? I doubted any of us would ever know for sure. All I knew at that point was the dead only demand that we respect their privacy and the living, despite all our efforts to uncover truth and meaning, are in the end helpless to do anything more than comply.

Then came the first dance. There was no music, but instinctively some of us began to clap rhythmically and then the others joined in. Without thinking, I began to sing *Hava Nagila* and was surprised when Fagin, my zaide and Rabbi Greenglass sang as well. Frieda, who had taken off her apron, now picked it up, twisted it into a taut length of cloth and held one end in her hand while Shylock took the other end. They danced a traditional *freilach*, moving around each other with great expression, as we accompanied with clapping and song. In the sky stars began to shift slowly, resembling nothing less than celestial cogs in some cosmic mechanism. Directly above us a group of stars moved into a formation. It appeared to constitute a six-pointed constellation, reminding me very much of a starfish.

This mystical phenomenon was abruptly interrupted by headlights in the distance racing up the dirt road leading from the highway as the roar of engines grew louder. This did not bode well. One by one, the wedding guests vanished into thin air like wisps of smoke, first Ned Tuplin, then Zaina's great-grandmother, then my zaide and finally Rabbi Greenglass. Then I noticed Fagin was gone. Shylock and Frieda were still circling each other in their lively freilach when they too were no more. Only Judas stood nearby.

"What's going on?" I said.

"The mission has been completed," said Judas as he too started to fade. "Now that it has, we will be forgotten by everyone. It will be as if Shylock, Fagin and myself had never appeared to them."

"Me too?" I asked. "Will I forget you?"

"We are part of you, Samson Grief. To forget us is to forget that you ever existed." And then he was gone.

"But what about me?" I cried as the SUVs screeched to a halt at the end of the dirt road. "Why aren't I disappearing? Why have I been abandoned?"

"It is your plan, Samson." Judas's disembodied voice was close to my ear.

"I am but your obedient servant." I could feel his invisible hand slip into mine.

Armed Blue Point Security guards scrambled out of their vehicles but stood their ground. One with a bullhorn positioned himself behind his vehicle's open door.

"You are trespassing on private property. You must surrender immediately. We will take you by force if we have to."

My instinct was to raise my hands so that they knew I was giving up, but only one hand would rise. Judas gripped my other hand and held it down. I suppose it looked to the guards like I was waving to them. I could only hope they weren't taking it as a sign of resistance.

"What the hell are you doing?" I said to Judas. "Let go of me."

"It is your plan, Samson," he repeated. "I am but your obedient servant."

"Come toward us," the voice bellowed through the bullhorn. "Slowly and with both your hands up."

"I better do what they say. I've got nowhere to run." I suddenly felt myself being pulled forward, my stumbling legs barely able to keep up.

"What are you doing?" I cried. "They said I should go slowly. I don't want them to think I'm..."

"It is your plan, Samson. I am but your obedient servant."

"What, are you stuck on some loop?" I cried. "I didn't plan for this!"

I could feel Judas pulling me harder, making me run even faster toward the guards.

"Slow down," the guy with the bullhorn warned. "Or we will take it as an act of aggression."

"Do you hear that?" I screamed as our speed increased and my feet were barely touching the ground. For a moment I wondered if we were about to achieve lift-off and take flight. That would have been my one ticket out of there. Of course, I also would have made as handy a target as any clay pigeon.

"It is... your plan... Samson," Judas said somewhat breathlessly. "I... am but your..."

"Yeah, yeah, I know! Then obey me, you New Testament nut bar. Let go! Now!"

I could suddenly feel his grip loosen from my hand, but I was still being propelled forward under my own velocity. I struggled to raise my hands in surrender but they were too busy flailing about while I tried to get my legs under control.

"It is your plan, Samson!" Judas's voice sounded farther away. Whether he finished his parting mantra I can't say because at that moment his voice was drowned out by a barrage of gunfire echoing through the night.

PART 5:

ISLAND FREILACH (AN EPILOGUE)

IT IS YOUR PLAN, he said. *I am but your obedient servant*, he said. Yeah right, and the Torah says it's cool to end the Yom Kippur fast with a BLT.

What did he mean by it being my plan? I didn't plan for any of this. Was he trying to tell me that everything that happened came solely from my own fevered imagination? Was I being gaslighted? Maybe he pulled the same stunt on Yeshua, insisting the betrayal, kiss and all, was really Yeshua's idea. I mean, if you think about it, isn't the basic conundrum of existence, the whole Predestination versus Free Will thing, just a form of divine gaslighting? On the one hand we're told our life's path has been laid out before us and yet, when we complain of our lot in life, we're assured that the power to change our fortunes was inside us all along.

Or did Judas play the betrayal blame game to assuage his guilt later on? Then again, maybe Yeshua did mastermind the whole betrayal that would lead to crucifixion and resurrection. And maybe it was my idea alone to run headlong towards certain death because I didn't want to face the consequences of being taken alive. All I know for sure is I have more questions now than when I was alive. Being dead isn't the answer to anything.

I'm still not sure where I am or how long I've been here. Some cosmic way station, I assume. Purgatory or limbo or bardo or whatever you want to call it. Not sure if Jews have a name for a place like this, although it's not unlike a Passover seder with the Exodus story entering its third hour and you're so hungry you'd gnaw off your own arm while waiting for the praying to end and the meal to begin.

It's mostly dark but I get the sense that there are others here, although I can't make anyone out very well. It feels like a medium-sized crowded room, similar to the pre-flight area in the Charlottetown Airport during a brownout.

But it's not all bad. While I've been waiting, I've been able to see both backwards into the past and forwards into the future. Maybe this is what it's like to have my third eye open (as far as I can understand that sort of thing)? Or maybe it's just an ability you get as a way to pass the time while you're here. I have to admit I spent most of my time so far focusing on the hindsight, which was how I was able to relate all that happened before I eventually wound up here.

I'm pretty sure this two-way vision isn't going to last much longer. Even now I notice the light starting to narrow and it suddenly occurs to me that this temporary aperture spanning both past and future is the real crack in everything, the crack that runs through the universe, the crack within us all.

Only the truly enlightened beings, the ones who have risen to a higher plane of existence, get to enjoy this panorama permanently. The rest of us schmoes – waiting to hop back on the perpetual treadmill of being born, living, dying then being reborn – only get a little taste of that enlightened good life.

The hope being that we'll try that much harder to live a better life during our next time round on the planet. Our island in the cosmos.

And this existential dance, this soulful transmigration or reincarnation or samsara or whatever you want to call it that we keep doing is our very own orbital freilach.

At any rate, I'll do my best to look as far ahead as I can in the brief time I'm allotted. Because I concentrated so much on the past and formulating a narrative out of what I saw, the future is more condensed and select and not in any particular order.

First of all, my death will be ruled a justifiable homicide in light of testimony by Blue Point guards that I was caught planting explosive devices and threatening to blow up the construction site. Despite the manufactured evidence, it won't be until a few decades later that my name will be cleared when certain emails between the head of Blue Point Security and Reuben Arsenault, detailing the conspiracy to frame me, come to light due to a deathbed confession by that Blue Point officer.

Reggie Muir will be found guilty of not only killing Krystal Wedge, but also his brother Kelvin. Testimony during the trial will detail the growing rift between the brothers after Reggie accidentally hit Aziza when they were only supposed to scare her. Later, when Kelvin tried to get Krystal Wedge to go public with her hush money story, as a way of exposing Reuben as being the one who paid her (Kelvin's way of getting back at him for encouraging Aziza to continue her Anne Surly webcasts), Reggie warned Kelvin that he was treading on thin ice. But Kelvin had put a bug in Krystal's ear, and after the brothers joined Blue Point Security, Reggie was promised a promotion if he took care of the Krystal problem, since she was threatening to tell her story to the press because she needed more money. After Reggie tied up Krystal and strangled her, then dumped her body in the sea, Kelvin decided to quit Blue Point Security but Reggie wouldn't let him. Kelvin didn't want anything more to do with his brother and threatened to expose Reggie unless he let him go. Reggie knew he had to keep Kelvin close because he knew too much. The tension between them only worsened, culminating in an argument where things quickly got out of hand when Reggie tied up, killed and dumped Kelvin's body the same way he had Krystal.

Suffice to say, Ceilidhlujah's progress toward Promisedom will be a long one, yet occurrences of some significance will eventually take shape. Things usually get worse before they get better.

The building of the Blue Point Detention Centre will be delayed by a series of freak accidents and structural problems, as well as lawsuits launched by the Mi'kmaq Alliance over the right of ownership of Rossiter's Field and neglect in the duty to consult in building the detention centre. Tamara Tuplin will call for an investigation into whether Premier Reuben Arsenault properly dissociated himself from the Freeland Corporation after taking power and if he violated the Landholding Act in purchasing Rossiter's Field and surrounding acreage.

The ensuing legal woes will follow Reuben and will eventually lead to him being ousted as leader of the New Judgement Party, then later detained while trying to leave the Island. Although he will manage to avoid prison through his lawyers' delay tactics, his health will suffer until he finally loses a prolonged battle with cancer.

While the detention centre will eventually get built, it will stay empty for a while, then become a place to incarcerate political prisoners from the U.S. and other countries. Due to an eventual erosion in its regulatory system, the prison will devolve into a de facto refugee camp for those fleeing oppressive regimes who cannot find asylum elsewhere. Its overcrowded conditions, resulting in a concentrated outbreak of the EMRADS virus (Extreme Mutation of Respiratory and Arterial Degeneration Syndrome), and rampant corruption will bring unwanted attention to Ceilidhlujah from around the world.

A global financial crisis, stemming from the inability to bring the EMRADS pandemic under control, will cause the economy to briefly surge and then spiral into a sudden collapse, wiping out Ceilidhlujah's status as an offshore tax haven. This will lead to the ultimate expulsion of the detention centre's inhabitants, thus spreading the virus Island-wide and creating a crisis of indiscriminate persecution and forced deportations. An extended lockdown, closing off the Island for almost three years, will finally bring the virus under control, but at great expense to the local economy, culminating in often-violent civil unrest and many lives lost.

A quick scan further ahead in time shows the permanent effects of the EMRADS virus will result in transmuting human biology to such a degree of instability as to necessitate the strict enforcement of a global accord to ensure environmental safeguards protecting life on the planet.

This will coincide with, and to some degree become a catalyst to, the detention centre being dismantled and ultimately converted into the long-awaited synagogue. It will be named Temple Epekwit'k, after the Island's final renaming when the Great Boat Party and the Mi'kmaq Alliance consolidate into the Epekwit'k Great Boat Alliance and takes power. The temple's opening ceremony will be presided over by Premier Tamara Tuplin, Minister of Culture

Damian Ishmael, Minister of the Environment Pearl Knockwood and Rabbi Dylan Markowitz (Stepan and Ilana Markowitz's great-grandchild), spiritual leader of Temple Epekwit'k and the Island's first residential rabbi, who will happen to identify as non-binary. In Rabbi Markowitz's opening statement, they will invoke the Jewish concept of *tikkun olam*, translated as *repair the world*. It will be in this spirit that, while primarily the spiritual centre for the Jewish population of Epekwit'k, the temple will also accommodate many social and educational programs for all cultures.

While Epekwit'k will continue to thrive as a sovereign nation, a new alliance with Canada will be forged. There will be many attempts by the federal government to rebuild a bridge to the mainland, all of them resisted by the Epekwit'k Great Boat Alliance as a way of perpetuating the Island's independence. In this way, they hope to be an example of peaceful reconciliation between Indigenous peoples and their settler counterparts, not just in North America, but across the globe. If this is what the Supreme One has been aiming for all along in establishing a new Promised Land, then as far as I can see at this moment, the promise may actually have a shot at being fulfilled.

Even though Frieda Greenglass will have no memory of Shylock or getting married to him, she will suffer a serious period of depression and leave the Island to stay with her rabbi brother, Avi, and his family in Moncton for a while. While there, she will seek professional help from Eva Litwak, a psychiatrist of Hungarian origin. Their doctor/patient relationship will only last a few months after they admit their attraction to each other. They will then embark on a personal relationship that will last until Frieda's death at age 98.

Zaina will stay in Hamilton for a few years, where she will help the Haddads settle in and learn more about her Druze heritage from them and the pocket community there. The Haddads will open a successful family restaurant with Zaina as their accountant. Although she will have found the Druze community she was looking for, she will feel restless and enrol in law school, graduate with honours and become an immigration lawyer. After practicing in Hamilton, she will eventually return to the Island where she will help reform the draconian immigration laws legislated by the New Judgment Party and initiate a revitalized program of bringing in immigrants with a focus on asylum seekers. I am observing all this with a certain amount of equanimity until I see that she will become involved with a Druze widower and marry. Not that I don't wish her happiness, but as one of the dead, I didn't expect to feel the loss and longing I had carried since the moment I laid eyes on her.

Following Zaina's journey back to the Island, I'm hoping to get some news about Aziza. But I see nothing. I search graveyards, expecting the worst, but find no stone with her name on it. I can only assume that after she hung up her straw hat and pigtails all she wanted was to disappear. Maybe I'm overestimating my temporary ability to look into the future, assuming nothing would be able to hide from my scrutiny. Still, I have to give all the credit to Aziza. If anyone can evade an all-knowing eye it's her. I can only hope she will find peace of mind somewhere in the world and somebody worthy to share it with.

My line of vision is beginning to narrow. Looking both forward and backward are becoming more difficult. I'm not ashamed to say I'm scared. I've never reincarnated before. Actually, that can't be right. I must have done it many times before, but I can't remember them. I guess that makes reincarnation a lot like painting a picture. Both are ways of entering the world anew. I've painted I don't know how many pictures, but each time I start a new one it's from scratch, like I've never done it before. I guess that's why I always kept doing it. For that new experience.

And yet we hang on to life because we dread starting over. That's the human condition for you, everyone wants a do-over but nobody wants to die. Sure, some of us have a fear that there is nothing after death, just a cold and eternal void. But some of us look forward to the possibility of another chance to get it right. To some of us, reincarnation is a treadmill, to others, it's a roulette wheel. Frankly, what I dread is not knowing what I'm going to come back as. I hope I'll be a person, any kind of person. But I could just as easily come back as a rock. Or a sea urchin. Maybe even a multi-armed starfish. I could go on and on but in fact that's already the basic nature of existence. I'm not saying it won't ever end. Just probably not in my lifetime. Pick a lifetime, any lifetime and I'll be there.

It's getting darker, so I should brace myself. The light is as thin as a length of thread, a freilach sash with two dancers – the past and the future – at either end. I can hear a faint strain of music coming from somewhere. The future, if I'm not mistaken. Just like the name of the CD that I would listen to every morning to get me in the right mood to work. But this isn't one of the Jewish lo-fi blues poet's songs. This is a song I often heard in the Crazy Diamond playing over the speakers from the Pink Floyd MP3-looping jukebox. I got to like this song after a while. Maggie told me it was written for one of the band members who died.

"...how I wish you were..."

Who knows, maybe it's coming from the Crazy Diamond 2.0.

Or maybe I'm making it all up. Listen and judge for yourself.

ACKNOWLEDGEMENTS

An early draft of this novel was made possible with the support of the Canada Council of the Arts, for which the author is most grateful.

In 2018 an earlier version of Chapter 1 appeared in *Chaffin Journal,* from the University of Eastern Kentucky.

The following texts were helpful to the author.

Ni'n na L'nu The Mi'kmaq of Prince Edward Island
by A.J.B. Johnston and Jesse Francis, Acorn Press, 2013

A Stream Out of Lebanon: an Introduction to the Coming of Syrian/Lebanese Immigrants to Prince Edward Island
by David Weale, Charlottetown Institute of Island Studies, 1988

Origins of the Druze People and Religion
by Philip K. Hitti, globalgreyebooks.com, 2018

The Lost Gospel of Judas
by Rodolphe Kasser, PDF from National Geographic website, 2014

Oliver Twist
by Charles Dickens, ebook produced by Peggy Gaugy and Leigh Little, HTML by Al Haines

The Merchant of Venice
by William Shakespeare, shakespeare.folger.edu

I want to take this opportunity to thank my dear wife Thelma. Her love and support allows me to fully enjoy the writing life I always dreamed of. Every word I write is a testament to the faith she has in me, for which I will always be grateful.

PHOTO CREDIT THELMA PHILLIPS

STEVEN MAYOFF (he/him) was born and raised in Montreal. His fiction and poetry have appeared in literary journals across Canada, the U.S. and abroad. He is the author of the story collection *Fatted Calf Blues*, winner of the 2010 PEI Book Award for Fiction; the novel *Our Lady of Steerage;* and two books of poetry *Leonard's Flat* and *Swinging Between Water and Stone.* Steven lives in Foxley River, PEI.